Little Aunt Crane

Also by Geling Yan in English

White Snake and Other Stories
The Lost Daughter of Happiness
The Uninvited
The Flowers of War

Little Aunt Crane

GELING YAN

Translated from the Chinese
by Esther Tyldesley

Harvill *Secker*
LONDON

9 8 7 6 5 4 3 2 1

Harvill Secker, an imprint of Vintage,
20 Vauxhall Bridge Road,
London SW1V 2SA

Harvill Secker is part of the Penguin Random House group of companies whose addresses can be found at global.penguinrandomhouse.com.

This publication is supported by China Book International

First published with the title *Xiaoyi Duohe* (小姨多鹤) in China by Writers Publishing House in 2008

www.vintage-books.co.uk

A CIP catalogue record for this book is available from the British Library

ISBN 9781846555909

Typeset in Futura and Fournier MT by Palimpsest Book Production Limited, Falkirk, Stirlingshire

Printed and bound in Great Britain by Clays Ltd, St Ives plc

Penguin Random House is committed to a sustainable future for our business, our readers and our planet. This book is made from Forest Stewardship Council® certified paper.

To the mothers, wives and daughters who suffer from war.

Prologue

The Chinese are Coming!

The smoke of war was rising in several places, in intermittent columns that rose on the mountain slopes that surrounded them on three sides. As the horizon changed from yellow to red, then to a dark reddish purple, the pillars of smoke turned to black, and the fires below burned brighter and brighter. The sky finally darkened completely, and aggressive, wordless bellowing could be heard from the flames: 'Oh! Oh! Oh!'

The sound of the women's wooden shoes filled the village as they hurried to and fro, backs stooped and knees bent, shouting as they ran: 'The Chinese are coming!' Since Hiroshima and Nagasaki had been flattened by atom bombs, the Chinese often came to fire off a few shots or throw a bomb or two. The women soon became accustomed to running at a crouch. Before losing the war, the men under forty-five had been enlisted in Manchuria's final recruiting drive; almost all those left behind were women. The women were calling their children home, but the boys of fifteen or sixteen were already at their stations by the wall that protected the village. The wall was a metre and a half thick, with two parallel rows of shooting holes, encircling the entire village. All six Japanese villages in the area had protective walls, built when the settlers first came from Japan; at the time they had thought the commanding officer was making a fuss about nothing: when Chinese met Japanese, the Chinese would hide if they could, and those that could not hide would bow and get out of the way. These days it was different: the people of Sakito village were now wailing 'The Chinese are coming!' just as desolately as Chinese all over China had been crying 'The Japanese are coming!' not long before.

Three days earlier, the inhabitants of the six Japanese villages had gathered together and set out for the small railway station. Yantun was the station's name, it was in the very northernmost part of Manchuria, and it was where they had alighted when they first came from Japan. Their plan was to take the last train for Busan in Korea, then the ferry to Japan, returning east by the same route they had taken when they came to Manchuria. Altogether there were over three thousand people from the six villages, a good many of whom had brought their livestock, for the weak, sick, elderly and young children to ride, or to carry luggage. After waiting at Yantun for a day and a night, a telegram finally arrived from the headquarters, ordering the villagers to return immediately to their homes: a large group of tanks had crossed the border with the Soviet Union, and they might run straight into them. Dr Suzuki from Shironami village leapt aboard the train, telling the villagers to ignore the headquarters' instructions: advancing and retreating were both a gamble, and true Japanese should choose to advance. The empty train drew away, with Dr Suzuki's furious, defiant face craning out of one of its open windows, still shouting: 'Jump aboard! Fools . . .'

The smoke drifted, and hung low over the skies of Sakito village, the autumn cold releasing its heavy acridity. The firelight gradually spread across the landscape, multiplying into countless torches that covered the hills and fields. It was like the entire population of China had come. Their howls were even more terrifying than the sound of gunfire: 'Oh . . . Oh! . . . Oh! . . .'

A boy lying prone at one of the gunholes fired the first shot. All the youths began to shoot in the direction of the torches, but these points of light were still several kilometres away. The torches were ever increasing in number; a single flame could multiply in an instant into a crowd. Yet the torches did not come close, and the howls and cries remained distant, like muffled thunder rolling at the edge of the sky.

The headman called the villagers together at the open space in front of the Shinto shrine. It looked like they would have to withdraw, whether they were supposed to be withdrawing or not.

Dawn was nearly upon them. In the far distance a train hooted once, it might be pulling dozens of wagons full of Soviet soldiers. The village head made an emergency announcement: they would take no luggage with them, nothing but their children. None of them could believe their ears – how were they supposed to evacuate Manchukuo without any luggage? The head was not the kind of person to overlook such an important detail. Besides, for such a big withdrawal they would need to make arrangements for food and lodging en route. There was a strange serenity on the women's faces, as though they could finally see an end after years of hardship. They had come from their homes in Japan many years before under the banner of the 'Pioneer Corps'; none of them realised at the time that their government had seized these apparently endless lands from the hands of the Chinese people. Now the Chinese had begun their great reckoning. A villager had been killed on the way to market several days earlier. It had been an ugly death: hair, nose and ears were all missing.

The fifty-one-year-old village head stood with a dozen elders at his back, waiting in silence for the clatter of wooden shoes to die down. He said that they should not ask each other questions or whisper together. The people did as they were told. He said again: Stand closer. Closer still. The crowd moved quickly to form a neat, orderly square. The babies were sleeping in their mothers' arms or on their backs, the slightly older children dozing as they leaned against the adults. The village head spoke in a very low voice, his throat dry and hoarse from a night spent smoking cigarettes. He said that he and the other elders had taken a vote and come to a decision. They must make an end before daybreak. The village head was not a gifted speaker, and when he could not find the words he just bowed over and over again. With an effort he made his meaning clear: the people of the Great Japanese Empire were the loyal subjects of the Sun, and to them the agonising shame of defeat was more painful than death itself. He said that the previous evening Soviet troops had shot three or four Japanese men in a nearby village, gang-raped over a dozen women and had stolen everything, leaving not so much as an ear of wheat or a single farm animal, worse bandits than the bandits themselves. And see the smoke hanging on the mountains! There was no way out. The Chinese might come charging down on them at any moment. As the Chinese themselves might have put it, 'The songs of the enemy could be heard on all sides.'

At that moment, a sixteen-year-old girl at the very back of the crowd slipped behind a beech tree, then crouched down and ran like the wind towards Shironami village. The girl had suddenly realised that she was not wearing her earrings. These earrings were made of gold, and she had sneaked them from her mother's jewellery box out of simple vanity and curiosity. Her mother's family lived in Sakito village, but her own home was in Shironami village on the other side of the railway. Ten days before, when the world was just starting to go mad, her mother had sent her to Sakito to help look after her grandfather, who was suffering from the after-effects of a stroke. Her grandfather had barely been able to walk, but late one night he had disappeared. The village dogs had found his body, half lying in the river, the rest of his body wedged in a crack in a boulder on the bank. Grandmother did not cry, for she realised how fortunate she was to have a husband who'd showed his care for her by ending his own life in this way.

Once she had found the earrings, the girl hurried back to the Shinto shrine, feet flying, wooden shoes clutched in her hands.

And so the girl missed the moment when everything changed. After she had slipped like a shadow into the pre-dawn darkness, the village head had said, speaking for the council of elders, that when they had heard of the vile actions of the Soviet troops, they had made a choice on behalf of the five hundred and thirteen villagers. He said that they had chosen the most dignified, least painful road to retreat from Manchuria. For the women, it was the only way to defend their chastity.

People were starting to get the feeling that something was wrong. The dozing children sensed that fate had nothing good in store for them, and they raised their heads to look at their elders. Two women clutched involuntarily at each other's hands. Another woman standing near the outside of the group stole a little bit further towards the edge, pulling her five- or six-year-old boy by the hand. Then she looked around and edged a little further. One more step and they could slip into the new poplar grove they had planted that spring. What did the village head and the elders have in mind for them?

Stern and grim, the elders stood behind the village head as he announced their decision. He said: 'We are Japanese, so we will die with dignity beside our fellow Japanese. The elders have done everything in their power to obtain sufficient bullets.'

Shock descended on the villagers. After a while, one of the slower villagers said: 'Does that mean killing ourselves together? Why?!' Some of the women were crying: 'I want to wait till my husband gets back from the front.'

The village head's voice suddenly became venomous and fierce. 'You would betray the whole village?'

By now the darkness was starting to fade; with every second the blackness was losing another layer of intensity.

At that moment, the girl who had just retrieved her earrings was standing ten paces away. She was just in time to hear the words 'killing ourselves'.

The village head said: 'You are proper Japanese, and you will die properly.' He had determined that one of the elders would do the deed, to give everyone a good death. This elder was a crack shot, he had survived both world wars, but now he would lay down his life for his country, as he had always wished. At this very shrine, where the sacrificial tablets of their ancestors lay, each of them would fall with dignity and honour, dying in their own community.

The women began to make confused, incoherent excuses, unwilling to accept a 'good death'. There are people who let the side down in every place, and Sakito village was no exception: these women thanked the village head, but asked him politely not to lead them to their deaths. The children didn't really understand, but they knew that 'a good death' was no good thing, and they opened their mouths wide, stretched out their necks, turned their faces to the sky and bawled.

A single shot rang out, and they saw the village head fall to the ground. Everything had been arranged in advance: the head would take the lead in being a good Japanese. His wife sobbed loudly, just as she had cried to her mother the night before she married the village head. Now she slowly laid herself down, weeping, beside her husband's corpse from which the blood was gushing, just as she had laid herself, weeping, on her marriage bed on her wedding night. In all the days of her life, no thought of defying her husband's will had ever crossed her mind. The women all began to wail: since the village head's wife had shown them such an example, where could they hope to flee? There was a second shot, and the head and his wife laid down their lives side by side.

The seventy-year-old elder lowered his gun, and looked down at where the village head and his wife had fallen together. All their children had died in the war, and now they were hastening to be reunited with them at last. Next came the village elders. They were very orderly, they came one after another, as they had done to receive their rice ball rations after Japan's defeat.The elders stood in line, backs unbent; one old man of eighty had a line of saliva dangling from his mouth, but his dignity was undiminished. A few minutes later, their descendants gathered next to their seniors, huddled together in a series of eternal family portraits. A strange calm fell over the crowd.

Every family came together, with the old people at the centre. The children were still bemused, but they felt a peculiar sense of security. The babies, who had been crying themselves hoarse, sensed this and quietened down, sucking their fingers, heads twisting slowly to and fro. Just then a voice cried out: 'Tatsuru! Tatsuru!'

Sixteen-year-old Tatsuru was watching the scene with horror-struck eyes. She saw her grandmother standing there all alone. The only thing any of them was afraid of was dying alone, with none of their own warm flesh and blood to cling to as they fell and to grow cold together. Tatsuru decided then and there that she wanted no part in these bonds of affection, families huddled in each other's arms, not even bullets parting them. By now the elder with the gun no longer looked human, his face and hands dripping with fresh blood. His training as a sniper had proved very useful; occasionally someone would mutiny against the collective out of sheer fright and attempt to flee the square, but his bullets pursued them with ease. After a time he perfected his strategy: first get the people down any old way, and once they were on the ground the thing was easy. He had prepared plenty of bullets, enough to dole out death to each person twice over.

The girl named Tatsuru saw the gunman come to a stop. She heard an odd noise close by; she was too overcome to recognise the sound of her own teeth chattering. The marksman looked around him for a while, then pulled out the samurai sword he wore at his waist. His marksmanship had not been perfect, and his targets had been less than exemplary, so he had to go over his work again to make sure, this time using the sword. Once he had finished, he examined the sword, ran a finger along the edge of the blade, and laid it down beside his body. Hot blood had soaked deep into the blade, blunting it. He sat down, unfastened a shoelace and tied one end to the trigger of the gun, the other to a rock. He took off his shoes, so sodden with blood that they must have weighed at least five kilos, to reveal socks that were also red. His bloodstained feet gripped the stone attached to the trigger, and kicked out.

'Crack! Crack! Crack!'

Days later, the 'crack' of the gun was still echoing in Tatsuru's brain.

When the heads of the five other villages heard Tatsuru's confused, incoherent account, their knees gave way and they sat down hard on the ground, their heads silhouetted against the stubbly skyline of the newly harvested fields, on a level with the rising sun.

After sitting still for ten minutes, the head of Shironami village rose to his feet. The other village heads stood up with him. Nobody made any attempt to dust themselves down. They had to go to the village to see if there was anything they could do – to close staring eyes, to straighten dishevelled clothing, perhaps one or two might need help to end their twitching and moaning, to put them out of their misery.

Seen through the leaves and branches of the trees, the five hundred and thirteen men and women, young and old, looked like they were camping out in the open, lying all together in a heap. The earth was dyed black from the blood that had been shed. The blood had poured out extravagantly, spattering the leaves and branches of the trees. There was one family whom the bullets had not separated, and their blood had flowed into a single stream, which had spilled from between two boulders to pool slightly lower down. It had coagulated into an enormous ball of blood beside the stones, bright red, extremely dense, congealed but not solid, like a jelly.

Tatsuru trailed along behind her own village head. The stench of blood filled her nose and throat, choking her. She had hoped to find her grandmother, but she very soon gave up on that notion: most people had been shot in the back and fallen face down, and she did not have the strength or courage to turn them over and identify them one by one.

The village heads had been on their way to Sakito to discuss their route to withdraw from Manchuria, but now they understood the final message of Sakito village. Sakito had always taken the lead among the Japanese villages in the locality, because they had been the first settlers to come here from Japan. Suddenly, the Shironami village head covered Tatsuru's eyes with his hand. In front of him was the corpse of the old man with the gun. The village head had known this sharpshooter and veteran of two world wars very well.

The man was leaning against a tree, the gun still cradled in his arms, though the stone tied to the trigger had fallen from the shoelace. The bullet had entered through his lower jaw, and his head had become an empty sacrificial vessel, pointing at the sky.

The head of Shironami village took off his overcoat, and laid it over what remained of the old marksman. By the look of things, there was nothing more the heads of the five villages could do. Just light a torch. Let there be nothing left for the Soviets and Chinese to violate.

The Shironami village head spoke. He said: 'This is the way it should be: the man in every village who is entrusted with the gun must carry out his responsibilities to the end, and make certain that the fire has been lit before he turns the gun on himself.' The village heads agreed, saying: 'This is the only possible way; we are left with no choice but to depend on his selflessness. It's certainly a pity that this old sharpshooter left his body to fall at the last into the dirty hands of the Chinese or Soviets.'

None of them noticed the girl called Tatsuru walking away quietly. As soon as she was out of sight, she broke into a run, her dishevelled hair streaming out behind her. She was not used to running; even as she fled she was horribly conscious of the immodesty of taking such big strides, showing her legs. Tatsuru would have to run five kilometres, and risk crossing the railway bridge with Soviets coming and going across it, to run back to the village and tell her mother what the head proposed for them all. She was not much of a runner, but she was going to have to race against the village head on her own two feet, so she could get there before him, to tell of that great red ball formed from a whole family's blood, and the empty skull of the old sharpshooter pointing skywards, over seventy years of memories, wisdom and secret thoughts spattered pinkish white on the trunk of the tree. She had to get there first, to tell her neighbours in the village about these things, to give them another choice besides a 'good death'.

Just as the railway bridge came into view, shots rang out again from Sakito village. Tatsuru's footsteps faltered for a moment, then she ran faster. The bridge was at the bottom of the slope, and she could already see several wagons standing on the track. A Soviet soldier was squatting in the doorway of one; he seemed to be brushing his teeth. Tatsuru had scratched her face on a tree branch, and it stung painfully from her sweat. She could not take the bridge over the river, she would need to go downriver and find a shallow place to cross. But the slopes downstream were covered in dense, wild thickets of hazel, and she had neither the time nor the strength to force her way through – and she wasn't a strong swimmer, what if she could not get across?

Tatsuru did not realise that she was sobbing. The world was so utterly hopeless.

She turned on her heel and dashed off in another direction. There was a village called Tunzi not far from here, where three Chinese men lived who often worked as hired hands for her family. One of them, a man of thirty or so, her mother called 'Fudan'. The men got on fairly well with her mother, sometimes they even went so far as to exchange smiles. Tatsuru could go to Fudan, and he would see her back home; the Soviet soldiers would take her for a Chinese. The Soviets would be far less likely to take liberties with a Chinese woman. Tatsuru had been to Tunzi once with Fudan, to visit a herbalist. But she could not speak a word of Chinese, so how would she convince Fudan to see her safely over a bridge guarded by the Soviets?

Tatsuru regretted her decision before she was properly inside Tunzi village. A large group of Chinese children were playing in the entrance to Tunzi, and when they saw her they gradually left off what they were doing and crowded towards her, staring, faces hard as iron. They had scowled in the past too, but never looked at her directly. One child said something in a low voice. She understood nothing else, but the three sounds that meant 'Little Jap' she knew well enough. Before she had made up her mind whether or not to run, a seven- or eight-year-old boy had already heaved a rock at her. After that stones, clods of earth and lumps of dung rained down, and it was too late to run even though she wanted to, and all her ways of escape were blocked. The only thing she could do was curl in a ball on the ground, wailing. Small boys are just like grown men: they have no idea how to deal with a weeping woman, and once Tatsuru started to cry, she became as pathetic and disgusting as Chinese girls to them. They stood around her, and looked on for a while. A hand came up and gently tugged at a lock of Japanese hair – look, nothing special – and let it go. Another hand yanked down the back of her collar to see her Japanese back: no different from a Chinese. Fairly soon the boys got sick of her crying, and ran off with a yell.

When Fudan saw Tatsuru, there was no need for her to say a word, he knew what he had to do. He must see her back home at once, there was no way he could let the neighbours see a Jap girl at his house. Fudan put one of his own ragged gowns around her shoulders, and rubbed a fistful of dirt into her face, a technique the girls in the village had used to keep Japanese soldiers at arm's length. Fudan was too poor to keep a horse or donkey, so he pushed her over the railway bridge in a handcart.

When Fudan brought Tatsuru to the village she was fast asleep. Her mother asked Fudan to put Tatsuru down inside the door, bowed to him and thanked him quietly over and over again. Her mother could speak perhaps thirty or forty words of Chinese; now she was using them for all she was worth. After Fudan left, her mother gently removed the gold rings from Tatsuru's ears, but even that did not wake her.

The minute Tatsuru woke she leapt up from the ground: Too late! The village heads must be back by now! The noonday sun was shining down, bleaching the country all around to a brilliant white; when Tatsuru's bare feet touched the earth she felt like she was gliding backwards. Her mother returned with buckets of water, running at a crouch to avoid making herself a target for ambushers. Tatsuru stamped her feet and reproached her mother angrily for not waking her: now it was too late.

The news Tatsuru had brought soon became common knowledge all over the village. The people of Shironami sent boys to carry the news to the other Japanese Pioneer settlements. There were no menfolk in Shironami, barely even any old men, so the village head had always been one man in charge of an enormous family of women. By the time he came back, it would be too late for him to lead them as the headman of Sakito village had. It was all too sudden; they would need at least an hour to pack their luggage. They could do without most things, but they had to take all their food, at least, and the rifles that had been issued to every settlement, five per village. No matter what, they had to flee before the village head. They conceded that the people of Sakito village were a fine example, but they did not want the Shironami village head to lead *them* to be such exemplary Japanese.

At sunset, the people of the five remaining settlements of the 'Great Manchuria Development Group' gathered in the playground of the Shironami village primary school. Everyone was asking questions and answering them at the same time. With such a crowd, nobody could take the lead. They had heard that there was a city with a receiving centre for Japanese, from where you could take the boat back to Japan. This group, mainly women and children, set off with only a schoolboy's compass to guide them. Soviet and Chinese raiders had carried off almost all their livestock, leaving only those that were too old or too young. These feeble beasts became mounts for the elderly.

They set off on the 250-kilometre march, the women taking tiny steps in their wooden shoes. A woman called Amon was eight months pregnant; she rushed from the front of the procession to the back, and then hurried to the front again, pestering everyone for news of her husband Kirinoshita Taro and her son. They were too tired to reply, or do more than just shake their heads. Tatsuru staggered behind her mother, carrying a bag of rice balls on her back. Her mother was carrying Tatsuru's four-year-old sister on her back, and pulling her eight-year-old brother by the hand. As she stumbled along, Tatsuru was privately exulting over her success that day: after all, she had beaten the village heads in a race. It never occurred to her that the village elders had needed half a day to deal with Sakito village, and she had already forgotten the gunshots she had heard that morning by the railway line, which had been fired by a group of Chinese guerrillas. This was a civilian armed force whose exact nature was hard to define, who did both good things and bad: resisting the Japanese, suppressing bandits, opposing Communists – everything depended on who happened to be in their way, not to mention who had the upper hand. They had been planning to enter Sakito village to see what they could find: if they found injustice they would avenge it, if they found enemies they would pay them back, if they found some way to take advantage they would take it. Instead they ran into five Japanese village heads returning to their villages, so they opened fire, and gave them what they were looking for, ahead of schedule.

Three hours after they had set off, the people were starting to miss their village heads. By this time dusk was falling around them, and the near 3,000-strong cavalcade had left the main road and was walking on an earthen track the width of a single cart. The procession had become long and scattered; mothers were constantly begging the cavalcade to stop, so that they could comfort their children, who could not walk any further. Women would say to their children, who were hanging back by the side of the road: Get up, quick, the headman's coming! If the village headman had been there, they thought, he might have been able to keep the children on their worn, bleeding feet. Just at that moment, gunshots rang out from the sorghum fields on either side of the road. The first casualties were two old people riding on animals, then several women took a bullet as they were running along the road. The children threw back their heads and howled. One old man who managed to keep calm shouted: Down on your stomachs, don't move! They threw themselves down on their bellies, but the old man had already been hit. The battle was over before they had a chance to fire the guns they had brought.

By the time the troop re-formed, they discovered they had lost more than thirty of their companions. Nobody had brought any digging tools; the relatives of the dead cut a lock of hair, laid the bodies in a ditch by the side of the road, covered them with a decent piece of clothing and continued on their way.

Every day there were ambushes. They all became accustomed to death; they no longer had the energy to cry over the dead, just silently unloaded the food they had been carrying. People also became accustomed to respecting the wishes of the gravely injured, putting them to death in the quickest, cleanest way. Others were not willing to die. Amon was one of these. When Tatsuru saw her, she was lying in a bed of her own blood, head pillowed on a lump of earth. Her newborn child was lying beside her, its short life over after just a few minutes.

She waved her bloody hands to everyone who passed, calling out 'Keep going!' No doubt she believed she was smiling, but her face was twisted into a grimace of pain. She said to everyone who came near: 'Don't kill me, I'll catch you up in a bit! I haven't found my son and husband yet!' A man in his fifties took pity on her, and left her a sack of rice balls.

The old people saved rice for the young. They also saved them bullets and trouble. As a group they came to an agreement, and threw themselves into the next river they crossed, where they vanished without a sound.

The villagers fumbled their way towards experience: by trial and error they discovered that their chances of getting hit were lower after dark, so they started to move on at night and make camp by day. On the evening of the fifth day, when they woke up, they found that several of the families who had been sleeping at the edge of the camp had been hacked to death with knives. One of the survivors said apologetically: 'We really were just too tired, we didn't hear a thing.' Someone else added: 'Even if we had heard, what then?'

Their route had dragged itself out to twice its original length, and they had run out of provisions. Tatsuru's mother taught the women to recognise edible leaves and wild fruit. She told them that it was rare for a Chinese to starve to death, because they knew how to make every kind of wild grass and leaves into food. This was a skill she had learned from the Chinese hired hands. Luckily it was autumn; they found a thicket of nut trees, where they gathered enough to last them two days. All the mothers of teenage daughters cut off their hair and found them dark-coloured boys' clothes to wear. Although the road became harder with every passing day, and their numbers were decreasing daily, they had already put nearly two hundred kilometres behind them.

Early one morning they came to a copse of silver birches. They were preparing to set up camp when shots rang out from deep within the birch wood. By now, they had learned to dodge swiftly behind the trees and lie flat, children safely hidden beneath their mothers' bodies. The enemy were very free with their ammunition, firing off their bullets a clip at a time. The war was over, there was no need to conserve bullets, they were shooting for the sheer joy of it, regardless of whether or not they actually hit anything. When the shooting reached its climax, they heard their attackers cheering in Russian. A few of the youths who had just learned to shoot started to return fire. They had had some gratifying successes with guns: once when they had run into an ambush they had shot back a few times, and the attackers had left them in peace. But on this occasion retaliating was precisely the wrong thing to do, like poking a hornets' nest. The Soviet soldiers had not taken them seriously at first, but now their fighting instincts were aroused.

The Japanese settlers fell back, abandoning the dead and dragging the wounded with them. The terrain was far from favourable, with a gentle downward slope behind them. They had retreated a hundred metres when Russian battle cries suddenly broke out from another direction. They were caught in a pincer movement. Now they were as likely to get a bullet if they moved as if they stayed where they were. The youngsters fired back erratically, no more than a few shots, but enough to reveal their positions to the opposition, and they were soon picked off, one by one.

The gunfire increased in ferocity. Having inflamed the Soviets' temper, they had no choice but to let them work it off for a while.

Did they not hear the sound of the children crying? Could they possibly not know that their opponents were a crowd of women and children? A grenade exploded next to Tatsuru's mother, and when the smoke had cleared, Tatsuru no longer had a mother, brother or sister. Her father had died in battle in the Philippines the year before. Perhaps it was a blessing that her present danger did not leave Tatsuru at leisure to ponder her newly orphaned condition. She was following the others as they tried to break out of the encirclement, keening in grief for her whole family as she ran.

By the time they had escaped from the ambush, only half of the villagers remained. Their losses on this occasion accounted for two-thirds of all they had sustained in their entire journey. Another hundred were wounded; they used up all their blood-clotting powder in one go that day.

They woke at dusk on the second day to find that all the wounded had committed suicide. They had plotted together in the night and, resolved not to hold everyone back, they had helped each other to stagger to a stretch of ground fifty metres away. They had employed all kinds of different means, but they had all become exemplary Japanese in that one night.

Another day passed, and the group advanced at a crawl over the mountain roads. They modified their route again and again, choosing the remotest roads, but this took them deeper into the mountains. The children had drunk no water for two days, and could no longer be coaxed to move. The babies on the mothers' backs were howling – no longer crying now, but the yowls of a wild cat on the point of death.

There was not a grain of rice left. Mothers who had had no water or rice for two days stuffed their dry, shrivelled breasts in the children's mouths: children at the breast and the older children too, including those children who had lost their mothers, anyone with breasts would do what they could for them. The procession had long since become shapeless and disorganised, straggling along the paths for more than a kilometre or two. They kept finding that children had wandered away, and adults had dropped dead in their tracks. The only thing that could induce the children to take a step was saying, 'We're nearly there, and once we're there we can sleep.' Their expectations were not so high now, anything was fine so long as they could rest their feet. They had stopped believing 'There'll be water to drink and food to eat when we get there' a long time ago.

It was September 1945 as this procession of dried-up ghosts was walking through Manchuria. All over the mountains and wilderness the autumn leaves flamed and burned a brilliant red. Autumn is very short in Manchuria; when they camped out in the open, there would be frost all round them in the mornings. They relied on wild fruits and leaves, belief and determination to reach their goal to keep body and soul together. After fifteen days' journey on foot, their numbers had already fallen to just over a thousand.

One morning they ran into the Chinese militia. Their march had taken them closer than they intended to a market town, disturbing the three hundred soldiers quartered there, all armed with Japanese-made guns and bombs. First they blocked their way and fired on the villagers, then they chased after them, still shooting. The villagers fled to a pine wood on the top of a mountain, as the sound of gunfire gradually faded behind them. The women had broken free of the attack carrying children on their backs or in their arms. Tatsuru had a three-year-old girl on her back; the child had a high fever, and her every exhalation was like a tiny ball of fire on the nape of Tatsuru's neck. The girl's mother, whose name was Chieko, was carrying her son of less than a year in her arms. Oblivious to the bullets, she sat down hard on the ground, white foam hanging from the corners of her mouth. Another woman went back to drag her along, but she resisted desperately, gripping onto a tree with both her feet. The child in her arms wailed piercingly; the woman's two wide, spiritless eyes seemed like empty caves. At that moment, she stooped over the crying child in her arms with a peculiar motion, and people near to her saw her knife-sharp shoulder blades rise up strangely. When she straightened up, the baby had fallen silent. The women around her did not make a sound, backing away as if in fear of her, as they watched her lower her dead child to the ground and haul herself upright, clinging to the tree for support.

After the woman called Chieko had killed her baby, she hurled herself at her little daughter on Tatsuru's back. Tatsuru shouted through her tears: Kill her tomorrow, let her live another day. Tatsuru was young and strong, and this murderess who had just slain her own flesh and blood could not catch up with her. Chieko's elder son ran up behind her, and lashed out at her with a wooden cudgel, catching her right on the head. She dodged him, shielding her head with both hands, then gradually she let her hands fall away, allowing her son of barely ten to beat her bloody.

And so the slaughter of infants began. From that moment on, women in the group began to strangle babies who were sick or too young. If on setting out children were found to be missing from a family group, nobody would make any enquiries. As mothers, they had to consider what they stood to lose or gain; they had to keep the children they could save. Even the mothers of wild animals have this special power, bestowed on them by the Creator: when they scent a predator approaching and know they are powerless to save their young, they are willing to kill their offspring with their own teeth first. The women's faces were dull and lifeless, their eyes full of a kind of hysterical mourning. Tatsuru never let Chieko come anywhere near her, she even tied the girl to her breast with her sash when she was sleeping. The morning after the attack, the girl who had escaped death at her mother's hands had actually recovered from her illness. Tatsuru had popped a pellet of wild chestnut paste into the girl's mouth, and told her that they had one more day's journey ahead of them, then they would be there. The little girl then asked Tatsuru what had happened to her face. She told her that this was not her original face, it was black mud from the river, smeared on for a mask. Why? Because they were going to pass through a town, and they couldn't let the Chinese men or Soviet soldiers see her real face. The girl told Tatsuru that she was called Sato Kumi, her family came from the Ueno district of Tokyo. Her mother had made her memorise this brief account of her origins on the road, so that the children would be able to trace their bloodline if anything happened to her.

That was the only conversation the two girls had before the final calamity.

They struck camp late at night. Kumi's mother did not wake. They cut off a lock of Chieko's hair, tied it to Kumi's body, and then set off.

The darkness faded away; another day came around. It was a perfect late-autumn day, and everyone was in unusually high spirits: they were almost there. The waist-deep wormwood bushes all around them were frosted a brilliant white as far as the eye could see. Everyone was exhausted, falling fast asleep before they were even lying down properly. They slept like the dead – a hundred stampeding horses would not have woken them.

Not even the sound of the guns woke Tatsuru straight away. But when she did wake up, she was no longer surrounded by the familiar faces of neighbours from nearby villages, but by unrecognisable corpses.

1

A dozen or so sacks had been laid out on a raised platform; it was impossible to tell from their shape whether there were people or animals inside. The man calling out his wares said he was selling them by the kilo, a jiao* would buy half a kilo of Jap woman, cheaper than pork. The price had been fixed in advance, and the heaviest of the sacks was no more than thirty kilos. The county Security Corps had sent a squad of men in black uniforms to maintain order and ensure fair trading. The playground of the primary school was crowded with locals; quite a few bachelors were keen on the idea but couldn't afford to buy. Thirty kilos of Japanese woman would set you back seven silver dollars, but a single man with seven dollars could get himself a proper Chinese wife: why would he want to bring home a female Jap devil?

It had snowed early that morning, but the roads and paths to Anping town were already black with footprints. People were still arriving, young men in groups of three or five, showing off for the

* In Chinese currency one yuan divided into one hundred fen. The jiao is the equivalent of ten fen.

crowd with bad-taste jokes, shouting loudly: 'If we buy one and she doesn't suit, is there a guarantee? Can we bring her back and swap her for another?' The reply was always the same: 'No exchange!' 'What if we end up with the wrong one after spending all that money?' A voice in the crowd would call out, 'What's all this right and wrong? They're all the same once you put the light out!' or, 'The wrong one? Women are like dogskin socks, the same whichever foot you put them on!'

The people laughed; a loud, frightening sound. The sack nearest the edge of the platform twitched a few times, and shrunk in on itself.

The man said that two days ago the Security Corps had exchanged fire with a group of bandits. They had killed several of them and the rest had fled, leaving a dozen or so pretty young Jap virgins behind, whom the bandits hadn't had time to do anything with. A bandit they had captured who had been wounded in the leg confessed that on this occasion they had committed no outrages, but they had shot about a thousand Japanese refugees – hadn't the students said all those years ago 'In resisting Japan there is no division between first and last'? This victory had netted the bandit leader half a pocket of gold jewellery, all taken from Japanese corpses. After that the bullets had run out, and they had let the remaining Japs go. The Security Corps did not know what to do with these teenage Jap girls, they were all starved to skeletons. The Security Corps had no spare money or rations to keep them, and yesterday they had notified all the village heads, so they could get the locals to buy them and take them home – if the worst came to the worst they could always use them to do the hard work about the place, turning mill wheels and the like. A donkey cost more than seven silver dollars.

The man from the Security Corps shouted impatiently: 'Don't leave it too late, or they'll freeze to death before you get 'em home.'

The crowd at the school gates shifted to admit three people: an old couple and a younger man. Those who knew them said to their neighbours: 'Here's Stationmaster Zhang and his wife! And their Erhai with them!' Stationmaster Zhang was in charge of the railway station. The station for Anping town was a stop on a small branch line from Boli to Mudanjiang, where trains halted for one minute. It boasted a grand total of one employee, who was staff, guard and stationmaster, all in one. Stationmaster Zhang in his green uniform was very conspicuous in the crowd of heavy black jackets. It was well known that Stationmaster Zhang ran profitable sidelines of his own from the station: the one minute the train stopped at the station was used for both loading and unloading, and sometimes he would push a group of people with no tickets aboard. His family had accumulated a fair amount of property in this way, so even the heaviest of the Jap women would be well within his means. Stationmaster Zhang's tiny, thin wife followed in his wake, pausing from time to time to stamp her bound feet at Erhai, who was trailing five paces behind. Stationmaster Zhang always called this son Erhai, or second child, but nobody could remember seeing the Zhang family's eldest child.

Stationmaster Zhang and Erhai's mother walked up to the platform, looked at the dozen or so sacks, and asked the squad leader of the Security Corps to give them a hand. They pointed to a sack in the middle, saying: 'Hold that one upright, let's have a look.'

The squad leader said: 'We can't get them upright, can't you see the sack's not big enough?' He knew that Erhai's mother was going to start haranguing him, so he said: 'Don't try to be clever, you want to see how tall she is, don't you? I'll tell you the truth, she's tall enough to reach the top of your kitchen range and wash the dishes! All Japs are dwarfs – that's because their mothers were she-dawarfs!' The crowd laughed again.

Flakes of snow started to drift down from the sky. They saw Erhai's mother say something to him. Erhai turned his face away. Some of the young men in the crowd knew Erhai, and now they started shouting: 'Haven't you got a wife, Erhai? Leave some for the rest of us!'

Erhai did not bat an eyelid at any of this. He was an extremely stoical man, and if he did not want to hear something he simply let it wash over him, but when something did rile him, he could be stubborn as a mule. Erhai had a pair of camel's eyes, always half closed, and when he spoke (which was rarely) his lips would barely open. Just then he was pushing his way through the crowd with his broad shoulders. He said through motionless lips: 'Pick one with a good sack, then when we get back home we can use it to keep grain in too.'

Stationmaster Zhang had decided on the sack from the middle. The Security Corps squad leader warned them repeatedly not to open the sack in front of everyone: if they wanted to inspect the goods they should do so in private. Once they'd got a look at the Jap woman inside, it would make it harder to do business with the others, whether she was pretty or ugly. As the squad leader said while counting Stationmaster Zhang's cash, at seven silver dollars, if she wasn't lame or blind she'd do just fine.

The people opened a wide lane, watching Erhai and his father sling the sack on a pole and stroll confidently out, carrying the pole between them.

Stationmaster Zhang had got things off to a good start. Before they had the sack stowed on the cart, two more sacks had already been carried away, and by the time Stationmaster Zhang's cart had reached home, the rest of the Japanese women had been sold. There was no more joshing and joking: after all, nobody in Stationmaster Zhang's family had made any jokes, they were there to do business, pure and simple.

Stationmaster Zhang's mule cart was waiting at the staging post opposite the primary school, and the mule was fed and watered and ready to go. They laid the sack out flat in the back. There was no doubt that there was something alive inside; they could sense it although it did not move an inch. Erhai did not want to tire the mule, so he had his mother and father sit with the sack on the cart, while he walked beside them. The snowflakes became thicker; each flake had its own weight, as if drawn by an invisible force from the sky to the ground. It was over a kilometre from the school to the station, and much of the farmland they passed along the way belonged to the Zhang family.

The bald, flat, empty fields soon turned to white beneath the thick, dense flakes, as man and cart made their way through the heavy snow of November 1945. People would recall this snow in years to come, saying that it came late that year, but it had been a fine snowfall for all that, heavy and fierce. Their memories of that year were very clear: everything became a symbol, for this was the year the Jap devils had surrendered, and the male Japs ran off, leaving all those orphaned, helpless Jap women and children behind. Even the Zhang family could sense that they were travelling on a path that was full of symbolism. In fact the snow had helped the women inside the sacks: nobody had the heart to watch them be buried in heavy snow, so they hurriedly made their purchases and took them home. The Japanese girl in Stationmaster Zhang's sack could also sense the violence of this snowfall and the hardships of the road. However, she did not yet know that the forefathers of the people who lived in this part of the world had come here too by the Shanhaiguan Pass that led to the rest of China, with nothing but a cart and an animal to draw it. In those days, people who could not make a living would head for the north. It had been just the same for the parents of the girl in the sack: those Japanese who could no longer make ends meet would go west, crossing national boundaries, making their way to this great wasteland, taking it by force from the people whose fathers had first tilled it. And so this place that some called Kwantung and others Manchuria had become the fatal narrowing in the road that forced them to travel cheek by jowl with their enemies.

Erhai's mother cast an anxious look at the unmoving sack, and asked Erhai whether he was wearing a jacket under his coat. Erhai said no. His mother had thought to make Erhai take off his coat to cover the person in the sack, but as he had nothing warm on underneath, she could not bear to see her son freeze. Erhai flicked his whip, the mule broke into a trot, and he started to jog alongside; he could tell what his mother meant.

Stationmaster Zhang's station was part of his house. The waiting room and ticket office together occupied the same area as six card tables, with a side door that led to the Zhangs' kitchen. When the heating was on, it warmed both his workplace and his home. Next to the kitchen was the stable, where they also stacked coal and firewood. When they unloaded the cart, Erhai carried the sack to the centre of the courtyard. The snow was falling hard, and he screwed up his face against it, his camel's eyes squeezed shut, long eyelashes already white with snow.

His mother called out: 'Come along, you're supposed to carry the sack straight inside – why've you dropped it in the snow in the middle of the yard?'

Erhai hurriedly picked up the sack, and walked with it towards the main room. He estimated the weight of this sack at under twenty-five kilos. Typical good-for-nothing Security Corps, cheating them out of nearly two silver dollars. As soon as he entered the room he noticed that something was wrong. He put down the sack and ran back into the yard, then to the west room. There was nobody inside. Xiaohuan was gone. Erhai knew without even opening the chests that Xiaohuan had snatched up a bundle of winter clothing and run home to her mother. Erhai thought she was right to run away: that would show his mother and father what a rotten idea they'd thought up. It was hardly Xiaohuan's fault that she could not have children, but his father and mother were determined to buy a Japanese woman to have children for the Zhang family in Xiaohuan's place.

At that moment Erhai's mother called from the main room: 'Erhai! Erhai!'

He sat down on the heated brick bed that northern Chinese call a *kang*, and smoked his way through the best part of a pipe of tobacco. His mother pressed her face against the glass, rapping with her fingers.

'Come here, both of you!' She, at least, was beaming with joy.

Erhai simply did not hear her, and his mother pushed open the door. She was used to her son not speaking when he was spoken to, but one glance at his room was enough to show her that there was trouble. She and her husband had already spoken more than once to Xiaohuan about what they had in mind: they just wanted to buy a Japanese woman to have children, that was all, and once she'd had them they would send her packing.

His mother promised to go with her son to collect his wife that day or the day after; they'd be able to persuade her to come back. But right now Erhai should open the bag and let the woman out.

Erhai half closed his eyes, glanced briefly under his lids at his mother, and rose slowly to his feet, muttering: 'What are you doing? Can't you open a bag?'

His mother merely said: 'It's not me and your father who'll be having children with her.' Erhai's mother knew her son: Erhai was very biddable in his actions, for all that he was not particularly filial in speech, and he was already getting to his feet to follow his mother. He had argued repeatedly with his parents over the purchase of a Japanese woman to continue the Zhang family line, but in his actions he had been respectful, and submissive.

Erhai and his mother passed through the yard, now piled high with snow, and entered the main room. Stationmaster Zhang had gone out to the platform; a goods train was coming through at two, though not stopping, and he had to give the signal.

The room was very warm – his mother had been next door to add more coal to the furnace and let more hot air into the flue leading to the *kang*. The shape in the sack shrunk into a ball, not moving a muscle. Erhai understood that when his mother told him to open the bag, there was at least something of the notion of 'lifting the bridal veil' about it. Besides, his mother did not dare do the deed herself. The Japs had surrendered now, but she was still a bit fearful of them. Never mind that they had been an occupying army of murdering, burning devils, any strange foreigner would have been frightening enough. Erhai could feel his heart banging away like a big drum.

When Erhai and his mother saw someone very small sitting there hugging her knees, they were both struck dumb. The waif's hair had been cut off an inch from her head, and by the hair alone she and Erhai might have been brothers. Erhai could have spanned her skinny neck with one hand, and her face was scabbed over with mud. Erhai's mother noticed that the little woman was wearing cut-off trousers that barely reached her knees, and that her legs were stained with recently dried blood. The waif looked at her, and one glance was enough to tell her that something was not right. Appalled, she said to Erhai: 'Go on then, tell her to get up!'

Erhai stood there speechless. His eyes were fully open now.

'Erhai, tell her to get up, quick!'

Erhai said to the waif sitting shrunk into herself on the floor: 'Get up.' He said resentfully to his mother: 'See what my father's gone and done! Who's to say if she'll even live?'

This was exactly what was worrying Erhai's mother. If the worst happened and a Jap died in their house, who knew what would come of it? Quite apart from the expense, explaining themselves to the authorities would be troublesome enough.

Erhai's mother held out both her hands, less than certain what she was doing, but she steeled herself to grasp the waif by the arms. She had told herself beforehand that this creature was seven parts devil to three parts human, but when her hands closed around those arms, she still experienced a moment of pure horror: this was nothing but a bag of bones. She dragged the waif to her feet, and as soon as she relaxed her grip, the young girl fell back down again. The men from the Security Corps had given a guarantee that all the women would be complete in every particular – how could they have sold them a cripple? She must have been shot in the leg, or damaged when her fetters were struck off, leaving her unable to stand upright.

They carried the waif between them to the *kang*, her legs still curled up under her. Erhai's mother ran her hands up the girl's trouser legs, as far as the tops of her thighs, but could find no trace of a bullet wound. She realised belatedly that it was menstrual blood. Relief flooded through her: at least the waif was female.

'Get her some hot tea, see if that won't help a bit.' Erhai hurriedly handed his mother a bowl of tea. By now there was no terror or repugnance in his mother's movements as she leaned the slight body against her own crossed legs, and slowly dribbled the tea into her mouth. Most of it ran out again, moistening the scabs of mud on her cheek, and leaving a smear on Erhai's mother's hand. She called to him to pour out a bowl of water, bring a towel and be quick about it. Erhai half filled a basin with hot water from a kettle that had been heating on the *kang*, and took a towel from the washstand.

When the tea was all gone, Erhai's mother moistened the cloth and wiped the mud from the waif's face, a little at a time. She understood this trick too well: during the Japanese occupation of the northern provinces, a truckload of Japanese soldiers would sometimes come to the copper mine at the north end of the town, and all the mothers of young girls in the village would rub coal dust and river mud into their daughters' faces.

Bathing revealed delicate, tender skin, with a touch of soft down below the ears. By the time the basin of water had become a muddy soup, it was possible to get a rough idea of the shape of the face. It wouldn't have been a bad-looking face, if it had been a bit fatter.

Erhai was standing to one side, watching his mother wash the mud off this face as one would wash a turnip: two wide eyebrows appeared, and a broad, plump nose. Perhaps because it was too thin, the face had too many teeth and too big eyes, leaving an expression that was close to a grimace.

Erhai's mother said: 'Very nice-looking. Just so long as she's not a cripple. What do you say, Erhai?'

Erhai ignored her, picked up the basin and left. He tipped the water away into a ditch, afraid that if he poured it away in the yard it would freeze and his mother would slip on her bound feet and fall. Erhai's mother followed him out, saying that she would make the girl a drink of egg soup first. You shouldn't put solid food in a stomach that had been starved for the first day or two. Then she sent Erhai off on a long series of errands, starting with going to the village to buy a few yards of cloth so she could make her a padded jacket. Erhai stuck his hands into his sleeves, and headed for the gate, at which point his mother remembered something and ran over the snow, staggering on her bound feet, to stuff a banknote into his cuff.

'I forgot to give you the money! Get the red flowers on a blue ground!' The general store in town had just two kinds of patterned cloth, one was a red pattern on a blue background, the other a blue pattern on red. As Erhai made his way towards the gate, Erhai's mother said: 'On second thoughts, make it the red one! Blue flowers on a red ground!'

'What are you spending all that money for? She might well be a cripple!'

'Being a cripple won't get in the way of having children.' Erhai's mother waved her son away. 'Blue flowers on a red ground, you hear me?'

'Xiaohuan will be even more upset.'

'What's to be upset about? Once she's had children, turn her out!'

'And how are we going to do that?'

'Put her back in that bag, carry her up the mountain and leave her there.' Erhai's mother chuckled, and it was plain to see that she was joking.

Erhai came back with the cloth to find both his parents at the entrance to the main room, peering inside through a crack in the door. Stationmaster Zhang heard Erhai's footsteps squeaking in the snow, looked over his shoulder and beckoned him across. His mother hurriedly gave up her place to him. Through the crack in the door they saw that the Japanese girl had got up, leaning sideways towards them, and was looking in the fist-sized mirror on the wall. Now that she was standing up she looked nothing like a female Japanese pirate, or a mother of Japanese pirates. She was pretty much the same height as the girls in the town. Erhai backed away. His mother appeared to be congratulating herself on a bargain.

'You see, does she look like a cripple?' she said quietly. 'She was just all cramped from being bundled up in that sack.'

Stationmaster Zhang lowered his voice and said: 'If anyone asks, say we bought her to do the cooking.'

Erhai's mother jerked her chin at Erhai to come with her. Erhai followed his mother into the kitchen, where he saw a big bowl of sorghum and rice piled high, topped with a heap of pickled cabbage and tofu. His mother said that she had gulped down the bowl of egg soup she had brought so fast that she'd been afraid she'd scald her throat, and ordered her son: 'Tell her to take her time, there's more in the pot!'

'Didn't you say she wasn't supposed to eat solid food?' Erhai said.

'How's she supposed to eat her fill if she doesn't eat solid food?' His mother had clearly forgotten her earlier warning in her glee. 'Tell her to take some water with every mouthful, she'll be fine.'

'Do I speak Japanese?' said Erhai. But his feet were already obediently carrying him towards the main room.

When he pushed open the door, his eyes took in two legs wearing a pair of black padded trousers that belonged to his mother. On raising his gaze slightly, he saw a pair of hands, with short fingers that were still rather childish. There was no need to do more; just by keeping his eyes open and fixed where they were, he could catch a vague glimpse of a waist. The waist shifted backwards slightly, retreating from him. Suddenly, the crown of a head appeared in front of Erhai's half-closed eyes. Erhai's heart started banging like a drum again: this was his first time to be on the receiving end of a bow from a Japanese. Very likely the bow was not meant for him, but for the big bowl of rice, cabbage and tofu.

Panic seized Erhai. His half-closed eyes shot wide open, and at that moment the head in front of him straightened up again. Erhai went red to the ears: he was looking straight into her direct gaze. Her eyes were too large, like a ground squirrel, probably because she had lost so much weight. Erhai felt a surge of both pity and repugnance. He put the big bowl of sorghum rice on the *kang* table, turned and left.

After leaving the main room, Erhai fled to his own room. A while later his parents came in, asking if he'd said hello to her. Erhai ignored them, and continued to rummage in the camphor-wood chest. How could making eye contact with that Jap woman just now have got him in such a state? He couldn't even justify it to himself. His parents, on the other hand, were beaming exultantly with the sly grins of born troublemakers. His mother said: 'This is no different from taking in a minor wife, we in the Zhang family can easily afford to do this.' Erhai's only response was to pretend he hadn't heard a word of it.

Stationmaster Zhang told his son not to worry, he and his wife would visit Xiaohuan's home together to patch things up. Since Xiaohuan couldn't have children, she wouldn't dare give them any trouble. In two years' time Erhai would take over from his father – he would be the new Stationmaster Zhang, and there would be plenty of lovely young girls ready to take Xiaohuan's place.

Erhai finally dug out a pair of dogskin ear muffs. His mother asked where he was going. He did not reply. It was not until he had picked up Xiaohuan's small cotton quilt from the *kang*, the one she used to cover her legs in the cart, that they realised their son was going to his wife's home.

'Who goes on a long journey in heavy snow like this?' said Stationmaster Zhang. 'Your mother and I will go tomorrow, isn't that enough?'

Erhai's movements as he tied puttees around his legs slowed noticeably.

'It's a journey of twenty kilometres! Suppose Xiaohuan won't let you stay the night, and you have to make another twenty-kilometre journey back?'

'All the same, we can't let Xiaohuan become a laughing stock, people saying that when she's out of the house, I'm at home with a Japanese woman . . .'

'That's not being a laughing stock.' Stationmaster Zhang spread both his hands wide.

Erhai looked at his father.

'That's the truth!' Stationmaster Zhang said. 'What did we buy a Japanese woman for? To have children, whether we say it to Zhu Xiaohuan's face or behind her back? Bloody hell, son, you're a grown man of twenty . . . All right then, off you go, running through the blizzard to your wife's home. Just see how she praises you for being so pure and noble.'

Erhai's mother did not worry in the least. He might speak sweet words to Xiaohuan, but in reality he would do what he was supposed to.

'I can't just stand by and watch you two bullying Xiaohuan like this!' Erhai said, slowly untying his puttees.

The snow fell all night without stopping. Early the next day, Erhai rose and went to top up the coal for the stove, where he found his mother teaching the little Japanese woman to make bricks of coal dust. It seemed that there was nothing wrong with her physically, she was just thin.

Erhai's mother turned her head, caught sight of Erhai and called: 'Erhai, you come and teach her!'

But Erhai had already left. He felt both queasy and amused; old women always love to pass responsibility on to someone else, he thought. It was in their nature, they couldn't help it. Any fool with a little muscle could make coal bricks. By the third day the little Jap woman was making coal bricks on her own; she had put on the new padded cotton jacket, red with a blue pattern, which Erhai's mother had sewn for her, and taken the leftover cloth to tie round her stubbly head, which reminded him of a conker. She had knotted the headscarf in a Japanese style: no matter how you looked at it, this was a Japanese woman. When Stationmaster Zhang came in from work, she knelt at the doorway, dressed in these new clothes, to welcome him home. Before two more days had passed she had figured out Stationmaster Zhang's work schedule; she would be there very early, kneeling at the door, to tie his shoelaces for him when he left. She did all this with such remarkable composure, solemn eyes staring straight ahead, that neither Erhai nor his mother said a word.

At last the snow melted. Once the roads had dried out and were passable again, Erhai and his mother took the mule cart to the Zhu family village. Of course Stationmaster Zhang could not go himself, who would be left in charge of the station? Besides, an important personage like a stationmaster could not waste his time on such a trifling matter. When he said he would go to collect Zhu Xiaohuan, he had just been saying the first thing that came into his head, and Stationmaster Zhang said many such things; nobody took them seriously. He sent Erhai and his mother on their way with gifts for their in-laws: two bottles of sorghum liquor, and a piece of ginseng he had been saving for years.

Erhai's mother told her son not to worry about the Zhus: everyone in the Zhu family knew how things stood, their only worry would be that the Zhang family was going to put aside their daughter.

'What would I do that for?!'

'Who said we're going to put her aside? Are we that sort of wicked people? I was just saying that Xiaohuan made the best marriage out of all the four Zhu girls, it's them who're scared of us.'

At the very beginning Erhai had not been at all fond of Xiaohuan. When he married her it had all been done strictly by the book; there had been nothing personal about it at all. For a while, he had even resented her, because the date of birth on her papers had been tampered with. After the wedding, Erhai learned from a classmate who lived in Zhu village that Xiaohuan had been the old maid of the Zhu family, so indulged that no one could do a thing with her; everyone knew she was a troublemaker, so no one dared to marry her. Fearing she would be left on the shelf, the Zhu family had adjusted her age downwards by two years.

Erhai could not remember exactly when he had first started to become fond of Xiaohuan. She did her duty: by the second month of their marriage she was pregnant. By the fourth month, the town midwife said that you could tell just by looking at Xiaohuan's midriff that she was carrying a son. From then on not just Erhai but even Stationmaster Zhang and Erhai's mother all began to tolerate Xiaohuan's bad temper, enduring it as they praised her with fawning smiles.

After she lost the baby, Xiaohuan's temper suddenly improved. The seven-month embryo had been as large and fully formed as a year-old child. Erhai had heard his mother telling the story over and over again to relatives and friends: how Xiaohuan had come across four Japanese soldiers, how she had become separated from her female friends as they fled, how she had climbed onto an ox that was grazing by the side of the road, and how the ox had carried her in a race with the Japanese soldiers. In the end it was hard to say if the Japanese soldiers or the ox should take the blame, but it was the ox that threw Xiaohuan up into the air, to land over three metres away. Xiaohuan went into premature labour.

Erhai's clearest memories were of the blood. They had carried out Xiaohuan's blood by the basinful; the old doctor from the county hospital had been covered in it like a garment. Spreading his two bloody hands wide, he had asked the Zhangs whether he should save the mother or the child: it was up to them, they just had to say the word. Erhai said: Save the mother. Erhai's mother and father said nothing. Still the doctor did not leave. He glanced at Erhai and told him in a low voice that he could save Xiaohuan's life but she would not be able to have children afterwards; there was too much internal damage. Now Erhai's mother spoke up: Then keep the child. Erhai bawled at the doctor's retreating back: Keep the adult! Save Xiaohuan! The doctor turned round, and told the family to come to a decision. Stationmaster Zhang announced formally on behalf of the Zhang family that if only one life could be spared, then he was to save the grandson and heir. Erhai seized the doctor by the collar: Why are you listening to him?! I'm the child's father, I'm the head of Zhu Xiaohuan's family!

In fact, Erhai had no recollection of having spoken these words. It was his wife who remembered them and recited them back to him later. Xiaohuan said: 'You really are as stubborn as a donkey – you gave that old doctor such a fright he nearly wet himself!' Erhai pondered these words afterwards. If he had truly said such things, this must go to show that he loved Xiaohuan. This was no common love: anything that could make him stand up to his parents, and risk cutting off the Zhang family line altogether, must be a strong affection indeed, deeply rooted in his heart and his guts.

❖

When they entered the Zhu family's courtyard, Xiaohuan's parents brought out stools, and invited their in-laws to sit in the sun and have a cup of tea. The Zhu family were one of the more comfortably off families in the village; they owned over five acres of good land and traded in oilseeds. It took a lot of shouting and furious scolding from Xiaohuan's mother to get her out of the house. She greeted her mother-in-law with a brief 'Ma', then turned at once to face her own mother, eyes full of surprise, saying: 'Who's this then in a new jacket? Did we invite him? What a thick skin he's grown!'

Erhai kept on drinking his tea, as the Zhu parents and Erhai's mother laughed hollowly together. Erhai felt like a weight had been lifted from his heart: Xiaohuan was treating the matter with good sense and clear understanding, behaving as if this serious grievance were a common-or-garden spat with her husband. He could tell from his in-laws' expressions that Xiaohuan had not informed them of the true state of affairs.

Xiaohuan had a round face with permanently flushed cheeks, and a pair of rather narrow eyes, with puffy lids half concealing very thick eyelashes, so that whenever he looked at her she always appeared to have only just woken from sleep. She had a very sharp tongue but a ready smile, and when she smiled a dimple appeared on her cheek, and the corner of her mouth turned up to reveal a gold tooth. Erhai had no time for people who inlaid their mouths with gold, but on Xiaohuan's face, that tooth glinting in the midst of her smile did not detract from her appearance at all. Erhai did not consider Xiaohuan a beauty, but there was something very appealing about her. She had an intimate, affectionate manner with everybody; even when she cursed you there was still something warm about it.

Xiaohuan's parents produced a packet of griddle cakes, saying that it should be enough for the three of them to eat for lunch on the road.

Xiaohuan said: 'The three of who? Who's going back with them?'

Her mother cuffed her around the head, and told her to get on, pack her bags and go home with her husband, for her parents didn't plan on keeping her. Only then did Xiaohuan shoot him a sideways glance, jerk her head and enter the house. A minute later she was back, with a headscarf and the legs of her padded trousers neatly tied. She had packed her things ages ago, of course; she had got everything ready before she heard Erhai and his mother coming through the gate. Erhai's lips twitched slightly up. He felt that Xiaohuan had made things very easy for him, first making a scene, then setting things to rights, and all done in the best possible way.

2

One April morning, the Japanese woman ran away. When Xiaohuan got up to go to the toilet, she noticed that the big bar on the main gate was undone. It was barely past dawn; Xiaohuan could not think who would want to be out so early. Yesterday evening's snow had been very light, covering the ground in a thin grey layer. Xiaohuan could see a line of footprints in the snow, which started in the east room, went into the kitchen and came out again, leading towards the main gate. The Japanese woman and Erhai's parents slept in the north room.

Xiaohuan went back to her room, shook Erhai awake, and said to him, 'That Japanese she-wolf! We fed her up and now she's run off.'

Erhai opened his eyes as wide as they would go, to indicate that he thought she was talking nonsense but he wanted her to carry on talking nonsense for now.

'She's run off, I'm sure of it! Your mother and father have been feeding good tea and good rice to a she-wolf – and now she's sleek and glossy she's headed for the hills.'

Erhai sat up with a grunt. He ignored Xiaohuan's stream of sarcastic remarks, about how greedy he was for that Jap woman, and how it seemed that little slip of a girl could still whet a man's appetite.

Erhai hastily flung on padded trousers and jacket, asking: 'Have you said anything to my father?'

She kept up her tirade: seven silver dollars, and you got to sleep with her dozens of times – you got yourself a damn good deal there, and no mistake. There are several unlicensed drinking holes in town where a whore and a bed for the night would set you back dozens of silver dollars!

Erhai glared at her. 'You shut your mouth. What'll we do if she freezes to death in this snowy weather?'

He left the room. Xiaohuan yelled at his retreating back: 'What's your hurry? Mind your step, don't trip yourself up and bash your teeth out, you wouldn't want to whistle when you kissed her, would you now?'

Erhai's mother looked over their belongings, and found that the Japanese woman had taken nothing with her but a few corn cakes. She was wearing the clothes she had worn in the sack. They could all remember how carefully she had washed and scrubbed her Japanese trousers and shirt, ironed them flat with the iron teapot and folded them neatly; she had been preparing luggage for her escape. Her thoughts of escape must have survived all through that long winter, despite the thick blanket of snow that had covered them.

Stationmaster Zhang said: 'So this Jap woman doesn't even appreciate our Chinese clothes? She'll freeze to death, you wait and see!'

Erhai's mother stared into space, clutching the red padded jacket with the blue flowers. They had lived together for half a year, she had treated her almost like her son's wife; how could she have kept her all this time without getting any loyalty in return? Two pairs of new cotton socks that had been Xiaohuan's had been laid out on top of the jacket; the woman had no gratitude at all. Stationmaster Zhang put on his hat, ready to go out the door. Erhai hurriedly jammed his own hat on his head and shoved his feet into his shoes, ignoring Xiaohuan, who was leaning against the door frame, enjoying a leisurely smoke, a wicked smile on her face, as if watching a good play. When Erhai barged his way past her, she deliberately staggered to one side in an exaggerated fashion, so she looked like she was dodging a large farm animal that had burst out of its pen.

Stationmaster Zhang and Erhai followed her footprints as far as the entrance to the village, where they merged with the tracks of horse and mule carts. Father and son tucked their hands in their sleeves, not knowing where to look next. Finally they agreed to split up and search. Erhai's heart was bursting with rage, which soon turned to resentment towards his parents: they had everything they needed in life already, so why did they have to go looking for trouble? How much of the family's precious resources had they spent on a half-dead Japanese woman? How many times had the family quarrelled over her? There was not so much as the shadow of a child to show for it, and he, Erhai, was in for a lifetime's worth of reproaches: Zhu Xiaohuan would have the moral advantage for the rest of her days.

He and the Japanese woman were absolute strangers to each other. The start of marital relations had done nothing to dispel this strangeness. The first time he came to her bed he had heard her crying. To begin with he thought that this was something he had to do for the sake of his parents, but once she started crying he became fierce and cruel in his turn. What was she crying for? Anyone would think *he* was the one bullying *her*. Here he was, doing his best to be considerate, and for what? He went at it softly and gently, yet she was acting all wronged, as if she was enduring his bestial behaviour. And so he might as well show her a bit of bestial behaviour. He finished very fast, while she sobbed softly. With an effort, he restrained himself from grabbing her by her hair, which was just starting to grow back, and asking her exactly how she thought she'd been wronged.

The next few times he found her lying like a corpse, neatly attired, chin up, toes pointing to the ceiling, as if she really had died. He had to take off her clothes for her. As he was stripping her, it suddenly dawned on him that his actions towards her were disgusting, despicable. She *wanted* him to be despicable. She had laid herself out so neatly, lying there like a dead thing, making him feel lower than a beast as he peeled off her clothes, as if he was raping a corpse. Mad with rage, he thought: Fine then, I'll be lower than a beast. Her father and elder brothers had been like beasts to Chinese women, this was no different.

There was just one exception. One night he had used up all his strength violating her; his first thought had been to roll off her body and jump straight down from the *kang*, but he suddenly felt the need to take a breather, to catch his breath. He felt one of her hands come up to rest on his back, stroking gently, a soft, timid hand. He thought of the first time he saw her, of that pair of childish hands with their short fingers. Yet more strength drained out of him.

By now Erhai had reached the gate of the Anping town primary school. It was still early, and the playground was empty. Without any hope of a result he enquired of the caretaker whether he had seen a Japanese girl pass this way.

The caretaker said he did not know whether it was a Japanese girl or not, but he'd seen a young person with a head like a feather duster walking away from the village. Wearing clothes with a collar like a monk's? Yes, just that kind of collar. Cut-off trousers? Yes.

Erhai returned home at dusk. Stationmaster Zhang had paid a visit to the Security Corps, to find out where the other dozen Japanese women had ended up. Two had been sold to neighbouring villages, and Stationmaster Zhang had gone there to make enquiries. He learned that both Japanese women had ended up living with poor bachelors, but for better or worse they had stayed, and both had a child on the way. It appeared that they could not have had any contact with the Zhang family's escapee.

In the following days, Erhai and Stationmaster Zhang visited several of the more distant villages, but with no result. On the evening of the sixth day, Xiaohuan came back from visiting a female friend in town, and saw a black shadow standing at the gate. She went up to her, grabbed her by her shirt and stormed into the yard, shouting at the top of her voice: 'She's back, she's back! Food's hard to come by outside, now she's starved off her fat she's come back to us for something to feed on!'

The little Japanese woman could not understand what Xiaohuan was saying, but her voice was as noisy as the celebrations at New Year. She stopped resisting and allowed Xiaohuan to drag her all the way to the main room.

Erhai's mother was sitting by herself, fiddling with mah-jong tiles and smoking, but when she heard Xiaohuan kicking up a fuss she put on her socks and jumped down from the *kang*. She walked up to the girl, but when she saw how thin she had become, the hand she had raised to slap her fell back down by her side.

'Xiaohuan, go to the station, tell your father, tell him to come home right now!' Erhai's mother ordered her daughter-in-law.

'Stay right where you are, don't you dare come in! You know you've done something shameful, don't you?' Xiaohuan said to the little Japanese woman.

At that moment Erhai came over from the west room. His mother said quickly: 'Come on, that's enough, if she's going to be scolded or beaten, that's for your father to decide.'

At supper time Stationmaster Zhang came back. He took out a piece of paper, and said to Erhai: 'Now then, write: *Why did you run off?* Those Japs all know our writing.'

Erhai did as he was told. The Japanese woman glanced briefly at the characters on the paper, but she did not move, save to lower her eyelids.

'She probably doesn't understand,' Erhai said.

'She certainly does understand . . .' said Stationmaster Zhang, his eyes fixed on her face beneath its thatch of hair.

'Don't ask. Do you need to ask? She must be missing her own mother and father,' said Erhai's mother. She picked up a big chunk of fat meat in her chopsticks and put it in the Japanese woman's bowl, then her chopsticks moved without a pause to a larger piece, which she deposited in Xiaohuan's bowl. It was like she was toying with an invisible pair of scales, with one of Erhai's two women on each side.

Stationmaster Zhang said: 'Erhai, this time write: *Why did you come back?*'

Erhai wrote down his father's question, a stroke at a time.

When the Japanese woman had finished reading, she remained motionless, eyelids lowered.

Xiaohuan said: 'I'll say it for her: I was starving, the corn cakes I'd stolen are all gone, so I came back. Have you made any more corn cakes? Make me some more, this time I want to take them off to Harbin, munching all the way.'

As soon as Xiaohuan spoke, the Japanese woman lifted up her head and looked at her. She had a pair of very attractive, very bright eyes. When she looked at Xiaohuan it seemed like she understood her well, and more than that, like she actually admired her a great deal.

Xiaohuan's mouth had never stood still from the day she first saw her; when bringing her a headscarf, she would say: 'Not as good as the headscarves you Jap devils use, right? You'll just have to make do, won't you? Would I have given up a good one for you?' If she gave her a pair of padded shoes, she would scold: 'There you go, a free pair of shoes, they're old but you can make do, don't turn up your nose at them. If you want to wear new ones, make 'em yourself.' Each time, the Japanese woman's eyes would brighten; she would watch her venting her spleen with verve and enthusiasm – and then she would bow from the waist, thanking her for her gift.

No one managed to get anything at all out of the Japanese woman that evening. The following day at supper time, she respectfully laid a sheet of paper on the table in front of the family. On it was written: '*Takeuchi Tatsuru, 16. Parents, elder brother, younger brother, younger sister, all dead. Tatsuru pregnant.*'

Everyone was stunned. Erhai's mother, who could not read, jabbed Stationmaster Zhang with her elbow, but he did not say a word. She nudged him again, with increasing impatience.

Xiaohuan said: 'Ma, she's got a bun in the oven. *That's* why she came back.'

'. . . Is it our Erhai's?' she asked.

'How can you say such things?' Erhai retorted angrily at his mother.

'Erhai, ask her, how many months?' His mother was afire with impatience.

'She must only just have got pregnant,' Stationmaster Zhang said. 'She ran off, realised she was having a baby and came straight back.'

'I've not seen her feeling sick, or throwing up, or anything like that . . .' said Erhai's mother, not daring to believe it.

'She must have known deep down,' Stationmaster Zhang said.

Xiaohuan glanced at Erhai. She knew how soft-hearted he was, and how troubled he would be at the words 'Parents, elder brother, younger brother, younger sister, all dead'. The little Jap woman called Zhunei Duohe* was an orphan, and only sixteen years old, no more than a girl.

'Quick, child, have something to eat.' Erhai's mother rubbed a bit of bean sauce on a steamed sorghum bun, added a strip of snow-white onion, and crammed them into Duohe's hands. 'You have to keep eating when you're carrying a child, whether you feel like it or not!'

The family picked up their chopsticks, one after another. None of them felt like talking, though all of them wanted to say: 'And we have no idea how her family died.'

That evening, Xiaohuan and Erhai felt that a burden had been lifted from their shoulders. Now that there was a child on the way, Erhai did not have to go to the Japanese woman's room any more. That night Erhai took Xiaohuan in his arms. Xiaohuan struggled unconvincingly, swatting him away and protesting half-heartedly, saying that the Jap woman might have whetted his appetite, but she, Zhu Xiaohuan, was the one who could satisfy his hunger.

Erhai stayed awake long after Xiaohuan was asleep. He was thinking that 'Duohe' was a peculiar name, but it looked nice written down. Maybe in future the name would trip more easily from his tongue. He turned over. The moon shone down, casting a patch of white onto the window. He thought to himself that once this Japanese

* Speakers of Chinese and Japanese cannot understand each other when they talk, but their writing systems share a lot of the same characters, which often have similar meanings in both languages. The name 竹内多鹤 can be understood in both Japanese and Chinese writing systems, but the pronunciation is quite different. So where a Japanese person sees the name Takeuchi Tatsuru, a Chinese would read it as Zhunei Duohe.

woman had given birth to his child, it would be easier to get to know her better.

The child was born at midnight in the first month of the new year. It was a girl, and a very easy delivery; they had hired a midwife from the county hospital who knew a little Japanese. Employing someone from the hospital was a calculated move on Stationmaster Zhang's part: he did not want the locals to know exactly whose belly the child had come from. As soon as Duohe's pregnancy started to show, she hid herself at home and did not leave the courtyard. Xiaohuan went back to her parents' to stay for four or five months, and did not come back until the child was a full month old. When people next saw Xiaohuan, she was swaggering through the streets with a baby in her arms, wrapped up in a pink cloak. When asked where she had got the baby she would reply: Do you need to ask? I picked her up this morning when I was out collecting dung! Or else she would say: I dug her up while searching for ginseng! If they said the child was pretty, then she'd respond: You're dead right there, looks like the ugly mother's turned out a pretty girl. If someone were to say unkindly: Xiaohuan, how come the little girl doesn't look like you? she'd reply: How could she look like me? If she took after me the matchmaker would be eating her heart out with worry, wouldn't she? How many idiots like Zhang Erhai are there in the whole world?

On the evening that Xiaohuan had returned to the Zhang home, she had gone straight to her room. Erhai's mother had come tripping in with self-satisfied little footsteps, and called Xiaohuan to come quickly and see the fat month-old baby girl.

'Is Erhai at *her* place?' Xiaohuan asked.

Erhai's mother knew what her daughter-in-law meant, and had made a hasty retreat. After a while Erhai was called in.

'All that effort for nothing, you've got yourself a girl. It'll cost you more to raise her than you'll ever get back from her dowry,' Xiaohuan had said.

Erhai had intended to take her by the hand to see the child with a heart overflowing with joy, but the words she came out with held him back at the door. He turned round and was about to leave, when Xiaohuan called out: 'Where are you off to now?'

He said, without a backward glance: 'To carry on making an effort!'

Xiaohuan dragged him back, and glared ferociously into his half-closed eyes. He just let her stare.

Xiaohuan stared for some time, then slapped his face. But she was not really hitting him; there was an element of flirtatious enquiry, mingled with accusation and resentment. Erhai slapped her right back without a word in response. Xiaohuan understood that her husband had not fallen in love with Duohe: he had the confidence of a man who feels that right is on his side and has no intention of putting up with an undeserved slap.

In the following days, Xiaohuan did not go to see the child. From her window she could see Duohe coming and going in the yard with rapid steps, head held very low, apparently doing nothing but carrying buckets of dirty water outside, and basins of hot water in. Duohe's chest was very heavy, and her face was as white and soft as buttermilk. Her body language was just the same as before the baby, she was forever bowing from the waist, but Xiaohuan felt that her expressions were completely different from the way they used to be. This was a Jap woman who felt she had someone to back her up, bustling and scurrying about with small steps in her wooden shoes like a woman who was her own master, giving herself airs of importance, walking all over the Zhang family courtyard and making it her own, like it was occupied territory.

One afternoon the sun came out, in a way you only see after rain. Xiaohuan got out of bed around ten, as was her habit, and sat on the *kang* smoking her first pipe of the day. From the yard came the sound of wooden shoes passing from the north room over to the boiler room. After that nothing moved for a long time. Only Duohe and Xiaohuan were at home, two women – two and a half if you counted the little girl of barely a month old. Xiaohuan got dressed, wrapped a shawl round her shoulders and carefully combed her hair. Then she walked into the courtyard, whipped off the shawl and shook off the loose hairs and dandruff. Just at that moment she heard somebody humming a little tune in the boiler room. A Japanese tune. She moved closer to the boiler-room window and saw, rising out of clouds of snow-white steam, two balls of pink flesh, a big one and a little one. Duohe's bathtub was in fact a Japanese Army-issue aluminium cooking pot, abandoned by the Japanese at the railway station after the surrender. The pot was deep enough, but not particularly broad, and Duohe had set a bench above the tub, so that it spanned from side to side. She sat on it, the child in her arms, and scooped out water from the tub to wash herself and the child. Holding a ladle made out of a gourd, she poured water first onto her left shoulder, and then her right. The water must have been very hot – with each ladleful, she would flinch away with a small, happy motion, a squeak would bubble up in her little song, like a little girl being tickled, and a smile would send her tune out of key. The water did not fall onto the child's body until it had passed over hers and adjusted to her temperature, so the water did not startle the child at all. Of course the child would not be afraid; she had spent nine months bathing in a bag of warm water inside her mother's womb. The ten o'clock sun was still in the east, and was shining through the hole left in the wall from where they had taken away the chimney at the end of winter, becoming a pillar of dazzling light that made a moon-shaped patch of brightness on the floor. The child clung to her mother's breast, peaceful and serene. Duohe's body was round and bulging, and it was not just her two breasts that were so full of milk they seemed about to explode: her whole body was full and round with milk, as if it might come flowing out at a touch. How many portrayals of this image of mother and child had there been over the generations? Pinched in clay, modelled in dough, fired into pottery . . .

She saw Duohe bend down to pick up a towel and wrap the child in it. She ducked hastily to one side. She had no desire for Duohe to see her gaping at them like that. And Duohe did not see her – the tune she was humming flowed on, smoothly and seamlessly, which showed that she was too preoccupied to look at anything. She stood up, dripping wet, and walked over to the column of sunlight. A young mother, dripping wet, her stomach no bigger than before the child, a line below her navel the colour of soy sauce leading directly into the thicket of bushy black hair between her thighs. There was enough hair growing down there to cover half a head. And there was enough growing on Duohe's head for two heads. She came from a barbarian, hairy race, which made the sight in front of Xiaohuan seem still more shocking. There was a strange twisting in Xiaohuan's guts, and she did not know if she was sickened by what she saw or not. No. All too clearly she was not sickened. The body of this young mother from an alien race, a body free from shame, showed Xiaohuan what a woman could be like. She had never really considered what exactly a woman was, and as a woman herself, she was too closely involved to get any sense of how matters really stood. Now she was outside looking in through the window at a woman who was like a little female animal. Xiaohuan was horribly upset, there was no way for her to put what she was seeing and thinking into any kind of order in her mind. If she were to get someone better read to assemble her thoughts and ideas, they would probably have come up with something like this: she was looking at a woman who was utterly female – skin and flesh poured full of milk, causing those parts that stuck out to bulge shamelessly, and then come together in the unfathomable place where her thighs met, descending into deeper darkness. Since the world began, how many hunters had become ensnared by the lure of those black bushy threads, dark and deep as a mystery? And it was not a lure without reason; its ultimate purpose was to give birth to a little ball of pink flesh.

Xiaohuan thought of Erhai. He had been lured in, and a part of Erhai had been transformed into this little ball of flesh. Xiaohuan did not know if she was jealous or moved, but for a moment all the strength drained out of her body and her heart. What would he want with this lure, if it could no longer give birth to a fruit of flesh and blood? If between her legs was a dark, dried-up barren land, just like Xiaohuan herself.

It was not until the Dragon Boat Festival that Xiaohuan officially met the child.

That day she had just got up, and Erhai came in carrying the baby, saying that Duohe was busy in the kitchen making Japanese red-bean balls, so he had to hold the girl for a while.

Xiaohuan took one look at him and said: 'Is that a winter melon you're carrying? Who carries a kid like that?'

Erhai shifted his hold to an even more awkward grip. Xiaohuan grabbed the bundle off him and made a cradle for the child with her arms. She looked at the fair-skinned, chubby baby girl, with her double chin and extra creases around her eyes – it had only been two months and already life had exhausted her, she could not even be bothered to open her eyes fully. It was so strange, how could Erhai's eyes have moved onto the face of a baby girl? And his nose too, and those eyebrows. Xiaohuan nudged one small hand out of the bundle of swaddling clothes, and her heart trembled: the fingers and nails were all Erhai's. The Jap woman did not have such long fingers, such strong, healthy, four-square fingernails. She did not realise that she had been staring at the child for so long; it was very rare for Xiaohuan to concentrate on anything for a stretch without smoking. She traced the child's forehead and eyebrows with her fingertips. It was Erhai's eyebrows that she loved the best, they were neither dark nor faint, and all their expression was in the arch and the tip. The baby had gone to sleep again. This child truly was no trouble at all. Those eyes were really just like a camel. Xiaohuan was perhaps even fonder of Erhai's eyes than his eyebrows. Was there any part of Erhai that she was not fond of? She had not been aware of it, that was all. And even if she had known, she would not have admitted it, even to herself.

After that, Xiaohuan always had Erhai carry the child over to their room. The thing she found most touching about the little girl was her sweet, tractable nature. She had never seen a baby that was so easy to soothe. Two lines of a song and she would chuckle, five lines and she would go to sleep. She wondered how she could be so pathetic? She had hugged another woman's child until she became a piece of her heart.

That day all the family members were choosing a name for the child. They could not keep calling her 'girlie this, girlie that', after all. Whenever someone thought of one, Erhai wrote it down with a brush pen, but they kept failing to come up with a name that everyone could wholeheartedly accept, although they had filled a whole sheet of paper with names.

'Call her . . . Zhang Shujian,' Stationmaster Zhang said.

Everybody understood what he meant. Erhai's official name was Zhang Liangjian.

'Doesn't sound nice,' said Erhai's mother.

'It sounds fine! What's wrong with it?' Stationmaster Zhang said. 'It's only different from Zhang Liangjian by one character.'

Erhai's mother laughed, and said: 'Zhang Liangjian doesn't sound nice either. Why has everybody always called Erhai Erhai, from primary school right the way through to now?'

'You have a go then!' said Stationmaster Zhang.

Erhai looked over the column of characters from start to finish. They were all either pedantic and overly literary or too countrified and commonplace. Duohe came in from nursing the child in the next room. Duohe would never open her garments to bare her breast in front of other people. She looked at everyone's faces.

Rolling smoke around her mouth, Xiaohuan said: 'What're you looking at? We were saying bad things about you just now!' She chuckled, and took the stem of her pipe from her mouth and knocked out the ashes. 'As soon as your back's turned we all start scolding and exclaiming over the Jap devils' wicked goings-on – we just can't help ourselves!'

Erhai told Xiaohuan to stop acting daft. Duohe was looking at them like that because she wanted to know what the child was going to be called.

Stationmaster Zhang flipped through the dictionary again. Back when Erhai was born he had gone through the *Analects* of Confucius to find the two characters Liangjian. At that moment Duohe uttered several sounds. Everyone looked at her. Duohe had never spoken aloud to anyone in the family before, although they often heard her singing to the child in Japanese. Duohe repeated those Japanese sounds over again, then looked from that person to this and back again, her eyes very bright. Erhai passed the pen over to her, and a piece of paper. She put her head on one side, pursed her lips, and wrote down on the paper 'Chunmei', a name that shared its second character with Kumi, the little girl whose life Duohe had saved.

'That's a Jap name, right?' Stationmaster Zhang asked Erhai.

'We can't go calling a Zhang child by a Japanese name,' Erhai's mother said.

'So only Japs get to be called "Chunmei"?' Stationmaster Zhang bellowed at his wife. 'We're still allowing them to occupy these two Chinese characters of ours?'

Duohe looked fearfully at the old couple. She had very seldom seen Stationmaster Zhang in such a fury.

'Those Japanese characters came from us!' said Stationmaster Zhang, jabbing at the paper with his finger. 'I say we *do* call her Chunmei, so there! I'm taking back what they took from us! So pipe down, the lot of you, that's settled.' He waved his hand and went out of the door to meet the next train.

From then on whenever Xiaohuan was at a loose end she would take the child in her arms for a walk in the streets. When it was feeding time, she would carry her back home, and when she was fed she would carry her away again. The child's pale, delicate skin became tanned by the sun, and she developed little red, raw patches on her cheeks from the wind. As time passed she became less peaceful, and drool and unclear babbling began to issue from her mouth, where teeth were just starting to sprout.

One day Erhai's mother went to the village on an errand, and saw an adult and a baby lying on the stage in the courtyard of the little theatre. She came closer, and saw Xiaohuan and Chunmei, both fast asleep.

Erhai's mother had always let her daughter-in-law have her own way, but this time she stamped her bound foot and started to shout. She said how could Xiaohuan do such a thing, did she want the child to roll down the steps, and do herself a terrible mischief? Xiaohuan woke up, gathered up the child in her arms, and brushed the dust, melon-seed husks and cigarette ends off the pink cloak. At this moment, Xiaohuan, who had always had the upper hand with her mother-in-law, found herself without a word to say. Erhai's mother snatched the child from her and headed straight home without even doing her errand, bound feet drumming on the ground as she went.

Ten minutes later Xiaohuan came home, having shaken off every trace of the stunned, tongue-tied look she had worn in the village, and quite recovered her taste for dressing down her mother-in-law. Was she condemning her because she was a stepmother? Was she saying that she carried the child out of doors every day and dropped her until the blood flowed from her eyes, nose and mouth? Even if Xiaohuan had harboured such crooked intentions she wasn't about to let anyone wag their finger in her face and scold her, and certainly not when her motives were entirely pure.

'Let's say what's on our minds: who wanted this girlie to go tumbling down and shed blood everywhere?' Xiaohuan said.

Since she had married into the Zhang family, Xiaohuan had never raised her voice in a quarrel like this. This time nobody thought about holding her back. Erhai took himself off to the fields to hoe the weeds,

Stationmaster Zhang went to walk the tracks, and he took Duohe along to give him a hand picking up rubbish from the railway line.

Erhai's mother pointed a finger at Xiaohuan. 'So is that step a place to go to sleep?'

Xiaohuan pushed Erhai's mother's finger aside, saying: 'And if I did let her sleep there, what of it?'

'Then you wanted to make the child fall and hurt herself on purpose!'

'How can you think such lovely things about me? If I wanted her to fall to her death, would I go to all that trouble? I've been carrying her around every day, all I had to do was hold the brat up by her legs, let go and drop her head first on the ground! Why wait until now?'

'I'm asking you! What did you think you were doing?'

Tears suddenly welled up in Xiaohuan's eyes. Her face twisted briefly into an unpleasant grin. 'I . . . do you really not know? I want to get a knife and slaughter that little Jap woman! Nobody can pay me back for that little life that came out of my belly! Never mind how many wicked things the Japs have done, I just want a life back, in exchange for my child who never saw the light of day!'

Erhai's mother knew that Xiaohuan was shrewish, but she had never experienced the full force of her venom. She had meant to reproach her for being sloppy and negligent, for putting the child down near such tall, narrow steps. Now she could see that Xiaohuan's eyes had gone completely wild, buried deep above their thick, heavy eye bags, and there was a good chance that she would forget herself and do something rash.

At that moment Erhai came back, panting for breath.

'What are you doing?' he said. 'I could hear the child crying half a mile off!'

'A half-Jap girl, you all think she's so special! Keeping the family line going! You get the bastard of those murdering, fire-raising Japs to carry it on for you!' Xiaohuan was beside herself, in an ecstasy of shouting and cursing.

Erhai took several steps closer, grabbed her and dragged her away. He managed to get the lower half of her body inside their room, while the upper half was still clutching at the door frame, that expression of insane joy still on her face.

'Have the Japs not brought enough disasters down on your family? Now you're actually inviting a wolf cub into the house!'

Erhai finally dragged the rest of Xiaohuan inside, and savagely shut the door. It never did to pay any attention to Xiaohuan at these times. He looked at her; she had collapsed on the floor, crying and carrying on, so he walked up to the *kang*, took off his shoes and sat down. He neither saw nor heard Xiaohuan's curses and fuss, ignoring them completely. Sure enough, by the time he had finished his pipe, Xiaohuan only had sniffling noises left.

'I can't carry on like this. I can't carry on living like this,' Xiaohuan muttered. Clearly her outbreak had more or less run its course.

Erhai refilled his pipe, and stolidly struck a match on the sole of his shoe.

'Now if I were to run off and throw myself down a well, you wouldn't even bloody drag me out. You wouldn't even go and get a rope. Isn't that right, Zhang Liangjian?'

Erhai gave her a look. She had already pulled herself onto her hands and knees, and was dusting herself down.

'Is what I say true or not? You wouldn't get a rope to haul me out, would you?!' Xiaohuan said.

Erhai wrinkled his eyebrows.

'Do you know why I'm always taking the child out?'

Erhai breathed in a mouthful of smoke, and exhaled. His eyebrows flicked up at the tips, indicating that he was waiting to hear what else she had to say.

'So when the day comes that you put that Jap woman back in the sack and throw her away, the child won't feel like she's lost her ma, as she'll already have got close to me. D'you see?'

Erhai's eyes briefly widened, scanning Xiaohuan's face for a while. His eyeballs behind their lids were in constant motion. Xiaohuan could see that her words had disconcerted and upset him. Xiaohuan, do you really mean that? Erhai asked himself and replied in his mind, I dare say she's just saying that because it feels right at the time.

Xiaohuan looked at Erhai's expression. She had ground him down, right down to the quick. She stretched out a hand to rub his cheek. Erhai dodged out the way, which made Xiaohuan feel frightened and hurt.

'You said that once she'd had a kid you'd put her in a sack and take her to the mountain and dump her. Did you say that or didn't you?' Xiaohuan said.

Erhai let her get on with it: say whatever you like, who cares.

'Once she's given birth to a son you'll throw her out.'

Xiaohuan could see it all. If at this moment she were to say, *Look at you, see how you're hurting! I'm just teasing you!* he'd feel a bit more easy in his mind. But she wasn't going to say that, not her! She was all in a muddle herself, unclear whether her words were just fighting talk, or whether she was speaking the truth.

When Xiaohuan next went for a stroll in the village, people saw that she had made a little straw hat for the chubby little girl, woven out of new wheat straw. Xiaohuan's fingers were nimble, even if she was a bit lazy. So long as you didn't put her to any trouble, she'd eat anything you gave her, cursing and laughing, and make do with it, but from time to time she would make an effort, and when the fit was on her she could help the village shop make over ten different kinds of fancy steamed buns. Everyone in Stationmaster Zhang's house worked, there was no master or mistress, there was only a Young Mistress, Xiaohuan, who was a lady of leisure, all they asked of her was that she would be happy, like a nice warm firepot, to bring a bit of warmth and liveliness wherever she went. When the people saw the plump baby girl with this straw hat on her head, looking absurdly appealing, they all said, 'That girlie's getting more like Xiaohuan all the time!'

'Are you having a go at me, or at her?' asked Xiaohuan.

'The little girl's got so fat with all that eating that her eyes never see the light of day!'

'What's with all the little girl this and girlie that? We've got a proper formal name now, you know, she's called Chunmei.'

People's tongues were not so complaisant once she was out of sight. 'Is Chunmei a Chinese name?'

'How come it sounds a bit Japanese? I knew a Japanese schoolmistress a while back called Jimei.'

'Where's that little Japanese woman Stationmaster Zhang brought back? How come we never see her go out of doors?'

'Maybe they bought her to be tied up and drop her pups in the house?'

One evening, Xiaohuan saw that Erhai had brought a big bucket of water to the room, where he proceeded to scrub his skin red. Whenever he washed like this, as though his life depended on it, Xiaohuan knew exactly what he was up to. Erhai was not willing to go dirty to the Jap woman's *kang*. Girlie was over a year old, and they were already feeding her millet porridge with goat's milk. It was about the time for Duohe to conceive a second child. Xiaohuan smoked her pipe, stared at him and sniggered to herself.

Erhai gave her a look. She made a pretence of opening her mouth, as if she did not know what to say, and just sniggered again.

'Brother, you smell fine just the way you are,' Xiaohuan said. 'Was it her that made you have a good wash? You should tell her that Japs are hairy but we Chinese are smooth, there's no need to go scrubbing as if you hate your own skin!'

Erhai played deaf, as usual.

'Or is your mother on at you again? Your father can't wait either. Seven whole silver dollars. Or is it you who can't hold it in any longer? I bet she's been lifting up her shirt, giving you an eyeful behind my back. Is that it?'

Erhai threw his flannel back into the bucket. 'Give Girlie her medicine, don't keep wittering on.' As usual, he neutralised her joking words, said in an attempt to let off steam. 'No sign of her cough getting better.'

Every time Erhai went to Duohe's to spend the night, Xiaohuan would look after Girlie and have her sleep in her bed. Girlie coughed all through the night, so Xiaohuan could not sleep.

Xiaohuan was twenty-seven, and no longer of an age to say 'That's it, I've had it with you, I'm off to marry some other man', but sometimes she would see herself in the mirror while combing her hair, and think that the round-faced woman in it was still worth a look. Sometimes she heard people compliment her: 'Xiaohuan looks good whatever she wears!' or 'How come Xiaohuan still has the narrow waist of an eighteen-year-old?' She had a beautiful neck, sloping shoulders like flowing water and long, white fingers like spring onions. Her face was not that of a top-ranking beauty, but once you were used to it, it was full of charm. When she was in one of her hot-headed moods, her estimation of her looks would become exaggerated, and she truly thought that she could reshuffle the cards she had been dealt with Zhang Erhai to start a new game with a new man. Since Duohe had been bought in, she often thought in this way.

But in reality Zhang Erhai was a man she could never leave or abandon. Besides, he was the only one in the whole world who could handle her; who else could she get to put up with someone like her? She and Zhang Erhai were too well matched. If she went, what a golden opportunity that would be for that Jap woman. Would she treasure everything about Erhai from his head to his heel the way Xiaohuan did? She never would; everything that was good about Erhai would be wasted on her.

Even if she could bring herself to leave Erhai, she could not bear to be without Girlie. Somehow she linked them together, all in a muddle. Xiaohuan had never expected that she would love a child so much, and she was uncertain whether her love for her was because she looked on her as half of Erhai. Looking at her and seeing Erhai's shadow, surges of warmth welled up in her heart, again and again, and she would clasp her so tightly that Girlie would suddenly panic, and with a 'Wah!' she would start to howl. Just like she was crying in her arms right now, kicking and struggling for dear life.

Xiaohuan gave a start, and hastened to comfort the child. Her heart was full of doubts: how could you love someone so much and yet not be yourself? Why did you have to cause him (or her) pain and be unable to prevent yourself from mistreating him (or her), or let him (or her) know that this pain is love? Does love have to be painful? She gently laid the sleeping child back down on the *kang*. Xiaohuan paid no mind to what Erhai and Duohe were doing, whether they were now sleeping sweetly, heads pillowed on each other's arms. She would never know Erhai's true attitude to Duohe – and if she had known she would not have believed it.

This attitude had changed somewhat after Erhai learned about Duohe's background and her helpless, friendless state, but not in any fundamental way. Every time he went to her room it was like a martyrdom, in which both Duohe and himself were the sacrifices. And all because of that damnable business of keeping the family line going. On every visit, the first thing he did was to turn out the lamp. Unless the lamp was out it was hard to put his face close to hers. Duohe was a bit better now, she no longer dressed as if for her coffin. She undid her clothes soundlessly in the darkness, and pulled the clasp from her hair, which now came halfway down her back when loose.

That evening, after Erhai came in, he heard her feeling her way towards him. Erhai's body tensed: what was she up to? She was squatting down, no, she was kneeling. Since her arrival at the Zhang family courtyard, she had scrubbed the brick floors of all the rooms until they were as clean as a *kang*: you could kneel anywhere on the floor. Her hand groped towards Erhai's trouser legs, and felt downwards until she touched his shoes. Erhai's shoes were very simple, he didn't need her to take them off for him. All the same he did not move, and let her get on with it. She removed his shoes and socks, and placed them on the side of the *kang*. Erhai then heard the sound of cotton cloth and padded cotton rubbing together. She opened up her outer clothes and her underwear. In fact, this was unnecessary – Erhai was not about to touch any other part of her body. That was an irrelevance – he came here only to conduct official business.

Duohe had put on weight after the birth of the child. Her body was no longer that of a girl; her stomach was rounded and smooth and her hips were much bigger. Erhai heard her cry out softly. He went a bit more gently. The only thing that had changed about him was that he no longer had any desire to cause pain to this lone young woman. Erhai never dared to consider the future. Once she gave birth to a son, would they continue to house this Japanese orphan, stranded far from her home?

Duohe's hands were very cowardly. She had set them on either side of his waist, rubbing at the layer of hot sweat there. This was what he couldn't bear, her two childish hands. Sometimes he would see them at the dinner table, and think of that moment at night. They were always very timid, rubbing his shoulders, back, waist in an exploratory way. One time they briefly brushed over his forehead. It was so pathetic, the way she wanted to know him. Duohe only laughed out loud with Stationmaster Zhang, Erhai's mother and Girlie. When she laughed it was even heartier than Xiaohuan, and she would sit on the ground, shaking her fists and kicking her legs with laughter, her hair coming down all over the place, provoking Stationmaster Zhang and Erhai's mother into laughter too, even though they could not make out what had set her off in the first place. She was unable to say what had made her laugh. Erhai would wonder at this: she whose family had died and left her alone in the world, but who was still able to laugh so well.

Duohe's weak hands patted his waist, like she was soothing her daughter to sleep. He suddenly heard her say: 'Erhai.'

The tones were wrong, but he could more or less hear what she meant.

He involuntarily let out an 'Mm?'

'Erhai,' she said again in a slightly louder voice, encouraged now she had a reaction.

'Mm?' he said again. He had already discovered the source of her problem: she was not rolling her tongue properly, and was trying to imitate the way the others said 'Erhai'r', with two rolled tongue sounds coming on top of each other. She had got the tones wrong too, it sounded like she was saying 'Hungry Crane'.

Erhai was almost asleep, when the next part came. She said 'Girlie', but in a very odd way that sounded like 'Pressed Potato'.

Erhai understood: she was showing off her Chinese to him. He rolled over and turned his face away, indicating very clearly that she would get no more teaching from him. Duohe's hands came up again, less timid this time, and grabbed at his shoulders.

'Nice day,' she said.

Erhai gave a start. This phrase was copied from his father. Stationmaster Zhang would go out to meet the first early-morning train, returning home when it was time for the family to get up, and he would greet them all with 'Nice day!' To a railway worker a 'nice day' was something important; when the day was nice the trains would stop and pass through on time, he would not need to hang about at the station, or to take too much trouble over his rounds, and at his age his complaints about walking the track were becoming increasingly bitter.

'Nice day?' She was hoping for a little praise or correction from Erhai.

'Mm.'

'Have you eaten?' she said.

This time Erhai did react. He almost laughed out loud. When people who wanted Erhai's parents to do them a favour came bearing gifts, Erhai's mother would immediately relieve them of their gifts saying: 'Have you eaten?'

'Make do.'

He did not even need to think about that one. Erhai could hear at once that this was one of Xiaohuan's catchphrases. No matter how good a job Xiaohuan made of anything, no matter how people praised her, she would always say, 'Well, make do.' Whether the thing was the way you wanted it or not, whether you were pleased or not, whether it tasted good or not, her mouth would always be full of 'make do'. Sometimes when she was in high spirits, Xiaohuan would whisk her way through all the rooms and the yard with a broom, saying 'Make do' over and over again.

Erhai thought, he could not pay any attention to her, if he started paying attention she would never let up. Then he'd get no sleep at all. He had work to do the next day.

She was looking up at the ceiling, saying over and over again: '*E'he, E'hai, Erhe* . . . Hungry Child, Second River . . .'

He hugged himself tightly and turned his back on her. The next day he mentioned the matter to his parents.

His father smoked a full pipe of tobacco, and then said, 'Well, we can't have her learning to speak Chinese.'

'Why not?' Erhai's mother asked.

Stationmaster Zhang stared at his wife. How could she fail to understand something so obvious?

Erhai understood what his father meant. Duohe was not to be trusted; who could say that she wouldn't run off some day? If she spoke Chinese, running away would be much easier.

'You can hardly keep her from learning to talk, can you? If a cat and a dog live together for long enough they both end up miaowing and howling!' Erhai's mother said, beaming.

'If she does run off she's got to give us a son first,' said Stationmaster Zhang.

'Is it up to you what she has?' Erhai's mother was still beaming.

The three of them smoked their pipes in silence.

From then on, whenever Erhai visited Duohe's room, she would always come out with a few disconnected Chinese words. 'A bit off' and 'out of the way' she got from Xiaohuan, along with 'well, that's just peachy' and 'oh my giddy aunt', both words from Xiaohuan's jokes and rages, which Duohe relocated into her own mouth. Though you had to listen hard in order to recognise them. Erhai did not even grunt at her, allowing her to experiment as she pleased. But he stepped up his pace, going at it many times in a night. In his heart he resented his parents, for he knew they were hurrying him along even if they never actually said a word.

Duohe, on the other hand, got the wrong idea. She thought that Erhai was becoming attracted to her; sometimes when she bumped into him in the daytime, she would dart a secret smile at him, and her face would be suffused with blushes. It was when she smiled that he realised just how alien she was; at those moments her smile conveyed her meaning in a way that was so very unlike a Chinese girl. But in what way it was different, he could not say. He just thought that when she smiled everything became even more of a mess.

This increased messiness was making her hands braver and braver during the night. It had got to the point where he could take no more. One night her hands grasped hold of his, and placed them on her delicate, slightly moist stomach. While his hands were still hesitating whether to shake hers off, her hands were already pressing his onto her bulging breast. He did not dare move a muscle. If he were to snatch his hands away, it would be like cursing her for her shamelessness, but if he did not remove his hands she would think that he had taken a liking to her. Xiaohuan was right there in the same house. How could he do that?

But even without Xiaohuan, he still would not have felt anything for her.

Back when his father was a worker walking the tracks at Hutou station, his elder brother Dahai fell in with a gang of Communist anti-Japanese partisans who lived out in the mountains and woods. Fifteen-year-old Dahai went with his brother to collect handbills from the partisans, and left them lying about on the trains. When they had just reached Hutou village, they saw that Japanese soldiers had tied up two partisans, who had been stripped of their shirts and trousers to reveal handbills tied to their waists and legs. The Jap devils hung them up at the door of the village post office, and they didn't even kill them properly, but poured boiling water over their heads. It took several buckets of boiling water, which soaked their skin and the leaflets until both were falling apart. Not long after that, Dahai disappeared.

His mother and father had spent all those years raising Dahai with nothing to show for it. For the sake of the worry they had suffered over him, and the tears they had shed, Erhai could not permit himself to become fond of a Japanese woman.

In the surrounding villages, Japanese soldiers had slaughtered people and burned their homes. They had trapped dozens of miners in a shaft of the copper mine and blown them up, just to kill a few anti-Japanese activists. And as for the airs and graces the Jap women who used to live in the village gave themselves . . . Even Japanese dogs knew that the Chinese could not be considered human, they were slaves from a defeated nation. One time a crowd of gorgeously dressed Japanese prostitutes was waiting at Anping village station, as their train was delayed, and they didn't even use the toilet in the station but took the only washbasin to piss in, several of them surrounding one squatting woman, shading her with their umbrellas, smiling as they peed. There was no need to be discreet around the Chinese men waiting for the train, because people are not discreet around mules or horses when relieving themselves.

Erhai ground his teeth. Let him not think of the ghastliest scene of all.

. . . Several Japanese soldiers, jabbering and shrieking away, singing drunken, out-of-tune songs, in front of them a Chinese woman riding on an ox, then falling from its back. By the time they reached her, a purplish-black stain was spreading across the crotch of her thick green padded cotton trousers. The woman's hair had come down, and below it her face was paper white. The woman paid no attention to the Japanese soldiers crowding about her, her two hands were thrust between her legs, as though to block the blood. The Japanese soldiers could see what was going on from her bulging stomach, and from the blood. There was no fun to be had with her, so they staggered off, still singing their tuneless songs. The man who had witnessed all this did not know Xiaohuan, but that was how he had described the scene over and over again to the people who came crowding round. While Erhai was running like the wind with Xiaohuan in his arms, that man ran equally fast behind him to tell him all about it, barely able to catch his breath.

How could Erhai allow himself to get fond of Duohe, a Jap woman?

She was pitiable, true, with nobody to turn to and no home to go to, but all the same . . . she deserved it!

When he thought of that word 'deserve', Erhai felt a momentary pang in his heart. He did not know who the pain was for, for Duohe, or for himself, for being capable of such harshness to a poor girl like her. What Xiaohuan said was true; Duohe owed her a little life. At the least, those compatriots of Duohe's who could commit murder without batting an eyelid owed Xiaohuan a life.

How could Erhai get fond of this Jap woman?!

With a burst of energy, Erhai viciously snatched back his hands. He jumped off the *kang*, groped for his clothes and shoes, and put them on, hopping from foot to foot. Duohe knelt on the *kang*, a dark shadow full of disappointment.

'Erhe?'

The hand that had just touched one of her round breasts felt as if there was a toad resting in its palm.

'Erhai . . .' At least now she had the right pronunciation and clear tones.

'Out of the way!'

She was silent for a moment, and then started to chuckle. Xiaohuan would say this phrase in her most cheerful moods. Sometimes when Erhai said something to her, she would make as if to kick him, and come out with those words: 'Out of the way!'

Erhai sat back down on the *kang* again. Duohe might have lived eighteen years, but her brain had not matured that far. He had just lit his pipe when Duohe leapt on him from behind, her jaw resting on the crown of his head, and both legs wrapped round his waist, her feet in his stomach. 'Out of the way!' she said, laughing. This evening she was making Erhai her playmate.

Erhai had never been so helpless. With Duohe, things always changed in this strange and baffling way, leaving him feeling foolish and upset. He waited until her craziness had worn itself out, then he knocked out the ashes of his pipe on the ground and clambered back onto the *kang*. All he could feel was Duohe's hair waving about, and her soft, soft hands, seemingly all over his face and neck. Very soon he fell asleep.

3

On a patch of wheat field between the village and the station, a battle was fought for a day and a night. One side wanted to destroy the railway, the other side to capture it, and nobody in the village really understood what it was all about. The crops in the field had been harvested, and all those straw stacks became the scene of the battle. Early in the morning of the second day the sound of gunfire ceased. Not long after, the people heard the whistle of a train, and said, *The soldiers that wanted to capture the railway have won.*

Xiaohuan had been cooped up in the house, and she could bear it no more. Carrying a bowl of maize-flour porridge, she picked up a salted radish in her chopsticks and slipped outside. There was no change to be seen in the straw stacks, the wide-open field was very still, and it did not look remotely like a battle had just been fought there. A flock of sparrows descended, pecked for a while at the grains of wheat that had fallen on the ground and then flew away again. Who knew where the sparrows had gone while the fighting was going on. At this moment the field seemed particularly vast; any piece of scenery in the distance seemed caught between the sky and the ground. A crooked scholar tree, a scarecrow, a half-collapsed shelter, all became coordinates on the horizon. Xiaohuan knew nothing of coordinates or horizons, she was only standing there in the autumn of 1948, stock-still and stunned at this ghostly scene.

The sky in the east turned red and brightened, and in a blink of an eye half of the sun was up. Xiaohuan saw a thread of golden light on the horizon. Suddenly she saw dead bodies, one after another, lying aslant or on their backs with their faces turned to the sky. So that's what a battleground is like. Xiaohuan took another look at the sun on one side and the retreating night on the other. This was a good place for battles, room enough to charge, space enough to kill.

The side that had killed and routed their opponents was called the People's Liberation Army. The PLA were a smiley lot, keen to lend a hand, and fond of dropping by people's homes. The PLA came to Stationmaster Zhang's home to visit and help out, and they would snatch whatever job you were working on right out of your hands. The PLA brought many new words with them; officials were called cadres, and the man who patrolled the tracks wasn't called the track-walker, he was the Working Class. Boss Lü who ran the wine shop in the village was no longer Boss Lü but a spy. The wine shop had been popular with the Japanese in the past as a place to stay, and no shoes or socks were allowed inside.

The PLA tied up the spies and traitors, took them away and shot them. People who could speak Japanese slunk around like thieves. The PLA also set up a series of tents, where they recruited the sons of the village for the people's own army, as well as students and the working class.

In the future you would be able to go to Anshan to refine coke, or smelt iron or steel, and earn enough money in a month for forty-five kilos of white flour. Many young people put their names down. Anshan had been liberated and was under military control;

the people who went were called the First Batch of Workers of the New China, elder brothers to the rest.

A PLA cadre saw Duohe beating cotton quilts with a wooden stick. He asked her what she was doing. Duohe looked at him, her eyes bright and visibly full of confusion. The cadre also asked her name. From the other side of the quilt, Erhai's mother hastily replied on her behalf. She's called Duohe. Which character for Duo? Which for He? Erhai's mother said, beaming, Comrade, all that stuff is far, far too difficult for me! I might as well be blind when it comes to writing. Erhai came out from the kitchen with a pot of freshly brewed tea, and told the PLA cadre that Duo was the character that meant 'many', and He was the character for 'crane', like the bird. The cadre said that this was a very literary name, especially for a working-class household. He beckoned to Duohe, and asked her to come and sit with them. Duohe looked at the cadre, then at Erhai, and bowed.

This bow was done in a way that the PLA found absolutely bewildering. There were people in the village who had bowed to them too, but it was completely different from this.

Another PLA cadre called Political Instructor Dai said: 'How old is this young girl?'

Erhai's mother said: 'Nineteen . . . She can't speak.'

Political Instructor Dai turned his head to look at Erhai, who was digging mud from the uppers of his shoes, and nudged him: 'Little sister-in-law?' They were friendly with Xiaohuan, so they knew that Xiaohuan and Erhai were a couple.

'Yes, his sister-in-law!' Erhai's mother said.

Duohe walked to the other side of the quilt. At that moment everybody stopped their conversation, and the 'crack-crack' of her beating echoed back from the brick walls and floor of the yard.

'During the Japanese puppet government, did the children here go to school?' Political Instructor Dai asked Erhai's mother.

'Yes.'

Erhai's mother knew what he was getting at, and pointing behind the quilt she said, 'Duohe's a deaf mute!' She smiled as she spoke. If they chose to take her words as a joke, that was fine by her.

The PLA regarded Stationmaster Zhang's family as the most dependable of the masses. They explained to Stationmaster Zhang that he was to 'take a leading role'. So they used his family as a starting point for finding out about the situation in the neighbouring villages, whose family had had dealings with bandits, which families tried to exert undue influence, which families had been influential during the puppet government. Stationmaster Zhang muttered to Erhai and his mother: But how is this different from old women's gossip? He thought that good relations with other people was the one thing they could never do without. In this village, getting on the wrong side of one person meant alienating a whole string of them, generation after generation. For this reason Stationmaster Zhang would often hide away outside when the PLA visited and tell his family to say no more than they had to.

The PLA had come that day to introduce to the Zhang family the great matter of 'Land Reform'. They told the Zhangs that land reform had already begun in many villages in North-east China. But when Xiaohuan came back from the village, she said, 'If you don't gossip like old women, other people are quite happy to. Political Instructor Dai's visit was actually to check on the business with Duohe. People in the village have been making reports to the PLA on people who bought Japanese women.'

Stationmaster Zhang's face fell, and he sat at the dinner table without saying a word. Once the meal was more or less over, his eyes swept over every face at the table.

'Don't tell anyone who gave birth to Girlie,' he said. 'Not even if they beat you to death.'

'I gave birth to her,' said Xiaohuan, smiling cheekily. 'Isn't that right, Girlie? Let's get you fitted with a little gold tooth, then who'd dare to say that we're not two peas in a pod?'

'Give it a rest, Xiaohuan,' Erhai berated her loudly.

'We weren't the only family to buy Japanese girls,' Erhai's mother said. 'There are people in all the villages round here who bought them. If we get into trouble, won't everyone else get into trouble too?'

'Who says there'll be trouble? But supposing something does happen, what then? With any government, there's bound to be things it likes, and other things it doesn't like at all. Getting ourselves a Jap woman to have children, while Erhai still has a wife of his own, how's that going to look?' Stationmaster Zhang said.

Duohe knew the words that were passing back and forth were about her, and that everyone's deadly serious expression was because of her too. Over the past two years she had come to understand a fair bit of Chinese, but with disputes of this kind, fast and serious, she could only catch half of what was going on.

'Then what were you playing at in the first place?' Xiaohuan said. 'So now it wasn't your idea to go and buy a Jap woman? Since she was brought home, has there been any peace in our family? Better to put her in a sack and take her to the mountain. Leave Girlie behind for me.'

'Xiaohuan, let's not talk nonsense, eh?' Erhai's mother said, all smiles.

Xiaohuan glared at her mother-in-law.

'Looks to me like we'd do best to get out of the way and be done with it,' Stationmaster Zhang said.

Everybody's chopsticks froze, and they looked at him. What was this 'get out of the way'?

Stationmaster Zhang passed his hand over his face, kneading the long, thin creases that covered it with his palm, to show that he was clearing his mind and gathering his energy. He would always re-arrange his features in this way when he was about to come out with something important.

'You move away. Move to Anshan. I know someone on the railway, he can help you get settled there. If Erhai puts his name down for the steel-smelting plant or the coke plant, they'll be sure to take him. Erhai went to middle school for two years!'

'Won't that be breaking up the family?' Erhai's mother said.

'I've worked on the railway for all these years, I can get you a seat on the train to see them any time I like for free. First let's see which way the wind blows – if the people who bought a Japanese woman are all fine, Erhai and the rest of them can move back again.'

'I'm not going,' Xiaohuan said. And as she spoke she shifted to the edge of the *kang* where they had been eating and shuffled her feet into her shoes. 'What would I do with myself at Anshan? Is my family there? Or Manzi, or Shuzhen?' Manzi and Shuzhen were her girlfriends, companions in idle gossip. 'There's no way I'm going. Did you hear that, Erhai? Will there be Shopkeeper Wang to give Girlie free sweeties to eat in Anshan? Is there a theatre there where they'll let me watch for free?' From the door of the room, she gazed down at the whole family, as if from a great height.

Erhai's mother looked at her. Xiaohuan knew that her mother-in-law's eyes were cursing her: All she cares about is eating her fill without having to lift a finger for herself!

'Erhai, did you hear me?' Xiaohuan said.

Erhai smoked his pipe.

'Let's be clear, you go tomorrow if you like, but you're going by yourself, hear me?'

Erhai suddenly bellowed: 'I heard! You're not going!'

The entire family gaped at him. He jumped off the *kang*, walked over to the washstand in his bare feet, picked up a half-full basin of water and hurled the contents out at Xiaohuan. Xiaohuan's feet leapt high in the air, yet she held her peace, and did not utter a word. Erhai would only get stubborn once or twice a year, and when the fit came upon him, Xiaohuan would not put up a fight with the odds so obviously against her. In due course when the time came for her to settle accounts with him, it would always be in compound interest.

Xiaohuan walked away, but outside the door she heard Girlie crying, and came back again, picked her up and walked cautiously past Erhai.

'Disgraceful!' Erhai's mother said. She was not just talking about Xiaohuan.

At this moment Duohe soundlessly got down from the *kang*, put the leftover rice and dishes on a wooden tray, and walked to the door, where Erhai squatted smoking. She halted there, and bowed; Erhai let her pass, and she went out of the door, her bottom leading the way. At this moment, if an outsider had been present, they would have immediately spotted that there was something wrong with this woman's movements. But the Zhang family were completely used to such actions from Duohe, they could not find anything eccentric in it.

After that, Erhai and Xiaohuan vanished from Anping village. Erhai's mother had one explanation in the village one day, another the next: 'Our Erhai's gone to his uncle's, he runs a factory.' 'Erhai has found a job in the city – from now on the government will be feeding him.'

There were a great number of the PLA stationed in the village, all of them southerners. This was a time when forces from the north and south were crossing each other's paths and getting mixed up. Many of the young men in the village had joined the PLA, and were pushing their way southwards. When Erhai left Anping village, he was part of a popular trend.

A year passed, and Stationmaster Zhang received a letter from Erhai, saying that the old couple had got their wish at last, they had a grandson. Stationmaster Zhang got his cronies on the train to take them a little quilt stuffed with new cotton, and an urgent message: No matter what, they had to take the child to a photographer's and get his photo taken. Erhai's mother was itching to see her grandson.

The day after Chairman Mao ascended the Tiananmen Gate in Beijing and announced the founding of the New China, another letter came. Erhai's mother saw a little photograph enclosed, and two trails of tears and one track of drool came flowing down. A strong, vigorous, fat little boy, hair all sticking up to heaven. Stationmaster Zhang said that he looked like Duohe, to which his wife said huffily, 'Such a tiny person, how can you tell?' Stationmaster Zhang sighed. He could see that she was trying to fool herself: she would rather die than admit to the half of her grandson's flesh and blood that was Japanese. She tucked the little photograph into her clothes, and went tottering on her bound feet into the village, where she told them that this grandson had almost cost Xiaohuan her life, he was so big! He could suckle for an hour at a time, Xiaohuan had been sucked empty! As she spoke, she smiled so hard that her eyes vanished into narrow slits. Only those close female friends who had gossiped with Xiaohuan said in private: 'Who believes that? Xiaohuan's parts were completely ruined, how could she give birth to a child?'

People asked Erhai's mother whether her son was earning a lot. He was a Grade One Worker in the coke plant, Erhai's mother told everyone, and a Grade One Worker eats and gets stuff for free, and lives in a house that belongs to the nation. So the people said: Erhai's really lucky. And it seemed that Erhai's mother was equally lucky, taking the words that she had made up herself to be real.

When the villages in the neighbourhood of Anping village were setting up Mutual Aid Teams, Stationmaster Zhang received another letter from Erhai. By now, Stationmaster Zhang was no longer in charge of the station, and his post had been taken over by a younger man. Now Stationmaster Zhang was Sweeper Zhang. Every day he swept his way back and forth with a broom across the waiting room the size of six card tables, and swept the empty space at the door of the station until dust filled the skies and the earth. The day he received Erhai's letter he swept more desperately than ever. Erhai's mother was going to cry herself into her grave. The baby had fallen ill and died the previous month. What was Erhai thinking, not getting round to writing about something so important for over a month?

Sure enough, Erhai's mother did almost cry herself to death. She brought out a pile of little hats and tiny shoes that she had sewn, and wept over each one in turn. She cried over Erhai's bitter fate, her and her husband's bitter fate, Xiaohuan's bitter fate, and she cried over those bloody Japs, death was too good for them, coming over to China to burn and kill, to chase her daughter-in-law and destroy her eldest grandson. She cried and cried, and finally got round to Dahai, her eldest son. Dahai had no conscience, dying like that after running away from home at fifteen, taking himself off to be a bandit or a pirate who knows where.

Erhai's mother made no more trips to the village after that.

One morning in the summer of the following year, a motorbike came down the broad earth track through the middle of the wheat field, with a man who looked like a government cadre riding in the sidecar. The motorbike drove up to the gate of the Zhang house, trailing a cloud of dust, and asked if this was Comrade Zhang Zhili's home.

Erhai's mother was sitting in the shade of a tree unravelling cotton-yarn gloves, but on hearing this she got to her feet. These years she had got a good bit shorter, and her legs had bowed into a pair of symmetrical teapot handles. As she shuffled her feet towards the door, the government cadre standing outside the gate could see a flock of baby chicks from between her two legs.

'Is that my Dahai come back?' Erhai's mother was standing about three metres from the gate, motionless. Zhang Zhili was Dahai's official name, the man accompanying the government official replied.

The government cadre walked up, saying that he was from the county Civil Administration Bureau. He had come to deliver Zhang Zhili's Revolutionary Martyr's Certificate.

Erhai's mother's brain was slow these days. When confronted with this cadre from the government all she could do was pucker her toothless mouth into a smile.

'Comrade Zhang Zhili died a glorious martyr's death on the Korean battlefield. This is his Revolutionary Martyr's Certificate.' The government official placed a brown paper envelope into Erhai's mother's claw-like hands. 'His spouse has taken the pension fund. His two children are still young.'

By now Erhai's mother had finally struggled her way into understanding. Dahai was dead, killed in Korea; his parents got the 'glorious', his widow and children got a sum of money. She did not feel able to have a proper cry, she could not let herself go in front of a strange government cadre with his southern accent – when she cried she liked to slap her thighs and howl. Besides, Dahai had run away when he was fifteen years old, and she had already wept over him. She had done with her crying at the time, and by now she had ceased to cherish any hope of seeing him alive.

The comrade cadre from the county Civil Administration Bureau said that from that day on the Zhang family were Glorious Dependants of a Revolutionary Martyr. Every month they would receive a sum of money from the government, at New Year there would also be pork and lard, in the eighth month they would be issued with moon cakes, and on National Day in October they would receive rice. The other dependants of revolutionary martyrs in the county would all enjoy the same treatment.

'Comrade Cadre, how many children did our Dahai have?'

'Oh, I don't really know. I seem to remember there were two. Your daughter-in-law is a volunteer in the army, in the military hospital.'

'Ah.' Erhai's mother stared intently at the comrade cadre, to see whether his next words would be 'Your daughter-in-law invites you to her home to see your grandsons!' But the comrade cadre's lips remained firmly closed.

As Erhai's mother was taking her leave at the main gate, Sweeper Zhang came back. She introduced the comrade cadre, and the two men shook hands formally, the comrade cadre addressing Erhai's father respectfully as 'Old Comrade'.

'You tell my daughter-in-law to come home and see us!' Sweeper Zhang said, shedding tears. 'Or if she's busy we can just as well go to see her and the grandchildren.'

'I can take care of the kiddies for her!' Erhai's mother said.

The cadre promised to pass on the message.

It was only once the sound of the motorbike was far away that the old couple thought to open the brown paper envelope. Inside was a little book with a red cover, embossed with gold characters. When they opened it, apart from the photograph on the Revolutionary Martyr's Certificate, there was another picture with a woman in army uniform. A row of characters were embossed on the photograph: 'Souvenir of Marriage'.

The Revolutionary Martyr's Certificate also said that Dahai was Chief of Staff of his regiment.

Erhai's mother started visiting the village again. Her son the revolutionary martyr had been a chief of staff, and nobody of such high rank had ever been seen in Anping village. On the day they went off to Jiamusi to see their daughter-in-law and grandchildren, Erhai's mother bought up half the village, from mountain delicacies to leather goods, puffed-rice candy, slow-cooked wild-rabbit legs and tobacco leaves.

By the time Zhang Erhai received the letter from his parents, sent before they set off for Jiamusi, he had not been Zhang Erhai for some time. He was now Grade Two Worker Comrade Zhang Jian. Zhang Jian was the name he had filled in when registering at the coke plant. As he picked up the steel-nibbed pen on the recruiting table, he had suddenly felt a compulsion to remove with one sweep of the pen the middle 'Liang' character of his formal name. In three years, Zhang Jian had risen meteorically from apprentice to Grade Two Worker. There were not many middle-school graduates like him among the workers, so in group newspaper readings or political study, the section chief would always say: Zhang Jian, you take the lead. At the beginning he thought that the section chief was picking on him, but gradually he started to show promise; in any case, once he had a few dozen words off by heart, it was always those same few words when you took the lead.

On the day the letter arrived, having said his piece, he could relax and think about family matters. How to keep Duohe and Xiaohuan at arm's length. What to do about Duohe, who went to the Neighbourhood Committee but never spoke. Whether to give in to Xiaohuan's strident demands to go out to work. But it was the business of Dahai the revolutionary martyr that occupied his mind the most. Who'd have thought it, his brother Dahai had survived into his thirties, become a chief of staff, married and had kids, without ever going home to find his father and mother before dying his glorious death. He thought that Dahai had really let the side down. When the study meeting broke up, an orderly who delivered newspapers and letters in his section had given him the letter written by his father. His few lines of large, coarse, bold characters were overflowing with joy: he said that he and Erhai's mother were going to Jiamusi to visit the grandchildren.

Zhang Jian read on. His elder brother had left roots for the Zhang family, so wasn't he off the hook? And Duohe was off the hook too; they could send her away. But where would they send her away to? Never mind that for now, the main thing was that he was going to liberate the proletariat – himself!

Zhang Jian went back to the family living quarters, not far from the production area. Xiaohuan had gone out again. Duohe came up with quick steps, knelt in front of him, removed his heavy suede boots for him, and carried them gingerly outside. Suede boots ought to be a light brown colour, but the boots of people from the coke-smelting plant would come out pitch black after the first day. He had had a wash in the factory, but people on the street could still tell that he was from the coke plant. All workers were tainted by it, the colour had leached into the deeper layers of their skin.

It was a very big room. Two wooden beds, joined together, had been placed on its east side, like a *kang*. At the west end was a big iron stove, and they had set up a sheet-iron chimney that coiled halfway round the ceiling, before emerging from a hole under the eaves. So long as they managed to keep the stove alight, the room was warm enough to make wearing padded cotton indoors unbearable.

It was the middle of August, so Duohe cooked the meal outside, and she had to take her shoes on and off every time she came and went, which made her busier than anyone. Xiaohuan was lazy. Provided nobody actually put her to work, she grumbled incessantly but abided by Duohe's Japanese rules.

He had just sat down when a cup of tea silently appeared in front of him. The tea had cooled nicely, it had been brewed according to the time he left work. After the tea arrived, a fan appeared too. By the time he took the fan, all he could see of Duohe was her back. Xiaohuan was the source of his happiness, but Duohe was the source of his comfort. The new workers' village had several dozen red-brick single-storey buildings, all new and built in a hurry, with a Neighbourhood Committee for every twenty or thirty buildings. In the Neighbourhood Committee, Duohe was Zhang Jian's deaf-and-dumb sister-in-law, who was always following behind her rowdy elder sister Zhu Xiaohuan, going to buy vegetables, or scavenging for coal. When Xiaohuan met with acquaintances on the road, she would make a wisecrack as she passed, and Duohe would always bow apologetically behind her.

Duohe brought over Xiaohuan's half-finished sweater. When the fit was upon her, Xiaohuan would unravel Zhang Jian's cotton work gloves and dye them, to knit a sweater for Girlie, with peacocks and ears of wheat in all kinds of different stitches. But her enthusiasm would pass quickly, and she always left her sweaters half done, for Duohe to finish. When asked how to do the fancy stitching, she could not be bothered to teach Duohe, who was left to puzzle it out herself.

They only had this room and an outer one, a shack thrown together out of oilcloth and broken bricks. Every family had made themselves a shed outside their door; only the style, materials and size varied from family to family. On two big wooden beds six wooden boards had been laid out horizontally, each over a foot wide and more than three metres in length. Girlie's pillow was at the foot of the bed, and Zhang Jian's was in the middle, while Duohe and Xiaohuan slept one on each side of him, just like the sleeping arrangements on a big *kang*. When they had first moved in, Zhang Jian had said they should partition the big room into two, at which Xiaohuan, revolted, had said: It's hardly worth putting up a wall to cover up your night-time goings-on! Xiaohuan had a murderously sharp tongue, but she could still be magnanimous in her dealings with others. When from time to time she was woken at night by Zhang Jian and Duohe, she would just turn over and tell them to keep the noise down, there was a child sleeping with them on the *kang* too.

When Duohe had given birth to her son it was Xiaohuan who had delivered him, and Xiaohuan had nursed Duohe through her month's confinement after the birth. Xiaohuan had called the son 'Erhai', and became much more friendly towards Duohe, having decided, in her own words, to give face to the Buddha, if not to the monk. When her son had died, she told Duohe to hurry up and have another: only by having another little 'Erhai' could she stanch the wounds of the whole family. The passing of little Erhai at barely a month old had torn a lump of flesh from all of their hearts.

From then on, whenever Zhang Jian wriggled into her quilt Xiaohuan would drive him out again: if he had plenty of seed going spare he shouldn't scatter it on ground where it wouldn't sprout, leaving Duohe's patch of fertile soil to go barren. Little Erhai had died the previous year, and Duohe's fertile soil was showing no signs of quickening. Duohe was redundant, Zhang Jian thought; now they had his elder brother's orphan children, the Zhang family had somebody to keep their incense fires burning.

'Erhai,' Duohe suddenly said, looking at him.

The first time she had seen him, they had been separated by a layer of light brown fog – the sack that had held her and given her a layer of protection from the snowy day. They had put her on the stage, and he had walked towards her. She was huddled up in the sack, and only got a glimpse of him. Afterwards she had shut her eyes, her head pulled in between her shoulders, like a chicken ready for the slaughter. She stored that glimpse of him in her mind, and reviewed it repeatedly. He was tall, true enough, but she had not been able to see his face, and she did not know if he was clumsy, or poorly proportioned. He was picking up the sack – was he carrying her off to be butchered? Her curled-up legs and frozen body were dangling in mid-air, in the sack, swaying along with his footsteps, and from time to time she would briefly bump into his calf. Every time she bumped into him she shrank, nauseated, into an even smaller ball. Pain started to revive, like countless tiny burrs, boring its way from the soles of her feet, her toes and her fingertips towards her arms and legs. He was carrying her, striding forward between a great mass of pitch-black feet and pitch-black silhouettes and laughing voices, making slow, deliberate responses to someone's jokes. She felt like that great mass might come up at any moment and trample her into the snow. Just then she heard an elderly woman's voice beginning to speak. After that came the voice of an elderly man. The smell of farm animals seeped through the seams in the sack. Shortly after that she was set down on a wooden board. It was the bottom of a cart. Dropped there in a heap like dung or dirt. The horse set off at a run, urged on by a whip, running faster and faster, shaking her down into something ever more tightly packed. A hand kept coming up and lightly patting her body, whisking away the snowflakes. It was an elderly hand, it could not stretch out fully, and its palm was very soft. Every time the palm of the hand patted her, she would shrink towards the back of the cart. Through the pale brown fog, she saw the corner of a courtyard, one wall studded with many black cowpats for fuel. Once again it was the tall man who picked her up and carried her through a door. The sack fell away from her, and she saw him. Another fleeting glimpse. It was only afterwards that she took her time looking over the man she had seen so briefly: he was like a big beast of burden, with a pair of eyes so much like those of an overworked mule. The fingers of the beast of burden were very close to her; if he wanted to touch her, let him try, there was nothing wrong with her teeth.

Lucky I didn't bite him then, she thought.

'Pregnant, I am,' Duohe said.

'Oh,' Zhang Jian responded, his eyes open wide. It really was a fertile field, continuing to produce plentiful harvests!

That evening Xiaohuan came back with Girlie. As soon as she heard the news she whirled round and trotted straight back out again, saying that she was going to get some wine. At supper they drank until sweat stood out on their foreheads, and Xiaohuan dipped her chopsticks in the spirits and dripped the liquid onto Girlie's tongue. Girlie's face scrunched up, and she threw back her head and laughed out loud.

'This time when Duohe's stomach gets big again, the neighbours are bound to suspect: how come the sister-in-law gets herself a big belly with never a sight of her husband?' Xiaohuan said.

Zhang Jian asked her if she had a plan, and she lowered her face. A plan? she said. Easy. Shut Duohe up in the house, and she would tuck a pillow in her waist and go strolling about everywhere. Duohe stared blankly at the table.

'What are you thinking?' Xiaohuan asked her. 'Of running off again?' She turned to Zhang Jian, and pointed at Duohe. 'She wants to run away!'

Zhang Jian looked at Xiaohuan. She was thirty if she was a day, and still she was incapable of being serious. He said that her trick wouldn't work. There was only one toilet for each row of houses, so several people had to share each pit; how was she supposed to go to the toilet with a pillow stuck up her shirt? Was Duohe not to go out of doors to use the toilet? Xiaohuan said that holding in a bit of pee wouldn't kill you. Rich families all sit on chamber pots in their own home. Zhang Jian told her to give it a rest.

'Or how about I go back with Duohe to Anping village, and have the kid there?' Xiaohuan said.

Duohe's eyes sparkled; she looked at Zhang Jian, then at Xiaohuan. Zhang Jian silently drew in two mouthfuls of smoke from his pipe, and nodded gently to himself.

'Our house is a long way from the village!' Xiaohuan said. 'There's lots to eat there, and the freshest chickens you've ever seen! The flour is fresh too!'

Zhang Jian stood up. 'Give it a rest, go to sleep.'

Xiaohuan paced around him, left and right, saying that whenever he was required to come up with a plan or take the initiative he was no bloody use at all. A big man like him, in the end he'd still always obey his smiling tiger of a mother. Zhang Jian let her ramble on as she pleased, stretched both arms wide and yawned hugely. He did not want to produce his idea before it was fully formed.

Once Zhang Jian came up with an idea there was no room for negotiation. The following day when he came in the door, and Duohe approached to untie his shoelaces, he told her to wait, there was something he had to say first: they were moving next month. Moving? Where to? A very long way away. Further than Harbin? Much further. Nobody in the section really knew precisely where it was, so he told them it was a city to the south of the Yangtze River. Why go there? A quarter of all the workers in the factory had to go.

Duohe knelt down, and undid the laces of his suede boots. South of the Yangtze River? She repeated those four characters in her mind. Xiaohuan and Zhang Jian's question-and-answer session continued. One said she wasn't going, the other said it wasn't up to her. Why did they have to go? Because of all the hard work he'd had to do to get the application accepted.

For the first time, Xiaohuan felt afraid. Go south of the Yangtze River? She had never even imagined that she might get so much as a glimpse of the Yangtze in her whole life. Xiaohuan had spent six years at primary school, but she did not have a clue about geography. The centre of her world was Zhujiatun, the Zhu family village, where she was born and grew up; Anping village was already foreign territory to her. When she had married into Anping the fact that it was just thirty kilometres away from Zhujiatun had been an important consolation. Now she was going to go to the south bank of the Yangtze. How many rivers and streams were there between the Yangtze and Zhujiatun?

That night Xiaohuan lay on the *kang*, unable to imagine a life where she could not run off to Zhujiatun. If she decided she had had enough of Zhang Jian she would have to carry on anyway: there would be no father, mother, brothers, grandmother or Manzi nearby. She felt a hand reach into her quilt, and take hers. Her hand was exhausted and useless, all temper fled. That hand held hers, and laid it against those lips that were so reluctant to move when he spoke. His lips were no longer as fleshy as when they were first married; all bone-dry creases now. His lips opened, and took her fingers inside them.

After a moment, he pulled Xiaohuan's arm under his quilt too, followed by her entire body. And he took her in his arms. He knew she was the pampered daughter of a country family who had never seen anything of the world, he knew how frightened she was, and what she was afraid of.

Xiaohuan had learned something in her thirty years. She had come to understand that with some things there was no point in making a fuss. They were going south.

4

It was a brand-new city on the south bank of the Yangtze River, surrounded by nine mountains, surrounding three lakes, and bordering the river on one side. Two of the mountains, called Flower Mountain and Jade Mountain, were like giant bonsai arrangements, one was about five hundred metres high, the other about six hundred, covered in fine pine woods, and on windy days you could hear the wind whistling in the pines even at its base. At the foot of both mountains and following their shape, a series of red-brick apartment blocks had been erected. Looking down on the green mountains and the red buildings from the summits was enough to make anyone want to burst into a chorus of 'Socialism is Great'.

All the residential blocks were a uniform four storeys high. Zhang Jian's family had the last flat in the row on the fourth floor. None of the neighbours could take a wrong turning and end up in their home, either deliberately or accidentally. The flat had two rooms, and a corridor where you could put a table to eat. If you leaned out over the balcony and turned your face to the left, you would find yourself surveying a gentle slope covered with golden-red flowers in full bloom.

Duohe had not set foot outside the door once in all her pregnancy. That afternoon, she pulled on Zhang Jian's canvas overalls to cover her bulging eight months belly. She puffed and panted her way up the slope, wanting to see the flowers that covered the mountain in a sheet of flame. When she came closer, she was disappointed to find that these were not the *katakuri* that had bloomed on the hills of Shironami village. *Katakuri* flowers bloomed every year in April, and were replaced by the more beautiful mountain lilies when summer came. Xiaohuan and Girlie always came back from climbing the mountain with pine cones, wild onions and wild celery, but they had never once brought back flowers.

Forced to lean back slightly under the weight of her alarmingly large belly, Duohe could not see the road beneath her feet, and she had to hold on tightly to one tree after another as she slowly climbed her way up the slope. The March sun was already quite hot, and before long Duohe had stripped down to just a tight-fitting vest. She made a bundle of the overalls, and slung them on her back, lashing them to her body with the sleeves.

Seen up close, the red-gold flowers had a thin layer of down on their petals, with long stamens poking out. When Girlie was curious about something, her eyes would pop open, and those camel's eyelashes that came from Erhai would become black stamens. Duohe often saw her own face reflected in Girlie's black eyes, dark as the bottom of a well. Girlie called Xiaohuan 'Mummy' and Duohe 'Auntie', but every time her gaze landed, itching, on Duohe's cheek, the back of her hand or the back of her neck, she would think that at six years old Girlie was not that easy to fool. Her brain was moving at an incredible speed, turning over the exact relations between these three people. It would not be too long before Girlie found her own answers, and their secret mother–daughter relationship would begin.

In the distance, the little train in the factory hooted melodiously, in a slightly higher key than a normal train, and slightly more muffled.

Duohe had no kin in all the world. All she could do was rely on her own body to create family for her. Every time she became pregnant she would pray, quietly and unobserved, on bended knees to her dead mother and father, while in her stomach more of her flesh and blood was growing.

A few months ago, when Girlie and Duohe were bathing together, the girl suddenly reached out a tender forefinger and drew it along that brown line on her belly, asking if this was the place where her stomach opened and shut. She said, yes it was. Girlie's finger applied more pressure as it moved along, painfully grazing her belly with her fingernail. But she made no effort to avoid it, and let her ask deeper questions. Sure enough Girlie said: When it opens up, a little person will come out. She smiled, watching her fascinated expression. Girlie spoke again, saying that she had come out of there, then that place had closed up, and when my little brother comes out it will open here again. Her fingernail sliced its way forcefully up and down, wanting to open it up then and there. She would see through all the lies grown-ups told.

With two bunches of red-gold flowers clutched in her hands, Duohe realised that every step down the mountain would be very difficult. She found a stone and rested, as the little train in the steel foundry drove from one end to the other with its drawn-out note, and then after a while drove past in the opposite direction, hooting again. Duohe closed her eyes. The noise from the train was the sound of her childhood. All the children of Shironami village had grown up listening to the little trains, and the Japanese goods they ate, wore and used had all been brought there by rail. All the parcels of neatly arranged, exquisitely wrapped nori seaweed and the bundles of carefully folded printed cloth. There was a deaf-mute in Shironami village who could do a first-rate imitation of the shrill call of the train. Duohe closed her eyes and sat on the stone, and imagined the sound of the distant train as the deaf-mute's voice.

And Dr Suzuki had arrived on the small train. He wore snow-white gloves, an inky-black top hat and a purplish-blue Western suit. When he walked, his cane took one step for every two taken by his legs, and neither the two legs nor the cane got in the way of any of the others, as he walked the country paths, transforming them into the colourfully lit boulevards of Tokyo and Osaka. Soon she learned that Dr Suzuki had four legs if you counted his cane – he had an artificial leg fitted to his left leg below the knee. It was only because he had all those legs to keep in order that he had retired from the front line. Duohe believed that Tokyo and Osaka must be very fine, because Dr Suzuki was fine just like them. All the girls had felt that way about Dr Suzuki: even after losing a leg in the fighting he was still so fine. In the final days of Shironami village, Dr Suzuki's real legs, false leg and cane were falling over each other in their agitation; he went from house to house, urging the inhabitants to get on the train with him and leave for Japan via Busan. He said that the Soviet Union had suddenly palled up with Britain and America, and was sweeping its way through Siberia, right at their backs. Everyone went with him to Yantun station, yet they watched the train carry Dr Suzuki away, so furious that even his hair was bristling with rage. Duohe thought that his final glance had fallen on her face. Duohe believed that the rather mysterious doctor could see other people's thoughts as clear as day. He must have known how much Duohe had wanted to leave.

Duohe was starting to feel chilly. The sun was already behind the mountain. A gang of children came down from the summit, with triangular red scarves at their necks. One child was holding up a triangular flag. He asked Duohe something in a loud voice. Duohe shook her head. There were too many of them talking at once. She noticed that all of them were carrying either clubs or nets. They asked her something several times more, but she continued to shake her head. She did not understand this *tianshu, tianshu* they were talking about. She knew the three characters on the triangular flag, but she could not see what they might mean when put together: 'Eliminate the Four Pests!'

The children ran on past her, down the slope. Every one of them shot her a sidelong glance, trying to work out just what was not right about this woman.

When Duohe stood up to head down the mountain, her foot slipped, and she slid downhill for several metres. Finally a stone blocked her way. She heard water gurgling, and turned her head to the side to see muddy yellow floodwater rushing past in a stone gully. She was afraid of taking another tumble, so she took off both her shoes. She had learned how to make these cloth shoes from Xiaohuan, but they were nearly worn out now, loose and slippery. A spasm of bellyache hit her, and she gripped her stomach tightly with both hands. Her belly was as hard as iron, distended and tense. She realised that at some point she had sat down on the ground, pressed on to the surface of the earth by her big belly, which felt like a small mountain. The pain in her belly spasmed chaotically for a short while, but very soon it found its direction, surging its way out to exit between her legs.

Duohe saw that in the murky yellow floodwater in the gully, red-gold flowers were tumbling.

She knew that she still had some time between the pains, she could shuffle her way home slowly. Having given birth to two children, she thought she already knew how to have a baby. At present the sky was clear, so blue it was tinged with purple, with the sun sinking behind the mountains, and the air was full of the calls of birds returning to the woods for the night. Once the contraction had passed, she would step over the gully and head in the direction of home. But the pain became more and more ferocious, tearing downwards at all her organs. She put her hand to her belly, she had to deliver this child safe and sound, she couldn't die. She had to give birth to lots of relatives for herself. After that she would never again be a friendless woman with no kin, alone in a strange land.

The bluish-purple sky pulsed dark and then light again in front of her eyes. The pain passed, her face was icy cold, beaded with sweat like a layer of rain. She looked at the gully beside her. To step over that rushing, noisy water would be like striding over the Yangtze River.

This was the time when people finished work for the day. The small roads at the foot of each building led to the main road to the factory, and every day high tide would come to the main road, and streams of people would go pouring forward. All were workers, dressed in canvas overalls, with towels tucked tightly round their necks. Duohe had never heard so many bicycle bells ringing all at the same time. This crowd separated out at the smaller roads in front of the buildings, where all the men in canvas overalls locked their bicycles at the entrance to the buildings. After that the bald, cement-built staircases would echo with the sound of men's heavy footsteps. This was the moment when Zhang Jian, returning home from the factory, would discover that Duohe was not there. Run off again? He would rouse his exhausted body, turn round and head straight downstairs.

When Zhang Jian came to this new city of iron and steel from

Anshan, he was transferred to the recently built steel plant, and after several months' training, he was now a crane operator. All of this was what Duohe had overheard him telling Xiaohuan. Duohe always made a mental note of the words she heard, and would turn them over in her memory in spare moments, slowly piecing together meaning from them. Where would Zhang Jian look for her this time? He knew she had never gone beyond the door of the flat, she had not been anywhere.

Another paroxysm of pain overtook her. She cried out. At the bottom of the slope the lamps were already lit. She cried out again. It comforted her a little. Her every cry went in the same direction as the urge. She was not very clear herself what she was calling out. At that moment she hated everybody, and most of all the Chinese man who had somehow impregnated her. Duohe did not like this man, and he did not like her. She was not after this man's affection, survival was all she wanted. It had been pretty much the same for her mother and grandmother. Their true family had been the people they gave birth to themselves, or who had given birth to them; all those birth canals were the secret passages by which family feeling was passed on. Sometimes when she and Girlie looked at each other, they would share a hidden smile, Xiaohuan had no part in it, not even Zhang Jian got his share.

She cried out, again and again. There was something in her mouth. It was her own hair, and she twisted her face to one side, and bit down on the hair that had fallen loose around her shoulders. Her mother had given birth to her, her little brother and sister, and then there was her grandmother who had given birth to her mother, and all the kin that had emerged from her birth canal: this was a gang that nobody else could get into. Because of this, her mother had not lost her mind when the notification that her father had been killed in action was opened out in front of her. It was for this moment that she had given birth to her family: when her husband left never to return, a crowd of child relatives at her knees showed her that she was not finished yet; every one of these little relatives could be a turning point that led you to better things.

Duohe was going to give birth to this tiny relative. She wanted to give birth to children until they made up the majority of the family, then let Xiaohuan try to lord it over them all! They would be like Girlie, watching for a chance to share a smile, a smile that was like a code which nobody apart from a blood relation could decipher.

She cried aloud, again and again.

Someone in the distance called back: 'Duohe!'

Duohe immediately stopped crying.

The person was holding an electric torch and carrying a tatty padded jacket. The light of the torch shone first on Duohe's face, then at once moved to illuminate her crotch. She heard them cry out.

Duohe had no time to wonder why it was Xiaohuan who had come, and not Zhang Jian. Xiaohuan's face pressed close to hers in a guff of tobacco, so that she could squeeze an arm in under Duohe's neck, and lift her up. Duohe was fatter than Xiaohuan, and the pregnancy weighed her down like a small mountain. Xiaohuan knew as soon as she tried that this was a vain hope. She told Duohe to bear up for a few minutes longer, she would go down the mountain and call Zhang Jian. With one bound Xiaohuan leapt over the gully, but before she had even caught her balance she jumped back. She covered Duohe with the tattered jacket, and told her to take the torch. If she lost her bearings, Duohe could signal to them with it. She jumped over the gully again with a kick of her legs. She had not got very far when Duohe cried out. Xiaohuan was terrified out of her wits by the sound, neither human nor ghost.

'That's your punishment for the evil you've done in this life! Running off up the mountain to look for your real mum and dad and your granny too . . .?' Xiaohuan let her temper go as she crossed the gully again with a bound.

Duohe's posture had changed. Her head was now facing the peak, with her feet towards the bottom of the mountain, her two hands propping up her body so she was half sitting, knees bent, and her legs spread very wide apart.

'Turning into a female wildcat! Dropping your litter here . . .' Xiaohuan went to drag Duohe, who seemed to weigh at least five hundred kilos. Recently her appetite had been outrageous, even Girlie saved a mouthful for her.

Xiaohuan made another effort, but not only did she fail to move Duohe, she was dragged over instead. As she picked up the torch, the light flashed briefly between Duohe's legs to reveal a bulge in the crotch of her trousers. Xiaohuan yanked the trousers away: in the light of the torch, a ball-shaped mass of soaking-wet black hair had already emerged. Xiaohuan immediately stripped off her own jacket to make a pad beneath Duohe's body. It was no use, the blood and waters had soaked into the mud, which was already plastered all over Duohe's body.

Xiaohuan heard her say something incomprehensible, though she knew that it was Japanese.

'Good, say whatever you like! . . . Push! . . . Say whatever's on your mind, I'm listening! . . . Push!' No matter how she knelt Xiaohuan could not get a purchase; one leg was pushing hard at the root of a tree, to prevent her from sliding down the mountain.

In fact, Duohe herself did not know what she was saying. If

there had been someone with a knowledge of Japanese beside them, they would have understood from these disconnected fragments of words and sentences that she was pleading with someone, a woman called Chieko. Duohe spat out each word through clenched teeth, begging her not to kill Kumi, to let Kumi live another day, Kumi was only three, if she was still not over her illness by tomorrow, there'd be time enough to kill her then. Just let her carry Kumi on her back, she didn't mind, she wouldn't be in the way . . .

'Fine! Good!' Xiaohuan replied to Duohe, all agreement, cupping that hot, damp little head in the palm of one hand.

Duohe's voice had already changed into another person's, she was begging in a low, husky, ghastly voice. Her voice sank lower and lower, and became an incantation. If that speaker of Japanese had bent over close to her mouth, they would have heard her cry out in a hoarse voice from deep within her chest: Don't let her catch up, don't let her kill Kumi! . . . She's a child killer!

'Fine, anything you say, say what you like, let it all out . . .' Xiaohuan said.

By now, Duohe was barely human. The entire mountain had become her birthing chair; she half sat, half lay, one hand gripping a pine tree, her wild hair veiling her body, her legs open very wide, pointing directly at the foot of the mountain: the tall chimney belching smoke, the train going past, the flaming red expanse of sky where a blast furnace was being tapped at the steel factory. From time to time Duohe arched her back, her great belly rose and then fell again. That little black-haired head was aimed straight at the countless lights at the mountain's foot, but it would not come out, despite both women's frantic efforts.

Duohe's flesh was all broken. In just this way, her mother had brought her into the world, willingly enduring a pain worse than death.

Xiaohuan was weeping, great, noisy howls. Duohe's appearance made her weep, she couldn't say why. The torch shone on Duohe's deathly face, her eyes open wide. What suffering could make a woman so ugly? What kind of extraordinary suffering could this be?

Little by little, the tiny head broke away from Duohe, into the palm of her hand, and after that came little shoulders, arms, legs and feet. Xiaohuan let out a great burst of breath, and bit through the umbilical cord with her gold-wrapped tooth. The little creature's wails rang through the forest like a miniature trumpet. Xiaohuan said: 'Duohe, a son! We have a son again!'

But Duohe's posture had not changed, and neither had the size of her belly. The pine tree she was clutching in her hands shook, rustled and hissed, her legs shifted upwards, then found their footing. Xiaohuan laid the sticky, slippery child down, and aimed the torch between Duohe's legs: sure enough, another little head had emerged! Xiaohuan screeched: 'It's twins! Aren't you amazing? Two in one go! . . .' She did not know what to do with herself, she was too shocked, and too delighted. How could it have fallen to her, Xiaohuan, to deal with something as huge as this?

Duohe pulled on two pine trees and bore downwards, then she sat up by herself, with a head that was already more than half out cupped in her hands. Xiaohuan held the crying child with one hand, and with the other she came to restrain Duohe. She was not clear why it was necessary for her to restrain her, perhaps she was afraid she would roll down the mountain slope, or it might be to help correct her birth posture – childbirth should take place lying down. But something hit her very hard, and she nearly fell into the gully.

Several seconds later it dawned on Xiaohuan that the blow had come from Duohe. Duohe had kicked her.

The torch had been flung to who knows where. Xiaohuan was holding the first baby, who was wriggling like a fleshy worm. The lights at the bottom of the mountain were like a wave of fire in Xiaohuan's swimming eyes.

The second child came out by itself. Duohe gently supported his head and shoulders in her hands, he knew the way now, and followed it out like a familiar road.

'Duohe, did you see that, two of them! However did you do it?'

Xiaohuan took off her own trousers too, and wrapped the two children tightly. Her frantic flailing gradually subsided, and some effectiveness returned to her movements. As she bustled about she told Duohe not to move an inch, just lie where she was, she would carry the children home, and then get Zhang Jian to carry Duohe down the mountain on his back.

The voice of the wind in the pine trees changed to a howl, and a long whistling sound. Xiaohuan looked at Duohe, who was practically at her last gasp, and suddenly thought of wolves. She did not know if wolves would come to the slopes of this little mountain. Let Duohe not become meat for the wolves now.

Xiaohuan stood still by the gully. Goose pimples burst out all over her body. They were not from the wind, but from fright at this thought she had not acknowledged. This thought that she did not dare acknowledge. Xiaohuan had lived for over thirty years – how many wicked thoughts had been born in her heart, and been extinguished there? More than she could count, but none of them had made her hair stand on end like this one. That thought was drenched in blood: a pack of hungry wolves fighting over a meal, all pulling in different directions, and once they were done there was no kinless, friendless orphan Duohe in this world. The timing could not have been better; a pair of sons had just come into the world.

Xiaohuan stood on the side of the rushing flood drain, listening to her own wicked thoughts flowing past, flowing away.

She walked slowly back to Duohe, and sat down beside her. The two babies had been tightly swaddled, and were no longer crying with fear at the boundless, empty expanses of the world. Xiaohuan took Duohe's hand. It was like the hand of a corpse, the palm rubbed dry and coarse by the branches of the pine tree. She told Duohe that she could not leave her alone for the wolves. No one could say for sure whether there were wolves in these mountains.

Duohe's breathing was slow and even, as though Xiaohuan had set her mind at ease. Xiaohuan did not know whether she had understood what she had just said. She told Duohe not to worry, neither of them would go, and Zhang Jian would come looking for them. Girlie had told Xiaohuan that Auntie must have gone up the mountain to pick flowers; Auntie had asked ever so many times what the flowers on the mountain were called.

Then Xiaohuan saw the moving light of torches. There were at least twenty people walking up from the bottom of the mountain.

Xiaohuan yelled: 'Over here! Help!'

The two newborn sons, scared out of their wits by the huge, unwieldy world, bawled out to each other in turn, two little trumpets, loud and shrill.

It was a group of policemen who had come to search the mountain. Zhang Jian had come banging at the window of the duty room of the local police station at ten o'clock, saying that two women from his home had vanished together. One was his spouse. And the other one? He came close to saying that she was also his spouse, but when the words came to his lips he said it was a female relative. Female relative? His sister-in-law. By the time the police had assembled all their people it was already close to eleven o'clock, and they sent a few men to the train station and the long-distance bus station, while the remainder went to search the mountain according to the leads provided by Zhang Jian. The uniformed police did not like this part of the mountain; when someone went missing in the pine forest no good came of it. People who had dabbled in corruption, people sick with love, couples who had quarrelled, all would take themselves off to the pine woods to hang themselves. Now they were flashing torches in all directions, far and near, asking why these two women had colluded to disappear together. Zhang Jian felt that every sentence he said in reply must be all wrong. His two spouses had run off together. It had taken him a very long time to get accustomed to the word *spouse*, but after he had heard it many times over he no longer felt that there was anything unrespectable about it. Right now he felt that this form of address was particularly well suited to his family, which in truth was not entirely respectable.

As soon as he heard Xiaohuan calling out, Zhang Jian guessed that something must have happened to Duohe, and therefore something must have happened to the child in Duohe's belly. He realised that he had already left the police and all those other people far behind him. Another guess pursued him: he would have to make that evil choice again, the way he had all those years ago. Keep the adult or keep the child. The next guess was that he would say to the doctor: *Then . . . keep the child*. After such a choice, he might perhaps feel for the rest of his life that he had committed a great sin, but he thought that this time he would not make the same decision as he had before. The beam of his torch found Xiaohuan.

Xiaohuan was standing on the far side of that stone-lined ditch in flowery underpants with two bundles in her arms, her mouth all bloody. The new moon had just risen from behind the mountains, and the bloodstain on the ground was black as pitch. By the time she had told him what had happened – Duohe had given birth – the police had started to appear, saying among themselves: *Had a baby? . . . Who gave birth? . . . Twins! . . . Alive?*

People gathered by the side of the ditch. Duohe had already stood up, and, with Xiaohuan and Zhang Jian's help, dragged herself into her clothes, which hung unevenly on her. She was half leaning into Xiaohuan's arms, one hand clutching a pine tree for support. The people said, *it's just as well we found you, now we can relax, how did you come to go climbing the mountain with such a big belly? So long as mother and sons are all right, that's the main thing, you must live a charmed life.*

They switched on the torches and shone them on the two children, and on their mother. Every time light from a torch came up, the babies' mother bowed deeply. And they returned the bow, although very soon after they started to feel that they had no recollection of ever having bowed in such a way before.

Everybody was laughing and joking, saying that Zhang Jian should hand out red eggs to celebrate the birth. They should be good for five eggs each at the very least, after having helped him comb the mountain in the middle of the night. One policeman, a morose, elderly man, was called Old Fu. Old Fu never cracked a smile; he felt that Zhang Jian had managed his household very poorly, and if it hadn't been for his sister-in-law, his wife and kids might well not have come out of it alive.

The matter was perfectly clear: of the two women, the one who had given birth was Zhang Jian's wife, and the one wearing red flowery underpants and carrying the children was his sister-in-law. It was just like making fried dough twists, once they were cooked it would require a lot of effort for Zhang Jian to tease the strands apart. All he could do just then was to say the first thing that came into his head, promising with a chuckle to take red eggs to the police station.

When they reached the foot of the mountain, the two policemen who were carrying Duohe continued past the turning on the little road that led to Zhang Jian's building. He became anxious, and asked them where they were taking her. To the People's Hospital – where else? She's had the children, what would she want with a hospital? Xiaohuan became anxious too, and hurried up to grab hold of the stretcher. The police insisted on a check-up, to see if anything was the matter with the mother and children. Even if they are all fine you still have to do your bit for hygiene – suppose the worst happened and something went wrong after giving birth on a barren mountain, what would we tell the Party organisation?!

It was well after midnight before they got Duohe and the two babies, and a frightened Girlie, settled down and asleep.

Xiaohuan told Zhang Jian to sleep as well, she would keep watch that night, to make certain that Duohe and the children were safe.

In the early morning pigeons landed on the balcony. Their continual cooing woke Zhang Jian from his doze. Xiaohuan had squeezed in next to Girlie and was fast asleep, while his head was occupying a small part of Duohe's pillow. The two little boys were both under Duohe's armpits. There they were, all sleeping in the same nest, old and young, male and female. He raised his head. Duohe was looking at him. He felt that she had spent a long time looking him up and down, from head to heel. Did she have to do it while he was sleeping, and all his defences were down? Outside it was broad daylight, but the lights were still on inside the room. Duohe's outstretched foot was pallid and swollen.

Zhang Jian walked outside, and bought a bowl of soya-bean milk at a stall on the corner of the street, where he got the stallholder to stir in two poached eggs and three big spoons of brown sugar, turning the soya milk brown. When he returned carrying the soya milk and eggs, Xiaohuan had moved nearer the centre of the bed, squeezing Girlie over to Duohe's side. Duohe's eyes were still fixed on him, watching him as he came down the corridor holding the big, coarse pottery bowl in his hands. He thought again, What does she mean by looking at me like that? He had come all this way just now without a hitch, but now the soya milk was splashing out.

They called the twins Dahai and Erhai (first born and second born), and when they were a month old, Zhang Jian widened the two wooden beds, to form two *kangs*. Dahai and Erhai both slept in Duohe's little room, and he slept in the big room with Xiaohuan and Girlie. Occasionally someone from the factory would come to discuss work with Deputy Group Leader Zhang, and the big room also became a sitting room. Working hard and avoiding speaking were Zhang Jian's strong points, and it was thanks to these points that he had risen to the rank of Deputy Group Leader of the Crane Drivers' Group.

From then on Zhang Jian never entered Duohe's room. At six and a half, it was easy to give Girlie orders. You would say to her, Go and get Dahai and Erhai, and she would first carry in one of her two little brothers, then the other, for Zhang Jian to kiss and play with. Erhai was slightly thinner, and that was how Zhang Jian told the twins apart. The brothers were superb eaters and excellent sleepers, and the next time Zhang Jian looked properly at Duohe, he found that all her surplus flesh had been converted into milk and suckled away by the two boys. Duohe was still Duohe, and every day from dawn to dusk she methodically went about her usual business. Girlie's clothes were ironed into perfect brightness and neatness, even a patched pair of checked trousers was ironed into knife-sharp creases. On the sixth day after she had given birth to the children, she had got out of bed bright and early, picked up a bucket of water, knelt on the floor with her bottom sticking in the air, and polished the concrete floor until it shone blue.

Zhang Jian had two friends at work, who had come with him from Anshan: Peng and Shi. Rivalries promptly broke out between them and their colleagues from Shanghai and Wuhan. The first time Xiao Peng went to Zhang Jian's home the twins were just over a month old. He wanted to get Zhang Jian to proofread his application to join the Communist Youth League. When the door opened he stood stock-still in the doorway. He asked what flooring Zhang Jian's family had put down, and they told him it was a concrete floor, same as everyone else's. Impossible, he said. He knelt down and rubbed the floor with one finger, saying, So smooth, it's like jade. Then he looked again at his finger, to which not even a speck of dust clung. He looked at the row of shoes at the door of the Zhang home, and again at the snow-white cloth socks on the feet of the Zhang family, and walked in gingerly on the tips of his oily, dirty suede boots. The second time he came it was with Xiao Shi, and they came prepared, having changed into their least holey and malodorous socks.

Some time later, when Xiao Peng and Xiao Shi again visited the Zhang home, they found that the Zhang family had prepared too; the Zhangs' sister-in-law silently set two pairs of wood-soled slippers in front of them. They felt like Zhang Jian's sister-in-law did not have a face, all they saw of her was the crown of her head, or else the back of her neck.

It was mainly because of Xiaohuan that they came to the Zhangs' home. Xiaohuan had treated Xiao Peng with such friendliness and warmth on his first visit that he stopped feeling homesick. It was only once Xiao Shi had heard his description that he came with him to meet her. She would wrap a big apron around her slender waist, and ask, with a cigarette holder stuck in her mouth at an attractive angle, what they would both like to eat, and she would make it for them. Xiaohuan never paid much attention to such everyday matters as oil, salt, firewood and rice; so long as the result tasted good, she was perfectly happy to use up half a kilo of oil in one session. So long as she had good lard, chopped in pieces and fried with plenty of soy sauce and onions, she could mix it with rice and put it on to steam, and the result was fragrant enough to lift the roof off the whole block.

Xiao Peng and Xiao Shi noticed that the Zhangs' sister-in-law never came to table, but took the three children into the little room where she fed them separately. One time the group in the big room had eaten themselves into a merry mood, and said, Bring the twin boys over so we can play with them. Half drunk, Zhang Jian raised his voice, and called out to Girlie to carry Dahai and Erhai over. A few minutes passed and Girlie's bobbed head appeared at the edge of the door frame, saying, 'Dad, my auntie says that I'd drop them. If you want them carried over, come yourself.'

When Zhang Jian had downed two or three ounces of spirits, he staggered next door, feeling like a little god, and saw his two sons lying in Duohe's arms drinking milk. Duohe was wearing a front-opening cotton top knitted out of yarn taken from gloves, and right now it was open all the way, exposing two pinkish-white breasts, which pillowed the round, bulging faces of the twin boys. Zhang Jian had never noticed what Duohe looked like when nursing children, but this time he looked and looked, this time his heart suddenly gave a lurch. Duohe said in that language of hers that she thought was Chinese that he could take them away, the boys had both drunk their fill. If he did not take them now they would go to sleep. Zhang Jian walked up, his hand brushed past the hollow of Dahai's throat.

When Duohe shrugged her shoulders, his hand touched her nipple. His hand was chilly.

What had happened that first night they were together? Had it been his hands that had first got to know her body? He had put out the lamp without looking at her. There was no brightness at all in the room, she was just a thin, small, black shadow. Her head seemed very big, her hair exceptionally thick. Although her hair was black too, it was not the black hair he was familiar with. It was barbarian black hair, a different species. The barbarian males had killed, burned and looted, and the lone, solitary woman they had left behind was no more than a thin, black shadow. He had closed in on her, then moved in closer still, looming bigger and bigger in her eyes. Darkness makes big, tall things even larger. In her eyes, he must have been the enormous black shadow of a man who killed, burned and looted. She had begun to cry. Slowly her legs had given way and she had collapsed on the *kang*. He had not been a barbarian towards her, he had not even been particularly rough with her, it was just that his movements were utterly devoid of interest. His movements were very effective, but absolutely indifferent. She had cried ever more painfully. The little, thin, black shadow had shaken and curled in on itself, like the grub of a green hawkmoth. He had started to get barbaric, to murder and pillage on this quivering black shadow.

She was not completely indifferent to him. At the least she regarded him as an occupying army. What thoughts did the women of the enemy nations have towards an occupying army? He felt she was looking at him in that way again, full of ambiguous thoughts. He raised his head, and sure enough, her eyes were deeply, profoundly barbarian, full of hostile provocation.

And that wasn't all that was wrong. Things were wrong within himself. His heart lurched over and over again, he could not move a step.

Zhang Jian came round with a start at the sound of Girlie's voice. Girlie was talking to Duohe in Japanese, saying that she did not want to wear the '*wanpiisu*'. Zhang Jian realised that it was a flowery dress. How could he have failed to notice the conversations that had always been going on between the two of them? From time to time half a sentence of Japanese would be slipped into half a sentence of Chinese. What would happen if they spoke this peculiar language outside?

'From now on you're not to say that any more,' Zhang Jian said to Girlie in a quiet voice.

Girlie looked at him with eyes identical to his own, ignorant and innocent.

Zhang Jian turned his face towards Duohe. 'Don't teach the children Japanese.'

Duohe also looked at him, apparently just as ignorant and innocent.

5

Xiaohuan had changed jobs twice in the space of a year. She first went to the factory as a temporary worker, where she learned to cut serial numbers, but having learned the way of it, she complained that it was too dull. In the time it took to finish one number she'd spent enough time with her own thoughts to last her a lifetime. You were supposed to do over ten numbers in a day, and that was a lot of lifetimes. She quit her job and lazed around at home for two months, her temper worsening perceptibly with idleness, and then she took herself off to work at a guest house. It was near the train station, and there were many guests from all over the country, which meant that she had plenty to chat about. It looked like she would not be switching jobs again for a while. The thing Xiaohuan disliked most about working in the guest house was the shifts. She had to spend sixteen hours at a stretch sitting in the duty room on the last Sunday of every month.

It was on a Sunday that it happened. Xiaohuan set off bright and early for work. She had just gone out when Zhang Jian got up. He leaned on the railing of the balcony, smoking, and heard somebody open the window behind him. Duohe. Her eyes were on his back, the back of his neck, and his head of thick, hard scrubbing-brush hair. Xiaohuan was not there. It was as if they could hear each other's hearts beating.

With the coming of autumn, the weather was still hot, but in a different way. The heat from the distant steel factory did not linger so long in the air. How good it would have been if there was no Duohe in this family, Zhang Jian thought mercilessly. He saw the neighbours going out, all in their family groups, the father riding his bike with the mother sitting on the seat at the back holding the baby, the eldest child and the second one on the crossbar, complaining, laughing, cursing as they turned the corner onto the main road below the building. He envied them desperately. His own bicycle could be done up too, he had already added a little chair he had welded himself to the handlebars for Girlie to sit on, and Xiaohuan could go on the back seat with Dahai on her back and Erhai in her arms. They too could be a family for people to envy. And yet they had to have this extra person, this Duohe.

When Zhang Jian had smoked two Donghai cigarettes down to stubs, he walked into the big room, and heard the voice of Girlie, who had just woken up, rattling away. As soon as she woke up she would go dashing over to Auntie Duohe's little room. Girlie seemed to be saying that her brothers were doing this or that and she wanted to do it too. Nobody could control Duohe's conversations with Girlie, the Japanese words so fluently mixed in. He walked to the door of the room, and assumed a forbidding expression.

'Girlie, in this house we don't speak foreign.'

'I wasn't speaking foreign.' Girlie raised two broad eyebrows, identical to his own.

'How come I didn't understand what you were saying just now?'

Girlie looked at him in bewilderment. After a while she finally said, 'Then *you* were talking foreign.'

He could feel Duohe's eyes on his right hand. He had hit Girlie twice, both times when he had been in one of his stubborn fits. Normally he adored Girlie, he had even worked bits of scrap metal from the fitters' bench into little tables and chairs for a doll's house for her. When he hit Girlie the two women formed a united front. Duohe took him by surprise from behind, battering his lower back with her head. Xiaohuan's mouth was a deadly weapon, a long string of vile words: Quite the lad, aren't you? In the factory you lick the leaders' arseholes to get yourself made a little group leader, but when you come home you pick the soft meat to pound!

His eyes on Girlie's feet, he said, 'Duohe, our family are Chinese.' Girlie was wearing a pair of white cloth sandals, the uppers made by Duohe and the soles by Xiaohuan. Girlie's perfectly clean toenails were visible outside the white cloth. Nowhere else in this town could you find white cloth sandals or pinky-white translucent toenails.

Duohe's silent, unobtrusive obstinacy could be seen all over the house: the concrete floor scrubbed to a gleaming blue-green, clothes ironed pencil-straight, the three children's shoes and socks without a speck of dust on them.

If everything could be untangled and done all over again, if there had been no war and the Japanese hadn't been so bestially cruel in China for so many years, Zhang Jian would marry Duohe. He would not care what country she was from.

He just stood there in front of her, startled by his own thought: He'd *marry* her? He was fond of her . . .?!

When they had eaten breakfast, Duohe, squeakily singing a Japanese song, strapped Dahai and Erhai to her chest and back and took Girlie by the hand. Only then did he react: the four of them were going out. Going where? To the park. Did she know the way? No, but Girlie did.

Zhang Jian stood up and slipped a shirt onto his bare back. Duohe was watching him, not daring to let a smile appear on her face, but suddenly it floated up. She dashed back to the little room, and Zhang Jian heard her unstrap the two boys and open the wooden chest. After a while the lid of the chest came down with a slam, and Duohe emerged in a patterned dress and a cloth sun hat, carrying a woman's handbag with frilled scalloped edging. She trotted about the little flat, her footsteps quick and rather clumsy.

This was the first time Duohe had had a proper outing, let alone a chance to take the three children out with Zhang Jian. She was wearing and carrying all her worldly goods.

The neighbours who were playing cards or chess in the corridor looked at the skilled crane operator from the steel factory, with his two children tied to him, one in front, one behind, walking with his sister-in-law all dressed up in her patterned costume, holding the seven-year-old girl by the hand, angling an oil-paper umbrella over Zhang Jian's head, to keep the sun off him and the two boys.

The people thought, there's something not quite right about this family group, what is it? But they couldn't be bothered to think it through, and soon returned to their chessboards and cards.

Zhang Jian took the woman and children on a train to the next station, which was on the banks of the Yangtze River. He had heard the people in the factory mention that there was this historic site here; at the weekend it was full of tourists from Nanjing and Shanghai, waiting in long queues at the snack shops, and even at the outdoor tea stalls you had to wait for a place.

They sat on stone seats, eating the rice balls that Duohe had hurriedly squeezed together for them, each one stuffed with a filling of turnip and soy sauce.

Duohe was chattering away in her incoherent Chinese. Sometimes

Zhang Jian did not understand, and Girlie acted as interpreter. The afternoon weather was hot and stuffy, so they walked to a bamboo grove, where Zhang Jian spread out his coat and put the children on it. Duohe was reluctant to spend time with her feet up, and said she wanted to go down to the stones in the river. When Zhang Jian awoke from a doze, the sun was sinking to the west, and Duohe had still not returned. He strapped on Dahai and Erhai, took Girlie's hand and walked out of the bamboo grove.

The front of the temple was surrounded by many people, all looking at a display of ornamental pot plants. Zhang Jian squeezed in among them, but could not see any sign of Duohe. He was grumbling and swearing to himself: she'd never gone out, but she still had to go and join in the fun, never stopping to consider her own limitations. At this moment he suddenly saw a patterned form through a gap in the crowd: Duohe's face, transformed by anxiety, looking around her in all directions, her footsteps still awkward.

Without quite knowing how it happened, Zhang Jian avoided her gaze. Thunder seemed to be rolling in his heart, so that his ears were ringing with the noise, as he asked himself despairingly: What are you doing? Have you gone mad? Are you seriously going to do what you said all those years ago, and abandon this woman? Nor could he hear himself applauding: Perfect timing! She's brought it on herself . . .

He led the children to a little restaurant, but as soon as he reached for his wallet, he realised with a sinking heart that he had given the one five-yuan note he had on him to Duohe in case she needed spending money. It would appear that he had planned the thing out in advance: by giving her five yuan he could buy himself a few minutes of easy conscience, at least she wouldn't starve for a few days. When he had seen her nursing, his hand had brushed her nipple, his heart had given a lurch, and at that moment a plan had come to him . . . or had it?

The sky was getting dark, heavy rain was on its way. The lady in charge of the restaurant was very honest and kind, and poured out cup after cup of hot water for him and the children. Girlie asked a hundred times, over and over again: Where's Auntie gone?

Zhang Jian left the children in the care of the proprietress, and dashed out into the rain. He ran up the mountain along little winding roads and back down again. The little road leading to the river clung to the side of the mountain. There were whirlpools there, a whole series of them, and once you fell in they would swallow you up, bones and all.

Zhang Jian started to cry. He had not cried since the age of ten; even when the child died in Xiaohuan's belly he had got by with a lump in his throat and a stinging in his nose. He was crying over how Duohe had never gone outside, or spent a jiao, and the first time she went out, the first time she had five yuan on her, she was abandoned. Did she know how to buy food? She could always let people take her for an idiot or a deaf-mute or someone who wasn't all there. Would people understand what she said, with her peculiar tones and words all over the place? She would not tell people she was Japanese. She knew how dangerous that would be. Or did she? Zhang Jian was crying for the children who from now on would have no mother of their own. Dahai and Erhai were six months old, and their accustomed food supply had been abruptly cut off. All the same, the children were much better off than he was; at the end of the day they were children and would soon forget, or hopefully they would. By the time the cement was no longer so clean it shone blue, and their clothes no longer carried the scent of starch and toilet water, or bore the marks of being ironed into knife-edge creases, his memories of Duohe would have faded a little.

He was shaking all over, as if soaked through with his own tears. In the place where the road and the river met, there were boats, hooting. He suddenly dropped his head to his knees, and he wept so hard that his chest cavity resounded emptily. How would he ever be able to forget the last smile that Duohe had turned on him? When she heard that he was taking them out, and went back to change her clothes and tidy her hair she had secretly applied some of the children's talcum powder to her face. Her final smile had been dappled, the baby powder washed away by sweat, and mixed in with dust.

When Zhang Jian returned to that restaurant, it was late, and supper was being served. Girlie was sitting on a bench, and Dahai and Erhai were lying on a bed made of four stools pushed together, asleep. The woman in charge said that Girlie had fed her brothers with steamed bread soaked in water, and had eaten a cold rice ball herself.

'Where's Auntie?' Girlie asked him immediately.

'Auntie's gone home,' he said. Drops of water were flowing down from his hair to his temples.

'Why?'

'She . . . has a stomach ache.'

'Why? . . . Why?'

Zhang Jian resorted to his old trick, he simply did not hear Girlie's words. One of the customers in the restaurant was a middle-aged man, who said he had had a chat with Girlie: she could say her name, the district she lived in, and which building. Zhang Jian strapped his sons to his body, while thanking the middle-aged stranger and the lady in charge.

'And what about my auntie?' Girlie asked.

He looked at his daughter. How long would it take for Duohe's words and expressions to vanish from his daughter's language?

'What about my auntie?' Girlie gestured at the oil-paper umbrella.

He went out holding the umbrella aloft; why get soaked on the way back?

'Did my auntie take the *kishya* back home?' Girlie asked when they got to the ticket window at the train station. He did not have to guess, *kishya* must mean train. He asked the ticket attendant to be kind, to take his work card and sell him a ticket now, and he would send money to redeem his work card later on. The ticket seller took one look at him and the three children. Their pitiable condition and honesty could be seen at a glance. He led them directly to the ticket sellers' room, to wait for the slow train at nine o'clock.

On the train it was still very crowded and noisy. People from the big cities who had spent a whole day being tourists and dining on fresh river fish in restaurants now set up tea stalls for themselves on the train, to eat dried strips of tofu, a local speciality. The train's final stop was Nanjing, and the loudspeakers were playing a comedy in Shanghai dialect about a member of the volunteer army coming home from Korea to get married. Those of the passengers who could understand it kept bursting into peals of laughter. The two boys were sleeping sweetly, but Girlie turned her face to the window, staring at her reflection in the dark glass. Perhaps she was watching her father's profile reflected in the window. Zhang Jian sat opposite her, with Erhai in his arms, one foot stretched onto the seat opposite to hold down Dahai, who was lying on the seat. Dahai and Erhai were identical to look at, but without knowing why Zhang Jian had a partiality for Erhai.

'Daddy, did Auntie go home on the *kishya*?'

'Mm.'

Girlie had asked this at least ten times. A few minutes later, Girlie opened her mouth again.

'Daddy, tonight I'm going to sleep with Auntie.'

Zhang Jian did not listen. He could feel his eyes filling up again, and he hurriedly distracted himself, smiling at Girlie.

'Girlie, out of Daddy, Mummy and Auntie, who are you closest to?'

Girlie looked at him with dark black eyes. Girlie was clever, she thought that when her elders asked this kind of thing they were setting a trap, which would always catch you whichever way you answered. Girlie did not reply, but that was what gave her away: if her heart had been more with Zhang Jian or Xiaohuan, she would have come straight out and said it without hesitation. But it was Auntie Duohe she loved the most. Girlie's feelings for this aunt with her unclear status and strange position were something that even she herself could not measure.

'Auntie's gone home on the *kishya*,' Girlie said, looking at her father. Zhang Jian could see in her eyes his own expression of curiosity, suspicion or fear.

'*Kishya* is what we call a train,' Zhang Jian said.

Girlie was already in her first year at primary school. How awful it would be if she took to going around saying *kishya* this and *kishya* that. But Girlie resisted his teaching, and after a while said again: 'If she takes the *kishya* home, Auntie won't know which building our home's in.'

'*Kishya* is train! Can't you speak Chinese?' Zhang Jian's voice suddenly rose over the jokes of the comedy actors, sending the tofu-munching tourists all around them into docile silence, as they listened to Zhang Jian saying: 'Train! What the hell do you mean with all this *kishya*! Train! Repeat it for me three times!'

Girlie looked at him, her eyes becoming rounder, her glance more powerful.

'Speak Chinese properly!' Zhang Jian said. An entire carriage-load of people were included in his scolding. His nasal cavity was swollen with tears, his brain tingled and bulged. He did not want to hear Girlie saying *kishya* every time she opened her mouth; that way there would be no hope that his memories of Duohe would fade.

Girlie was watching him. He could see that her full, tender red lips had hundreds of *kishya*s shut up inside them. Now the look in her eyes was not his. Was it Duohe's? It seemed that he had never paid attention. With a shudder, he suddenly saw it. The look in her eyes from her maternal grandfather, or her maternal great-grandmother, or perhaps a maternal uncle or great-uncle. It was a heroic but potentially murderous expression.

Zhang Jian forced his eyes away. Duohe's shadow could never be cleaned away. His parents had spent seven silver dollars, thinking only to buy a belly that would bear them sons and daughters. Was it that simple? They were really too stupid.

Duohe had wandered off and got lost. This was a ready-made explanation. A half-truth. Or perhaps not quite a half-truth. With Girlie and Xiaohuan, Zhang Jian stuck to his story like grim death: Duohe had wanted to go to that big rock in the river – lots of people went – then she had got herself lost. When Girlie heard these words she cried herself to sleep. A seven-year-old child, she was full of hope: the People's Police would find Auntie and bring her back in a few days. Daddy and Mummy would find Auntie and bring her back. Auntie would go to the People's Police by herself. In a seven-year-old heart, there was hope to be found everywhere in the world. So Girlie got out of bed, brushed her teeth, washed her face, ate breakfast and went to school the same as usual. She did not seem to have any suspicions over 'Auntie getting lost'.

Xiaohuan's shift had ended at midnight. As soon as she came home and saw him spring, panicked, to his feet with a bawling Dahai in his arms, she understood. She came over, gathered up Dahai and said 'Pah!' to him. He asked what she meant by that. She said he had actually gone ahead and done that wicked thing. In the morning, once Girlie had left for school, Xiaohuan told Zhang Jian to phone his section and say he was taking a day's leave.

'Have you any idea how much work a group leader has to do? I can't go asking for leave!'

'If you can't ask for leave then resign as group leader!'

'If I resign who's going to keep this big family?'

'If you can't keep us you know what to do about it. Put us in a sack one by one, go up the mountain, get lost and then dump us.'

'Bollocks!'

'The old society's over, there's no more people trafficking, otherwise you could put the kiddies and the wife in a sack, weigh 'em, sell 'em, and you needn't have to earn money with blood and sweat as a group leader. The kids have all fattened up nicely from drinking milk, you could get enough to keep you in rice and fuel for half a lifetime!'

Xiaohuan raised her round face, as she took from a chest the little flowery bag and sun hat that she used when going out.

'Where the bloody hell do you think you're going?'

'Get your shoes on and come with me.'

'I'm not going to the police station!'

'No, going to the police would mean turning yourself in, right?'

'Then where are you planning on going?'

'Wherever you went to ditch her, that's where you and I are going.'

'She ran off by herself! It's not like she's never run away! You're the one who calls her a little Jap she-wolf that no amount of feeding can tame!'

'A little she-wolf couldn't fight off a big Manchurian tiger like you.'

'Xiaohuan, she got in the way in our family, it was uncomfortable. Let her go.'

'Even if our family isn't comfortable it's still a family. However uncomfortable it is, it's still her home. Can she survive if she leaves here? All over the country they're arresting American and Kuomintang secret agents, and Japanese spies and reactionaries! We often get plain-clothes police in our guest house, they turn up in the middle of the night to check the rooms, they even check the pit in the toilets. Where's she supposed to go?'

'Then who told her to get herself lost?'

Zhang Jian was determined not to relent, or to let his heart soften. This was the time that was going to be the most painful for him, and the first few days would be the hardest. The twins made a fuss at being weaned from their mother's milk, and turned their noses up at porridge, but by the second meal they were ready to toe the line. Why had he wept so loudly when he was sitting on the stone steps by the side of the river? It was over the chunk of his heart that he had lost for Duohe. He had cried so much that this part of his heart was dead from pain, for better or worse: you had to bury it, and after that you had to go on living, you had to look after the people who were still alive, adults and children both. He was determined never to let his mouth or his heart soften and say: let's go and look for her.

In any case, even if they did go looking for her, they would not necessarily find her. Unless they went to the police station and filed a report, and if they did that there would be big trouble. The Zhang family had been plain, ordinary, law-abiding folk for generations, they had never had much to do with the law. Buying and selling human beings, forcing a woman to have children and abandoning her . . . would not all those things bring down death and ruination on the whole family? He did not dare to think any further.

'Zhang Liangjian, I'm telling you, if you don't get her back, then it's murder. You know she won't be able to survive if you dump her outside. It's premeditated murder.' When Xiaohuan was upset she called him by his full name, as if she were reading out his sentence. She had picked up a fair few new words since she had gone out to work, and 'premeditated murder' was one of them.

'Are you going to look for her or not?'

'I'm not going. We won't be able to find her.'

'Won't be able to find her? *I* see.' Xiaohuan was sneering now, and her gold tooth was gleaming with a cold, threatening light. 'You stuffed her in a sack and put her in the river.'

'Is she as obedient as that? Throwing herself into a sack! For God's sake.'

'You coaxed her into it. Otherwise how would she go along with you so nicely onto the train, and let herself get carried off by you so sweetly to the rocks by the river?'

'Zhu Xiaohuan, that's a damn lie! You know how I feel about you . . . When the children get older life in our family will be even worse!' Zhang Jian's half-closed eyes were so weak and melancholy.

'Don't try to push the blame onto me and the children. You laid violent hands on this woman for the sake of this family? How are we supposed to bear that kind of monstrous emotional debt? This isn't the kind of favour we can accept. If that's the way you see things, I'll take the children back home to my mother's house. It might become a habit – next time you'll snatch the kids, hide up in some hole, and watch them get themselves lost! You're quite the pet in the factory right now, you need to be progressive, and those half-Japanese bastards are standing in the way of your mighty progress! Eliminating them isn't murder, it's righteous nationalism!'

Xiaohuan stomped her feet into her shoes and walked out of the door. Zhang Jian followed her out. When the two of them reached the riverside it was ten o'clock, but there was not a tourist anywhere. Xiaohuan made enquiries of a custodian: had he seen a woman of twenty-six or twenty-seven, of middling build? Was there anything special about her? She wore her hair coiled up in a great big bun. Anything else? The whites of her eyes are unusually white, and the pupils unusually black, she bows when she talks, and when she's finished speaking she bows again. Also, when you see her she's not quite like a typical Chinese female comrade. In what way? In every way.

Zhang Jian pushed his way forward, saying that the woman was wearing a dress with a pattern of red, green and yellow dots on a white background.

The custodian said he had no recollection. How many tourists had there been yesterday? They'd even had five or six foreigners.

Zhang Jian and Xiaohuan wound their way up and down the mountain several times. They encountered people trimming the flowers and trees, sweepers, ice-cream peddlers calling out the wares they carried on their backs, but everybody shook their heads at this woman who was different from Chinese female comrades.

The reefs that stretched out into the river were more than half submerged. Ships passed back and forth, hooting. Zhang Jian thought that Duohe was dead, and he was the one who had done the deed. Faced with the choice between his two spouses, this was the only thing he could have done.

They searched for a whole day. They could not carry on searching without a thought for hunger or thirst, nor could they carry on leaving the children in the care of the Neighbourhood Committee. Zhang

Jian and Xiaohuan took the nine o'clock slow train south. He saw Xiaohuan lean back with her eyes closed. He thought that she was catching up on the sleep she had missed at work, but then she suddenly hunched her shoulders, as if she had cramp, and opened her bright, penetrating eyes. As soon as they fell on Zhang Jian, she leaned back again. It seemed that she had realised that the man sitting opposite her was not worthy of her trust: she had been on the verge of saying something, but then stopped.

In the following days, Zhang Jian gradually realised what she had been going to say. She went to reception centres for indigents in the surrounding cities and counties, and checked among the people they had taken in, but she did not find Duohe. With Duohe gone, Xiaohuan had to ask for leave to take care of the two boys and Girlie. Dahai and Erhai were not accustomed to Xiaohuan; Xiaohuan changed their nappies twice a day, whereas Duohe had changed them six times. Also because Xiaohuan did not wash nappies regularly, they were often not hung out to dry for long enough, they had to endure half-damp nappies, and soon they started to suffer from nappy rash. Girlie dropped out of the children's choir, and every day she would run straight home as soon as school was over, her sheet-iron pencil case banging and clattering on her bottom all the way. She had to help wash vegetables and rice, because in the afternoon Xiaohuan took her brothers on visits to the neighbours, to teach them how to make little hedgehogs and goats out of steamed bread with red-bean filling. People would not take Xiaohuan seriously when she said things like 'my sister's run off with someone'.

In just over ten days, the cement floor which had always gleamed greenish blue with cleanliness was covered in a layer of oil and dirt. Xiaohuan never cleaned up properly after scattering fatty meat when making dumplings in the corridor. At mealtimes she was always the first to sit down, and by the time the two others had joined her, she would remember that she had not brought the food through. When she brought in the food, she would forget to put out chopsticks for everyone. And while she worked she was always cursing at the top of her voice: that vegetable stall sold mud with the vegetables; those black-hearted sods in the rice shop, they mixed sand in with the rice. Or else it would be: Zhang Jian, we're out of soy sauce, just nip out and get me some! Girlie, you're so lazy there's maggots growing between your bones, the basin of nappies I told you to soak for me has been there for a full day!

Xiaohuan's job in the guest house had only been temporary in the first place, and after two weeks away from work she was issued with a warning. Xiaohuan could not abandon the two boys, her only choice was to grit her teeth and resign from a job she actually liked, and which had been so hard to find.

One day Zhang Jian drew a basin of water, sat on the side of the bed and washed his feet with soap. Xiaohuan sat down, looking at his two feet, all weighed down with cares, as they stirred water that was greyish white with soap.

'Has Duohe been gone twenty days?' Xiaohuan said.

'Twenty-one,' said Zhang Jian.

Xiaohuan ruffled his hair. She was not willing to mention that washing the feet with soap in this way was something Duohe had compelled him to do. Zhang Jian had never put up any serious resistance to Duohe. Who would? Duohe's compulsion was of the silent kind, she would come tripping over with a basin of hot water, put it next to your feet, then set down a cake of soap. Half squatting, half kneeling, she would take off your socks. When she lowered her head to gauge the water temperature, anyone would surrender. Twenty-one days without her, and they still washed their feet according to her methods. How much longer would be needed for Xiaohuan to get Zhang Jian completely under her own jurisdiction again?

And would she get all of him back under her control?

After a month, Zhang Jian started to find this home unbearable. That day he had been on the night shift. When he woke from sleep he filled a bucket of water and started to scrub the floor, wiggling his bottom just like Duohe. It took several minutes to scrub a patch of floor bright and clean. As he was scrubbing, he heard a female neighbour's voice cry out: 'Aiyo! Isn't that Auntie? What's the matter, Auntie? How did you get like this?' The female neighbour's voice was shrill, as if she had seen a ghost.

The door opened behind Zhang Jian. He looked over his shoulder, and saw her come in: a begrimed, splotched figure. You could see at a glance that the patterned dress had served for a month as quilt, sheets, towel, bandages, nobody would ever believe that it had once been white. The neighbour was behind Duohe, her hands held open but empty, not daring to support this dirty, debilitated creature.

'How come you're back?' Zhang Jian asked. He wanted to crawl up from off the floor, but he could not. He had collapsed right there on the spot from relief and a kind of delayed fear, as if he had been pardoned.

Duohe's hair hung loose about her shoulders like a ghost. Just then, Xiaohuan came out of the kitchen, put down the spatula she was holding, dashed over and flung her arms around Duohe.

'What's happened to you?' She burst into tears, one minute taking Duohe's face in her hands and looking at it, then clasping her to her breast, then holding her at arm's length again. That face was very dark, beneath a surface layer of greyish white. There was a dead expression in her eyes. Xiaohuan had thought that she would never forget the way Duohe had looked when she first came out of the sack, but in fact she had forgotten. It took the Duohe she saw at this moment to remind her how terrible she had looked back then.

The neighbour was sharing in the grief and gladness of this family reunion with a heart full of suspicion, but her mouth was repeating: 'You're back, that's good, you're back, that's good,' over and over again. Nobody in the family paid any attention to the pity and disgust in her eyes as she looked at Duohe. The neighbours' guesses had been confirmed: there was something wrong with her brain.

The door closed on the neighbour. Xiaohuan got Duohe settled on a chair, bawling to Zhang Jian to make some hot water with sugar. Xiaohuan had always been lax about hygiene, but right now she thought that a bit of hygiene was just what Duohe needed. Having packed Zhang Jian off to get hot sugar water, she also called urgently to him to wring out the nappies in the wooden bathtub, she was going to give Duohe a wash.

Duohe leapt from her chair, and pushed open the door of the small room with a clang. The two boys were lying on a pile of cotton wadding, because nobody had got round to changing their urine-soaked quilt and sheets. The atmosphere in the room was thick, a heady mixture of food, excreta and urine. The children had been gnawing the corners off playing cards, and chewing on steamed *mantou* bread, and the bed and floor were covered in crumbs. Duohe lifted up a boy with each hand and sat cross-legged on the bed, so the children were at once positioned safely and securely. She undid the buttons on the bodice of her dishcloth-filthy dress, and the twins immediately bit down on that pair of nipples without opening their eyes. A few seconds later, both of them spat out the nipples. Duohe once more stuffed them back into their mouths. This time they immediately spat them out. Dahai and Erhai had been having a nice sleep, then woken up to suckle on two dry nipples, like two shrunken grape skins whose juice had all been drained, and now they suddenly turned hostile, crying and shrieking, beating with their fists and kicking their feet.

Duohe did not move a muscle, or make a sound, holding on to them calmly but stubbornly. Her flaccid breasts swayed with every struggle. Those breasts looked like they belonged to a fifty-year-old; the flesh had been dried out by suffering, and her ribs were clearly visible in neat descending rows below her collarbones.

Duohe stuffed her nipples into Dahai's and Erhai's mouths again, and once more they spat her out. Her hands pressed against Dahai's mouth, forcing him to suck; it seemed that if he kept on suckling for long enough, her milk would return, sucked back from the deep places of her life. So long as the children drank their milk, their relationship to her would be something that even the gods could not overturn, a law set down by heaven, and her position would be superior to that man and woman in the other room.

She had failed with Dahai. So she moved on to Erhai. One of her hands ruthlessly pressed down on the back of his head, the other hand pushed the nipple upwards towards his mouth. His head was under attack from left and right, and his smothered face was turning purple.

'Why are you doing this to yourself? How could you still have milk?' Xiaohuan said.

How was Duohe supposed to understand logic or be rational? She was being completely unreasonable with her two baby sons.

Finding himself with no means of retreat, Erhai simply staged an assault, biting down on the nipple that persisted in persecuting him. Duohe cried out in pain, 'Ow!' and let her nipple slip from her son's mouth. The two useless nipples that nobody wanted hung there, snubbed and tragic.

Zhang Jian could bear it no more. He picked up Erhai in his arms, cautiously telling Duohe the children had already got used to eating rice porridge and soft noodles, and they were growing pretty well, as she could see. They hadn't lost so much as an ounce of flesh.

Duohe suddenly put Dahai down. In a blink of an eye she was on him, tearing at Zhang Jian's clothes. She might be just the shell of a woman, but when she moved she was like a wildcat. She hung onto Zhang Jian's broad shoulders, one fist battering at random his head, cheeks and eyes. Her feet had grown claws too, and ten long toenails left bloody tracks on Zhang Jian's calves. Faced with this sudden onslaught, and terrified the child he was protecting in his arms would get hit by a stray punch, Zhang Jian was beaten until everything went black in front of his eyes.

Worried that Dahai would be frightened, Xiaohuan held him close and retreated to the door. Before long Duohe had beaten Zhang Jian into the corridor, where he knocked over the pail of water, trod on the scrubbing brush and staggered backwards. The iron spatula was kicked across the floor, clattering as it went.

Duohe was weeping and howling as she beat him, and there were words of Japanese in her cries. Zhang Jian and Xiaohuan thought that these must be dirty words. Duohe was saying: So close, so close! She had come so close to not being able to come back at all. She had come so close to rolling off as she clung to the train that carried watermelons. She had come so close to losing control and soiling her dress when she had diarrhoea. She had come so close to allowing Zhang Jian's plot against her to succeed.

Xiaohuan was watching closely, and when the opportunity came she snatched Erhai out of Zhang Jian's hands. She knew that right now it would be impossible to hold Duohe back. She had become a creature somewhere between human and ghost; she would naturally be possessed of an inhuman strength. Xiaohuan whisked the leftover tea and cold food off the table, to keep the damage from the fight to a minimum. If Xiaohuan had been in her shoes she would not have hit this man, she would have taken the razor he used for shaving to him.

Duohe relaxed her grip on Zhang Jian. He was attempting to justify himself with lame arguments, saying she had run off by herself and got lost. But Duohe couldn't hear what he was saying; the twins had cried like resonant trumpets since their birth, and now they were getting bigger the trumpets had become full size, and they were blowing in chorus, each vying to outdo the other.

Duohe went for the spatula on the floor and slashed at Zhang Jian with it. He ducked, and the spatula hacked into the wall. At this moment he was locked in a life-and-death struggle, not with Duohe, but with the people of Shironami village. Theirs was a unique, hellish rage that could only be produced by a long period of silence and calm. The people of Shironami village had taken over Duohe's body, and the spatula she was brandishing became a samurai sword.

'Let her hit you a few times, she'll be all right once she's seen a bit of blood!' Xiaohuan persuaded Zhang Jian from the side.

But her voice was buried beneath the wailing of the children, and Zhang Jian did not hear a word of it. Even if he had heard he would not have necessarily paid any attention. He just hoped that Duohe would use up her strength lashing out at empty air. He looked for his chance to spring into the big room and close the door, but when it was half shut Duohe managed to block the door with her body. It became a vertical pair of scales, with one person inside and one out, and the weight on both sides equally matched. Zhang Jian thought it was quite terrifying, the way a woman like a willow blown by the wind could hold her own against him in a fight: Duohe's hair was loose and streamed around her, and her heavily tanned face was a greenish-purple colour, beneath the greyish white of starvation and lack of sleep. She was exerting too much strength, her mouth was stretched into two lines, exposing her teeth, unbrushed for over a month. Xiaohuan had never seen such a terrible sight. She yelled at the top of her tobacco-smoked lungs: 'Bloody hell, Zhang Liangjian! Are you made of bran? Will you fall to bits if you get a couple of slaps? Let her hit you a few times, and then it'll be over with.'

All Duohe's toes seemed to be gripping into the concrete floor, holding her crookedly against the door. Then she suddenly gave up; the door banged open wide, and Zhang Jian collapsed in a heap.

She had lost the interest and energy needed to call him to account. The silence of the villagers of Shironami could be a still more terrible thing.

Zhang Jian got to his hands and knees. Duohe's feet were right in front of him. These were the feet of a refugee fleeing from famine; the ten toenails were all black mud, and scales and spots of compacted dirt like those of a snake had formed on the surface, running all the way to her calves, mingled with mosquito bites.

Xiaohuan wrung out a facecloth and offered it to Duohe. Duohe's eyes were fixed straight ahead, and she did not take it. Xiaohuan shook out the facecloth and swiped it across her face, saying over and over again: First have a rest and get your strength back, then you can have a go at him. She rinsed the blackened facecloth and came up to wipe Duohe's face for her again. Duohe did not move an inch; it was as if her head belonged to somebody else. Xiaohuan's mouth never stopped: Hit him? That's letting him off lightly! You should get a penknife and carve him up slowly! Bloody useless lump, isn't he? A big man takes the four of you out and doesn't even realise when he's one short! Look at him, the lord and master, but when has he actually taken charge of anything? There's always someone to take charge for him, in big things and small!

Xiaohuan aimed a kick at Zhang Jian's backside, and told him to go and heat some water right away. By the time Zhang Jian had boiled a big pot of water, carried it into the toilet and fished out all the nappies from the tub, Xiaohuan's smoky voice was still chattering away: And to think they made him a group leader in the factory. In charge of two dozen men. Put him in charge of three kids and one adult and he can't even keep the figures straight!

Xiaohuan pulled Duohe into the toilet. Everything she did was done neatly and prettily – provided it was something she wanted to do. With a few swipes of the scissors she cut and shaped Duohe's hair, then she pressed her down into the tub and scrubbed her from head to foot with a loofah. The dirt on her feet and calves would take time to get off, so Xiaohuan repeatedly splashed handfuls of water onto her, then plastered on a thick layer of soap and left it a while to soak. You could only end up in a state like this after a very close brush with death. But all the time she was chattering away about the children: in Girlie's homework book each exercise gets a hundred per cent. When Dahai and Erhai hear the loudspeakers outside singing 'Socialism is Great' they stop crying. Girlie was chosen by her class to present the volunteer soldiers with flowers when they came to give a talk. Now and again she would raise her voice and ask if the next kettle of water was hot yet.

Altogether they turned three tubs of water black before they produced anything close to the Duohe she had been before. A heavily tanned, leggy Duohe. After cutting away her hair, her head was wrapped in a towel containing lice treatment. Girlie seemed to come back from school with lice every other day, so Duohe had always kept some lice treatment handy.

Outside the door someone was shouting for Zhang Jian.

Before they had time to open it, a hand had pulled the kitchen window up. The Zhang family kitchen, like that of the other residents, looked onto the common walkway which was open to the air. The face outside the window was Xiao Peng's. Xiao Peng had been sent to the local technical school to study Russian, and when Xiao Shi happened to be on the night shift and they were free during the day, the pair of them would go to Zhang Jian's home. If Zhang Jian was in, they would play chess or a card game called Chase the Pig; if Zhang Jian was working the day shift they would amuse themselves bantering with Xiaohuan. When Xiaohuan was out, Duohe would serve them in her silent way with two cups of tea and two pieces of home-made pomelo-skin sweets. At first neither of them could get accustomed to the taste of those sugary, salty, bitter pomelo sweets of Duohe's, but after a while they would ask Zhang Jian or Xiaohuan as they drank their tea: No pomelo sweets today then?

As Xiao Peng and Xiao Shi came in, their eyes immediately fell on a purple bruise on Zhang Jian's face. They asked him which of those Shanghainese bastards he'd given a seeing-to. Xiaohuan said that Zhang Jian had been beaten by his wife; the couple had come to blows on the *kang* and they didn't know their own strength. Just then Xiao Peng and Xiao Shi observed scratch marks on Zhang Jian's arms. They did not believe Xiaohuan, and said the first thing that came into their heads: Sister Xiaohuan, *you* know how to fight anyway, he didn't make a mess of your face. Xiaohuan winked one eye and said with a grin: He didn't have the heart – who'd keep him company on the *kang* otherwise?

Zhang Jian had had enough, and roared in a muffled voice: 'Shameless!'

'They're our brothers, what're you afraid of?' Xiaohuan looked towards Xiao Shi and Xiao Peng. 'Great lads of twenty – in our village they'd be fathers already!' Just like in the past, she turned her head and called out: 'Duohe, have you made the tea?'

Yet Duohe did not appear as in the past, softly and noiselessly, smiling broadly and bowing deeply, carrying in a wooden tray in both hands, laid out with teacups, saucers and toothpicks.

Xiaohuan herself went to the kitchen, and clumsily carried out two cups of tea. Xiao Shi and Xiao Peng had always thought that there was something a little bit odd about this family, but today the atmosphere was getting stranger by the minute.

While they were playing chess in the larger room, Xiao Peng, who was sitting out, saw a thin, dark woman walk past. He looked again, and it was Duohe. She had lost the big bun on her head, which was now wrapped in a patterned towel, and was dressed in blue-and-white-striped trousers and shirt, which flapped around her stick-thin body like flags. He hadn't been to the Zhangs' for a month, what had happened to them . . . ?

'Why, that's never Duohe?' Xiao Shi cried.

Duohe stopped in her tracks, and adjusted the positions of Dahai in her arms and Erhai on her back, hitching them up. She looked at him, her mouth still soundlessly singing something. Xiao Shi thought, let her not be talking to herself. He and Xiao Peng had heard the neighbours say that Zhang Jian's sister-in-law was a bit disturbed.

A few days later Xiao Peng and Xiao Shi went to Zhang Jian's home to while away their Sunday, and they saw that Duohe was almost back to normal. She had cut her hair into a fringe that came to her eyebrows, her thick black hair all tucked behind her ears, and her face was tanned. She seemed to suit this dark face, like a student.

She smiled silently just as before, smiling until her mouth broke open as far as it would go, bustling with little tripping steps about the cement floor, which was polished to a blue sheen. It took a kick from Xiao Shi to tell Xiao Peng that he had been staring at Duohe for too long.

Xiaohuan came in from outside, a nurse's cap covered in dirt and dust on her head. The Neighbourhood Committee was mobilising all the workers' dependants to support socialist construction, to go and break rocks to lay a road to the door of the People's Auditorium. When they came to mobilise Zhang Jian's family, Xiaohuan went out, swearing and muttering, leaving Duohe at home.

'A hammer came smashing down on top of my big toe!' she said cheerfully. 'I should be grateful I was wearing that pair of Zhang Jian's suede boots. I've still got ten toes left!'

As soon as Xiaohuan was back the atmosphere became more cordial. Once again she donned her apron, ordering this and sending off for that, making life more pleasant for everyone. She earned five fen an hour breaking rocks, but for every hour she would smoke a jiao's worth of cigarettes. When she came back home she assumed the aspect of a wage earner, as careless with her money as any wealthy woman. She fried five eggs, all the family had, then minced them with bean noodles and garlic chives for filling, and made two hundred dumplings.

While eating his dumplings Xiao Peng still kept measuring up Duohe, who was in the little room.

Xiao Shi said with a laugh: 'Hey, your eyes are popping out of your head, don't go and swallow them!'

Xiao Peng blushed, got to his feet with a jerk and gave him a kick. Xiao Shi was short in stature, with a round nose and round eyes in a girlish face, and when he had taken his oath on entering the Communist Youth League he had had just such a mischievous look to him. Xiao Peng, on the other hand, was a classic strapping North-easterner. Xiao Shi actually thought that Duohe had changed for the better; without that antiquated bun on her head she was very easy on the eye, with a pleasing quality to her that was different from other women.

'Sister Xiaohuan, why don't you set Xiao Peng up with a girl?'

Xiao Peng stood up again for another assault, but Xiaohuan held him back.

Xiaohuan said: 'Sit down, sit down, I'll fix the pair of you up.'

Zhang Jian had been slowly shelling pumpkin seeds while all this was going on. He would peel three or four, then tip them into his mouth. Then he would take a long draught of spirits until he was pulling a woeful face. On hearing this, his half-closed eyes slid sideways to glare for a moment at Xiaohuan, and he said: 'Our Girlie's right here, listening!'

Xiaohuan pretended not to understand that Xiao Peng and Xiao Shi's noisy quarrel was aimed at Duohe, saying that in the guest house where she used to work there was a cashier, with two big thick plaits: when should she bring her over for her two brothers to check out?

Xiao Peng was none too pleased; he drank in silence, and did not eat his dumplings. Xiao Shi said not to worry, Sister Xiaohuan, both he and Xiao Peng knew how to put their best foot forward with women, neither of them would have any trouble. Zhang Jian, who had been drinking steadily until his face was flushed and stern, said that if the two of them wanted to visit his house they should behave in a decent manner; if they did not they wouldn't be allowed to come again.

When Xiao Peng and Xiao Shi left, it was already eight o'clock in the evening, and there were only three hours before Zhang Jian had to leave for the night shift. He slept for a while, then got up again and steeled himself before his fingers finally pressed on the door of Duohe's room, pushing it gently open.

Duohe was knitting a top out of yarn. She had not lit the lamp, using the light that came in from the street. Her face was mostly in shadow, but the look in her eyes held him back. She had misunderstood him. That wasn't what he was after. He stood in the doorway and said in a quiet voice: 'I've applied for a residence permit for you. Once you have a residence permit you can't get lost wherever you go.'

The chilly pressure of Duohe's eyes on his body became a little warmer and softer. It might be that she did not understand what a residence permit was, but she had spent these years relying not so much on an understanding of language as a kind of almost animal instinct. This instinct led her to believe that a residence permit was something vital, that it was a good thing.

'Once you have a residence permit, you can go out any time you want.'

Her eyes thawed, and they swept back and forth over his face.

'Get some sleep.' He pulled at the door with one hand, about to withdraw.

'Get some sleep,' she replied. An outsider would hear the awkwardness in these words at once. It was not just the diction and pronunciation – she was returning a greeting or salutation, as if 'get some sleep' meant 'goodnight'.

But to Zhang Jian these words were perfectly normal, and he could find no fault with them. He closed the door on her, holding his breath, twisting the metal doorknob to the left a whisker at a time, retracting the brass tongue, then he turned back the doorknob, allowing the tongue to inch its way out, muffling the clunk of the door in his thick, solid palm, completing the set of actions needed to close this door in almost total silence. The children were fast asleep, he did not want to wake them. Or that was how he explained it to himself.

But Xiaohuan had another explanation. When she heard him groping his way to bed, she started to laugh quietly. Laughing at how he'd got himself kicked out of bed by her. He'd done nothing of the kind. If he was up for it that was fine by her, she wasn't jealous anyway. How could she be jealous at a time like this? He was just telling her about the household residence! If he stuck to just doing the business without going on about it he had her unconditional support, otherwise would he have been able to have kids by her back then? Bollocks to unconditional support! And would he want to do that with her at a time like this? What was he, a pig? Couldn't she see the state she was in when she came back home?

Xiaohuan merely sniggered, and ignored his explanations.

Zhang Jian was not remotely sleepy. He sat on the bed, his big knees drawn up almost to his lower jaw. He felt so utterly useless and so completely in the wrong that it was driving him out of his mind. If Xiaohuan came out with just one more off-colour remark he would jump off the bed and leave.

Xiaohuan leaned against the wall, lit a cigarette, and began to smoke, contentedly and with relish. When she had finished her cigarette, she let out a long sigh. Then she began to talk in a rambling way about how women were all very base: once they had had intimate relations with a man, they let their own fate be absorbed into that of the man, whether the woman admitted it or not. Besides which, it was not just a case of intimate relationships, she'd given birth to a brood of his children! She might refuse to admit that she'd given her life to him but it was no use: she was kidding herself!

Zhang Jian sat there, not moving a muscle. From next door drifted the sound of a child's half-roused crying. He did not know if it was Dahai or Erhai. The bigger the twins got, the more alike they looked, a moment's inattention and you'd get them mixed up. Especially when they were naked. Duohe was the only one who could tell them apart at a glance.

Xiaohuan lit a second cigarette and passed it over to Zhang Jian. He did not take it, but groped for his pipe on the windowsill, packed it with tobacco and lit it. How could Xiaohuan have such a clear understanding of where the truth lay? Zhang Jian remained alert. Her talk moved gradually from disconnected comments to Duohe herself. Duohe's a Japanese woman, true enough, but I bet you a whole carton of Donghai cigarettes that she let her life become absorbed into that of her man a long time ago. Whether she's fond of the man or not is a matter for another day, it makes no difference anyway, but suppose she wanted to break her own life away from the man's life, she couldn't do it. If you want to reconcile with Duohe there's only one way to go about it, and that's to get intimate with her. Any woman would put on a superficial show of pushing her man away, no doubt there'd be a couple of punches or a kick or three, but it was all fake. *She* might not know she's faking it; she would be thinking she's really pushing you away, venting her spleen, working off her grievances, but in fact she's already reconciled with you; you wanting her will go a lot further with her than any amount of 'sorry' or 'apologies'.

Zhang Jian listened, taking it all in. Xiaohuan was partly right. She was no fool when it came to the important things. He lay down close to her, his head pressing into her waist. Her hand reached out to his head and tousled his hair. In the last two years she had been prone to attentive, affectionate gestures of this kind, which were also to a certain extent an expression of superiority, treating him as a member of the younger generation, or a little brother. Still, the way she ruffled his hair at that moment made him feel exceptionally comfortable. He fell into a soft, deep sleep, and when he woke his mind felt clean, bright and calm. It seemed that he had not been in such good spirits for a very long time.

At eleven o'clock, Zhang Jian set off in good time for the night shift. He put on his shoes in the hallway, and the noise of his canvas work clothes rubbing together woke Duohe from a shallow doze. The sounds made by a man going out to work at night to earn a living for the whole family make a woman feel extremely safe.

❖

Duohe lay on the bed, listening to this man walking towards the door, off to earn a living, his aluminium lunch box gently clattering. He must have bumped into the door frame while groping for the door in the dark. The sound caused a wave of drowsiness to wash over her.

Over a month earlier, she had climbed up from the stones by the riverside, found the road back to the bamboo grove, made her way in and realised that she had taken a wrong turning. She turned back again, and took another road. She had found the place where Zhang Jian and the children had rested, and saw a shoe that Dahai or Erhai had dropped. She turned round and groped her way out, and she had searched every place where there were crowds. Before long, she had walked herself into familiarity with the several kilometres that had been entirely new to her; she had even searched all the public toilets several times. In this park, whose tourists were gradually thinning out, she suddenly saw why Zhang Jian had brought her all this way to the riverside. In order to abandon her. She realised that these small, very steep stone steps on which she found herself sitting were far removed from everything else. The village of Shironami where she was born and grew up was so far away. Beyond Shironami, still further to the east, was her motherland, Japan. There was also a Shironami village in Japan, where generations of her ancestors were buried. She had been able to find Shironami village again in Girlie, Dahai and Erhai; through their eyes she could still see all the joys and sorrows of those far-off ancestors buried in the Shironami village of her motherland, that silence and calm that was peculiar to the people of Shironami, that mad happiness and violent rage that only they had. Every time she rubbed the boys' hair, she would think of her father and brother come back to life again in the form of her children, borrowing their tiny bodies to warm her, and giving her a means of support. Duohe had sat on that little path of stones facing the Yangtze River, between the distant sky and the distant water, and thought about how the three little Shironami villagers she had given birth to were now separated from her, as if they were at the ends of the earth.

By the time she had followed the stony path up and down again, the park was empty. She wanted to ask for the train station, but she did not know how to say the words 'train station'. She walked to a tea stall that was just packing up, where she dipped her finger in spilled tea and wrote the two characters 火車 on the table. The owner of the tea stall was an old lady of sixty, who smiled at her and shook her head, her face red with embarrassment, meaning that she was illiterate. The old lady called over a passer-by, and asked him to read the two characters written on the tabletop. The passer-by was a young lad pulling a cart, he thought she must be deaf and dumb, and patted his handcart with big gestures and exaggerated expressions, to show that he would take her there in his cart. When she got off the cart, her hand went into the side pocket of her dress, and she twisted the five-yuan note between her fingers, not knowing if she should get it out to give to the young man. Finally she decided not to give him money, but to give him a few extra bows instead. Her deep, ninety-degree bow, knees held tightly together, both hands brushing the knees, seemed to put the young man in a panic, and he hurried away, pulling his cart behind him, turning round from far off, only to unexpectedly find himself on the receiving end of another bow. This time he ran off without even daring to turn his head. She very quickly discovered that he had brought her to the wrong place. Because she had only written 'train', and not the third character for 'station', the young man had put her down at a place where two train tracks met. Before long a goods train came through. The goods train suddenly slowed down at the crossing. Several children who had been sitting beside the reedy ditch jumped on board. The children shouted to her: Come on up! Come on up! She broke into a run, and the children stretched out their hands and pulled her up. Once she was on board she asked: Of Yushan? Yushan going to? The children exchanged glances, unsure what it was she was asking. She felt there was absolutely nothing wrong with her words, but still they did not understand, and her confidence ebbed away. In the howling gale, she reassembled that sentence in her mouth again, and asked in a voice half the volume: Going to Yushan? One of the boys took the lead, and nodded to her. They seemed a bit disappointed to have used such a lot of energy to pull up a woman they could not even communicate with.

Beneath the tarpaulin the wagon was full of watermelons. The children pulled the tarpaulin aside and made themselves at home among the fruit, the tarpaulin becoming a roof and a quilt to cover the seven or eight of them including Duohe. It was only then that Duohe understood why their speed had decreased when they reached that section of track: they had just passed a place where the track had been washed away by the rains, and was now under repair. Duohe lay prone on the melons, her body rolling from left to right, and through gaps in the tarpaulin she could see the worksite brightly lit by lamps. She understood what Zhang Jian had wanted when he'd looked at her that morning: he had wanted her body. He had leaned on the railing of the balcony smoking, she had opened the window behind him, but he still had not turned his head. In the end it had been too much; he had turned to look at her, they were two metres apart, but his lips had already kissed her. He had wanted to enjoy her one last time.

To her surprise, Duohe let the gently rolling melons rock her to sleep.

The cold woke her. She did not know where the tarpaulin that had covered her had gone. She turned her head, the children were nowhere to be seen, and a good number of melons had got down from the wagon with them. The train was plunging into endless black night, charging forward into even deeper darkness; she did not know the time, or the place. But she did know that everything was working in Zhang Jian's favour, letting him have his way, letting him separate her and her children. She was finally parted from her motherland, from Sakito and Shironami and from every departed member of her bloodline.

The train started and stopped in the poisonously hot sun, started and stopped in heavy rain. She steeled herself many times to jump down, then steeled herself as many times to stay on. After meals of watermelon for days in succession, her whole body was seeped through with red and yellow watermelon juice, and watermelon peel was sticking to her matted hair, which had been blown out of its bun by the wind. Her head was full of the roaring of the wind, and the rasping sound of the train rubbing against the darkness. That noise poured into flesh, bone and blood vessels, and flew into the air with two tracks of tears. She lay supine on the icy-cold, rolling watermelons, thrown from left to right by those untrustworthy, irresponsible spheres. Many years before she had been put in a sack, and flung on the back of a galloping horse by bandits, and her despair then had been no less than the despair she felt now. She lay on the melons, facing the sky, thinking of Amon.

Amon was the woman who had lain by the roadside giving birth.

Amon's long hair had come loose, her face was like wax, her lips a ghastly pale as she lay there in the Manchurian September dusk of 1945. She was lying there like a heap of blood-soaked rubbish: a kimono seeped through with blood, two bloody legs, a bloody child with the steam still rising from it. She had walked all through her labour, right up to her delivery, and the baby was at its last gasp, the long umbilical cord twining like a vine attached to an underripe melon. Amon would not let anyone come close, showing her teeth and gasping hoarsely: 'Keep going! Get a move on! Don't come over! Don't kill me! I'll catch up in a bit! Don't kill me – I haven't found my husband and son yet!' gesturing over and over again with her bloodstained hands. It was not until long after they had passed by her that people realised that her bared-tooth grimace had in fact been a smile. She was smiling as she begged them for mercy. Her bloody hands were balled into fists, waving up and down in turn, beating time to her hoarse cries: 'Keep going! Keep going! . . .' in a voice like ripping cloth.

There had been nothing dignified about Amon; she wanted desperately to find her son.

And so an equally undignified Duohe appeared in front of the travellers who were coming and going from all over China, her loose hair matted into a black cape, her sour-smelling dress a mass of green flies.

That station with its clouds of flies was called 'Wuchang'. She did not know how many times they had changed engines before they reached this stop. From the buildings, houses and the more densely concentrated telegraph poles that had started to appear, she could see that this was a big place, bigger than either of the towns she had lived in. The watermelons and leather were being unloaded a wagon at a time. Soon they would reach hers. It suddenly occurred to her that she had used dozens of the melons, for washing her face and hands and as a chamber pot. Together with the watermelons the children had taken, there must be a hundred, at least, that were no longer usable. Those hundred and more melons would be laid to her account. Do you have proof that you have not eaten or ruined those hundred watermelons? Do you have proof that you were not working in collusion with bandits along the track to throw off those melons, and that soon you will divide the spoils with them? Duohe did not understand how Chinese law punished things like this, but she knew that no law in all the world would lightly forgive such things.

She took her chance, and climbed down from the wagon. By the time the people unloading the previous wagon had had a chance to react, all they could see was a blotchy shadow, dirty, with loose, streaming hair, flashing by and disappearing in a cloud of steam from a passenger train that had just pulled in. She clambered between the wheels of the carriages, whose undersides were hung with the black dust of a thousand kilometres, which rubbed off to join the red and yellow melon-juice stains on her white dress with its red, yellow and green spots.

As she walked among the passengers, they forgot all about the heavy luggage on their shoulders and turned their heads to look at her repeatedly.

This was when the melon meals of the last few days hit home. The shock of the surge in her guts left her cold all over, and goose pimples burst out on her hands and neck. She knew how to ask for the toilet in Chinese. But she did not understand the answers people gave her when they finally understood what she was saying. Everybody spoke with completely different tones and accents, kindly repeating something to her over and over again. She thought they must have heard the gurgling sound in her guts. She clutched her stomach, half bowing, not daring to move a muscle. In the end a woman in the crowd grabbed her sticky hand and took her to the toilet.

As she was squatting over the trench, it suddenly crossed her mind that she had no toilet paper.

That woman was surprisingly considerate and understanding; she opened the partition door and passed her a sheet of paper with people's faces printed on it. There was still plaster dust on the back, showing that it had just been ripped from a wall. There was a red cross over the faces, who stared in goggle-eyed astonishment at their final fate. If she had had any alternative at all, she would certainly never have put paper with faces on to such a use.

When she left the toilet, light-headed and leaden-footed, she was approached by two people in gauze face masks. She had spent enough time squatting in the toilet for the woman to guess what was the matter. The woman was talking to the people in the masks in a loud voice, saying something she did not completely understand, and pointing to Duohe. Now they were closer she could distinguish their sex. The man said in Chinese with peculiar tones that Duohe was seriously ill, and that she should go with them. The woman said that the station clinic was not far, just a few steps. Both their eyes were smiling above their big masks. Duohe found that she had already started to go with them.

Groaning men and women were lying on the benches of the clinic. Two more people were lying on white beds with wheels. When Duohe was brought in, the woman in the mask said something to one of the men who was lying on a bench, who pulled in his legs, and the woman in the mask told Duohe to sit in the place where the man's bare feet had just been. Duohe had only just sat down when the man put his feet back again, forcing her to sit on the floor.

The woman in the mask brought a thermometer from the inner

room and put it in Duohe's mouth. This thermometer made Duohe feel safe. In the years since she came to the Zhang family, the only thermometer when she had a fever had been the palm of a hand. The palm of Xiaohuan's or Zhang Jian's hand (and in the past it had been Stationmaster Zhang or Erhai's mother's hand) would press down briefly on her forehead, and that was her temperature taken. This was the first time since she had left her village that her mouth had come into contact with this chilly, fragile stick of glass. She closed her eyes, drinking in the slight tang of the ethyl alcohol: that taste was her memory of Dr Suzuki. Just then the man in the mask walked over, lifted up Duohe's eyelids and looked carefully. His fingers were as light and dextrous as Dr Suzuki's.

According to the thermometer, she did not have a fever, her temperature was more or less normal. The woman in the mask was a nurse, and now she came over, saying she wanted to take some blood. While she was swabbing Duohe's arm with ethyl alcohol, tying on a rubber tourniquet and sticking in the needle, she told Duohe in her slightly distorted Chinese that there was a bad outbreak of schistosomiasis just now, and trains coming in from the east always carried a few who had it badly.

Duohe could not really follow what she was saying, but she could guess that there was some terrifying disease about just now. She asked the nurse what schistosomiasis was.

The nurse looked at her, seeming not to understand.

She thought, was her speech really so hard to follow? Could she have got her words backwards? She plucked up her courage and asked again, this time changing the order of her sentence.

The nurse asked where she was from.

Duohe did not speak.

Having taken her blood, the nurse brought a cardboard folder with a form laid out on it. She said that this was a medical history, and she must fill it out. The headings she had to fill in were: Name, Address, Family Members, Marital Status . . . Duohe picked up the pen, and put it down again. Without knowing why, she started to cry. No matter what she wrote it would not be accurate. The only address Duohe could remember was that of her home in Shironami village. From the moment when the people of Shironami village set their feet on the bloody road of refugees, filling in that section had become an impossibility. After that hand grenade had fallen next to her mother, brother and sister, how was she supposed to fill in 'Family Members'? Since Zhang Jian had abandoned her on the rock by the Yangtze River, since her breasts had swelled into iron balls because there was no one to suckle them, since her secret conversations with Girlie had been cut off, and the space in her arms for Dahai and Erhai was empty, the four characters, identical in Chinese and Japanese, for 'Family Members' were the four characters she least wanted to see.

The female nurse stood next to her, watching her cry. After a while, she squatted down, trying to find Duohe's eyes in the gaps between her hands which she held in front of her face. More time passed, and the male doctor came over and asked whatever was the matter.

The five patients lying on the benches and beds had all ceased their groaning, listening to her cry.

She was weeping so hard she could not catch her breath. Several times she choked up, so that no sound at all came out, and the doctor and the nurse, believing that she had finished crying, opened their mouths to ask 'Where is your home? Do you have any identity papers?' Then she would take another breath, the floodgates would open, and she would continue crying. She wept until all the muscles and bones in her body were dislocated and cramping; in her tear-drowned eyes, the male doctor's two anxiously shuffling feet became a pair of unrecognisable foreign objects.

She cried until the last of her energy was spent, leaning against the leg of the bench. The doctor and the nurse were whispering something in low voices; she did not care, and even if she had cared she would not have understood. The language they spoke together was full of squeaks and glissandos, it was completely different from the Chinese of Zhang Jian and Xiaohuan.

They changed back to the language they had been using with her: Has something happened at home? Did you meet a bad man? Her appearance led them to suspect that she had been physically abused. Had she just recently had a narrow brush with death? She must have had a terrible shock. They understood: anyone who had suffered excessive shock would be unwilling to talk about it for some time.

They gave her an injection. By the time they had pulled out the needle, the two human shapes in front of her eyes were already starting to blur at the corners of her vision. In another blink of an eye, they and the dimly lit space had mingled into a continuous greyish-white blur.

When she came to, woken by her swollen breasts, it was morning. She took a look around her, to find that she was no longer in the clinic, but in a hospital ward. Outside the window rain was falling. There were three more beds in the ward, and she did not understand why she had the room to herself. They had changed the clothes she had been wearing for a pair of shapeless, sexless pyjamas printed with the Red Cross and the name of the hospital. Her patterned dress was balled up on the empty bed opposite. She thought of those five yuan. She did not know just how big a sum of money five yuan was, but right now it was all she had.

Rather to her surprise, the five yuan was still in the cloth bag with the frilled border, which like her dress bore sticky water stains and the sour smell of watermelon. She stuffed both the money and the dress under her pillow.

It seemed that her movement had brought someone over. He was wearing a white uniform with insignia on the collar. She realised who it was: a policeman. She had seen the police; around New Year and at festivals they would come to the residential blocks and stand at the foot of the building telling the dependants and children hanging over the common balcony: 'Increase your vigilance, prevent the enemy from making use of this opportunity to commit sabotage – if you see someone suspicious or a stranger report it immediately.'

This policeman was in his early twenties, and he studied her as he settled his pith helmet on his head. He asked if she was feeling any better. His language was different again from the male doctor and the female nurse, with another kind of intonation to it, so he had to repeat himself three times over before she nodded. Then she gave him a bow.

'For the moment, just concentrate on getting better, eh?' the policeman said.

This time she nodded after the second repetition, and after that she bowed again.

'Don't be so polite,' he frowned, which meant that he was getting rather impatient with her, and at the same time he gestured with his hand. She understood his expression and gesture first: he did not like the way she bowed too much. 'We'll talk again when you've recovered.'

After that the policeman made another sign: lie back down on the bed, he was going. She lay down and looked at the ceiling, which was in urgent need of plastering, wondering whether the policeman was well intentioned or hostile. It seemed that he was neither of these things. It seemed that he was both at the same time. The ceiling was a mass of fine cracks, the plaster flaking away in places. What would the policeman make of her after their conversation?

And what was a policeman doing here? Was he the kind of policeman that exhorted them to 'report suspicious people or strangers immediately'? That male doctor and female nurse must have reported her to the police after they had given her the sedative. She was a suspicious person. No wonder she was in a ward by herself. Suspicious people threaten the safety of normal people.

A very young nurse came in, pushing a small trolley. She pulled over an iron stand from the corner of the room, took a bottle of medicine from the trolley and walked to the foot of the bed. Her big eyes widened for a few seconds, then returned to the medicine bottle. She very earnestly put three or four holes in Duohe's arm, before at last she got the needle in. After two hours, when the drip was finished, Duohe crawled to the foot of the bed, and saw a card hanging there: *Name: ?; Sex: Female; Age: ?; Place of Origin: ?; Cause of Illness: Acute gastroenteritis.*

This was a highly questionable patient. This patient was being kept under observation. Did the policeman outside the door have a gun? The moment this suspicious patient went out of the door, and dashed along the corridor, a bullet would bring her down to the shiny artificial stone floor. This corridor was seven or eight metres long; she had got a rough estimate of its length from the sound of the little nurse's trolley when it was being pushed in. What about the toilet? Just use the chamber pot underneath the bed. She couldn't, she was not used to chamber pots, she had to have a toilet. It's not up to you whether you are accustomed to something or not!

For a suspicious person, even biological needs can seem suspicious. Looking out of the window, she could tell from the height of the white poplar trees that her ward was on the first floor.

She stealthily got down from the bed, her eyes scanning the room in search of her shoes. She had been wearing a pair of sandals, with uppers made from white cloth, to which soles made out of rubber tyres had been added at the shoemaker's stall, so you could walk soundlessly in them. But they were nowhere to be seen. Once a suspicious person was without her shoes, she was easier to keep a watch over.

She shook out her sour-smelling balled-up dress, and rapidly changed out of the uniform pyjamas. Once again she felt the banknote in the little bag.

The hardest bit was getting the glass window open without any noise. It was even harder than jumping to a branch of the white poplar tree and from there sliding down to the ground – Duohe's two slightly inward-facing soles were not ideally suited for walking, but they were perfect for trees. There had been four wooden poles at the gate of the Village Committee of Shironami for the children to climb, and Duohe had often beaten the boys. The hospital building was old, and the wood had warped, making friction between the window and the frame inevitable. Opening the window was bound to be very noisy.

But this window with its cracked paint was the only exit, the only way that led to Girlie, Dahai and Erhai. With her hands, she exerted a gentle pressure on the join between the window and its frame, causing the hinged windowpane to gradually come free. After that she stood on the bedside table, grasped the handle of the window, and pushed up, using the weight of her body to control it, and to muffle the sound. She had pushed the window open. The noise was like a thunderclap to her senses. She turned to stare at the door. The door did not move, and there was silence from outside. Perhaps she had not made any noise after all. The soles of her feet were already on the bricks of the windowsill. With one more step, she was facing the white poplar tree.

Could she span the gap to the tree with one leap? Would the fork of the tree be sturdy enough? There was no time to be too particular, she had to jump, even if she was jumping to her death.

When she slid down from the tree, a woman in a white apron carrying two buckets of water on a pole was watching her. She ran right in front of the woman, causing her to start back violently, splashing out slops from the two big buckets. Backing off in that way must mean she was scared of her, Duohe thought as she ran. It would appear that suspicious people made normal people afraid. Perhaps she was a madwoman in her eyes.

Duohe was running, with no thought for direction, north south east or west had no meaning for her at all. Her only direction was one that could put as much distance as possible between her and the hospital. A line of rickshaws was parked at the side of the road. The rickshaw men poked their faces out through the gaps in their awnings, watching this woman with loose, wild hair and bare feet walking rapidly by, but no one dared to call out to her for custom.

An oil lamp was shining in a dimly lit general-goods shop. She strode in, and the proprietor straightened up from behind the counter, and said some words to her that she did not understand. The language was polite, but the look in his eyes told her that he did not regard her as a normal person. She asked for paper and pen. Paper and pen came. She wrote down the name of that small town by the banks of the Yangtze River. The shopkeeper shook his head. She also wrote down: *I go*. The shopkeeper had never had such a peculiar communication with anyone in all his fifty years. He shook his head again.

Duohe pointed to one of the pastries on the counter. The shopkeeper immediately took out the pastry as requested and put it in a paper bag, and when he raised his head a sodden, ragged five-yuan note was lying on the counter. The shopkeeper counted out many notes of all sizes, and put them one at a time in front of her, saying words she did not understand as he set each one down. But she knew he was counting out numbers. One note was marked with '2', two notes were marked with '1', the remainder was a pile of smaller notes, all marked with different numbers. A quick calculation told her that she had spent five fen on this pastry. That was to say, she was in possession of a considerable sum of money.

She thought that now she had brought him some business the shopkeeper would answer her question. She pointed to the name of that city, and to *I go*. The shopkeeper still shook his head, but at the same time he raised his voice and called something out. Duohe could hear a voice replying from somewhere. A hole opened in the ceiling to reveal a young boy's face, who said strings of words that Duohe did not understand; but also told her: that place is a long, long way away, you have to take the ferry! The hole in the ceiling closed up again.

The shopkeeper repeated: Take the ferry! This time his language was a bit easier to understand; when he said it the second time Duohe nodded vigorously.

Duohe thought, it plainly was not a ferry that had brought her and the watermelons to this place. She wrote again on the paper: *train?* The shopkeeper conferred again with the boy in the ceiling, they both thought that it would be possible by train too.

The shopkeeper hailed a rickshaw for Duohe. After half an hour, the rickshaw pulled up at the doors of the station. Duohe did a quick calculation: that big pastry had cost five fen, so a rickshaw puller probably earned twenty pastries in a day. The price of ten pastries ought to be a respectable payment. Sure enough, the rickshaw puller gave her a smile full of crooked teeth as he took her three jiao.

When she passed her pile of big and small notes over at the small ticket window, a woman's voice said that her money was not enough.

She pressed her face close to the little window. She thought she had misunderstood. By thrusting herself closer she could see the ticket seller's fat body and half of a face. The woman asked, was she buying a ticket or not? If she wasn't, then let the people behind her buy them.

'I buy!' This was her first time to speak Chinese so loudly and forcefully.

'You haven't enough money!' The ticket woman's face appeared, sideways on.

'Why?!' she asked. Her voice was even louder and coarser, and she pronounced it with a strong North-eastern inflection, in perfect imitation of the Zhang family. In fact she was saying, Why can't I go home? Why can't I go back to be with my daughter and my sons? Why are my two breasts swollen enough to burst while my children are crying with hunger?

All this made Duohe's 'Why?' sound full of violence. She *was* going to Ma'anshan, and she *had* to have a train ticket, never you mind why.

'Why?' The sideways-on woman's face at the hole disappeared. With a clatter the whole window opened, as her finger came slashing down. 'You ask all those people behind you why. You're missing more than half the money! Can't you read the price list? Ticket prices are set by the state! You're not Chinese!' The crowd of onlookers was getting bigger. A pair of bare feet, a head of long, messy, dirty hair, a dress soaked in watermelon juice and then in rain caused the distance between the crowd and Duohe to increase too.

A small child asked her something in a loud voice. The people burst out laughing. Those words 'You're not Chinese' had served as a warning for Duohe. She had to leave. As she was turning round, that child seized his opportunity to scurry up, seize a fistful of her hair from behind, and then run away again, screeching happily. And so it went on with her walking, and him grabbing. Finally she won; her utter lack of reaction made the child lose interest in his game.

In the waiting room she bought a map of the national rail network. On it she found the Yangtze River, and Wuchang, which was where she was right now. Then the tip of her index finger stopped at that little town on the south bank of the Yangtze. What roundabout route had she and the watermelons followed to reach this place? In fact that city and Wuchang were connected by the same Yangtze River!

Now she had that map she could go back to Girlie, Dahai and Erhai. Even if she had to walk. Her two sons had no milk to drink, she would get back even if she had to crawl. She spent slightly over one yuan on a pair of shoes in a shop near to the station, the cheapest kind. She needed an umbrella too, but she could not bring herself to spend more than one yuan.

She slept for a while on a bench in the waiting room. When it started to get dark, she set off on foot along the railway tracks, heading eastwards. The rain slackened, but it was very cold. The buildings and telegraph posts went from dense to sparse and then to none at all. She walked into a small station. A short while later, a goods train drew in, and she climbed aboard, to find that the train was loaded with wood. Every time the goods train passed through a station, she kept a careful lookout for the station name, and compared it with the name on the map by the lights of the station.

At midnight she jumped off the train carrying wood. Because this train had turned off at a junction. She waited outside a little station for the next goods train, but no other train pulled in.

The little station had no waiting room, only wooden railings with a shelter tacked on. She went to sleep on a bench under the shelter. The sun had just risen, and the fields and farmhouses were extremely peaceful beneath the green mountains tinged with blue. Even the buzzing of the bluebottles was part of this peace. The flies gradually increased in number, landing on a piece of sweet melon skin on the ground until it was a greenish black. Duohe, lying on her side, watched all those threads of smoke rising from the houses, and the sky and mountains reflected in the water of the rice paddies. If she let her eyes drift out of focus, the scenery became more familiar; since Duohe had left Shironami village, she had always been looking for things similar to Shironami and Sakito. Now the distant village scenes resembled her home in the September sunshine that used to come after the rain. And so Duohe slept deeply, despite the hordes of buzzing flies.

She slept for over ten hours at a stretch, and when she woke she had forgotten what she was doing in the shelter attached to this little station. But she knew that while she had been sleeping, nothing had touched her apart from flies.

It took her until the fourth day to find another goods train to climb aboard, this one carrying fertiliser. But two hours later she was discovered. In the course of the questioning she came to understand that fertiliser was worth money, so people would often sneak aboard to steal it. She came to see how suspicious she was in the eyes of her interrogators. She had already realised that the more she spoke, the greater their doubts, so she let them ask anything they wanted until they lost their tempers. Gradually, she saw that in their eyes she was no longer suspicious, but disabled. Deaf and dumb and mad.

From then on she didn't dare to steal onto trains. She walked back home, stepping over the sleepers, it was much safer that way, and more peaceful. She would rest her feet in every station along the track, and sometimes the rain got heavier, so she would take shelter there. Train stations really were good places, there were always benches for her to sleep on, and cheap food. There would be passengers hurrying by, but just as their vigilance and interest was aroused, they had already passed her. Even though she only ate one meal a day, she started to run out of money. On the last leg of her route she ate raw maize, raw sweet potato, stealing and eating whatever came to hand.

She didn't notice when the dress was torn ragged, or when her shoes fell apart on her feet. Those cheap shoes had been cheap for a reason: they had cut corners with the soles, which were nothing but cardboard inside. She only noticed her chest, which was losing weight every day, and was no longer full like before. She walked like a woman possessed. What was the matter with these weightless breasts? Were they drying out? Would she end up giving dried-up breasts to her famished children? Just like the mothers of Shironami village, whose dried, cracked nipples could no longer block their children's wailing.

When she finally reached the city, Duohe had imagined herself losing her way in the crowd of identical buildings, but the reverse was true, and she headed without hesitation towards one block amid all those uniform red walls and white balconies. She had become a mother dog, drawn in by a mysterious sense of smell towards her sons and daughter.

When she gathered up her two sons, smelling pungently of urine, she discovered that her milk *had* dried up. There was a stabbing pain in her left nipple: Erhai had bitten her! That Chinese pair had come between her flesh and blood. They all said in Shironami village that the Chinese were sneaky and full of guile, and this was indeed the case. A pair of hands came up and lifted Erhai away; they were Zhang Jian's hands. A voice, rather hesitantly, told her that her two sons were already used to eating rice porridge and soft-boiled noodles, and just see how well they're growing. They hadn't lost even an ounce of flesh. The voice was Zhang Jian's. What was he trying to say? Did he mean that having lost mother and milk, lost a heaven-sent guiding link, her sons were living just the same, and growing just as well? Did they have any uncertainty about who their true mother was?

In the blink of an eye, she was lashing out at Zhang Jian. She hung from Zhang Jian's big, broad shoulders, flailing random blows at his head, cheeks and eyes with one fist. Her feet had grown claws that raked with all her might at Zhang Jian's feet.

Zhang Jian was carrying Erhai, and he hurriedly retreated into the big room, for fear that the child would get hit. Duohe blocked the door with her body, and did not let it close fully. She and he were locked in a stalemate for several minutes, each on one side of the door, until Duohe suddenly dodged out of the way, and the door flew open with a clang.

Duohe had given up. She suddenly felt that any attempt to punish him was too base, too small a matter.

Over five hundred villagers of Sakito village were good Japanese, dying together as they had lived, several generations all together under one roof. The blood of several generations had flowed into a mass, you can imagine how thick that must be. It had worked its way through cracks in stone to form a ball, even bigger than the wine cups her father had used to drink sake. The ball of blood was trembling, with a delicacy of texture unique to things caught between solid and liquid, ready to break apart at a touch. The first thread of sunlight stretched out from the fork between the two mountain slopes. That was an extremely tender light. The light shone into the sphere of blood, and both the light and the blood ball quivered for an instant, but that horrifying beauty lasted for just the blink of an eye. After that, the sun came fully up from between the mountains, and it was delicate and tender no more. Several village heads who were straightening out the corpses passed by, one of them trampled on that blood ball, and it was not so fragile after all: it had set. Those feet moved out of the way, and it was smooth and round and bright and clean, just as before; it would seem that it had already acquired a history, just as amber and agate require a long, long history in order to form.

Duohe let the hands that clutched at Zhang Jian fall away, her eyes opened very wide, but the glance was timid and full of fear.

What need had she, Duohe, to come to blows with him in this way? A proper Japanese would not go to all this trouble; she would be able to make him understand that it was too late for everything without making a sound.

Chieko was bent over her year-old son, her long, thick hair fell down to cover them both, a cover that no wind or rain could penetrate. The mother's body, starved thin and frail as paper, folded in on itself. It was rolling into a snail shell, rolling the flesh of her heart up inside itself. Only a love for the child that was intense beyond all reason could produce such a movement. That snail shell twisted itself tighter and tighter, and the wails of the boy became quieter and quieter, sealed up in the shell. Chieko's shoulder blades rose up in a terrifying way, and suddenly fell into repose. At that very moment, the child's crying broke off. The snail shell broke apart to reveal a face that seemed to have been released from a heavy burden. She had chosen the best for her son among all the unendurable ends: let the person who gave him life take back his life, there was something fitting about it. In that instant, all the mothers around her saw the light, and with that they were relieved of their heavy burden. They could at least prevent their children's pain from getting any worse; they could draw a limit to the exhaustion, terror and starvation their children were suffering. Chieko's thumbs and forefingers had locked on the boy's neck, and changed all the unknown suffering yet to come into something already known – in their situation, the torment of not knowing in itself was greater than the terror, exhaustion and hunger. Chieko with her long hair flying loose had not gone mad at all. She started to pursue her daughter, opening her soft embrace and her iron-hard forefingers and thumbs, from a wholehearted wish to let her three-year-old daughter Kumi enter into her eternal care as soon as possible. The women chasing Chieko gave up their pursuit. One by one the young mothers leaned against the trees, with dishevelled hair and dirty faces, clothing faded and worn, thinking about the final mother love that Chieko had taught them. They set off on the road again, wind and moonlight filtered down through the leaves and branches of the tall beeches, with occasional wails from wildcats. And so it was that the silent killing of the infants began . . .

A hand pulled her into the toilet. It was Xiaohuan's hand, as red and healthy as her face, and as dimpled. Duohe did not listen to what Xiaohuan was saying, she just watched that pair of rosy, smiling hands tip a pail of hot water into the wooden bathtub. What came next was all wrong: Xiaohuan started to talk about Girlie in a very everyday manner. 'When you see her later on, make sure and praise her, eh? She's been getting a hundred per cent in all her subjects, the teacher drew a five-pointed star next to the hundred per cent too! The only thing she's no good at is craft class, they told her to do a paper cut-out of a cat, she brought it home, and got me to do it all for her!' As she was speaking she dipped the loofah she was holding into hot soapsuds, and violently scrubbed Duohe's back, causing her to lose her balance and lurch from side to side, scouring the skin and flesh of her back until they hurt as if they had been scalded, but it was an extremely comfortable pain, a very beautiful pain. '. . . D'you know how wicked that Dahai is?' Xiaohuan was scrubbing so energetically that her ideas had lost all coherence: '. . . he's a wicked little lad . . . he can play with his own winkle, just lying there! When I took them out, that naughty boy Erhai saw the neighbours had put out shrimps to dry, and he grabbed them and stuffed them in his mouth. Tell me this, how did he know that those shrimps were for eating? I remember when you were carrying those two, you really craved shrimps, is this kid a miracle or what? He can even remember what his mother likes to eat.'

Duohe interrupted, blurting out that when she was little she too had liked to eat her grandmother's dried shrimps.

This took her very much by surprise. How had she got herself into a conversation with Xiaohuan? Now, just when she was making plans to perish together with her children! At that moment Xiaohuan yanked her from the water, lifted up one side of the bath and poured the dirty water into the toilet, tutting to herself, and saying with a smile: 'Now there's a pity, there's enough in that water to fertilise two mu of fields!'

Duohe looked at the grey layer of filth from her body on the toilet floor, and involuntarily laughed too. It had truly taken her by surprise, how could she be laughing? Wasn't she just that moment considering the best way to make the three children pass away with her without the slightest pain or the least fear, to be good villagers of Shironami . . .?

At this moment Xiaohuan suddenly thought of something, dropped Duohe and rushed out of the toilet, pulling the sheet-metal door behind her with a clang. It rang out with a cheerful sound, like a great gong. Not long afterwards there was another banging of gongs, and Xiaohuan opened the metal door, a little parcel of red cloth in her hands, which contained a red thread tied round a tooth. It was Girlie's first milk tooth. Girlie had wanted to wait until Auntie had come back before she threw it onto the roof to make her teeth grow straight. Duohe ran a tentative finger over that little tooth that had passed back and forth over her nipple so many times, thinking, this won't do, she might now not be capable of doing that beautiful deed that would take them from this world.

That night, when Zhang Jian's two friends Xiao Peng and Xiao Shi had gone, and Zhang Jian had left for the night shift, Girlie sneaked into the little room.

'Auntie?'

'Ai.'

'Have you got a *himitu*? Is there some secret you aren't telling us?'

Duohe did not speak. Girlie crawled onto her bed, so she crossed her legs, and Girlie sat down on them.

'Auntie, did you go to get married?' The seven-year-old face was looking directly into hers.

'Eh?'

'Get married?'

'No.'

Girlie relaxed. Duohe asked her who she had heard this from. Girlie changed the subject.

'Auntie, marry our Teacher Wang. Teacher Wang is my form teacher.'

Duohe burst out laughing. She had not imagined anything like this, that she could still chuckle out loud.

'Teacher Wang is *suburashii ne*, just great!'

Duohe asked in what way.

'Teacher Wang gave me a milk sweet from Shanghai.'

Duohe hugged her, rocking back and forth. The two bodies, one big, one small, rocked like a see-saw in an amusement park.

'And another thing, I like Teacher Wang's fountain pen.'

Duohe held Girlie close. It was twelve o'clock at night. As she had originally envisaged it, she would already be dead, Girlie, Dahai and Erhai along with her. Duohe clasped Girlie to her, thinking that fortune had truly been on her side; if she had died, she could not have heard such amusing words from Girlie. She was actually being a matchmaker for her. A seven-year-old matchmaker. Girlie raised her head, and gave her a sweet, beautiful, gap-toothed smile. Duohe found that her Shironami villager's enthusiasm for death had cooled completely.

A month later, Xiaohuan told Duohe that Girlie's class teacher, Teacher Wang, would be coming home for a visit. As soon as Teacher Wang walked through the door Duohe had to stop herself from laughing: this Teacher Wang who Girlie had wanted her to marry was a woman, with two long plaits. Girlie looked at Teacher Wang as she sat on the side of the bed in the big room, then she looked for a while at Duohe standing in the doorway, her eyes full of the smug satisfaction of one who had brought a romance to a happy conclusion. When Teacher Wang had left, Girlie asked Duohe if she was willing to marry Teacher Wang. Only then did Duohe collapse on the bed, waving her fists, kicking her legs and laughing out loud.

It was another Sunday, and Xiaohuan was the last one out of bed. Once she had bathed, she took the three children out. She said she was going to take them on a boat to pick water chestnuts, but it was obvious to Zhang Jian that she was giving him some space for a few hours of domestic bliss with Duohe.

Through the half-closed kitchen door, he could hear the scratchy, hissing noise of an iron hitting damp clothing, and with the sound, a smell of starch laced with cologne came rushing out. He pushed open the door.

Duohe looked at him through the white steam. It was early October, her broad-sleeved shirt was looped up with two elastic bands, showing most of her upper arms. Those arms had never rounded out again. Perhaps she would never recover her former appearance: round, white, tender and childish.

'I'm going out to buy grain. Do you want me to pick anything up while I'm out?' he asked, drooping his eyelids in his usual way.

She was nonplussed: when had he learned to ask for instructions from a woman? And asking him to 'pick something up' was unheard of. Sometimes Xiaohuan would go to browse the shops, and drag Duohe along. The two of them would go empty-handed and return empty-handed, all they wanted was to fondle all the silks and satins and cottons in the shops, and having compared them in front of the mirror, to discuss which ones they would buy when they had the money. It was all Xiaohuan debating with herself in front of the mirror: Is that red or not? It's called date red, it wouldn't look all that alluring on me, eh? And how many more years will I be able to wear red? Just the next year or two. When I've saved up five yuan I'll come and buy some, would it take a whole five yuan? Four's plenty. She would drag Duohe in front of the mirror, take this length of cloth or that one and hold it up against her: You need a good strong blue, look how delicate the pattern is, would four yuan be enough for a padded jacket or a smock? Let's wait and save the money a bit at a time. To save money was the Zhang family's greatest goal. Once they had saved the money they would bring the grandparents over from Jiamusi. The Zhangs' daughter-in-law was an army doctor, she had remarried the previous year, and she could not keep her former father- and mother-in-law living with her forever. But it would take them a while to save up for two tickets.

Duohe shook her head, and buried herself in her ironing once more. Out of the corner of her eye, she could see Zhang Jian's back, clad in blue overalls, faded from frequent washing, gathering his resolution for a while, then he turned round and walked away. The grain shop was ten minutes' walk from where they lived; Zhang Jian could be there and back in five minutes on his bicycle. He poured the grain into the wooden chest under the kitchen range, and produced a small paper bag from his pocket, his long, thick fingers fumbling with embarrassment.

'This . . . is for you.'

Duohe opened the paper bag. Inside were two sweets wrapped in sparkling, multicoloured cellophane. She watched those long, thick fingers retreat and clench into a fist, as if hating themselves for courting a snub. Just as he withdrew his hand, Duohe was reaching for the iron from the stove, she seemed to have burned him. She immediately set down the iron, and took his hand in both her own.

'It didn't burn me,' he said. In fact he had burned the tip of his finger.

She examined it carefully. She had never looked so closely at this man's hands. There were thick calluses on the palms, and the joints of the fingers were very big, the fingernails strong. A pair of handsome, dignified hands, but a tiny bit foolish too.

Without quite knowing how it happened, Zhang Jian had already taken her in his arms. Xiaohuan was right, this was the best way to make peace. Duohe's grievances had found an outlet at last. She cried silently, as if her whole body was made of tears. Xiaohuan had said, you wanting her will be more of a consolation than anything else. He wanted her several times, one after the other. Xiaohuan had really acted selflessly, taking out all three children by herself, just in order to give them a few hours together. He could not let Xiaohuan down after she had been to all that trouble.

Duohe kept her eyes closed throughout, her short hair plastered to her face with tears and snot. She mumbled that she was going to give him more children, maybe ten or more, like she was reciting a charm, taking an oath, trying to placate him.

At the beginning he did not understand what she was saying. When he finally did understand, his ardour immediately vanished. If she got pregnant again, where would they hide her? And even if they managed to keep her hidden, how could they afford another child? Their present large family was already a huge amount of work, and he could not bring himself to touch any of his subsidies, overtime payments or night meal expenses, already for the night meal he only ate cold *mantou* bread brought from home. He had nothing left to wring from himself as it was.

Duohe really was a piece of fertile ground, seeds scattered there never went to waste. She stood at a distance at the junction that Zhang Jian had to pass on his way home from work, where a mound of gravel was piled. She saw Zhang Jian's bicycle coasting down the slope from the railway, and stood on the pile of gravel, calling out to him. Zhang Jian stopped the bicycle, and she came sliding down with a rattle and a rush, staggering with a mad happiness.

'I . . . Sanhai!' She was so happy that her language had lost all rhyme or reason.

'Sanhai?'

'Sanhai, third boy, in stomach!' Her red nose, half transparent from the cold, had fine wrinkles on it, and that childish smile had returned.

Zhang Jian drew in a breath of cold, dank early-winter air. She walked up to him, inclining her head upwards from time to time, as if he were from an older generation, and she, his junior, was owed a few words of praise from him. Zhang Jian's head was full of numbers, thirty-two yuan a month: even with overtime, night meal allowances, and all the subsidies added in, that would mean forty-four yuan at most. Would they still be able to eat red-cooked aubergine? Soy sauce was as costly as gold. All around him, people kept greeting him: 'Are you done for the day?' He didn't reply to their greetings, ignoring even those glances that rested briefly on him and flew over to Duohe. He suddenly thought of something Xiaohuan had said: whatever your life's like you still have to muddle your way through it.

'Come on!' He patted the back seat of the bicycle.

Duohe sat down, and held onto the sides of his canvas work overalls with both hands. She was an unremarkable-looking woman, but that stomach of hers truly was a prime piece of fertile land, children loved it in there! His father and mother had taken a blind chance, but they had drawn themselves a winner when they picked that sack.

In the evening Xiaohuan leaned against the wall smoking, ruffling his hair with one hand, and told him not to worry. Even if they had to eat bran and vegetables they would bring up the child somehow. However many came they would raise them all. More sons meant more wealth, they'd never heard of anyone complaining of too many children! Duohe would be pregnant in the winter and spring, and when she started to show, they'd rent a house nearby in the countryside, and hide out there for the birth. Country people were easily dealt with, a note or two of money would stop their mouths. Zhang Jian turned over: Do we have two notes? Does money come that easily?

Xiaohuan did not make a sound, but her hand continued to ruffle Zhang Jian's hedgehog-like hair over and over again, as though she had a plan all prepared in advance.

But Duohe miscarried. Just before Spring Festival the three-month-old foetus shook itself loose from her body as she was going up the stairs. She dragged herself up to the fourth floor, leaving a pool on every concrete step. As soon as she made it through the door she heard neighbours discussing it: Has somebody died? How come there's blood everywhere? The gossip came to the Zhang family's door: Oh, how dreadful, something's happened in Zhang Jian's home! Half the walkway was blocked with people beating on the door, pushing at the window and shouting. Duohe lay quietly in the steaming hot pool of blood. Wondering whether she would still be able to have a Sanhai, or a fifth child, or a sixth. Whether she would be able to birth herself a crowd of relatives, to see in their eyes the father, uncle, grandfather and grandmother from whom she was parted forever, and the village scenes, the fields and the flowering cherry trees . . .

The number of people concerned about the family grew and grew. Someone pulled open the kitchen window, the way Xiao Peng and Xiao Shi did; someone else was yelling: Go and borrow a stool! Another person shouted: Is Sister Xiaohuan there?

Xiaohuan had just decided that her stroll with the two boys had gone on long enough, and as she came close to the entrance of the building, she saw a big rump with a patch sewn on squeezing through her kitchen window. She raised her smoke-singed voice to ask whose bum that was, and who was pinching her family's gold bars and silver dollars in broad daylight? They'd just had a brand-new radio go missing from her home!

People were leaning on the railings of the common walkways, all talking at once about bloodstains on the stairs.

Xiaohuan promptly abandoned the pushchair, and dashed up the staircase, a boy under each arm. She knew at once that something had happened to Duohe, and what that might be. By the time she had reached her own front door, she was past caring to ask who that bum belonged to, and who had had such a nerve. She opened the door, and shot out a hand behind her back, closing it tightly. The blood on the floor had already become puddingy. Duohe was in the small room, lying on the bed, an elliptical patch of dark red beneath her. Xiaohuan set Dahai and Erhai down, and hurriedly returned to the small room.

She rubbed away the sweat on Duohe's forehead with the palm of her hand. Neither spoke. What need was there to speak? Xiaohuan grabbed the boys' nappies from the balcony, wadded them up, and shoved them into Duohe's trousers. Duohe looked at her, and she looked back. With that first look, Xiaohuan knew she would be all right, she was just tired, and to speak more would only exhaust her.

Xiaohuan went to the kitchen, and stoked the fire in the stove. The people outside the window were still worrying. Let them worry, she had to brew some hot water with sugar for Duohe as quickly as she could. It was not until Duohe was clutching a big jar of sugar water in both hands that Xiaohuan remembered she had dumped the push-chair at the bottom of the stairs. She ran down, to find the pushchair gone. It had been made by Xiao Peng and Xiao Shi; the body of the carriage was two wooden chairs fastened together, with a horizontal bar that could be opened and closed to hold the boys in. The carriage was made with ball bearings, it was unusually attractive and easy to use.

Xiaohuan scattered coal ash on the bloodstains, and swept every-thing clean from one floor to the next, all the while cursing the neighbourhood at large: Steal our kids' pushchair to sit your own brats in, would you? Well, I hope your kids get great big ugly boils from sitting on it, I hope their bums are covered in poisonous carbuncles, each one with eight heads, flowing pus and dripping blood until they drown in it! So you see that a woman in our family's not well, and think you'll come up and pick on her? I'll splash that woman's blood on your doorstep! I'll give you bad luck for the rest of your life! Let you have sons without a pizzle, daughters with no eyes!

Xiaohuan cursed with blazing eyes and head held high. The neighbours' children came out one by one holding their dinners, standing on the common walkways, forming an attentive audience. Xiaohuan had been a public curser of some note in the Zhu family village. The children were eating, watching and listening, and from time to time they would offer a few suggestions: Auntie Xiaohuan, it's a bum full of big fat maggots, not poisonous carbuncles! Or: Auntie Xiaohuan, why don't you say a stomach of bad offal?

When Zhang Jian heard that Duohe had miscarried he let out a secret sigh of relief. But more than a month later, Duohe had still not stopped bleeding. Zhang Jian and Xiaohuan both started to be afraid, and discussed calling a doctor. Xiaohuan helped Duohe to a privately run women and children's hospital. After the diagnosis Duohe went straight to the operating theatre, the miscarriage had been incomplete. After the operation, Duohe stayed in the hospital.

Every day at dusk, Xiaohuan brought the three children to see her. On the afternoon of the third day, Xiaohuan entered the ward, and found it empty apart from Duohe. She was asleep, her hair sticking out all over the place. Xiaohuan dipped a comb in water and tidied it for her.

Duohe suddenly said that she had saved a little girl, saved her from the hands of her own mother, who had been trying to strangle her. The little girl's name was Kumi, and she had been three years old at the time. So how old was Duohe then? Sixteen. Why did the mother want to kill the little girl? At that time many mothers had killed their own children. Why? Because . . . because killing them themselves was at least better than having someone else kill them. Who would kill them? These were people from a country defeated in war, anyone would kill them. The head of Sakito village had got a sharpshooter to kill all the villagers, several hundred of them.

Xiaohuan did not move. She sat down. It was a fine day, with the scents of early spring drifting in through the window. After all these years living here, it was only now that her yearning for her old home in the North-east faded somewhat. How long would it take Duohe, who had lost her village, her parents, her brothers and sister, before she would be able to let her longing fade? She listened as Duohe described with difficulty how she had watched the suicides of the people of Sakito village, and how the people of Shironami and the other Japanese villages had set off on the road of no return. Duohe's Chinese was far from adequate to describe such a terrifying, devastating story, in some places Xiaohuan had to rely on guesswork to piece the meaning together. It was as well that she could not describe it fully and freely, otherwise Xiaohuan would not have been able to carry on listening.

A nurse came in, and Duohe stopped her tale. Xiaohuan could see that her hands were shaking in a frightening way, like those of an old woman. After the nurse left, Duohe continued to talk. The Japanese that remained had barely seemed human. The children who had not been killed by their mothers starved or froze to death one by one – they had already walked from autumn into winter. The fast horses of the bandits came charging up, they seized the girls, nobody was able to struggle, or call out. There was just one old man – the only old man to have survived – who said: The gun! Pick up the gun and shoot the girls! But the gun had been lost long since . . .

Xiaohuan marvelled at the pain in her heart: the cruelty and ghastliness of this story did not belong in this world. How could the Japanese have such a passion for death? How could a village headman send the people of an entire village to their deaths? Or a mother take charge of her child, sending him to his death?

By the time she had heard Duohe's story to the end, her mind was a blank, and remained so until she was back home, where she found Zhang Jian sitting at the table, pouring himself wine and drinking it alone. Her tears immediately flooded out.

Zhang Jian asked several questions, but could make nothing of the answers. Girlie was scared stiff. At first she said: Mummy, have something to eat, the food's all gone cold. Later she did not dare to make a sound. She had never seen Xiaohuan cry so painfully; she was the kind of person who makes other people cry. Xiaohuan cried for a while, then took up Zhang Jian's wine cup, drained off two cups of pure sorghum liquor, blew her nose and went into the big room to lie down. She did not tell Zhang Jian Duohe's story until he had come to bed.

When he heard of Duohe running with three-year-old Kumi in her arms, pleading with her executioner of a mother, he pounded a tattoo on the bedboard, and cried out: 'Aiya!'

That night Zhang Jian and Xiaohuan did not sleep. The two of them were both propped up there smoking. After smoking for a while, Zhang Jian would recall this or that detail of the story, and ask Xiaohuan again; after Xiaohuan retold the detail, he would say he felt he had lost all hope: it really was that horrible a tragedy. Some details he asked for several times over, and with every confirmation he became even more upset. But he still continued to ask without pause, hoping that he had misheard.

Zhang Jian did not get to sleep until nearly dawn. In the morning he went to work dizzy and with a throbbing head; anyone in his group who made the slightest mistake he dealt with severely, accepting no excuses. Duohe, a girl of just sixteen, had experienced such horrors. The way Duohe had looked when she first came out of the sack appeared like a ghost in front of the crane, in front of his lunch box, in his clothes locker, in the spray of the shower. He hated his parents: they went and spent seven silver dollars on a girl, and now look, her story was driving him close to madness. If they had told him her life story when they first bought her, that would have been much better. He would have resolutely pushed her out. And who would she have gone to then? If he had known her history a bit earlier, he would have changed the attitude with which he treated her. But how would he have changed it?

6

The day before Duohe came home from hospital, Zhang Jian went to Jiamusi. Stationmaster Zhang, who had always been in rude health, had suffered a stroke, and was lying half paralysed in his former daughter-in-law's home. Their daughter-in-law the army doctor was a good daughter, she said that the old couple had better stay with her. When Zhang Jian went back home and said all this to Xiaohuan, she said knowingly: 'Your dad's paralysed, so he can be half a maid, while your mum cooks, washes the clothes and sweeps the floor. In the army when there's one more person in the household they allocate more rations, so she gets both money and labour. See what a fine bargain she's got herself!'

After a month's leave to see his family, Zhang Jian returned to work at the factory, where the Party secretary of his section told him that his application to join the Party had been approved: passed pretty much unanimously, as all agreed that Zhang Jian kept his head down and worked hard, with a plain and simple attitude to life. Zhang Jian was prone by nature to choosing the easy way out, those above and below him could all find good points in him. Sneaky people found that it was very easy to loaf on the job with him, he would not quibble, but just do a bit more himself. Difficult, quarrelsome people thought that he was slow: you could have a bit of fun at his expense without getting a reaction, knock off his hat and he wouldn't lose his temper, cut in front of him on your bike and he would just let you hit him. From his taciturnity leaders could tell at once that he was steady, which showed he was a hard and willing worker. When they gave him the happy news of his admission to the Party, he said: 'How can I be worthy?'

As he went out through the main gate of the factory it was drizzling. He rode his bike as if his pedals had wings. When he ran into acquaintances on his way, he almost changed his usual greeting of 'Come off work?' into 'Joined the Party?' Joining the Party was a good thing, a very good thing indeed. If you were not a Party member you would never get a chance to be head of a work section. Zhang Jian did not crave high office, but he wanted to earn a bit more, so the family could have a slightly better life.

He bought a bottle of spirits for six jiao on the way. A jiao more extravagant than usual. After this he let his feet take him round the corner into the free market. They were packing up, and the only thing he could find to wash down the wine was boiled peanuts in five-spice.

He wrapped the peanuts in a handkerchief, caring nothing for the fact that he would shortly have a five-spiced handkerchief, and got on his bicycle, but just as he was about to set his foot on the pedal, he jumped off again. The free market was held in a very long, arched shed of reed matting, and he was at the far end, when a familiar figure walked through the bright and tender light. He had never been one for fancy talk, but this time he could not help himself. That form was truly very beautiful. He got back on his bike, and wobbled leisurely out of the shed, following that figure. Slowly he got closer, until gradually they were shoulder to shoulder. He turned his head to one side, she gave a start, and then immediately a smile.

Why had being away for over a month made all memories count for nothing? In his memories she did not stand out from the crowd. But then again, when had he ever seen her in a crowd? Her dense, black hair, cut level with her ears, and her thick fringe were enough for him to tell at a glance that she was no local, she did not belong there. The marks her days on the road had left would never disappear from the lines of her body. But the miscarriage and operation more than two months ago had added a layer of smooth plumpness to her clear lines. Her cheeks were glossy like a growing girl. And her white shirt with its pattern of thin blue checks set her off so well: to look at her, she was the cleanest person in the world, just out of the water. She was truly beautiful. Zhang Jian recalled the few books he had read in his life, so he was not left completely without words to express his sighs of emotion and appreciation towards her. Of course, none of these words reached his mouth, he just asked her where she was going and whether she had got caught in the rain just now.

Duohe said she was on her way to Girlie's school. Girlie had left her wellies and umbrella behind. She was going to find them and bring them back for her. And Xiaohuan? Xiaohuan was punishing Girlie, keeping her standing in the corner, she couldn't get away.

It was now half past six in the evening. The days were already getting longer, and as it fell behind the mountains, the setting sun was leaving its last traces of red on the tops of the newly planted poplar trees.

They walked together in silence. He did not say that he was going with her to the school, she knew as a matter of course that he was accompanying her. Their silence made both of their hearts feel tired.

He tilted his head, looking at her eyebrows, her eyes, the bridge and tip of her nose and her lips peeping through the black hair . . . how could it have taken him until his thirties before he gave her a proper, thorough look, and saw what made her different?

She also inclined her head. It was as if the left side of her face was sore from all the looking, an uncomfortable sensation.

Their eyes met, and both were scared stiff. He thought, had he loved any girl before he met Xiaohuan? Had he had those kinds of presumptuous thoughts all men have about the young female leads when watching the opera? What was the matter with him, that someone he had known for eight or nine years could cause his heart to pound in this way? Did that mean he had never known her? She could see that his heart was pounding, for her own heart was leaping too.

They had only just looked at each other, but she was starting to seek out his eyes again. First she looked from his hands to his arms with their rolled-up sleeves, then to his shoulders. When her eyes crept up to his face, he looked back at her. This time they gazed for a little bit longer. Both of them were very greedy for this exchange of glances. Every time he looked at her, he noticed a peculiarity about her eyes: the black part was unusually black, the whites unusually white; the front was very round, almost without corners, but then they narrowed, and the outer corners were two long, curving folds. You could not call this pair of eyes pretty, but they were distinctive and unusual. Another careful look revealed the thickness of her eyelashes; two black circles that formed a frame for her eyes.

He looked and looked, and his heart continued to leap and lurch. But all the same, he was no longer terrified like last time. Last time he had been so panicked that he had actually abandoned her. That truly was the kind of thing a beast would do. He did not want to think about how such a beast should be punished.

The more they looked at each other, the greedier they became. They took twenty minutes to walk what should have taken them five. On the road they met an old lady selling gardenias, and Zhang Jian got out five fen and bought a flower. He told Duohe to hang it from the button of her shirt. He was not at all taken aback by his abnormal behaviour, it was like he was born to be a pampered official's son, frittering away his money on women and romance. He would need to wait until he had the leisure to analyse this behaviour before it could surprise him. Right now his mind was desperately busy, busy receiving every amorous look and gesture, busy with his own affectionate glances or quietly fondling her hand, waist or shoulders to return her affection. There are so many things that can be done between a man and a woman. Far more than just the usual business. On the street with the people coming and going, just quietly fondling the palm of her hand was making his heart soft and prickly. That palm was so supple and tender, and there was an inexpressible sweetness to it, like all stolen things. Compared to when he was lying beside her carrying out their official business, the ecstasy was greater by far.

When the two of them arrived at the school the sky was already darkening. Once the gatekeeper had ascertained their reason for being there he let them in. Zhang Jian remembered that Girlie was in the third class of the first year. The first-year classrooms were in a row of Soviet-style rooms next to the playground. The school was brand new, just like the city, and if you did not understand the definition of 'socialism', all you had to do was take a look at the cream-coloured school buildings, and then this new city's red-and-white blocks of flats and iron-grey blast furnaces.

The big glass window of Class 3's room overlooked the gatehouse;

look hard and you could see the old gatekeeper eating supper at his post. Zhang Jian asked Duohe if she knew Girlie's seat number. She did not. Mostly, pupils were seated in classrooms in order of height, the tall ones sitting at the back and the little ones in front. Girlie was of middling height, so her seat should be in one of the middle rows. They opened and checked all the middle desks, but did not find a thing. Then let's look in all the desks, one at a time.

Just as they were about to leave, they both came to a halt at the door, as if they had left something behind.

In the warm-hued darkness, full of the colours of the setting sun, they looked each other over very clearly: every little detail, each hair, each freckle that they had seen just now, had become an intimate secret between them. They embraced gently. Gradually, they leaned all the weight of their bodies into each other's arms, savouring the delicious taste a little at a time. A good flavour tasted in secret was like a delight piled on top of delight.

Zhang Jian carried Duohe in his arms to the desk closest to the door. Duohe said in a quiet voice: We can't, we can't, the gatekeeper is so close, he'll see us.

Zhang Jian undid her buttons, and fastened his mouth on hers. It was precisely the fact that enemy forces might appear at any moment that made his whole body catch fire. His hand touched her midriff, and his emotions gave another lurch. This time it was in the deep places of his lower abdomen. He was deliberately tantalising himself, so that the swinging, lurching feeling in his groin swung ever higher only to leave him dangling in mid-air, and the more it went on the more ingenious tricks he was forced to come up with in order to keep going. He felt as though his whole body was flying through the air on a swing. What was this thing that was tormenting him? This torment was like heaven.

He felt that she too was completely different from the way she used to be. In the past she had only taken him as a male body, a male body that could mate with a female body, but now it was different, she took him as something unique in the whole world, something unique that belonged to her alone. It was a uniqueness that one could miss out on so easily in the vast sea of people. At this moment everything was different; caresses became caresses unique to them, every touch sent her into fits. Who said that women could not take the lead? Her body was drawing him over from a very long way away, pulling him in. That patch of fertile ground seemed to have buried him and hidden him within.

He closed his eyes and rode the swing as it rose and fell, his heart full of the alluring glances Duohe had cast left and right. She was both amorous and barbaric, and that was what Zhang Jian found the most novel and stimulating of all.

How could the flavour be so fine? A person's heart could fall in love with another heart; could his fleshly body have fallen in love with her body?

When it was over both their bodies were soaked through, yet they could hardly bear for it to end. As she was putting on her clothes she asked what time it was. Who cares about the time? I suppose it must be after eight? Never mind the time.

As they were walking past the sentry post, the old gatekeeper looked them up and down, concluding that they had been up to no good in there. If not stealing things then sneaking an assignation. The latter, by the looks of it.

When they reached the entrance to their building, the two of them exchanged glances. Zhang Jian jerked his chin. Duohe understood, and walked briskly up the stairs. Halfway up, she plucked the gardenia from her button. The crumpled flower had already become a sacrifice to flesh grinding against flesh, but she still hated to throw it away, so she tucked it in the pocket of her shirt. When she went into the apartment she gave Xiaohuan a panic-stricken smile. Xiaohuan was chatting with Xiao Peng and Xiao Shi, and paid her no heed. Xiao Peng looked at Duohe with a resentful expression in his eyes, as if he was reproaching her.

Xiao Shi greeted her very easily, saying: 'Oh, you're back, Auntie.'

Duohe looked at the three sleeping children. On Dahai's and Erhai's necks, a day's worth of prickly-heat powder, mixed with sweat and dust, was stuck in the fatty folds, making rings of greyish-white concrete. Girlie too had gone to bed without washing herself, but she had washed her white shirt, and hung it on the light bulb to dry without wringing it out, so it was dripping a big patch of water onto the straw mat. Duohe sat down in the middle of the sleeping children, and listened anxiously for the slow, heavy clump of Zhang Jian's big shoes in the stairwell. He had made her go home first, while he stayed back to be bitten and stung by flies, idling away enough time. That's to say, he wanted to conceal what had just taken place between them from Xiaohuan. Did she not want to conceal it too, hiding the gardenia in her pocket? It was not like the gardenia could tell on her. But when people treasure their secrets, and are loyal to their secrets, they feel that nothing can be depended upon, that anything could give them away.

Zhang Jian had become her secret lover. They had lived under the same roof for eight or nine years, eaten thousands of meals out of the same pot, and been man and wife to each other on the *kang* over a hundred times. But this new unfamiliarity had washed away all the old scars, and given them a new beginning. Without this unfamiliarity, how could there have been today's encounter in that dark classroom? From now on, they might be at home in the flesh, but their minds could elope every day.

All the while she was listening for the sound of Zhang Jian coming up the stairs. And all the while she could not hear it. His betrayal was more complete than hers. From the room next door came conversation and laughter. Could those three really not see anything strange about this? Duohe had gone out to look for an umbrella and been away for two or three hours, and Zhang Jian had quite simply vanished.

Soon after nine the two guests took their leave. On the communal walkway they bumped into Zhang Jian, carrying his bicycle upstairs on his shoulder. Duohe heard Xiaohuan say, Hey, why did you carry the bike up here? Where are we supposed to put it? Duohe thought, Zhang Jian's mind must have been elsewhere, preoccupied with making up lies, and he had carried the bike upstairs without noticing it.

Duohe thought that for a man like Zhang Jian, telling such a lie was a hundred times better than coming right out and singing a love song. And he was lying to Xiaohuan. When she had first entered the Zhang household Duohe had seen that the two of them were so close they were practically the same person. If Zhang Jian told a lie to Xiaohuan, it was like lying to himself.

They met in the empty classroom, and discovered that there was no need to use the main gate at all; the school's boundary wall was low enough to get over with minimal effort. They met in bushes in the park as well, and in the reed-filled ditches by the railway, and the pine woods on the slopes of the mountain. One day, he put her on his bicycle, and they rode for two hours, until they reached a graveyard, planted thickly with cannas and dahlias. He laid a sheet of newspaper down behind the flower beds for their marriage bed. It was always after he came off the night shift that he took her to these places. If he was on the day or afternoon shift, he would take her up the mountain behind the town. One time, when the two of them were all over each other, a group of children out playing on the mountain appeared from nowhere; he hurriedly flung his clothes over her, as he pulled out all the money from his pockets, and threw it at the children.

They did nothing to give themselves away to Xiaohuan, who never noticed a thing. Duohe had picked up a few new skills after her month as a vagrant, and was now capable of going out to buy coal, grain or vegetables. Xiaohuan was happy for her to do these tasks, which held no enjoyment for her, and gradually it became normal for Duohe to go outside for a walk when she was bored. Xiaohuan knew that Duohe always pretended to be deaf and dumb when away from home, because the way she spoke had caused trouble for her in the past. Anything she could not get across, Duohe would write down: *Coal too damp, make it cheaper*; *Meat too lean, other people buying fat meat – same price! No good!* . . . With a bit of thought and guesswork, anybody could understand her.

Sometimes Zhang Jian would bring things he had prepared as an alibi for Duohe: a bundle of dried yellow flowers for soup, a handful of preserved eggs, or a few *baozi* dumplings, which he got her to take home after their assignations, so that Xiaohuan would think that Duohe had been wandering about all that time for the sake of buying a few *baozi*.

One day Girlie was off school with a reaction to her smallpox vaccination. Xiaohuan tried to get Duohe to come out for a stroll, leaving Girlie in charge of Dahai and Erhai, but Duohe had arranged to meet Zhang Jian that morning, as his night shift ended at eight. By this time, Duohe had become an accomplished liar. She said she wouldn't feel easy in her mind, leaving Girlie in charge of her two brothers when she wasn't feeling well.

Xiaohuan was scarcely out of the door before Duohe left, hard on her heels.

Zhang Jian caught sight of her when she was still a long way off, and the hands that he had been holding clenched at his hips immediately relaxed. Above his head, an enormous Japanese pagoda tree spread over him like an umbrella, from which dangled a bead curtain of insects, cocooned in leaves.

He took her to the factory Workers' Club on his bicycle. By now, love had driven away all his caution. The club was showing a film at nine. Their assignations had taken them to all sorts of places, but they had never yet been in a cinema. It did not bother him that she did not understand any of the Chinese coming from the loudspeakers; he went right ahead and took her to the pictures anyway, just like all the other people in China who were courting or carrying on secret affairs. And like the other courting couples watching the film, he bought two bottles of fizzy drink, a bag of honeyed Chinese dates and a packet of melon seeds.

It was the first screening of the morning. There were not that many people about, mostly university students home for the holidays. There were a few pairs of young lovers too, all with fizzy pop, dates and melon seeds, the only three items available at the club's small shop.

The lights went down, and all the courting couples started to become restless. Zhang Jian's and Duohe's hands sought each other out, twining and twisting back and forth; nothing could satisfy them, but nothing could stop them.

The fizzy drinks and snacks were getting in the way. Zhang Jian put them down on the vacant seat beside him, but they were precariously balanced, and in the end he left them on the floor. They seemed to have discovered a thrill that was different from normal. Actually, they would always find a different satisfaction every time they discovered a new location – the more down at heel and rough and ready it was, the bigger the turn-on, and the more intense the satisfaction. The cinema was a turn-on of an entirely new kind, and Zhang Jian's touch was driving Duohe wild.

The film ended, the audience departed, and Zhang Jian and Duohe left too, giddy, as if walking on air. When they reached the lobby, Zhang Jian saw a door to their right, which seemed to be leading backstage. He shot her a glance, and she ducked through after him. Inside it was very dark, with backdrops from the workers' amateur dramatics group lying around everywhere, some showing trees and mountains, others showing city streets. There were cracks in the curtains from which faint rays of sunlight cut through the darkness; the contrast between light and shadow gave the place a spooky air.

The smell of mildew went straight to their heads. Duohe missed her footing, her hand clutched at a curtain, and the mildewed silk crumbled away in her hand. Clearly, the workers' theatre troupe had not been active here for a very long time.

Zhang Jian arranged the sets, and spread out his overalls. His hands lacked accuracy and efficiency, his movements were both fast and clumsy, the actions of a fool in the grip of an excessive joy. He had not been so tense on his first night with Duohe. It was almost too black. Too much darkness is not a good thing, it takes the eyes a very long time before they can see the shapes of people and things. That first time it had not been so dark, there had been a little bit of light coming in from the back window.

Outside the back window, the snow on the slope was like a mirror for the moon that shone in. That night was his first night with a woman of another race. He saw the shadow of the Japanese girl, very small, yielding to her misfortunes. It was precisely the kind of daintiness and meek submission that men all over the world found unendurable; a complaisance that would melt as you took it into your arms. The muscles in his calves were clenching over and over, any minute now he would get cramp. He hated himself for being so useless: it wasn't like he had no experience of women. He wanted to reach out for the lamp in the dark, but halfway there his hand changed its mind and groped for his pipe. He needed the lamplight to see to untie his belt, which had got caught in a granny knot. But if he lit the lamp wouldn't he scare her to death? And scare himself to death as well. With a burst of effort he snapped the string of his trousers. Sure enough, she was meek and yielding, never making a sound, and as soon as he took her in his arms she dissolved. He knew she was crying, but her tears as she gave herself up to her fate did not trouble him at all. The palm of his hand passed once over her face, he had meant to wipe away the tears, but it suddenly became more than he could bear, his palm could cover her entire face, all he had to do was apply a little pressure and he would smother her. His calf was still rock hard, any minute now the cramp would start. How could he be so useless?

It was no longer dark backstage. They could see one another clearly. At this moment, the hunger that they had provoked in each other during the film was tremendous. The two of them rolled on the work overalls, as if they were both dying to swallow the other whole.

When it was over, he started to talk of what he called their first night. She immediately pressed her palm over his mouth. All her memories of that night were dark.

There were no lamps, there was no light. The dry heat of the room could not circulate in the blackness. His body was a guff, and as he removed his clothes one at a time, the smell became stronger, and hotter. After that he became one dark movement after another. One of the movements was to seize hold of her wrist. His two big hands grasped tightly, as though he was still afraid she would struggle, even this far along. She said: I'm scared. He did not understand. She was afraid of changing from a girl into a woman in this thick darkness, where he would take from her the thing that she would only lose once in a lifetime. She said again: I'm scared. He wrapped his arms securely around her narrow waist . . . she started to cry, the tears ran down to her ears, and he made no attempt to wipe them away.

Now she could not remember clearly whether he had wiped away her tears or not. He said he had, she said he had not. Could they not even remember this? Best not to remember too clearly, they could remember it any way they wanted now. They dragged themselves up, and realised that they were ravenously hungry. It was only then that they recalled the dates, fizzy drinks and melon seeds, none of which they had taken with them. Never mind, let's go to a restaurant for a bite to eat. He had not yet taken her out for a meal. Lovers always feel that wine should be drunk today, with no thought for the morrow, and at this moment Zhang Jian and Duohe, who had never spent much money, would have squandered the fortunes of the entire family without caring a straw for it.

There were several small restaurants opposite the club. They were in no mood to be picky, and sat themselves down in the closest. Zhang Jian ordered two dishes: fried slivers of pork and fried slivers of potato, with a five-ounce bottle of white spirits. Duohe asked for a cup too. When they had downed the wine, the couple's eyes could not leave each other's faces, and their hands could not leave the other's hands. The two of them were oblivious to the reproaches and shock of the other patrons: public displays of affection were unheard of in the workers' area. Their ears were deaf to all remarks. It would appear that going to a little restaurant for an ounce or two of wine had taken on a new meaning, and brought them a new excitement.

From then on, every so often Zhang Jian would take Duohe to the cinema and have a meal in a restaurant. Their rendezvous was now generally backstage at the club. Even if the big screen was up and a film was showing it did not interfere with their pleasures. They arranged the stage sets into something rich and magnificent, a spacious castle covered in ivy, a chaise longue like Westerners used. They were constantly on adventures and treasure hunts behind the stage, they kept unearthing new material, and so their trysts became ever more classical and dramatic. Once as they were lying on their chaise longue they heard thunderous slogans. A meeting had started up onstage without them noticing. On emerging from behind the scenes, they discovered it was a commendation ceremony: the central Party leaders had commended Zhang Jian's factory for producing superior-quality steel, from which a tank had been built.

The great sums of money consumed by their assignations gradually became a hole that Zhang Jian could not possibly fill, try as he might. More overtime, more night shifts, drinking less, giving up smoking were all to no avail. His debts in the factory became heavier and heavier. Before, he had taken two *mantou* every time he went on night shift, now he even dispensed with that. He would only splurge on tasty food and drink when he and Duohe could enjoy them together.

One day he and Duohe were sitting in a snack shop run by a

Shanghainese. Duohe said she had overheard Xiao Shi and Xiao Peng discussing how Zhang Jian owed a lot of money at the factory.

Zhang Jian let go of her hand.

She asked him how much he owed.

He did not speak.

She said from now on there would be no more eating out.

He said he just owed two or three hundred yuan, he could soon pay it back if he just put his nose to the grindstone.

She said they would not be watching any more films either.

He raised his head, his forehead a great pile of wrinkles. He told her not to keep on about it, he was going to take her to Nanjing to stay in a hotel too. This was the first time in their two years of trysts that he got fierce with her.

When the Neighbourhood Committee came to recruit workers' dependants to engage in labour, Xiaohuan said once again with a cheeky grin that her children were too small, her liver, spleen and lymph glands were all enlarged, and that she couldn't possibly go. Duohe walked out of the small room. She was willing to go and crush ore, to earn that wage of five fen an hour.

This was an age that disdained leisure. Ten-year-old Girlie was always dashing in and out; every day she would run a very long way to collect waste iron, wearing two pairs of shoes to rags in a month. Duohe took a truck with a big crowd of dependants to the quarry, where she hit the ore with a hammer, or tipped it out into an empty railway wagon. Duohe worked with a towel round her head and a straw hat over it, the same as all the other dependants. What made her different was that she wore no oversleeves like the rest of them, she had a loop made of elastic crossed over her chest to form two loops at either end which held the sleeves in place on her upper arms, revealing her snowy white forearms. The women of Sakito and Shironami villages all mulched the fields, raked the soil, ground corn and fed the livestock with two arms exposed in colder weather than this. The women were divided into two teams; one pounded ore, the other carried it. The two teams would swap shifts once a day. The hardest part was walking up a single-plank bridge, to tip the processed ore into the wagons, and it was easy to slip. Duohe very quickly became a noticeable figure about the place: she carried the ore on her back in a wooden bucket with a movable bottom operated by a lever, and would walk to the topmost point of the single-plank bridge, where she would turn round so her back was to the wagon, give the lever a tug, and the bottom of the wooden bucket would open up, dropping the ore straight into the goods truck.

The dependants asked Duohe where she had picked up this innovation. Duohe gave a little smile. This was an invention of her Shironami village. The dependants thought that the Zhangs' young sister-in-law was not afraid of hard work, she never gossiped, and her moral character was first-rate. Too bad that she was daft as a brush.

Duohe handed over the money she earned to Zhang Jian. Zhang Jian looked at her in such a way that it felt like he was planting kisses all over her face. They had not had an assignation for a very long time now. When they did occasionally meet it was like a second honeymoon, made all the sweeter by absence. Their favourite place for trysts was still behind the stage at the Workers' Club. Some new sets had been added backstage; the workers' amateur dramatics group had just put on a new play, with a bed and a big wardrobe. At nine o'clock in the morning, the cinema was showing a film, and they bought tickets, but squeezed their way backstage. Silently and stealthily, they built up their nest. In their frequent visits here, they had unearthed two more doorways behind the stage, both leading to open country.

In the damp cold of deep autumn, two warm bodies must clasp

each other close in order to survive. Swept away by the intoxicating feeling of coming together after a long absence, he actually spoke words that he would normally scorn – 'I love you!' He did not just say it once, he kept saying it until Duohe even believed it. Duohe had never heard this phrase, did not know that it had become a cliché, and she was so moved she felt like she was about to die.

He embraced her tightly. This encounter was so perfect, perfect in every way. He took a rest, and slid down by her side, his chin filling up the hollow of her throat.

A beam of light from a torch suddenly stabbed inside.

'Who's that in there?'

There was a rushing sound in Zhang Jian's head. Keeping his back to the source of the torchlight, he somehow found himself clutching Duohe to his chest, enveloping her completely.

'Get out of here!' Zhang Jian's voice was low, deep and malevolent.

'You get out! If you don't come out I'll shout for help!'

Zhang Jian's brain was turning with lightning speed; there had been no interruption to the sounds of the film from onstage, the cinema would not lightly cut short a film to deal with a matter of this kind, as that would throw all the later screenings into confusion. A cinema would not lose good money in this way. Though the audience might not mind stopping the film for a good show of catching fornicators in the act. He could feel that Duohe had shrunk into a small, tight ball, and one gently quivering, ice-cold hand was clutching at his shoulder.

'Turn off the torch, or I'll chop you with a knife!' Zhang Jian's voice was full of certainty. While he was bluffing, he found himself wondering how he could have come up with 'chop you'. Had his mind turned to a row of swords and spears among the props on realising that he was cornered?

The voice wavered slightly: 'I'll call for help!'

Still covering Duohe with his body, Zhang Jian rolled them both from the bed to the floor, saying, 'You just try it then – call!'

'You come out!'

'Turn off the torch!'

They lay face down on the ground, making a much smaller target for the torchlight. Zhang Jian shifted towards the stage spears in their rack. Then he stretched out his long leg, enough to fetch over a lump of iron covered in cloth. When the light of the torch caught up with him it was too late, Zhang Jian already had the lump of iron grasped in his hands.

'Turn off the torch!' he said.

'If I don't turn it off what are you going to do about it?'

'Then don't – just try it.' As he spoke, the light glanced off the lump of iron in his hands.

The torch immediately went out. The speaker obviously thought that there was no need for him to risk his life to test what his next insane move might be, for a dog can jump a high wall when cornered, and even a rabbit can bite. There were quite a few members of the steel factory's militia who were handy with a gun or a knife, and they often held shooting or bayonet-fighting contests with the militia from other factories.

'Come out! Or I really will shout for help!'

Zhang Jian shoved Duohe's clothes at her, and gave her a push. Her hand still clutched, uncomprehending, at his shoulder. Speaking softly in her ear, he told her to leave quietly by the back door on the north-west side, he would catch up with her very soon.

She took it for the truth. The film onstage was playing lyrical, beautiful music, and Duohe fled on the wave of that rising melody. Time passed, and Zhang Jian knew that it was no longer just one person waiting for him. But he had not expected to find the entire staff of the club, all except the projectionist who was showing the film. On the screen, the actors were still living out their happy lives.

A button on Zhang Jian's work clothes was fastened askew, his peak cap was pulled down very low, and long shoelaces were trailing from his suede boots. In the eyes of the indignant people in front of him, he was a classic villain. He knew it too. And yet to his surprise he did not feel remotely like a villain, rather, he felt like a hero in a tragedy. He had sacrificed himself to safeguard his beloved, and if he was not tragic then who was?

'Where's the other one?' the man holding the torch said. He was not afraid of Zhang Jian now. Even if he did decide to chop somebody, there were seven or eight people to share the danger.

Zhang Jian thought Duohe was quick on the uptake. She would already have run into the thicket of elms that were just shedding their leaves. She would be waiting for him now, neatly dressed. A woman with a past like Duohe's would not have survived until today if she was not quick.

'The other what?' It was like Zhang Jian could barely be bothered with him at all. Those camel's eyes were outstanding for showing derision. Sure enough, the workers were outraged by his looks of proud disdain. If this big North-easterner did not surrender by himself, taking him down would probably be hard work.

'Stop playing stupid! We're asking about that fancy woman of yours!' said one of the northerners in that little cluster of people, who the club workers called Director Xie.

'Who's my fancy woman?'

'I saw it all! Don't think you can get out of it!' The one holding the torch was a southerner of forty or fifty.

'Why ask if you saw the whole thing? You call her to come out!' Zhang Jian said.

'Then you admit she's your fancy woman?'

Zhang Jian ignored them. He wished he hadn't got into a debate with them. The reason why he had been tight-mouthed from a very young age was because early on he had observed that people were not worth paying attention to – if you went along with their train of thought, and started to bandy about with them, you would very soon find yourself on the receiving end of their crude, unpleasant words. His feelings for Duohe had become carrying on with a fancy woman – Duohe, a fancy woman? They had dirtied her just by mentioning her! Zhang Jian could bear hardship, exhaustion or pain, but he could not bear to be dirty.

Some of the people went off to search in the maze of scenery, while the others kept watch over Zhang Jian. A member of staff reported back: the back door was not locked, the fancy woman might have run off that way. That fellow must be covering her escape. He's a depraved, cunning old fox. If they had not received notification that the Great Leader was coming to the steel factory on a tour of inspection, who would go checking those dark corners? And there they were thinking that special agents from the US or Chiang Kai-shek had buried a bomb here or something, when all the time it was a man and a woman in a tryst!

Zhang Jian's section had been sweeping and tidying every day too, putting up red paper flowers and great pompoms of red silk ribbon to welcome the inspection by the Great Leader Chairman Mao. But in the past people had also said that the provincial head or the mayor was coming, and no such person had ever appeared beside the blast furnaces. So this time the workers hadn't really believed it. Hearing people in the club talking like this now, Zhang Jian thought, means the Great Leader really is coming. The club was under the direct control of the factory headquarters, so their news was up to date and reliable.

The searchers returned in dribs and drabs. They had set off in pursuit from that back door in the north-west corner, but they had failed to catch up with the loose woman. Director Xie said eloquently that it would seem she was fleet of foot as well. It made no difference – now they'd caught this one, she wouldn't fly very far.

Zhang Jian was taken to the factory headquarters. In the corridor he bumped into Xiao Peng. Xiao Peng's eyes flew open in astonishment at the sight of a group of people escorting Zhang Jian, some clearing the way, some acting as armed guards. He asked one of the club employees who was part of the armed escort what had happened. He was carrying on with a loose woman! Director Xie promptly asked Xiao Peng whether he was on familiar terms with this degenerate element of the factory. Xiao Peng kept silent, but shot a glance at Zhang Jian's looming back, and saw his shoelaces swinging back and forth, dragged into two muddy ropes. Xiao Peng's Russian studies had been cancelled halfway through the course, and he had been sent to the factory headquarters to do any work that came to hand while waiting to be reassigned. He followed the group into the security section, the door closed, and he joined the crowd of secretaries, typists and cleaners which was blocking the door, their bodies all half tilted to hear the interrogation that was going on inside.

The interrogation was sometimes so quiet that it was almost soundless, then sometimes it burst into a deafening roar, like a loudspeaker with a faulty connection. No matter whether the questions were bellowed or quietly spoken, Zhang Jian did not utter a word from start to finish.

Finally they heard Zhang Jian open his mouth: 'What's a problematic lifestyle?'

The interrogator explained to him: he had a spouse, but was carrying on with another woman as well.

'I don't have any problems with my lifestyle,' Zhang Jian said. 'I only do that with my spouse.'

'You go running off to the club to enjoy yourself with your spouse?'

The people outside all laughed, the female typists blushed from ear to ear and wrinkled their noses: this filthy language really wasn't fit for their ears.

'Well, what made you and your spouse take a fancy to the backstage? Go on, enlighten me.' The interrogator thought that the accused was taking the most appalling liberties.

Zhang Jian again brought his skills with silence to bear. The questioner threatened him: offending against morals and decency and blackening the face of the working class before the Great Leader Chairman Mao's inspection will incur a heavy punishment. A Party member would be expelled from the Party, a non-Party member's wages would be docked. If he did not come clean and admit to his fault in a decent manner, rather than making up lies to bamboozle the security section, that was adding another degree to the offence. Not talking? Fine. It's good that you like silence. We'll say nothing for three minutes.

'I'm asking you again, who was that woman with whom the problematic behaviour was taking place?'

'My spouse.'

This time it was the turn of the security head to be silenced.

'Your spouse? Then what did she run off for?' Director Xie from the club asked. His logic seemed to be a bit clearer than the head of security.

'Run off?' the security head said. 'If it was his spouse they wouldn't go to that kind of dark corner in the first place. When they could do it at home under the quilt, so clean, so warm?'

The listeners at the door burst into a roar of laughter. A thought suddenly came to Xiao Peng. He backed out of the crowd, jumped on his bicycle and pedalled at lightning speed towards the residential area.

No wonder Zhang Jian and his sister-in-law were always coming home one just a bit later than the other. Zhang Jian, who seemed so quiet and unassuming, was quite the ladies' man, gobbling up all the tender grass on his own home turf. There could be no other explanation for any of this.

When he reached Zhang Jian's home, the neighbours told him that Xiaohuan had gone to the canteen run by the Neighbourhood Committee. Xiao Peng followed their directions, and found the canteen, two big rooms above the grain shop. Next to the window of one room several big stoves had been built up out of bricks. The other big room of the Neighbourhood Committee had been converted into a crèche, where a few dozen children were rolling about on reed mats and singing, '*If you want to wear a flower, wear a big red flower.*'

Xiaohuan, having joined the group on the spur of the moment, could not then immediately take herself off again. All the female cadres in the Neighbourhood Committee kept giving her pep talks to encourage her to stay on and be their head chef. They gave her lectures, explaining that 'labour is glorious', and made her watch the dependants practising a little song-and-dance routine: '*She rubs her face with scented powder, she combs her hair until it shines, but just because she takes no part in production, everybody calls her dirty.*' After two weeks' work Xiaohuan started to go to the hospital to get sick notes for a day here, half a day there.

As soon as Xiaohuan saw Xiao Peng, she ran over, bright-eyed and beaming, waving two fists coated in white wheat flour.

'Miss your sister Xiaohuan, did you?'

'Where are the children?' Xiao Peng asked.

'In the crèche.' Xiaohuan tossed her sloping shoulders in the direction of the big room next door. With a twist of her body she ran back to the stoves, uncovered a steamer, and took out a roll from inside. 'Fresh out of the pot!'

'Sister, listen to me.' Xiao Peng was retreating towards the door. 'Zhang Jian's in trouble!' he said in a low voice.

'What's happened?' Xiaohuan immediately untied her apron, and hung it on the railings in the corridor. 'Is it serious?'

Xiao Peng motioned her to go with him straight away. On the staircase, Xiaohuan missed a step, and almost fell on top of him. In one breath she asked several times over: 'Where's he injured?' When they reached the foot of the stairs, Xiao Peng looked at her.

'It's not that kind of trouble. If only it was. Injuries can be mended,' Xiao Peng said.

Xiaohuan's mynah bird's mouth was silenced now. She understood it all.

Xiao Peng talked her through what he had heard outside the door of the security office. Xiaohuan looked at his earnest, portentous expression, and let out a titter of laughter. Xiao Peng thought that this woman was crazy past the point of common sense; didn't she know that after this her husband would never be able to hold his head up again?

'And there was I thinking he'd run out with me! I waited here and waited there and never saw him anywhere, I thought he must have taken a wrong turning. Come on, get a move on, take your sister to your factory headquarters!'

Xiao Peng mounted his bicycle, and Xiaohuan sat on the back seat. They had been riding for more than five minutes before Xiao Peng finally said: 'Sister Xiaohuan, do you mean to say that the person who was with Zhang Jian in the club . . . was actually you?'

'If it wasn't me, would I be prepared to bring down this crock of shit on my head for his sake? Is your sister Xiaohuan such a push-over?'

'But then . . . the pair of you . . .'

Xiaohuan started laughing again. This laugh was a little bit dirty, a little bit wicked.

'Xiao Peng, little brother, wait until you have a woman of your own, then you'll know, when a monkey's desperate he can't control himself at all!'

Xiao Peng did not speak. He did not believe what Xiaohuan was telling him, but he did trust his understanding of Xiaohuan's character: it was impossible that she would make a concession of this kind for another woman, not even her own sister.

Xiaohuan bounded up the steps of the factory headquarters, twitching at her clothes and tidying her hair as she walked along the corridor in the direction of the security office. Xiaohuan's hair, yellowed from too much perming, was held back behind her ears with a kerchief, and even well into her thirties she was still a good-looking woman. When they reached the door of the security office, she turned the handle and went straight in without knocking.

The door opened wide, Zhang Jian was sitting opposite the desk with his back to the door. Like a lead actress coming onstage, Xiaohuan sauntered in.

'They say you've put out a reward for me. So here I am!' Her slightly red, slightly swollen eyes were smiling into curved lines, but with a certain ferocity shining through. 'What article in the law of the land forbids a husband and wife from carrying out their marital relations? Sleeping with your wife at home is called marital relations, but go outside and sleep with your wife and it's called problematic behaviour? Is there anyone here who hasn't got himself a wife yet?' She cocked her head and swept her eyes over the faces in the room. 'If there is then please leave, what I'm about to confess isn't fit for you to hear.'

The secretary in charge of the security office looked at this woman, slender and graceful, but also quite capable of taking off her shoe and laying waste with it.

'You are Zhang Jian's spouse?'

'Legally married, a proper matchmaker and everything.'

At this moment Xiaohuan was standing by Zhang Jian's side, her hips tilted, and she gave his shoulder a nudge, to show that she wanted him to shift over and make a bit of room. No sooner had Zhang Jian moved over to the right than she sat down with a bump, half of her bottom landing on the corner of the chair, the other half pressing against Zhang Jian's leg. She chattered away aimlessly with the head of security and the club workers, about how she had married into the Zhang family, and how she and Zhang Jian's mother hadn't got along, which was why she had made Zhang Jian move here from the North-east. Zhang Jian noticed that while she was gossiping away she was looking all around her, everywhere but at him. In these people's eyes, Xiaohuan was fierce, lively and full of charm, but he knew that her heart had taken a blow; she hated him.

'You're man and wife, you've got three children already, don't you care about losing face, running off to do it outside?'

'We can't do it anywhere except outside.' Xiaohuan's shamelessness was making all the men in the room blush. *She* was not afraid, and no matter how meaty her talk became, they would still be hanging on her every word. 'You go to our home and take a look – if your bum's a bit on the large side don't even think about turning round! And we've got three children, our lass is almost as tall as me now. The least little noise and our Girlie asks: Ooh, Mummy, has a rat got into the house? Well, hey, we're all married here, aren't we?'

She was gesticulating wildly as she spoke, so that not even the official in charge of security dared to interrupt. She was a female firebrand, the kind of country woman who was more than capable of pulling down a man's trousers in the course of a good-natured quarrel, and when she was not happy, she would have the nerve to pull down her own trousers and stand in your doorway, cursing and blocking the way.

'All the families have the same little bit of room, and they've all got nests of children. If they were all like you and took it out of doors, how could anyone bear to look at this steel factory? Our Great Leader Chairman Mao is coming to inspect, would you have him inspect *that*?'

'Yes, if the Great Leader were to come looking, he'd know that the houses of our working class aren't big enough to live in, so we all have to seek out corners to breed up the next generation.' Xiaohuan was having a fine old time, talking away, slapping her thigh and Zhang Jian's thigh and laughing loudly. While she was laughing she ordered one of the workers from the club: 'Pour me some water!'

The head of the security section temporarily confined Zhang Jian and Xiaohuan in his office, and went personally by motorbike to Zhang Jian's work section. The Party secretary there had sponsored Zhang Jian's application to the Party, and he stuck by his original statement: Zhang Jian was not afraid of hardship or hard work; when at his post he never left the crane except to relieve himself. The section head also rode his motorbike to the building where Zhang Jian lived, and asked the neighbours about the relationship between the Zhangs, and their general conduct. The neighbours all said that the two of them were practically joined at the hip; when Zhang Jian went out fishing, Xiaohuan could not bear for him to go, and chased him from the fourth floor to the ground. Xiaohuan enjoyed a good row: when Zhang Jian insisted on going she would pour a pitcher of water down on his head over the walkway railings.

The security head thought, Looks like they're a real treasure, one in ten thousand. He assigned another security officer to observe and monitor their behaviour and conversation. The result was that there was no conversation between the two of them, not so much as a sentence, even their positions did not alter: the man sitting on the cane chair under the window, the woman on the wooden chair by the wall, big eyes staring at small eyes.

They had no idea that without moving a muscle or making a sound, separated by a distance of a few metres, this man and woman had already said it all. Just as Duohe had discovered many years earlier, the pair of them were so close they were like a single person. Sitting face-to-face like this, Zhang Jian felt that he was sitting with his other half, the other half of him that had not been possessed by Duohe, and never could be possessed by Duohe.

Xiaohuan's nose had gone red. He saw her raise her head and look at the ceiling. She was not willing for her tears to flow. She did not mind shedding tears in front of Zhang Jian, but she was unwilling to weep in front of outsiders. Outsiders were concealed in the crack of this door, and the cracks of the walls, here, there and everywhere; it was just that they could not see them. Xiaohuan delighted in crying in front of Zhang Jian; women get into the habit of shedding tears in front of people whom those tears might move. Many years before, this man's one sentence – 'Save the mother' – had led her into this habit.

On that day, Zhang Jian had held aside the temporary cloth curtain hung up over the door, and walked in the room. She already knew her place in his heart, knew she could use her power over him. From then on she would exert her power over him from time to time, and bully him in small ways. The door curtain was a bed sheet; Xiaohuan's mother had woven the cloth herself, and then had it printed with white plum blossom on a blue background, as part of her dowry. The door curtain shut out a dusk that was the same as usual: in the dusk there were the voices of mothers calling children home for supper, the clucking and crowing of chickens in front of their coop, and the sounds of Erhai's mother blowing her nose and of Erhai's father's dry cough. The twenty-year-old Zhang Erhai stood inside the door curtain, his shirt bleached yellow with washing. His stomach, chest and sleeves still bore the remains of Xiaohuan's blood, and that of his son, dead before he saw the light of day. How had he died? Please don't tell her. The blood had already dried, the traces of that awful deed were now a dark reddish brown. The young father stood by the sheet with its white flowers on a blue background for a good while, looking at everything except his wife, who they had to put their son to death to save. And he had not just killed his son, he had also defied his parents, to bear the evil name of unworthy, unfilial son, breaker of the family line. Xiaohuan's tears flowed swiftly and violently, like a thaw in the mountain wilds at the start of spring. From then on they only had each other. The child was gone, and they had offended the people involved and people uninvolved too. She had so many tears, even she had not realised that to let herself go and cry could be such a relief. The Zhang Erhai in those tear-filled eyes was bigger and taller than he was in reality, as if soaking in her tears had made him grow. Two kerosene lamps were reflected in her tears, and he walked over to her through the mass of shadows from the flames of the lamps. He stretched out an enormous paw; she did not know whether he was wiping away her tears or her sweat. She took his hand in both of her own, and placed it on her mouth; the palm of the hand was very salty, with sweat running from every line. She did not know how long had passed, she had strength to howl with grief to her heart's content, wailing for that son in a piercing voice. She howled and howled, until her mind moved on to other thoughts. 'You stupid bastard! What did you save me for? With our child gone, will your parents let me live on? Those gossip-mongers, those finger-pointers, can they let me live?' Terrified by her weeping, the twenty-year-old Zhang Erhai had bundled her up in his arms in a clumsy, awkward hug. After a while she realised that he was howling too, but entirely without sound.

At this moment the man in front of her was no longer Zhang Erhai. There was a lump in Xiaohuan's nose and throat, and her head swam. That Zhang Erhai was no more, he had become Zhang Jian, and this alone was sufficient for her to let go and wail in mourning.

Zhang Jian knew he had done wrong. He had wounded her.

He had done nothing wrong to anyone else, and he would rather die than be forced to admit it. But to Xiaohuan, he had done wrong.

She had never, ever thought that he would be so heedless of dignity, make such a spectacle of himself, behave as disgustingly as it was possible to be. Had she not cherished him sufficiently, not loved him enough? They did that kind of thing behind her back, and concealed the matter from her, treating her as an outsider. Just how long had they been concealing it? Quite some time. More than two years.

As if she would have made difficulties for them! Was it not she, Zhu Xiaohuan, who had urged him to go and make peace with her? Was it not she, Zhu Xiaohuan, who had reasoned with him: women are always half reluctant and half accepting? Was she the kind of person to have the wool pulled over her eyes? Had it not been she who time after time had made space for them?

But this was different. Making a space for them was not the same thing.

Why was it not the same? What kind of thing was it?

It was not the same thing in the heart. It was hard to say for sure about things within the heart.

Did that mean that his heart had changed, that he had ceased to be faithful?

No! It was not that simple! What is this thing called a heart anyway? Sometimes we don't know ourselves.

His heart had changed indeed.

An injustice as great as the heavens!

When had the heart changed?

Zhang Jian was looking at Xiaohuan. The look in his eyes was both fearful and confused: has the heart changed?

If it had not changed how could he have been the way he was with Duohe, unable to look at her, or touch her, because as soon as he touched her his whole body caught fire? Had the change begun with that chance meeting in the free market over two years ago? No. It had started earlier. After Xiaohuan had told him Duohe's life story; the very next day, he saw Duohe tacking quilts for the children in the little room. A meaningless tenderness surged up in his heart.

At that time she was kneeling on the bed with her back to him, the button that held closed the round-necked shirt with no collar she wore around the house was open, exposing the hair beneath her hairline, very soft, like the downy hair of an infant. Just that section of neck and that little bit of hair caused him to be seized by an unreasoning impulse, to come over and gently hold her in his arms. No matter how young they were, Chinese girls never seemed to have that hairline, or that baby hair. Perhaps because they rarely knelt in that peculiar posture, so that section of neck had no exposure. He found it so strange, he detested anything that was Japanese; in the past, whenever Duohe had acted the slightest bit Japanese it would always increase the distance between them. And yet, since he had learned about her life history, he had changed, and Duohe's downy hairline and the way she knelt filled him with tenderness! During these two years, he and she had shared joy and love, had sent speechless messages of love with their eyes, then a few moments would pass, and it would occur to him that it was this Japanese woman he loved, and it was this moment of awakening that had him beside himself with emotion, close to tears: she was a woman from a foreign land, who he had got by such a fluke! It was not until he had lost that enmity that he had truly made her his. He had passed through so much defensiveness, loathing and coldness before he could start to fall in love with her.

Her story had caused his heart to change, and made him disloyal to Xiaohuan.

So how did he plan to deal with his wife? Would he make her continue as an outsider, living in that tiny flat? She, Zhu Xiaohuan, a leftover bitch? Dog she might be, but Xiaohuan was the best dog at eating shit ever. She had stayed with him in the security office while he made a spectacle of himself, she had stayed with him when he had behaved so badly, bringing shame on the Zhang family's ancestors.

Three hours of detention, and the matter was settled by leaving it unsettled. Zhang Jian rode home on his bike, carrying a frostily compliant Xiaohuan. On the road neither spoke, the words had already been used up in the looks that had passed between them. Next would come the penalty, and dealing with the offender. Zhang Jian had no choice but to submit to Xiaohuan's punishment, and whatever else she had in store for him.

As they were crossing the railway, Xiaohuan told Zhang Jian to turn to the right. The railway track was lined with wild rice and reeds, and Shanghai workers' dependants would often come here, whole families, old and young, to cut wild rice for cooking or to take to the market to sell. In the early winter, the leaves of the surviving wild-rice stems were withered and yellow, and rubbed against the big, bushy bulrushes with raspy, brittle sounds. Zhang Jian walked with Xiaohuan, stepping over the sleepers one at a time; it was impossible to push the bicycle along, so he gritted his teeth and carried it on his shoulder. A train was approaching in the distance along the winding track, and it let out a drawn-out hoot. With a wail, Xiaohuan burst into tears.

Zhang Jian put the bicycle down, and came up to her. Her ever-present shrewishness and willingness to make a scene came on again; she hit and scratched him, refusing point-blank to get off the railway line. The train was shaking the rails, causing them to vibrate and creak. Xiaohuan was crying so hard that she could not catch her breath, but from her disconnected speech he could hear: Whoever dodges out of the way is the bastard son of a turtle! Death is clean! Let the train roll us into mincemeat together, and save us a world of trouble!

He gave her a slap round the face, and carried her in his arms off the track.

The train went speeding by, a cup of leftover tea came spilling out of a window, horizontal in the wind, dropping tea and tea leaves in equal proportions onto their faces. It was only when the train had passed that he heard clearly what Xiaohuan was bawling:

'The two of you must have come here, for sure! Oh what fun you had in these reeds! And not afraid of getting a chill or schistosomiasis either! If you got sick you'd come home and pass it on to me and the kids!'

Xiaohuan's permed hair had become a tangled black bulrush. Seeing Zhang Jian looking at her in shocked amazement, she grabbed his trouser leg, and ordered him to sit down with her.

'Damn the man, now he's pretending to be a telegraph pole! When you were having a lovely time here with Duohe she must have been like a wriggling carp, looping and swooping like a kite, like a jade dragon riding the clouds!'

Zhang Jian sat down close to Xiaohuan. After a while, she turned her face towards him. He had come off the night shift at eight in the morning, and gone to meet Duohe without getting any sleep; now dark was coming on again, and at twelve o'clock the night shift would be waiting for him once more. Winter fog rose up from the reed-filled gully. She saw exhaustion in those camel's eyes, as if they had passed through a hundred kilometres of desert. The two black circles under his eyes, the two deep hollows in his cheeks, where the beard had been barely touched by the razor. At this moment his face really was not much to look at. Pulling the wool over people's eyes, cheating and hiding away in holes and corners was truly no easy task, the man was visibly thinner and older. She noticed that her hand was resting again on his hedgehog-like hair. His heart was so full of wild ambitions that he cared for nothing else, and his hair grew as wild as his ambitions. Xiaohuan thought, actually, there had been some change in her heart towards Zhang Jian too. The change seemed to have started after Duohe got pregnant with Girlie. That evening, Zhang Jian, who was still Zhang Erhai at that point, gathered up a pair of shoes, a waistcoat and two battered novels he was fond of, and returned to his and Xiaohuan's room. He had done what he had to for the sake of the Zhang family, and from now on he would carry on his life with Xiaohuan. When he climbed onto the *kang* and wormed his way into the quilt, they clung tightly to each other, but Xiaohuan's body had lost interest. She told herself this was her cherished Erhai, she should not be distant. But her body was no more than painfully polite to Erhai, she denied him nothing, but that was all. From then on her body was just caring, attentive and considerate, but the interest was no longer there. She began to resent herself, look at you, so petty! This is Erhai, isn't it? But her body refused to fall in with her reasoning, and the more energy she put in, the more at a loss she became. It was then that Xiaohuan secretly wept for herself. She wept for the former Xiaohuan, who only had to lie in Erhai's embrace to feel fantastic from inside to out, from body to heart; everything she could wish for was hers. This word 'fantastic' could not be replaced with any other word. But the days passed, and she felt that she was no longer just a wife to Zhang Jian; gradually, she became a women of unclear status. It seemed that all women's roles had mixed together and fallen to her: elder sister, younger sister, wife, mother, even grandmother. Her tender love for him was that of all these women. And what was more, her many different statuses had transformed her tender love towards every member of the family.

She stretched out to take his pipe directly from his pocket, filled the bowl, stretched again, fished out his matches and lit the tobacco. She inhaled several mouthfuls of smoke, and tears welled up again: he did not even sleep or eat, cheapening himself in this way! His hand slowly went to clasp her waist. She reached again to take out a handkerchief from his work overalls. She was too familiar with him, and with the contents of his pockets, she did not have to rummage about. The handkerchief was folded straight and four-square, and still retained the smell of cologne mixed with starch. No handkerchief in the family could escape Duohe's iron. Any member of the Zhang household, big or small, left the home as flat and smooth as if they had just walked out from under the iron.

Xiaohuan smoked the pipe of tobacco, then rose to her feet, pulling Zhang Jian with her. She ordered Zhang Jian to take her to a 'dark corner', just to see what kind of place it was where you could behave like beasts, like cats and dogs mating out of doors, and how they had gone about their dog-and-cat existence for over two years. Zhang Jian rode his bicycle to the Shanghai snack bar next to the People's Hospital. From the back window you could see the lake, and the mountain slopes on the far side.

He led her to a little table at the window. The cheap crocheted tablecloth was spotted all over with dirt. Anything that came to this new, developing city was very soon given a revolutionary makeover, and when that happened, the Shanghai style was no longer Shanghai and Nanjing was no longer Nanjing, everything ended up with the same feel, rough and ready, slapdash and with no attention to detail.

Xiaohuan thought, Here's the two of us sitting here, what are we supposed to say? He could understand Duohe's way of talking well enough, but it hardly made for smooth or easy conversation. In any event it was all just squeezing hands, and rubbing feet, and exchanging languishing glances. His heart had changed, right enough, otherwise how could he, who had never learned to spend money in half a lifetime, be willing to spend so much to sit here and squeeze hands, play footsie and exchange looks? His heart *had* changed.

The waiter came up and asked for their order. Without so much as a glance at the menu, Zhang Jian ordered a steamer of soup-filled dumplings. The dumplings arrived, but neither of them could eat. Xiaohuan's nose was burning with unshed tears again. Zhang Jian told her to hurry up, or the soup in the dumplings would congeal. She said she was parched, too thirsty to eat a thing. Zhang Jian called the waiter again, and asked him what soup this restaurant specialised in. The waiter said that before the shop was taken into public ownership, its best soup had been chicken and duck blood, but it had been taken off the menu.

Xiaohuan bit a mouthful of soup-filled dumpling. Zhang Jian told her that in the past the dumplings had only been half the size they were now. Xiaohuan thought he was very familiar with the place: how many meals had he eaten here? When he was due to work all night she would put two steamed *mantou* bread rolls in his lunch box, but he would often bring them back untouched, still in their wrapper. When drinking wine at home he went from six jiao for a half-kilo to four jiao, and then to three. Afterwards he just went to the free market to buy the peasants' home-distilled spirits, which was like drinking ethyl alcohol mixed with water. And yet he was prepared to spend money on these tiny dumplings with soup slopping about in the mincemeat. The lakeside view outside the window didn't come for free either, half of the money spent on these dumplings with no filling went on scenery. Once the heart had changed, what need was there to eat? You could eat your fill and get drunk just looking at the scenery.

'I've thought it through. All I can do is pack in my job and go back home,' Zhang Jian said.

'Give it a rest. Those people in our home town know you bought a Jap woman, if we go back they'll look on our three kids as Jap devils. The house is old now too, it's practically falling down.'

They had recently received a letter from Zhang Jian's parents. The old couple had finally woken up to their unspoken status as servants, and had gone back to the house in Anping village. The letter said the house had been unoccupied for a long time, that it was empty and on the verge of collapse.

Zhang Jian looked at the pitch-black surface of the lake outside the window. The silence was stifling.

Xiaohuan also knew that the three of them had become trapped. Perhaps things would have been a bit easier if Duohe had not told her story. She ground her teeth, and a surge of fierce malice welled up in her heart: why did Duohe have to tell the story of her life? Such wickedness, what the hell did it have to do with her? And what the hell did it have to do with Zhang Jian? Could you even call that heart of Zhang Jian's a heart? It was as soft as a persimmon in October, cooked to a mush, could it survive being trampled so cruelly underfoot? He had brought Duohe here with its view of mountains and lakes outside the window, and his mushy persimmon heart had turned into a gush of sweet water in front of her. She thought, Oh, my Erhai!

Her hand caught hold of his under the table. She clutched too tightly, until it turned cold.

That damnable life history of Duohe's! That damnable situation of hers, living all alone in the world; if she threw her out Duohe would never survive. It would have been so much better if she hadn't known her past! She could have kicked her out, and whether she lived or died would have nothing to do with Xiaohuan. Xiaohuan wasn't useless like Zhang Jian. He looked so big and brawny, but his heart was a mushy persimmon. She, Zhu Xiaohuan, had the courage of a slaughterman. If a woman stole her man from under her nose in the family home, she would take her right out and butcher her; she had been killing chickens since she was small, and was an outstanding killer of rabbits and ducks.

When the two of them left the restaurant, it was already eight o'clock. Xiaohuan suddenly remembered that Girlie had asked her to go and watch her play the drums. The Great Leader Chairman Mao was coming on an inspection, and students had been selected to form a drum troupe. Today they were having their dress rehearsal in the playground of the Number 3 Primary School. Xiaohuan told Zhang Jian to hurry up and take her there on his bike, even if they just made it for the tail end of the performance. Parents from every family were going, Girlie would be upset if her parents didn't make it.

The Number 3 Primary School was identical in every respect to Girlie's Number 6 Primary: cream-coloured schoolhouse, light coffee-coloured doors and windows. That Soviet architect had drawn up a plan for a school, and built over a dozen identical buildings. It was also one of his plans that had caused several hundred identical residential blocks to rise up under the slopes of the mountains and beside the lake. The four hundred drummers who had been chosen were all wearing white shirts and blue trousers, with a red neckscarf. It was early winter, so the schoolchildren were all wearing padded or lined jackets under their white shirts, and the shirts were wrapped as tightly as bandages around their bodies. They neatly changed the rhythm of their drums as their formation changed its shape, all those little faces daubed with too much rouge; at first sight this was a courtyard full of hopping, prancing, apple-cheeked little folk-tale illustrations.

Xiaohuan found Girlie in the third row. Girlie's face immediately split into a grin. Xiaohuan pointed at her stomach, and Girlie glanced down to see the multicoloured belt of her trousers had come loose from underneath her white shirt, and was swishing around flexibly. Girlie's smile broadened, like an opening flower.

Zhang Jian squeezed in beside Xiaohuan. The people around them were all parents and guardians, stamping and gesticulating and chatting together. One of them recognised Xiaohuan and asked her in a loud voice: Has your girl been picked to go up and see Chairman Mao? Xiaohuan shot back mercilessly: *My* girl got lucky, did *your* son? Another hand reached over to pass Xiaohuan a melon seed. Zhang Jian thought all those visits to the neighbours had been time well spent – wherever she went she would never lack for cigarettes or melon seeds.

The children came down for a rest. Girlie asked Xiaohuan and Zhang Jian whether her back was hunched. Xiaohuan said she was fine, jumping about so sprightly.

Girlie said: 'That old teacher says I'm hunchbacked.'

Without looking at her, Zhang Jian said: 'It's good to be a bit hunchbacked, that means you're like me.'

Xiaohuan watched Girlie go back to her classmates. Everyone in this family held it together, and if any of them were to take themselves off, the whole thing would collapse. See how cheerful Girlie was – if anyone left, what would become of her? The family in Girlie's heart would collapse. Just like if Girlie left, or Dahai or Erhai, Xiaohuan's family would collapse. Wasn't it too late now to start dividing up who was who? You could no longer tell them apart.

She said to herself: Hey, make do, for the sake of the children.

But deep down she knew it was not that simple, how could it be? She had said the same thing to Zhang Jian, that she was doing it for the children's sake. She looked at him. The past years had been so dubious and unclear, so hopelessly stupid and cowardly, that for the people who had become entangled in it, all hopes of escape were in vain. How could he not want to break out, and rip and tear his way to an honest life, even if it left them bleeding?

7

The ore under the hammer shattered very neatly, breaking into four pieces when she wanted four, three if she wanted three. Duohe thought, you could make both the metal hammer heads and the wooden handles into a part of your own body, and apply your strength just so, all controlled by the nerves. The stones could become familiar too, after an autumn and winter spent sitting there tapping at them, they would split however you wished.

There was no need for her to ask the group leader for leave any more. Last year she had often written on scraps of paper: '*I am asking for half a day's leave, as I have family business to attend to.*' Zhang Jian had come up with the words and phrasing for her. He was afraid that she would write her lies in a way that was harder to understand than other people's, and he would be left waiting at their rendezvous. He was also afraid that her lies would not be pure Chinese lies, and would attract the team leader's suspicions regarding her identity. This was not like going to the butcher's or the grain store. The people who led the dependants to the worksite were all women, key activists whose political sense of smell was much more acute than the proper cadres. These women had exposed two cases of sabotage when Chairman Mao came on his tour of inspection. In one case they had discovered a bust of Chairman Mao in a rubbish bin. It had been smashed, and then bandaged up with sticking plaster. In the other case they had caught a group in the mines teaching middle-school students how to put together a radio that could receive English and Japanese. Duohe's group leader now depended heavily on Duohe's efficiency: she would sit down for a morning or afternoon at a stretch, wordlessly tapping away, and get through enough ore for three. On alternate days when she transported ore, she never took time out there either, and was more reliable than a good machine: pack the stones, onto the bridge, turn round, pull open the bottom of the bucket, straighten up, and the stones would fall into the wagon. By early spring, Duohe had been breaking ore with the other dependants for a full year, and she would still bow deeply when she saw any of them, smiling broadly, as if seeing you was the happiest thing in her day. People whispered to the group leader: Duohe's different from us Chinese. Chinese people can get friendly enough with you in an hour that you can eat food straight out of their lunch box. She's just particular about hygiene, that's all. Then there must be something wrong with hygiene.

People gradually noticed that Duohe was a bit slow on the uptake. You would call out to her: Duohe, bring that pot of green-bean soup over here, would you? Puffing and wheezing from the strain, she would move over an enamel bucket that it took two people to lift. You could say to her: That path's horrible underfoot, level it out with a shovel while everyone's resting, and she would pick up the shovel and get to work, without so much as a hint of a question: While everyone else is resting? Aren't I part of everyone too?

When the dependants got together, they would always be discussing who beat his wife, and which family's wife and mother-in-law were locked in a psychological battle. One day somebody shouted to Duohe as she was coming down from the single-plank bridge with the empty bucket on her back: 'Zhu Duohe! Your big sister's so clever, she knows everybody, how come she hasn't found a family and got you married off?'

'That's right! Zhu Xiaohuan's been a matchmaker for so many people!'

'All the people Xiaohuan set up end up getting married! Take the family next door, the husband's got a younger brother with a harelip, and it was Xiaohuan who introduced him to a wife. A peasant, from the outskirts, her family grows vegetables. She met her in the market, and she's not bad-looking either!'

'Back in the old days, Xiaohuan would be coining money!'

'Then what's she playing at, leaving such a pretty snow-white girl on the shelf? She'll grow old in the home at this rate.'

Duohe looked from one to the other. Their speech was too quick, and some of them were southerners, all speaking together in a gaggle, two or three at a time. She had not understood any of it.

'I'm talking to you, Duohe, how old are you?'

This time she understood. She first held up two fingers, then put her hands side by side and held up nine. Her expression and movements were absolutely sincere, like an idiot showing that she knows her numbers. After that she gave that smile of hers, the same big, sincere, unchanging smile she used with everyone from strangers to people she knew very well.

Everyone gave a start. There was no warmth in their relationship with Duohe; when they were with her they could not breathe freely, they felt held back and suffocated.

'Why don't I introduce you to a husband tomorrow?' a woman from South China said. 'I've got a cousin in the Nanjing Chemical Engineering Institute, he's well into his thirties, just a little bit bald on top. By the time you get to your thirties, you want someone gentle and refined, and white and tender, just like Duohe.'

'Duohe, how come you never tan?'

Duohe had already filled her bucket with ore, and was walking away towards the rail track.

'Do you powder your face?' a woman from the North-east said. 'The Japanese face powder they used to have back in my home town was ever so good, it'd make any face white and fine. After the Japs surrendered you could find that powder all over the street.'

Duohe did not even hear what they were saying. She had only just pieced together the southern woman's words into sentences. By the time she had tipped the stones into the wagon, she understood what her speech had meant. She wanted to introduce her to a bald man in his thirties. Chemical Engineering Institute. Liked pretty women. With soft skin and white flesh just like Duohe.

Everyone wanted to marry off Duohe. Including Zhang Jian and Xiaohuan. If she could give up her children, if she could fabricate a believable life history, they would probably already have married her away.

Over four months ago she had watched from the grove of elms behind the club as a crowd took Zhang Jian away. By the time Zhang Jian appeared in front of her again, she knew that everything had changed, beneath a surface layer where everything remained the same. That day he switched shifts from the night to the day, so he had a whole day free. In the past he would have guarded this whole day with his life: he would be able to take Duohe a long way away, as far as the riverside where he had once abandoned her. But that day he went straight to sleep after the night shift, and Duohe did not even hear him going to the toilet or washing his feet. He slept right through from eight in the morning until six in the evening. Duohe had the two boys settled at the table eating their supper when she saw him come out of the big room, his nose dark and face swollen from sleep, dragging his feet as if through a swamp on his way to the toilet. It was like he had not seen Duohe at all. When his sons called out to him he ignored them too. When he emerged from the toilet and the boys called out again, he turned round, leaning on the door frame, as though he had slept himself into paralysis. Now standing, he was a heap of mud propped upright, and if he did not lean against the door he'd be certain to collapse.

Duohe called out to him. Duohe called him in a very special way: Erhe, second river. She had called him this for more than ten years. Ehe, Ehai, Erhe. Xiaohuan had corrected her many times, but later she said with a smile: Let him be Second River, then. Duohe worried that she was saying his name wrongly, so she took pains not to say it out loud too often, and when she did, it proved that she was forced to do so by the pressure of circumstances, as a matter of great urgency.

He leaned there, a mass of wrinkles piled high above his eyebrows.

'I'm worn out,' he said.

She looked at him in shock. Had he been tortured? What punishment had he suffered? There was so much pain in his eyes. At that moment the door was unlocked, and Xiaohuan came in, bringing back *mantou* bread made from mixed grains, and rice porridge. She was grousing away in a towering rage: There's no bloody advantage to working in the canteen at all, unless you count never getting short measure. Call this crap fried aubergine? Every single bloody aubergine's eight months pregnant, a bag of seeds! Xiaohuan was just the same as normal, full of sarcastic remarks about the canteen that was struggling to keep going. It was like nothing had changed. Zhang Jian went straight back to the big room, and went to sleep again.

Another week passed; Zhang Jian was still sleeping unusually heavily and long, as if he wanted to recover all the spirit and physical strength he had spent in his assignations with Duohe. When he occasionally spoke to Duohe, it was to say: Dahai can really eat, he's just five and he can eat two two-ounce *mantou*! Or: Is Erhai peeing down the stairs again? Just now someone was cursing away below! Or: You don't have to iron my work overalls! At the factory you have to crawl everywhere, they'll be a right mess in no time!

Duohe was always looking at him. He had never pretended to be confused, or not to understand all the words in her glance: *What are your plans? Didn't you say you loved me? You've taken away my heart, now you've poured it back, but my heart has gone wild with ambition, it can't be contained in such a small place!*

He no longer gave her hints about meeting. She sent him secret signals, and he pretended not to see. She sent him signals because she wanted to speak to him face-to-face, so he could give her just a few words to set things straight. What had they done to him in the factory? Did Xiaohuan know? Was this the way he would be from now on, returning to a state of casual acquaintance, to their relationship that was neither one thing nor the other?

That spring came very early, the quarry was green on every side. Duohe sat in the middle of a crowd of rowdy dependants, listening to them offering to match her up and making enquiries about the secret of her skincare. Duohe always took forever to get a rough idea of what they were talking about. By the time she more or less understood that one of the women was talking about face powder, that woman was already there right in front of her, and by the time she understood what she meant to do, it was too late, that woman had stretched out a finger to rub her face, then examined her fingertip. Only then did Duohe understand: these women had a bet that Duohe had powdered her face.

Duohe looked dumbfounded at that crowd of women, all in their thirties.

The dependants all scolded the woman who had stretched out her hand. It was not a proper rebuke, but a joking one, siding with the guilty party, saying that she had taken liberties because she could see that Duohe was honest and a bit dim!

That woman said, 'Aiyo, so soft! Come and stroke Duohe's face if you don't believe me!'

The others asked Duohe if they could stroke her. Duohe was thinking, they wouldn't go that far, surely, but the women had already approached, each with a hand out. Duohe saw all those different mouths speaking, all saying nice things. Duohe herself briefly rubbed the places they had touched. Once she had walked away, the dependants said: There's something not quite right about her – ask to stroke her face and she just stands there all respectful and lets you do it.

Duohe was the first to clamber aboard the truck back to the dependants' quarters. The women's behaviour just now had made her feel lonelier than ever. She was wearing a straw hat just like theirs, and as old and battered as theirs after a year of being blown by the wind and shone on by the sun; she was wearing canvas overalls identical to theirs, their husbands' cast-offs, so all of them were bulky and oversized, but they would always see something different about her.

The truck started up. With every rut and pothole it flung her together with all the other women, so close that you were forced into profound intimacy, but she could feel the antipathy of their bodies towards hers. Before she and Zhang Jian had loved each other, she had never thought that she would want to blend into a society of Chinese, or want Chinese people to recognise her as their kind. She had not even felt alone. She had her children; her own flesh and blood that she had given birth to and was raising for herself – flesh of her flesh, the blood in their veins was half Takeuchi family blood. She had once thought that so long as they surrounded her, the village of Shironami would surround her too. But all of this had changed. She had fallen in love with Zhang Jian, and placed her life in his. It seemed that whether or not he was the father of her children was of no real importance, it was an irrelevance, the crucial point was that on the soil of this foreign nation, she had fallen desperately in love with this man from another country. How many times had the two of them run away together in the course of those two years? She could no longer return to where she started from. The Shironami village she had built up in secret was destroyed. And she was the one who had destroyed it. Because she had hoped that this land which had birthed Zhang Jian would take her in, would assimilate her unconditionally. Because by falling fatally in love with Zhang Jian, she had accepted his motherland without reserve.

All the dependants in the truck were screaming with laughter. She had missed the joke. She could never blend in with them.

Zhang Jian's love for her, breaking out so suddenly and so suddenly extinguished, had turned her into the loneliest of people. The truck came to a stop, and the women got out like bees from a hive, pulling one another, the first off waiting below to catch the others, shouting to the last ones: Jump, I've got you! Duohe slowly shifted her way towards the end of the truck. What was the hurry? Zhang Jian was not waiting to welcome her with burning kisses. When Duohe finally got off the truck, the other dependants were already far away.

Duohe walked up the big slope, but did not turn off at the small road that led to her home. She walked all the way along the slope, until the sound of bicycle bells could no longer be heard behind her. Increasingly dense green bristlegrass rose up ahead of her, further on still came pine trees. Following the steepening slope beneath her feet, the scent of the pine trees became ever more humid, cool and dark.

On the rocks, moss and lichen formed layers of grey, green and white. Behind her, she could hear the hooting of the little train. The moss on the stones, the long call of the train, the scent of the pine trees, what more did she need than this to take her back ten years and more, back to Shironami which was gone forever? These few things were enough. Dr Suzuki had come on a small train, and a small train took him away again. The sixteen-year-old Takeuchi Tatsuru did not know whether she was the only person who wanted to jump onto the train with Dr Suzuki. It was not so much that she had seen clearly the hopelessness of their situation; she just wanted to do something to let Dr Suzuki, who had always been so gentle and courteous, cool his anger a little, to let him feel that he had not done all that talking in vain, that there was still a girl of no particular importance who was willing to take the train with him. She also wanted him to see that she was not one of the blank-faced villagers he was cursing for fools. She had already pulled her mother and younger brother and sister up to the door of the train, when her mother suddenly realised that the hand that had been pulling her, dragging her out from the community, belonged to her daughter Tatsuru. Her mother shook her arm vigorously. At that moment there was a difference in height between her and her mother, brother and sister: her foot was resting on the footplate of the train, and Dr Suzuki's artificial leg was just another half-metre away. A dozen thoughts came into her head. She did not realise that she had got down from the footplate. It was only once the train had pulled out that she had the time to order her thoughts.

And right up to that moment years later, she had still not ordered her thoughts. The scene around her which had sparked her idle fancies brought her back to Shironami in earnest, and it suddenly occurred to her that when she stood on the footplate of the train, looking at Dr Suzuki's artificial leg, she had wanted to form a connection with that mysterious limb. Of all the mysterious things about Dr Suzuki, this was the most mysterious of all. She had wanted to spend some time very, very close to it.

The scent of the pines got weaker for a while and then strengthened again. The wind in the trees was moist, as it rubbed on her forehead and cheeks. What did that mean? That the young girl Tatsuru had wanted to spend her life taking care of Dr Suzuki? If her mother's arm had not shaken her away from the train and she had taken another step up, instead of down, she would have been a different Tatsuru. A Tatsuru whose heart would not have been shattered for the sake of a Chinese man.

The pine trees up ahead were getting increasingly dense. She grabbed hold of a branch and sat down on a rock where the moss grew thick. Her feet were not that far away from the stone flood drain. The days were getting longer, and it was not yet dark. This city never got completely dark; if steel was not being tapped here, iron was being tapped there, or else they would be rolling out a big piece of iron somewhere. So there was always one miniature sunrise or sunset after the other.

Duohe slowly made her way home down the slope. It was only now that she felt her legs were so heavy she could barely move them forward, and her knees were wobbly, giving way with every step. Carrying stones on her back really was very hard work.

Duohe suddenly stopped. She saw herself as a young girl.

The young girl Tatsuru was attracted by a remarkable spectacle: a mass of blood flowing from a finger-thick crack in a stone, flowing towards the rising sun, gradually congealing beside the stone into a ball: a ball of blood the size of a melon, half transparent, and gently quivering. The blood of several generations under one roof was so dense, so thick, flowing into this thing between solid and liquid. Several generations had lived under one roof, so close they could not tell who was who, body temperature, pulse beating, convulsions, at the last became a ball of blood. When the young girl Tatsuru heard the village heads' final plan for the inhabitants of their own villages, she fled the village, and ran towards the fields. Stacks of sorghum came towards her, one after the other, then slipped past and were left behind. She had never run so fast. In the wide-open spaces her running raised up a wind; there was stubble from the sorghum under her feet, each stem wanting to pierce her, to transfix the sole of her foot. Her hair was full of her running, her clothes were full of wind too. The wind went from cold to hot, to a roiling boil.

How could the young Tatsuru have imagined that she was running towards this crowd of hundreds of identical red-and-white blocks, towards the arms of a Chinese man whom she had won and then lost again? Running towards this night.

It could all be made very easy. Find a tree, right here on this mountain, hang up a rope and tie a noose. She would need to find a good rope. All decent Japanese used good knives and good bullets for this kind of thing. Ceremony was more important than anything else, because how many weighty ceremonies of this kind would a person have in their whole life? She had missed out on marriage, the most important ceremony for a woman, but for this ceremony she could not just make do. She had to find a good rope.

When she was nearly back at her own building, Duohe saw a crowd surging out from the staircase. From far off she heard Xiaohuan's smoke-and-oil voice: 'Somebody, go and borrow a cart for me!'

The waiting crowd drew closer. Duohe saw that Xiaohuan was carrying Erhai in her arms. Someone in the crowd said: 'Oh, his auntie's back!'

Duohe squeezed past these people who were not helping at all, just adding to the confusion. All the way she could hear people discussing it: It seems he's not dead! But how could he be alive? By the time she had squeezed her way closer, she saw that Xiaohuan's eyes were staring straight ahead of her like a blind woman's as she clasped the child in her arms, coming over with stumbling but very rapid steps. All she could see was the crown of Erhai's head. Xiaohuan's tightly fitting knitted cotton top had ridden up from carrying the child, creeping up as far as her chest to reveal a strip of long, narrow waist. Xiaohuan was utterly unaware of this, she had not even noticed that she was wearing one wooden slipper and one cloth shoe on her feet.

Duohe finally got close to Xiaohuan, stretched out her arm to take Erhai from her and at once got hit by Xiaohuan's elbow: 'Get out of the way!' It was such a sharp elbow, sharp enough to chisel through her arm.

In Duohe's slow listening and understanding, the discussions gradually came together: Erhai had fallen from the fourth-floor balcony. He and Dahai had been flying paper planes off the balcony, and somehow he had gone right over the railing, and straight down.

Duohe paid no attention to anything. She squeezed her way once again to Xiaohuan's side and called out: '*Jirōchan!*' Nobody understood what she was shouting, her secret Japanese name for her son. Her two ore-dust-stained hands became sharp claws, as she caught hold of Erhai's arm, still shouting: '*Jirōchan!*' She was unable to stop, and Erhai's eyes which had been closed throughout unexpectedly opened.

In an instant Xiaohuan came to a halt, two lines of tears dropping rapidly onto Erhai's face. The deathly, staring eyes had a little life in them now.

Erhai closed his eyes again.

Xiaohuan sat down with a bump on the road, rocking the child in her arms, crying and calling: 'My Erhai! What's wrong with you? Where does it hurt? Tell Mummy!'

Try as she might, Erhai did not open his eyes, and his greyish-white little face looked like he was sleeping. There was not a speck of blood on him or on the old blue shirt, bleached almost white with frequent washing, whose sleeves had been lengthened with another, much fresher strip of blue, and patched at the elbow in black. This was a child from a poor family, but from a very neat and self-respecting poor family. The patches were done so ingeniously, the clothes pressed with an iron into knife-sharp creases.

Xiaohuan said to Duohe: 'Call him again!'

Duohe called out to him, twice. She called Erhai by his official name, 'Zhang Gang'.

This time Erhai did not open his eyes.

'Call to him the way you did just now!'

Duohe stared dully at Xiaohuan: she did not know what it was she had said.

At that moment a man came over pedalling a flatbed tricycle. Xiaohuan climbed aboard, with Erhai in her arms, and Duohe got on as well. The closest clinic was at the factory headquarters. On the trike, Duohe stretched out a hand at intervals to feel the pulse at Erhai's neck; it was still beating. Every time she took her hand away, Xiaohuan would glance at her, and she would nod once, to show that Erhai was still alive. Xiaohuan was chivvying the driver along: 'Big brother, be quick! All our three lives are in your hands, mothers' and son's alike!'

When they arrived at the clinic, the emergency doctor examined Erhai, and said that the child did not seem to have been seriously injured. Not a single bone had been broken, there were not even any signs of internal bleeding. There was only one point of uncertainty, and that was his head.

Just then a nurse brought a jar of fruit for Erhai. She opened it, and fed the syrup to him a spoonful at a time. There was nothing wrong with his swallow reflex. Could a child fall from such a high place and have nothing the matter? Xiaohuan asked. It looks like there is nothing the matter; if he had sustained internal head injuries, he would not be able to eat. Who falls from the fourth floor and has nothing wrong? You can only call it a miracle. Perhaps the child's weight was too light, and the evergreen trees at the bottom of the building broke his fall a bit. What to do if there was a problem? Going by all the results, no problem could be found.

The doctor told Xiaohuan and Duohe to take the child back home, and come back if there were any new developments.

'What developments might there be?!' Xiaohuan got up from the chair along with the doctor.

'I don't know . . .'

'You don't know and you're telling us to go home?!' Xiaohuan grabbed a fistful of the doctor's white coat.

Like the scholar in the popular saying, who is left unable to express himself when faced with a crude, uneducated soldier, the doctor looked at this North-eastern woman. When she turned savage, her lips clenched, and there was no sweetness in the deep dimples on her cheeks, rather they emphasised her malevolence. The doctor became fierce in his turn. 'You, take your hands off me!'

'Just tell me, what kind of developments might there be?' Xiaohuan grabbed a bigger handful of white coat.

'How would I know? Be reasonable, can't you?!'

'I will not!'

The doctor turned his head and shouted to the baffled female nurse: 'Nurse Ding, call for someone to take her away! She's causing a scene!'

Now Xiaohuan was lying on the ground, nobody knew how she got there. 'He pushed me! That little bastard pushed me!'

All of the ten or so people in the clinic came running over. The female nurse testified that the doctor had not pushed Xiaohuan. Xiaohuan accused her of a cover-up. The head of the clinic had to step in, and the result was that the clinic would provide an ambulance to take the little boy and the two adults to the People's Hospital for a thorough check-up. They were experts there, and had more equipment.

That doctor wiped his hands on the front of his white coat, scrunched up into a dishcloth by Xiaohuan, muttering: 'What developments could there be? He ate all the syrup from a whole jar of loquats!'

The emergency doctor at the People's Hospital was a woman. She pressed and manipulated here and there on Erhai's body with light, gentle hands, and when she had done with her prodding and twisting, she nodded her head and smiled at the two women who were craning their necks to see. Her smiling face behind the big white face mask was extremely gentle. After that she wheeled Erhai into the X-ray room. She carried on examining him until ten o'clock in the evening, and only then did she walk over to the desk, sit down behind it and start to write.

Xiaohuan watched her with bated breath. Duohe looked at Xiaohuan and took hold of her hand, not knowing if it was to console her or seeking consolation from her. Xiaohuan's hand seemed to be utterly without feeling, with none of its usual strength. Duohe felt that hand give an involuntary twitch, then twitch again; it seemed that every stroke of the lady doctor's pen was writing in Erhai's book of life and death. Rather, it was writing in Xiaohuan's own book of life and death. Xiaohuan was utterly absorbed, she had even forgotten to close her mouth, and you could see a faint gleam from the gold tooth. Duohe on the other hand was more composed than Xiaohuan. After all, she had been to middle school and, judging by all the test results, Erhai was not in danger.

The woman doctor pulled down the face mask, to reveal all of her smiling face.

'The child has no injury. Everything is normal,' she said, as she rose from the desk.

Somehow Xiaohuan was back on the floor again. This time she fell to her knees at the doctor's feet, clasping her legs through a layer of white coat as she burst into noisy sobs.

'Oh, Doctor! Thank you!' she howled.

The doctor was bewildered by her, both frightened and rather put out. 'What are you thanking me for? There was nothing wrong with the child in the first place . . .'

Xiaohuan, however, paid no attention to anything except clutching her legs and weeping: 'The Goddess of Mercy came down to earth . . . Brought our child back from the dead . . . Such goodness and kindness!'

The doctor tried to lift her to her feet, but in the end Duohe had to lend a hand before they could pull Xiaohuan, dissolving into a puddle of tears, upright again. The doctor handed several prescriptions to Duohe, and told her that the child was anaemic and should eat pig's liver. The medicine on the prescriptions was to prevent internal bleeding, and should be taken for three days; if everything was normal they could stop the medicine. Xiaohuan, her face swollen with tears, agreed with the doctor: 'Ai, ai.' Very much to Duohe's surprise, everything, from Xiaohuan's appalling behaviour to her ignorance, was taking her further and further away from her thoughts of finding a good rope.

The door to the emergency room flew open with a crash, and Zhang Jian came in, in oil-stained overalls, a safety helmet on his head and a towel round his neck. You could see at once that he had come straight down from the crane. He had been on the evening shift that ran from four o'clock until midnight, and a neighbour had come to the workshop with the news.

He rushed straight over to Erhai, who was lying on a trolley. Erhai was the apple of his eye. You might say that he had no reason to have a preference between his two identical sons, but he always felt that there was something intangible about Erhai that charmed him. Sure enough, Erhai, who was full of surprises, had performed another miracle.

He hugged and kissed Erhai. The child feebly opened his eyes to look at him, and then closed them again. The doctor said that the child had had a great shock, it might take him a while to get over the damage to his nerves.

Once they were back home Zhang Jian flew into a silent rage at the two women, glaring fearsomely at them both. In Xiaohuan's words: this was his mule's temper coming on again. When he looked at people in that way it was exceptionally unnerving, like at any moment he might grab one of the half-bricks they used to pen in their coal to hit you, though in reality he would be more likely to hit himself.

He looked at the two women until their hearts were prickling and chilly with fear.

At last he spoke: 'Can neither of you keep a proper eye on the children?'

'Who told the Neighbourhood Committee to start up a canteen?' said Xiaohuan. 'If Duohe didn't go out to earn that five fen, we wouldn't even have pig's lard to eat!'

Zhang Jian smoked for a while in brooding silence. Finally he announced his decision: Duohe would immediately resign her job. If they couldn't get pork lard they would eat the cheaper fat from pig's innards, if they couldn't afford cotton-seed oil then they would eat no oil at all; they could not keep dumping the children on Girlie. Girlie had been hiding, terrified, in a neighbour's house ever since Erhai was taken to the hospital. Her mother Xiaohuan had three phrases for her: 'I'll strip the hide off you!', 'I'll beat your bum ragged!' and 'I'll pierce your mouth with a big needle!'

Xiaohuan was now standing outside the neighbour's door, shouting at the top of her voice: 'Hide in other people's houses for your whole life if you think you've got what it takes! I'll have your skin when you come home, see if I don't!'

Duohe tugged Xiaohuan's arm from behind. Although Xiaohuan's methods of managing her children were no different from all the other families in the block, it embarrassed Duohe. There were many things that Xiaohuan was not afraid of, of which the most notable was losing face. She pulled Xiaohuan back towards their own door, overturning a low table as she did so, and a chess set laid out on it went flying, sending some of the pieces straight through gaps in the railing to fall in the gutter at the foot of the block. The owners of the chess set cried out, saying there were two pawns missing. Xiaohuan's mouth paused in her scolding to yell at them: 'You're only a couple short, aren't you? Just carry on playing, make do!'

Duohe did not move. Why find a good rope? Just carry on living, make do!

8

Beggars were starting to appear on the streets in increasing numbers. No household dared to open up when there was a knock on the door, for fear that they would find one standing there. Sometimes you would get three generations of beggars all at once.

Duohe no longer went to the ore site to earn her five fen an hour. The canteen closed down too, and Xiaohuan went back home with a 'Thank heaven, thank my lucky stars, and thank Chairman Mao as well', and reverted to her lazy life of late nights and lie-ins.

These days when Xiao Peng and Xiao Shi happened to drop by for chess and a chat, she would not bind her apron around her narrow waist, saying briskly that she'd make them some food. Now all she had to offer them were gold and silver rolls, using sweet-potato flour instead of maize flour, and maize flour in place of white. Dahai and Erhai would be seven soon; Girlie was already starting to look like a big girl, all large eyes, her four limbs like straw stalks, forever waking up hungry in the middle of the night.

Before their visits, Xiao Peng and Xiao Shi would often fill the pockets of their work overalls with green beans or soya beans, bought at a high price on the black market. Xiao Peng had gone back to technical school for another year, and had returned to the workshop as Technician Peng. One day he went to the Zhang house to play a card game they called Chase the Pig with Xiaohuan and Xiao Shi. Duohe came into the room to top up their tea, and backed out once she had finished. Xiao Peng rolled up the clean white sleeves of his work clothes, and said in a loud voice: 'Thank you, Little Sister.'

The others were all startled by the sudden rise in volume. Duohe flashed a baffled smile in his direction too. Then Xiao Shi let out a guffaw, grabbed hold of Xiao Peng's left wrist and held it up high: 'New watch! Shanghai brand! How come none of you saw it?'

Xiao Peng's face flushed the colour of pig's liver, but he did not hit Xiao Shi, just swore at him angrily: 'So what if it's a new watch? You little bastard, ogling away!' At the same time he shot a glance at Duohe, and Duohe gave him another smile.

Duohe's smiles never held anything back, and she made men like Xiao Peng harbour a mistaken belief that he was the man who had amused and pleased her the most that day. For all these years, Xiao Peng had tried to figure out how Duohe was different from other women. He always felt that she had a background that was somehow inscrutable to him. She was different from ordinary women, and the differences were so subtle, so slippery, that by the time you got a hold of them, they had long since slid away.

'Duohe, you come and play a round or two, I'm off to buy something to eat,' Xiaohuan said, stretching out one foot to search for her shoes underneath the bed.

Duohe smiled again, briefly, shaking her head. Xiao Peng noticed that when Xiaohuan spoke to Duohe she pronounced every word carefully, with none of her usual quickness of speech.

'Sit down, sit down, we'll teach you!' Xiao Shi said. 'Even people with brain fever can play this game!'

Duohe watched him shuffle the cards. The children were still at school, she had washed the clothes and ironed them, and there was a while before supper time. She sat down hesitantly. When picking cards from the deck, Xiao Peng's hand kept brushing against hers in passing, and he would glance fleetingly at her. If Xiao Shi was not talking he was humming songs, or he was boasting and bragging about how good his cards were: Xiao Peng was going to lose his shirt to him, and every other stitch he had on too.

Duohe was struggling to understand Xiao Shi. She would lose half a sentence, understand half a sentence, and then the meaning of another would come too late. Before Duohe had learned the card game, the children were home from school. Girlie, who was in her first year of middle school, came running in with Dahai and Erhai, now in the second year of primary school. Duohe hurriedly got to her feet, bowed in farewell to the two guests, and told them to carry on playing, while saying to the children: 'Wash your hands!'

The three of them walked unwillingly into the kitchen. At once, Girlie shouted out: 'Erhai's sneaked some *pan* to eat!'

Erhai came scurrying out of the kitchen, carrying four twisted steamed rolls in his hands, though it was hard to say if they were made of chopped onion rolled into steamed bread or breadcrumbs rolled into onions, as he scattered a trail that was more onion than flour in his wake.

'Put down that *pan*!' Girlie shouted, chasing after him.

Girlie was a Three-Good Student, she had good morals, good grades and good health, and she was like a little mother to the two boys.

'I'm going to count to three, and you stand still!' she ordered. 'One, two, three!'

Erhai came to a halt, and Dahai took his chance to snatch the steamed rolls from his hands. The flour was not sticky enough in the first place, and a lot of onion had been mixed in, so that as soon as they left his hands they fell apart. Erhai was on him in an instant, wrapping both hands around Dahai's neck, and biting down on his shoulder.

'My *pan*! Give me back my *pan*!' Erhai shouted.

Xiao Peng and Xiao Shi could see that they were no longer play-fighting, but fighting in deadly earnest, and hurried up to pull them apart. Then they asked Girlie what *pan* was. Girlie told them: It's just *pan*. Where do they say that? What dialect is it? I don't know – that's what my auntie always calls it. Xiao Peng and Xiao Shi exchanged glances: How come this word doesn't sound like Chinese?

After supper, Zhang Jian and Xiao Peng played chess, and Xiao Shi sat watching, ready to take over from the loser. Xiao Shi asked Zhang Jian: 'Where is Auntie Duohe from, exactly, and how come she talks about *huajuan* like it's in a foreign language?' Zhang Jian knitted his eyebrows and stared at the chessboard. Nobody found it strange that he did not respond.

But Xiaohuan called out from the sewing machine where she was mending clothes: 'What did his sister-in-law say that you didn't understand?'

Xiao Shi said with a smile: 'See what sharp ears Sister Xiaohuan has! She manages to listen in when we're talking, even over that noisy sewing machine.'

Xiao Peng said, laughing: 'Sister Xiaohuan, we really don't understand the words his sister-in-law says.'

Xiaohuan said: 'Really? Then I'll tell you – that's how they talk in the Land of Gibble-Gabble! My little sister's been to the Country of Gibble-Gabble!'

Xiao Shi and Xiao Peng both laughed and said that the language of Gibble-Gabble was so difficult, almost as bad as the language of the Jap devils.

They often went on like this, nobody much caring whether they were talking nonsense or not, provided it kept boredom at bay. Duohe sat on the bed in the big room knitting socks for the children, topping up the three men's hot water at intervals. There had been no tea to drink in the Zhang family for quite a while now. All the money for tea leaves had gone on grain. In the autumn Duohe would often go to the outskirts to gather a kind of grass seed, which could be fried over a slow heat until it turned yellow, then brewed into a fragrant tea. But by now it was early summer.

It was Xiao Shi's turn to play chess with Xiao Peng. Zhang Jian went to check on the children, who were doing their homework in the other room. Out of the corner of her eye, Duohe saw Xiao Shi give Xiao Peng a kick; he did not move, but Xiao Shi did. He stood up, took a drawing pin from the picture of Chairman Mao above the dining table, and set it down on Zhang Jian's chair. Zhang Jian came back, and was about to take his seat, when Duohe suddenly understood. She let out a shrill cry. Xiao Peng and Xiao Shi had never known that soft-voiced Duohe was capable of such a powerful soprano: 'Erhe!'

Zhang Jian turned, but by then Duohe had run over and was holding up the drawing pin that should already have jabbed into his bottom, her face as red as blood.

'Go! You, go!' Duohe said to Xiao Shi.

Xiao Shi kept sniggering with embarrassment. 'I was just having a bit of fun with him . . .'

Duohe grabbed a fistful of Xiao Shi's sleeve, yanked him up from his stool and hauled him towards the doorway.

'You, go! You, go!'

Xiao Shi was stunned. He had never seen Duohe lose her temper, nor had he known that she possessed such stubborn strength. Both Zhang Jian and Xiaohuan held her back, but she did not relax her grip on Xiao Shi's sleeve. There was no shortage of people in the work section who enjoyed making Zhang Jian the butt of their jokes: some put sand in his shoes, others stole cotton gloves from his toolbox. When it was time for political study, often someone would draw a picture of an ape or a comical figure from legends on the back of his chair in chalk. When Zhang Jian was caught backstage at the club, these people who were already so fond of taking the mickey out of him became even more lively and energetic. Perhaps it was only Xiao Peng who understood that Zhang Jian was not as gentle and kindly as was generally supposed. His silence was because he would not bring himself down to their level; he seemed to have more important matters on his mind.

But what matters were these? Xiao Peng could not even begin to guess.

Xiaohuan and Zhang Jian finally rescued Xiao Shi from the onslaught. Xiao Shi was grinning cheekily, bowing and scraping left and right. Xiao Peng thought, who knows when this silence of Zhang Jian's that keeps him aloof from the world might explode, and who knows which poor bastard will suffer damage from that explosion.

It was also clear to Xiao Peng that Xiao Shi had hoped to attract Duohe's attention with his little joke. But the two of them were always covertly competing, striving for a smile from Duohe, even a wordless smile. Could it be that the two of them wanted to court her? Xiao Peng was shocked by this notion: how could he marry a woman who was quite a few years his senior? Besides, there was the marriage his parents had arranged for him back home when he was still a child; he could not dodge his responsibilities. He was twenty-six now, how much longer could he put it off?

Xiao Peng did not even know if he liked Duohe. It was just that lingering charm of hers, so different from his female colleagues, that made his heart itch. He looked at Xiao Shi, still slimily justifying himself and professing brotherly affection for Zhang Jian, and suddenly it became clear to him – Zhang Jian and Duohe were lovers. Small wonder that one drawing pin could transform her into a leopardess, springing up to tear with her teeth at anyone who harmed her leopard. Everything was clear now: Xiaohuan had been covering up for them in that incident at the club, and Xiao Peng could see who had given birth to the children.

Xiao Peng thought that he had soiled himself by associating with this shameless, dysfunctional family for all these years. When he and Xiao Shi left the Zhangs', he decided not to go there again. But he was back the next day, and every day after that, more regularly than in the past. He did not know why. He did not mention his conjectures to Xiao Shi; he despised Xiao Shi's chattering, gossiping tongue, and the fact that he could not see more than five centimetres below the surface.

One day in August after work, he bathed, washed his hair and changed into a short-sleeved sailor's striped shirt with holes under the armpits that he had mended with sticking plaster. He arrived at Zhang Jian's building, just in time to see Duohe coming down the stairs with a wooden bucket on her back. He asked her where she was going, and she pointed in the direction of the grain store. He said, 'I'll help you carry your grain, shall I?' She smiled. He immediately turned his bike around.

When they reached the door of the grain store she pointed ahead again, into the distance. 'There.'

Xiao Peng followed her. She had a very interesting way of walking, with small, shuffling, but very quick steps. This close to her, his feeling that she was unlike other women intensified.

'How much further is it? Come up on my bicycle.'

Duohe gestured to the huge wooden bucket on her back. 'Bucket,' she said with yet another smile.

Xiao Peng thought for a minute, and told her to take off the bucket. He watched her unfasten it, feeling that there was something very peculiar about it, that it was not like the utensils used in normal homes. He picked up the bucket with his left hand, held onto the handlebars with his right, and set the bicycle in motion, wobbling as he went.

By the side of the road, a crowd of people was picking over something that turned out to be a pile of newly harvested peanuts, a lot more mud than nut. One of the neighbours had passed on the news that there were peanuts for sale around the building, and Xiaohuan had borrowed five yuan from another neighbour and told Duohe to go and buy some. The children were undernourished, and Dahai had been suffering from a swollen liver for the past six months.

Xiao Peng and Duohe grubbed in the mud with both hands, and scraped up three or four kilos of peanuts. Duohe was just about to tip them into the basket to be weighed, when Xiao Peng held her back, poured the peanuts out of the bucket, and picked away the thick layer of mud that the peanuts had been rolled in. He smiled at Duohe. Duohe understood, and squatted down to pick through them with him. Xiao Peng thought, at her age, how can this woman not understand how much cunning there is in the world? If not for him, would she have spent the money on mud?

The peasant selling peanuts pointed over with the long stick he used as a balance for weighing, almost jabbing Duohe in the face with it. He shouted: 'No sale, no sale! I won't sell to anyone who starts picking and choosing!'

Xiao Peng seized the balance stick in his fist, telling him to stop poking people with it. The peasant said he had already made it clear beforehand, there was to be no picking and choosing! Xiao Peng and the peasant fell into a tug of war over the balance stick. 'So if we pick them over then we deserve to get poked in the face with your stick? And a female comrade's face too – you can't just go jabbing away whenever the fancy takes you! What if she's blinded, whose fault would it be then?' 'I never blinded her!' 'Oh, this bastard doesn't care even if he puts her eye out!'

The peasant was a simpler soul than Xiao Peng. Xiao Peng's first words of accusation had shifted the topic, but he unquestioningly followed the flow of Xiao Peng's logic.

'Her eyes aren't blind, they're just fine, aren't they?' the peasant said to his panic-buying customers.

'That's just because you don't have what it takes to carry through your evil intentions! Did you all hear that? Our nation is going through hard times, and these crafty peasants are taking this opportunity to suck the blood of the workers, their elder brothers!'

Xiao Peng seized the stick in his hands, and the peasant stamped his feet beside him, begging him not to go baton-twirling with his scales, he was going to break it.

'They're a black-hearted lot, those peasants from the outskirts! Taking advantage of us when we're short of grain and oil, raising the market price for all their life's worth.'

'That's right!' voices replied from among the buyers.

A North-eastern dependant, mud smeared all around her mouth, said in a loud voice: 'These peasant brothers of ours are so ungenerous, they sell us these few little peanuts, and even plaster them with thick mud first!' Just now she had taken advantage of the tug of war to shell the muddy peanuts and cram them into her mouth at top speed. She wanted to fill her belly, that would mean one more meal saved for her children.

The deep-seated and bitter grudges which had built up over many years between the workers' dependants and the peasants from the outskirts exploded. The peasants knew that the workers from Shanghai could not do without fish and shrimps so they inflated their price until it was as high as Shanghai prices. When they sold greens they soaked them in water, and if you confronted them they would quibble: What do you mean too much water? That's just softening it up! It'll melt in the mouth!

Brandishing the stick, Xiao Peng said to the dependants: 'We workers are the proletarian class. When famine strikes all we can do is carry on, though our bellies are empty, but they still have their private plots of land! They're the propertied class!' Xiao Peng cared nothing for whether the great principles of which he was speaking were in fact principled, or whether they were persuasive, but he cut a fine figure, and even the peasant was beginning to suspect his own motives.

Xiao Peng swished the balance stick about as he brought into play his stage voice from the amateur drama group, educating the peasants from the propertied class. His eyes kept glancing at Duohe. Duohe was wearing a white-and-blue-checked shirt; the white was very white, the blue faded until it too was almost white, the original long sleeves had become so tattered they could no longer be patched, and had been cut into short sleeves, but that cleanliness, neatness and smoothness made her very eye-catching in a crowd of workers' dependants. Duohe was watching him, round-eyed, seemingly astonished by his suddenly revealed talent. Whether it was his talent as a rabble-rouser or his talent as an amateur actor made no difference, the light in her eyes was illuminating him all the while.

Duohe gave a chuckle, and Xiao Peng felt as though two ounces of spirits had shot straight to his head. He certainly could not immediately abandon the stage which he had just built up. He heard a crack; the stick which was as thick as a sapling snapped in his hand, and jabbed painfully into his knee. He paid no heed to the pain, as he led the working class to throw off their oppressors. He divided the peasant's peanuts into equal portions, everyone would produce three yuan, and he declared to the peasant, as if proclaiming the will of Heaven: if that's not enough for you, you won't even get that three yuan.

The peasant cursed them roundly for bandits.

Xiao Peng did not get angry, he laughed heartily, and said that in the old society the landlords and idle rich had cursed the Communists in just that way.

After that people crowded joyously around Xiao Peng, as though he really was leading a great uprising. Xiao Peng nodded and waved to the dependants, but his senses were all focused on Duohe. He wanted Duohe to see: What is Zhang Jian compared to this? Is he possessed of such splendid eloquence? Does he have this crowd-pleasing charm?

At the technical school, Xiao Peng had read several novels. He was certainly not like Shao Jianbo towards Xiao Bai Ge.* Nor was he like Jiang Hua with Lin Daojing.† To him, Duohe was a strange

* A reference to the novel *Tracks in the Snowy Forest*, published in the 1950s. This novel describes the Communists' fight to stamp out bandits (including remnants of the old Nationalist government), and includes a lovely young female orderly called Xiao Bai Ge (Little White Dove). Translator's note.

† A reference to the novel *The Song of Youth*, the tale of a young woman, Lin Daojing, set in the 1960s, who is trying to find a path in life, and finally turns to the Revolution. Jiang Hua is a revolutionary comrade who becomes more than a friend to her. Translator's note.

creature with vast, mysterious powers of attraction. Her unclear, halting speech, her odd footsteps, and her astonishing naivety were all just parts of what made up her allure. Sometimes he had speculated with Xiao Shi that her intelligence was stunted, but as soon as you saw her eyes, that suspicion promptly dissipated: not only was she in full possession of her faculties, she was actually rather sensitive to the feelings of others.

He strapped the half-full bucket of peanuts onto the crossbar of his bicycle, and walked with Duohe. The summer sun was very late in setting, and the metal that was being turned out of the blast furnaces added another sun to the city. The uprising he had just led had left him sweating all over, the sailor shirt was sticking to his back and chest, and the sticking plaster he had used to patch the holes was soaked through and had curled up and dropped off during his arm-waving, foot-stamping performance. Each one of his vehement, impassioned gestures had made the holes a little bit larger, exposing unruly armpit hair.

Duohe glanced at him from time to time, and gave him a smile. Her lack of words was lovable too. How was it that ordinary women had so much to say when they hit their thirties? Finally, Duohe spoke.

'Clothes broken,' she said. Her eyes were so earnest, although she was still smiling.

He had talked of novels, songs and poetry all the way, and her response was 'Clothes broken'.

'Here.' She pointed to her own armpit.

There was a very small patch under her armpit too, which was now saturated with sweat. For some reason, Xiao Peng found himself aroused by this mend she had made and her armpit soaked with sweat.

He came to a halt. She stood still too, without knowing the reason why.

'Mend it for me.'

She looked fixedly at him, a layer of sweat like fine droplets on her nose, and her thick fringe damp with sweat. She understood that the words coming out of his mouth made little difference to anything, they could just as well have been blown away by the wind. There was no need to say the words that did make a difference.

Tears suddenly welled up in her eyes.

He became afraid. If she took things too seriously, then it might well be too difficult to pick up the pieces later.

They walked back to the flat, and Xiao Peng said breezily to Xiaohuan that he had helped Duohe to carry her things, and Duohe had agreed to mend his clothes for him. Duohe's tears left him disturbed all evening. If she were to take him as her saviour that would be a nuisance: she would throw herself at him, body and soul, and drag him into domesticity. Had he stooped to pick up Zhang Jian's leftovers? Was he really that cheap? At that moment Duohe was washing his sailor shirt clean and ironing it dry, then she took it to the sewing machine and patched it for him. Listening to the tapping of the sewing machine he thought: Look at her, already she wants to drag you into spending your life with her!

That evening Zhang Jian and Xiao Shi were both at work, so Xiao Peng was the only one there, and he was no match for Xiaohuan's banter, all he could do was listen to Girlie reading out the essay she had written. Girlie had a big book full of fine, stirring sentences which Xiao Peng and Xiao Shi had copied from newspapers, magazines and books. Every time Girlie wrote a composition, she would look through it. So when she wrote of bumper harvests it was all 'golden sands flowing through the village', 'you would think that white clouds had fallen onto the cotton fields', 'beating the jujube tree with staves, fruit falling like a rain of carnelian' . . .

Everybody thought these sentences were first-rate; only Xiaohuan said as she listened: 'Then how come we're still so hungry? How come our Dahai's liver's all swollen up? How come their dad's as skinny as a praying mantis?' Or she would say with a chuckle: 'No wonder – the village is full of golden sand. You can't cook sand into a meal! Carnelians falling out of the jujube trees – can you eat those? That's why there are beggars dead of hunger outside the door of the department store every day.'

Sometimes Girlie was unable to write by the time Xiaohuan had finished her tirade, so she called her backward, with rightist tendencies.

Xiaohuan said: 'So what if I'm rightist?'

'Rightists have to sweep the toilets, if they won't do sweeping they climb up the high chimney and jump off!' Two engineers in the factory had been made rightists, and had swept the toilets for a while. One after the other they had jumped off the fifty-metre-high chimney.

By the time Girlie had finished reading her essay, Duohe had mended Xiao Peng's sailor shirt. She handed it over to him, and he gave her a piece of paper, written hurriedly under the cover of Girlie's essay, an invitation to watch a film, the afternoon showing at half past four.

But the film finished and Duohe had not come. At first, he had been making something out of nothing, in search of a little extra secret tenderness, but getting stood up by Duohe made him suddenly turn neurotic. *She* was cold-shouldering *him*? She had the nerve to make him waste the price of two cinema tickets; one ticket had bought an empty seat, the other an empty shell – throughout the film his spirit was with Duohe, and he had been unable to follow the story. Was she looking for death? Did she dare to arouse his anger? He knew what was what, he could have exposed the filthy tangle of relationships between the Zhang family to the security office! Was she keeping herself pure for Zhang Jian? This woman was so faithful despite everything he had put her through, and Zhang Jian thought he deserved her?

When Xiao Peng next went to the Zhang household, he did not go up the stairs, but waited around for Duohe to come down. He knew that Duohe often went to the vegetable market near closing time, to gather up the old outer leaves of the vegetables. Sometimes she went to the meat stall too. After a day's worth of meat had been cut away, the skin would be sold off cheap just before they shut up shop, and Duohe would queue in the great crowd of dependants to try her luck.

He saw her walking away from the meat stall carrying a piece of skin, curled at the edges, which had been hung up all day for the flies to bite. He went up to her.

Duohe backed off a little, but immediately gave him a very big smile.

'Why didn't you come to the film?' he asked.

She smiled again briefly, and shook her head. What was it about that childish air of hers? Had she eaten rice for thirty years and more for nothing?

She was still smiling and shaking her head.

'It's nothing – friends going to see a film, it's perfectly normal.'

She was watching his lips, her eyebrows scrunched up. Xiao Peng recalled the tone of voice Xiaohuan and Zhang Jian used when speaking to her, so he slowed down and repeated his words.

'It's not,' she said.

Her 'it's not' could mean any number of things. He sensed that he was becoming neurotic over his relationship to her. He was afraid that her 'it's not' implied: 'You're getting too emotional over something that's all in your head.' He did not know how it had come about, but he knew what it meant to feel pain.

That day he did not go back home with Duohe. The pain was starting to devour him. But avoiding Zhang Jian's home and not seeing Duohe made the pain worse. Regardless, he ignored Xiao Shi's goading and his cruel mockery, and was determined to stay away from Duohe. At the turn of the year, Xiao Peng returned to his home town, where he married his fiancée. On the marriage bed he vented his fury on his new bride, saying to himself with every move, 'I'll give you pain! I'll give you pain!'

On his return to the factory, a letter came from his father saying that his wife was pregnant. He became even more ferocious towards himself. He ground his teeth, closed his eyes tight, beat the left side of his chest, saying again, as if reciting a curse: 'I'll give you pain! I'll give you pain!'

He had told no one about his marriage, not even Xiao Shi.

The only time when Xiao Peng could forget his pain was when he saw that photo of himself with the Great Leader. It had been taken when Chairman Mao came to the mouth of the furnace, and addressed the factory leaders, saying that this newly arisen city was the hope of the nation. Behind Xiao Peng's back were gleaming sparks of molten iron, and although he was right at the edge of the picture, it was all so full of youthful vigour and romance. They were going to build up this little town into a new-style enterprise of iron and steel. The nation depended on people like Xiao Peng. Chairman Mao waved his hand, just like Lenin and Stalin had waved. This majestic poetic feeling was the only thing that Xiao Peng could use to kill the pain. His own hand gripped the hand of the Great Leader, a real hand with a temperature of 36.5 degrees and a pale pink palm.

His hand had passed on the body temperature of the Great Leader to over a hundred people. As soon as anyone arrived for the night shift, they would shake Xiao Peng's hand. A hand which had shaken that of the Great Leader would bring him mighty, almost supernatural powers. How could there be room in such greatness for this trivial pain of his?

Another summer came. Xiao Peng, wearing the sailor shirt that Duohe had mended for him, rode his bicycle from the single men's dormitory outside the factory. Dogs had started to appear on the streets again. By the look of things, the dogs had sniffed out that they were living in somewhat safer times, they were no longer liable to end up in someone's cooking pot. When he reached the doorway of the department store, sounds of singing and beating drums came drifting over. A few dozen beggars from the poorer part of the province north of the Huai River had organised a Fengyang flower-drum troupe and were putting on a performance. A black dog held a battered straw hat in its mouth, standing in front of the audience, and then sitting down. There was no money in the straw hat. It was packed with buns and heavy, and the dog's neck stretched upwards desperately in order to prevent the food in the hat from tumbling out. When the straw hat was full, a woman came over, took down the hat, and shared out the *wotou* and *mantou* buns between a dozen or so children who were sitting or lying around. The dog stood quietly to one side, its shrunken belly twitching rapidly, a big slab of tongue hanging out. The woman passed the empty hat to the dog, and the dog went back in front of the audience, sitting up and begging.

A boy's voice came from the audience: 'Give some to the dog!'

Xiao Peng looked in the direction of the sound. The speaker was Erhai. His head was wrapped in a bandage, and he was carrying an iron hoop on his shoulders. During the summer holidays, Erhai was never without a collection of war wounds. Dahai, half a head taller, was standing next to him. Xiao Peng thought, Let me not see Duohe!

But sure enough, she was there. Erhai ran into the circle of people, picked out a chunk of sweet-potato bun from the straw hat the dog was holding in its mouth, and held it beside the dog's muzzle. Duohe darted out from the crowd to pull him back. Completely unmoved by Erhai's largesse, the dog tossed his head and carried on with his task. An old man from the flower-drum troupe walked over, pointing to the black dog with the flute in his hands. The dog immediately stood up and set down the hat; the old man pointed again, and it suddenly ran over to Erhai. Duohe hugged him close with a cry of 'Ah!' The dog rolled on the floor, four paws pointing skywards. The old man told Erhai that he could feed the dog now.

Erhai put the sweet potato in front of the dog, it turned round, stood up, and swallowed the sweet potato in two gulps.

'Is this dog for sale?' Erhai said.

'Can you afford it?' the old man asked.

Xiao Peng saw Duohe dragging Erhai out of the crowd. At eight years old, Erhai was not a tall boy, but his little legs were all muscle. Those legs were kicking on the ground, and it took Duohe ten seconds to drag him a single step. Dahai was standing behind Duohe, hoping that people would not take the two of them for twins.

Xiao Peng walked over, smiling broadly. 'Erhai, do you want this dog? Your uncle Xiao Peng will buy it for you.'

A lock of Duohe's hair had fallen onto her face; she took out her hairslide, pulled it open with her teeth and smoothed her hair behind her ears. Xiao Peng did not look directly at any of these actions, but he felt that Duohe was performing them for his benefit, striking all these different postures for him.

Without another word, Erhai broke free of Duohe and, pulling

Xiao Peng's hand, went back into that crowd of flower-drum beggars. A policeman had just arrived, saying that those places north of the Huai River were really such a nuisance. The three years of natural disasters were over, but still they sent these beggars to spread their lice and fleas!

The beggars gathered their bundles, picked up their children, led the dog away and scattered. They were used to playing hide-and-seek with the police, and they would be back as soon as they were gone. There were three identical new-style department stores in the town, all with air conditioning; when the beggars staged a performance there it was the next best thing for them to a holiday somewhere cool.

Duohe bowed to Xiao Peng and said: 'Have you come off work?'

Everybody greeted each other like this: 'Going to work?' 'Coming off work?' But Duohe used the greeting in a way that was decidedly peculiar. Xiao Peng half-jokingly sketched a bow in return. 'Off for a walk?'

Duohe pointed to Erhai's head, to show that this was the reason for their outing: they had just changed his bandages. Hers was the powerless smile of a gentle mother, a mixture of love and irritation. She was still wearing the previous year's shirt with its fine blue-and-white checks, only it was even older, the blue checks all washed away. If she had not been so fond of cleanliness, it would not have been fit to wear. He found it strange: where had his pain got to? He was simply overjoyed. He had not seen her for a year, and just standing together like this, saying a few inconsequential words, and watching the beggars' song and dance was enough to make him cheerful.

Music was drifting out once more from the door at the back of the department store. Erhai dragged Xiao Peng over.

Xiao Peng took out fifteen yuan which he had set aside to send to his wife and child, and looked for the old man they had just met. On seeing the money, the old man removed the flute from his mouth and said: 'Fifteen yuan, and you think you can buy my dog?'

'So how much do you want?'

'This dog of mine belongs to the god Erlang.'

'Never mind whose dog it is, are you selling or not? This boy of mine wants it – it's only worth a dogskin quilt for my bed.'

'This dog is worth more than two girls who can sing and play flower drums.'

'Who's buying your girls?'

Duohe tugged his arm, pulling him away.

'Fifteen yuan? That's not even enough for a dogskin quilt!'

Xiao Peng took out another five yuan from a different pocket. He had bought two months' worth of meal coupons for eight yuan, all he had left was this five yuan.

'Twenty?' The old man looked at Xiao Peng's pocket, considering whether he could wring any more profit from it.

'Don't push your luck. Twenty yuan can buy one hundred kilos of rice!' Xiao Peng said.

'We don't eat rice,' the old man said.

Duohe's hand continued to tug at his arm. Even once she had pulled him away, her hand still lingered. Erhai was lying in a despairing heap on the ground in a puddle of rainwater, pounding his fists and drumming his feet, shouting: 'I want the *inu*!' over and over again.

Xiao Peng asked Dahai: 'What's an *inu*?'

Dahai said: 'Dog, of course.'

Duohe said something quietly to Erhai, which sounded like coaxing mingled with threats, but Xiao Peng did not understand her words. After a while of this, she looked at Xiao Peng with a wry face, as if to say: 'See what you've started.'

Xiao Peng shot into the department store and bought four sweets, ran out and gave them to Dahai and Erhai, and also promised Erhai that he would definitely buy him that black dog. At the beginning of September, Xiao Peng bought a black puppy in the outskirts of the city and kept it in the dormitory while he trained it to stand, sit and carry a hat in its mouth. His three room-mates became fed up with it, and threatened to put the dog in a stew, and Xiao Peng along with it. By the end of the year, the black puppy had grown as big as the flower-drum beggars' dog. He got on his bicycle, leading the dog, and arrived in triumph at the Zhang home.

The family were eating supper. They had put a coal stove in the corridor, and on it sat an iron pot, with tofu and preserved vegetables bubbling away inside. People were clustered all around it, adults sitting, children standing, all eating until their eyes and noses were streaming. Xiao Shi was sitting beside Duohe, adding a green-bean cake to the mix.

Xiaohuan pointed to Xiao Peng, saying, 'Who's this person? Do we know him?'

Xiao Peng moved aside, to reveal the dog that was following him.

Erhai threw down his chopsticks and came running over, both arms outspread, then he knelt in front of the dog and hugged it close. Duohe and Xiao Peng exchanged glances.

Xiaohuan said: 'Aiyo, we don't see hide or hair of you for over a year, and now you come bringing meat? Perfect, dogmeat to eat at the start of winter, and a dogskin quilt thrown in!'

Erhai grabbed a *mantou*, tore off half and held it out to the black dog. The dog did not move. Xiao Peng took the *mantou* from him, and presented it again, and only then did the dog eat. When it had finished, Xiao Peng told it to stand up, run in a circle, sit and beg. Erhai wanted to feed it another *mantou*, but Xiaohuan rapped on the pot with her chopsticks. 'We've only just started to get proper food for people to eat, and now we're feeding a dog?'

Duohe glanced at Xiao Peng. Xiao Peng knew that she wanted him to stand up for Erhai, and give him some support.

Zhang Jian finally opened his mouth. He said: 'We can't keep it.'

Xiaohuan added: 'There's no room. The twins are still sharing a bed with their auntie, they kick her black and blue in a single night! Even if we don't kill it, we'll have to give it away after a couple of days!'

'If anyone tries to kill my dog, they'll have to get past me first!' Erhai suddenly said, in a choked voice. He was down on one knee, shielding his dog's head with both hands.

Xiao Peng had never before noticed how wild this boy's eyes could be. He had observed his character, and how his passions were always more extreme than ordinary people; if he loved something he would bring such ardour to that love, if he hated something he hated with a scorching heat.

'Mummy, let's each of us have a mouthful less food,' Girlie said.

Only Dahai ate his dinner without a sound. He was a child that never gave them any worries; at most he would go to the neighbours to borrow a basketball, and bounce it up and down the communal walkway to hone his skills.

Xiaohuan came to a decision. They would keep the dog for now, and if they really could not cope they would give it back to Xiao Peng. Xiaohuan sent Xiao Peng to the kitchen to get himself a bowl and chopsticks. She added a big scoop of pork fat, and a generous pinch of salt.

After supper Xiao Peng and Xiao Shi cycled back to the dormitory together.

'What's all this? It's been over a year, and you start a second offensive?' Xiao Shi said.

'What about you then? General offensives without a pause, only they get beaten back every time.'

'Huh, you think she's that hard to get to grips with?'

Xiao Peng's heart skipped a beat. 'You haven't –'

'Her skin, her flesh, like flour for rice balls, delicate and sticky –'

Xiao Peng jumped off his bicycle to throttle Xiao Shi on the spot. 'You've touched her?' His voice did not change, but there was a stab of agony in his heart.

'Don't believe me? Try it yourself if you don't!'

'I tried ages ago!'

Xiao Shi rode the bike away with a rush, and then swerved violently back towards him, whistling as he went. The sound was piercing and sweet.

'Oh my . . . !' Xiao Shi said. 'That flavour . . . can I tell you? You've really tried?'

Xiao Peng did not dare to look in Xiao Shi's direction. As soon as he looked there would be trouble. He would knock him down with his bike, that short-arse with his doll's face, whom all women liked but none took seriously, and then he would find something to bash his brains out with. The railway line was just ten metres ahead of them, and the train was whistling as it rounded a bend a kilometre or two away: a heaven-sent opportunity for Xiao Peng to grind that doll's face into mincemeat. That bastard had got the upper hand; now even if Xiao Peng did get Duohe, he would only be catching Xiao Shi's dirty water a bit further downstream. Zhang Jian and Xiao Shi were both pissing on his head. And there he was, still hoping that the Great Leader Chairman Mao's hand and the sparks of iron that filled the sky might relieve his pain.

One clear autumn afternoon, Xiao Peng came to the road leading to Duohe's home. The great famine was over now, but the Zhang family's great famine had yet to be relieved. The two boys' capacity for food was astonishing, and while one was eating to grow taller, the other was eating to grow an ever wilder nature. So Duohe still had to go to the state-run vegetable market at the close of business to buy up pumpkins that were more than half soft, greenish potatoes and cabbages gnawed to nets by insects. Everyone knew her in the vegetable market, they could see that she was civilised and polite, never any shouting or fuss, and would keep back a pile of rubbish specially for her, which she would gather with a shovel into the wooden bucket she carried to sort through at her own pace. Xiao Peng followed her through that reeking market, and he saw her go into the butcher's shop where she added rubbish from the butcher's to the rubbish from the market: a handful of pork bones that had been shaved white. By the time she had walked out of the fishmonger's, a cloud of flies had started to pursue her, and there was not enough space on the wooden bucket for them all to alight, so they came to rest on Duohe's hair.

Now she was walking into a little restaurant, emerging moments later with a paper packet in her hands, from which oil was seeping. She had gathered up the leftovers and chewed bones from the restaurant, taking them back to feed Erhai's beloved black dog. The flies landed on her shoulders, and on her back.

She is such a clean, pretty, quietly elegant beggarwoman, he thought.

'Duohe.' Xiao Peng caught up with her as she came out of the eating house.

As soon as she saw him, she came running up, bringing with her a body's worth of flies. That there should be a woman anywhere in the world who knew so little of how to hide her happiness! Then came another deep, deep bow.

That little shit Xiao Shi, even he had got his hands on her. But he, Xiao Peng, with more compassion in his heart, had played his hand a step later, and all he got for his pains were leftovers.

How was Duohe to know that at this moment his heart was like an oil cake turning over and blistering in a wok of boiling oil, as she chattered and smiled in a way that made her seem not quite mistress of her tongue, about how Erhai adored the black dog and how touched she was by Xiao Peng's generosity? He felt that he was going through the motions with her: A dog? Just a small thing, hardly worth mentioning! She continued to chatter away, thanking him for understanding the child – Erhai was very unhappy.

Erhai was unhappy? Now that she had pointed it out, he could see that this was the case. When he'd fallen from the fourth floor three years ago, he hadn't damaged so much as a hair on his body, but his joy had been lost as he fell. So Duohe's sudden warmth towards him, quite the reverse of her usual silence, nattering on at him in a display of friendliness in her odd language, was all because of Erhai. Xiao Peng would never be able to guess who Duohe was close to, or why, and the more he was unable to guess, the less he could bear to accept it; the less he could bear it, the more pressing he became in his pursuit, and the more neurotic he became towards her as a result.

'I just came to tell you that I'll be waiting for you here tomorrow,' Xiao Peng said.

Duohe's smiling face stretched forward briefly, then pulled back again.

'You owe me a film.' Xiao Peng's face was stern and blank, giving her nothing to guess at, and nothing to escape from. 'You must come and see a film with me.'

Two gleaming circles of tears formed once again in her black, limpid eyes, which moved back and forth.

Damn it all, this woman was really cheap! Treat her properly, like a decent human being, take her somewhere as elegant as a cinema, and she felt so hard done by as to shed tears. If that low-down wretch Xiao Shi had lured her into his dog kennel, kneading her like glutinous rice cakes, then she should let him have a knead too.

'Are you and Xiao Shi courting?'

Her eyebrows wrinkled, her gaze focused on something, her lips slightly parting and coming together. It was like she was silently turning his words over in her mind. Her eyebrows suddenly shot up, and the two glistening circles of tears promptly disappeared. She said over and over again: 'I didn't!'

'What's wrong with courting?'

'I didn't!'

'He's told me everything.'

She looked at him. He could feel Girlie, Dahai and Erhai all surveying him through her eyes, to see when he would let down his guard and burst out laughing, bringing this joke to an end.

There was no need to say anything more now. Xiao Shi had been having him on: Duohe was blameless where Xiao Shi was concerned. And Xiao Peng cared about this blamelessness, even though he was not planning on marrying her, which made his infatuation with Duohe still harder to explain. There were a dozen or so top technicians, and he was the one with the most potential to be groomed for leadership: because his family had been poor peasants for several generations, he was a Party member, and he had represented the technicians when he had gone with Chairman Mao to the mouth of the furnace. What reason did he have to be so hung up on a woman like Duohe who couldn't even speak properly?

The following afternoon Duohe came to the cinema. She had deliberately done herself up, her hair washed until it gleamed, and wearing a pleated cotton skirt with a round-necked knitted cotton top. The top had been dyed black, and a cord threaded through the neck, with a pompom dangling from each end. The skirt was a black-and-white check. Duohe did not have Xiaohuan's alluring waist, full of charms both in motion and repose; her figure had no obvious curves or straight lines, she was all vague transitions. Viewed from behind she appeared thoroughly clumsy and dull. However you looked at it, there was no way she could be Xiaohuan's little sister.

So who was that woman called Zhu Duohe really?

At the door to the cinema, Xiao Peng pointed to an enormous poster and told her: This is a new film, it's called *Bitter Flower*, they say it is full of 'fight'. 'Fight' was the word young workers used to describe intense war films.

Duohe's expression changed, becoming extremely anxious, as she looked from one film still to the next. Finally she stared at the picture of a Japanese Army officer for a very long time.

In the cinema Xiao Peng found himself in an awkward predicament: Duohe's hands were clasped together in front of her chest, and he could hardly touch her bosom in order to steal a hand away. She seemed to have immersed herself completely in the film: when the plot and music reached a moment of crying or shouting, she came close to crying and shouting too. Xiao Peng was about to make a move and take that hand which was blocking her mouth. This was a good opportunity: the woman was heartbroken, so he could enfold her in his arms as naturally as water flowing downhill, and let her give way to her heartbreak in comfort. Without this step, none of the other steps could be taken. Xiao Peng was getting ready to brace himself, Do it!, when he suddenly heard Duohe say something. He pricked up his ears, and heard her say another word. As though she were copying the Jap devils in the film and speaking Japanese. No, it sounded more like she was correcting their language. Perhaps it was neither of those things, and she was speaking without meaning to. A Japanese word. An authentic, fluent Japanese word.

Duohe was Japanese. Duohe? He should have guessed long ago that this was no Chinese name.

Xiao Peng's deduction gave him such a fright that he sat there paralysed. How could Zhang Jian and his family ever have had the nerve? Harbouring a Japanese woman, for more than ten years, and giving birth to a litter of Jap whelps. Take a look at the Japanese people on the screen – could you call them human? They were devils, gabbling away in their strange language, killing without batting an eyelid.

His hand, which had been itching throughout, was paralysed too, and lay flaccid on his thighs, as his sweat slowly seeped into the legs of his work trousers. Why did Duohe have to be Japanese? Anything else would have been fine. He, Xiao Peng, was sitting with a Japanese woman in a dark cinema watching a film, about to knead her hand with the hand that had shaken the Great Leader's?

When he and Duohe left the cinema, he slowed and followed behind her. He saw clearly that beneath her peculiar surface layer a Japanese woman was concealed; in fact there was nothing peculiar about it now. She came from the same stock as the Jap devils in the film. Xiao Peng understood the mystery surrounding Duohe now: no matter how polite and reserved she was, there was also a part of her that could never be tamed. No matter how earnestly she smiled, there was something unnatural about it. And this lack of fluency showed through in Erhai: his cold, cold ardour, his listless obstinacy, his barbarian affection and rage towards certain people and certain things, this was where they came from.

Outside it was getting dark, a drizzly autumn dusk, a clichéd kind of weather suitable for lovers. Xiao Peng led Duohe through the drizzle to his dormitory. His room-mate was cooking a meal for himself on a kerosene stove in the corridor, but as soon as he saw that Xiao Peng had brought back a woman, he hastily said that he would go to a fellow Sichuaner's dormitory to have his meal there.

Xiao Peng asked Duohe to sit down at his desk, and found a few film magazines for her. Then he brewed her some tea. The water in the Thermos was not particularly hot, and the tea leaves clogged up the mouth of the cup like floating rubbish.

'You're not Chinese, are you?' He gave her a look. That same look fell on the dirty socks his room-mate had left soaking in the washbasin.

But Duohe did not turn pale with fright as he had predicted. A Japanese woman in hiding whose secret had been exposed, he would have thought she would be on her knees in front of him begging for mercy.

'I found out a long time ago,' Xiao Peng said.

Duohe put the cup down on the desk, and smoothed the creases on her skirt.

Xiao Peng thought, What is she thinking? Does she assume she can avoid the question and that'll be the end of the matter? Will I let her off as lightly as that?

'How did you come to stay behind in China?'

Her lips repeated his words silently for a moment, making sure she had understood.

'Sold.' Her simple, direct response once again was far from what he had anticipated.

He saw her eyes start to glitter again, without any attempt at disguise. Don't cry, don't play games with my heart, Xiao Peng silently reproached her.

With the greatest of difficulty, she began. She would come out with a sentence and then halt; sometimes she could not get her intonation right, and had to try again using different tones, until she saw a flash of understanding on Xiao Peng's face, at which point she could continue. She gave the bare bones of the story, everywhere there were gaps, but Xiao Peng was still stunned by what he heard. Three thousand refugees, women and children, blood all the way, dropping dead, death and cruelty to themselves and each other, it did not seem like a story of human beings. And what human could bear to go on listening to it?

And Duohe was the one who had survived this great calamity.

Xiao Peng had not known that his heart could ache over things that had nothing to do with him. Perhaps Zhang Jian and Xiaohuan had gone through the same kind of heartache?

Duohe got to her feet. Her bow was deep and prolonged, and he came over to stop her – this kind of bow was a flaw that could give her away, people might grope their way along this flaw, and finally destroy her. But his gesture of restraint changed halfway into a not particularly romantic embrace. As he held Duohe's slightly resisting body, he felt the pain recede a little. He gripped her more tightly, in order to make the pain in his heart clear up completely. If he could just avoid thinking about his own wife and child back home, or about Zhang Jian or Xiaohuan, he could be romantic.

He took Duohe back to the Zhang family's building on his bicycle. When they parted he said that he had always loved her, otherwise he would not have kept coming to this building. In the space of eight or nine years, how many ruts had the wheels of his bicycle made on this road from the factory? These ruts were the proof. He was afraid she did not understand this technical student's language of love, pedantic phrases from the printed page, spoken as slowly and effortfully as promises to love until the mountains crumbled and the seas ran dry.

Duohe understood. She bent double in another deep bow. He took a hasty step forward, and she just happened to straighten up at that moment, so that his hand connected with her face.

'I'm no Zhang Jian. You're not a slave to be a concubine for me or to give me children either, so don't do that.'

Duohe turned round and walked into the pitch-black stairwell.

He thought how he was a young man who had attended a high-level technical school, studied Russian, had spent time with the Great Leader, and despite the wife back home whom his aged parents had married him to, his relations with Duohe could nonetheless be very much part of the New Society. If all else failed, he would risk killing his old father with rage and his old mother with weeping, and put aside his country wife, who had been gone from his memories for some time.

He turned his face into the drizzle and headed towards the factory, pedalling his bicycle in the rhythm of a march. The wind grew stronger, the rain grew fiercer, and the rhythm of his pedalling changed to a sea shanty. Duohe had had three children – so what? She was quite a few years his senior – what of it? Everything that was out of the ordinary just made him prouder still, because only exceptional people could have an exceptional romance.

The factory lights in the rain appeared unusually bright. Every raindrop became a tiny lens, reflecting multiple images of the heavens and the earth, multiplying the light of the lamps countless times. Rain could only create this soft sound and atmosphere when falling on the hubbub of somewhere like the noisy factory area, just like Duohe's tears as they fell onto the broad embrace of that hard man Xiao Peng. With that boy's body that still lacked a man's final steadiness, Xiao Peng jumped off his bike, and stood in the bustling, busy, magnificent light of the lamps that stretched as far as the eye could see, standing in the slow rain of 1962 which had just left famine behind.

❖

The following day, Xiao Peng received a note from Zhang Jian. A slip of paper in Zhang Jian's forceful handwriting: '*Wait for me at lunch.*'

Just as Xiao Peng had expected, the first thing to come out of Zhang Jian's mouth was: 'How was the film?'

'Pretty good.' He stared at Zhang Jian: you dog fucker, are you trying to keep me under your thumb?

Zhang Jian walked towards the meeting room, a lunch box of rice piled with fried shallots in his hands. The room, full of piled-up stores and tools, only had two keys; one was for the section leader, the other for the group leader.

As soon as Xiao Peng entered he sat down on an empty oxygen cylinder. Otherwise Zhang Jian would have asked him to sit and he would have lost the upper hand.

But Zhang Jian remained standing, the man and his shadow towering above him. 'What are your plans for her?'

So this was going to be all interrogation, with one of them high and one low. Just as he went to stand up, Zhang Jian pushed him back again, telling him, 'Sit down to talk.'

'Can't say that I'm planning anything with her.'

In an instant Zhang Jian's face darkened. 'What else do you want to do?'

'Go to the pictures.'

After this all his awareness was centred on Zhang Jian's suede boot as it came hurtling towards him: the sole had parted company with the upper, and had been sewn back on, leaving a half-circle of brilliantly white new twine at the front of the sole, and the back heel was made of two black chunks of rubber tyre.

'What're you doing?!' The kick sent Xiao Peng rolling underneath the oxygen cylinder, his knees bent at an angle that fitted it exactly.

'What am I doing? Kicking you!' Zhang Jian said. 'If there's one thing I can't abide it's a man who shirks his responsibilities. You get together with her, that's fair enough, so go and get rid of that woman of yours back home.'

Xiao Peng discovered that Zhang Jian, who would not usually say boo to a goose, could speak pretty fluently and had plenty to say for himself. He was still more surprised to find that, for all he could spend a whole day without a word, he was able to worm out people's secrets like they were in the palm of his hand – how had he discovered the business of his wife and child back home?

'Then why don't you put aside Sister Xiaohuan?' Just as Xiao Peng was thinking of getting back up, Zhang Jian lashed out again with his foot.

'Donkey fucker – put *her* aside?'

There was no sense to his words, no logic of cause and effect, but his peremptory firmness left no room for argument, and Xiao Peng felt that he had lost another round in the debate.

'If you can't put aside your wife, then you put an end to it right here and now, don't ruin her.'

'What gave *you* the right to ruin her?'

Zhang Jian was at the door, his hand already on the lock. He played deaf again to Xiao Peng's fatal question.

Xiao Peng was in so much pain that he could not stand up. He thought that he should expose Zhang Jian and be done with it, let the Public Security Bureau take him away for a bigamist. But then Duohe would be taken too, and vanish from this place forever. In the heart of the twenty-eight-year-old besotted lover Xiao Peng, all the world could vanish, so long as Duohe did not disappear.

From then on, whenever he had spare time he would lurk at the foot of the Zhang family's building. Occasionally Erhai would come out with his black dog, and he would ask the boy a few questions about how his auntie was getting on. Erhai's black eyes would look him up and down without blinking, and once Xiao Peng did something that he immediately cursed himself for: he took Erhai in his arms, and kissed him on his eyes.

By the time he had mounted his bicycle and fled the scene, still reproaching himself bitterly, tears were flowing. He, Xiao Peng, was part of the first group of technicians trained up by the New China, and now what demon was tormenting him into this state?

After he had suffered this lack of control with Erhai, Xiao Peng, filled with self-loathing, had a struggle with his conscience. He had to make a final decision: either go home to put aside his wife (sending her fifteen yuan a month just as before) and marry Duohe, or else forget completely the good times he had spent in Zhang Jian's home for the last eight years.

That day in the factory, Xiao Peng walked between the lights from the spot welding and oxyacetylene torches. A face appeared from behind a welder's shield, then immediately hid again behind the mask. Like he could hide his whole body behind a face shield. Xiao Shi was hiding from him. He moved on several paces; on the criss-crossing rail tracks of the iron foundry trains were coming and going carrying steel ingots. Xiao Peng thought, how could heaven be sending him such enlightenment: it was clearly Xiao Shi, who had been like a brother to him, who had told his secret! He was jealous of Xiao Peng and Duohe; he had prised out the secret of Xiao Peng's wife and child back home in the North-east, and had told Zhang Jian.

He waited until a train had passed, and stormed over the tracks. Xiao Shi had just finished a job, and was knocking fragments of waste away with a hammer, when Xiao Peng walked up and said: 'I'll give you hunger, you little bastard! No way is that flesh like sticky rice balls; it's like pig's lard that's been melted and then set again, it melts at the touch of your tongue!'

Xiao Shi continued to put on his air of total indifference, shaking and swaying his head and smiling.

'Did you tell the secret? Do you even know what a secret is? She told all of her secrets to me!' Xiao Peng was walking on the sheet iron, and the noise was deafening.

'What secret?'

'I wouldn't tell you, not even for ten big packs of Da Qian Men cigarettes, that's how secret it is!'

'Oh, *that* secret. Of course . . .' Xiao Shi looked around him. There was an ear-splitting racket of metal hitting metal, to which was frequently added the noise of the trains in the factory as they went past, and the whistles of the cranes. Even if they had been yelling at the tops of their voices, the people next to them would still not have been able to hear.

'What secret do you know?' Xiao Peng was fully alert now, and he stared at Xiao Shi.

'You've only just found out about that secret now? I've known for ages, from that year and more when you weren't visiting Zhang Jian's!'

So this woman had been confiding her life's history of blood and tears to everyone, and Xiao Peng had never received any special treatment. He was overwhelmed for a moment by a feeling that he had been snubbed. Xiao Peng thought how his ardour had been so foolish. Xiao Shi and Zhang Jian must have been laughing themselves sick behind his back.

He sat down on the railway tracks, pondering his role as a romantic clown, a tragic loser. Perhaps he was the only one whose heart had broken over Duohe's life story. He had become a laughing stock.

Everywhere there was a confusion of glaringly bright welding torches; the sound of metal beating on metal was more powerful and magnificent than a thousand drums and gongs. In the middle of the New Society, Xiao Peng sat curled in on himself, heartbroken, at the intersection of several rail tracks. Everyone was celebrating as if for a festival amid the fireworks of the sparks of the welding and the drums and gongs of iron and steel, but Xiao Peng the laughing stock sat there, with no sense of north, south, east or west, and with no idea of his next step.

The clanging sounds of the metal were beating against his heart, lungs, liver and guts, his spine and his skull. The sounds belonged to an age of greatness, to an age where magnificent festivals were everywhere to be found. Suddenly several wagons came reversing over the rails. Xiao Peng got to his feet, intending to cross over to the other side of the railway, to get out of their way.

But someone grabbed hold of him.

'Where are you going, you bastard? Tired of living?' Xiao Shi pointed to a train coming from the other end, which at that moment was intersecting with the reversing wagons.

If Xiao Peng had crossed to the other side of the track, he would have been squashed dead by the train: he had come very close to being ground into sausage meat beneath its wheels.

'Bloody hell,' he murmured, brushing aside Xiao Shi's hand. Brotherly feelings like his and Xiao Shi's did not allow for tears of gratitude.

'I thought there was something wrong with you, sitting there like you were sick!' Xiao Shi said, following after him. 'You were going to lie down on the railway line for a woman? That's a bit much, don't you think?'

'To hell with your bit much! Piss off!'

Xiao Shi knew he was grateful: in that moment he had not only hauled back Xiao Peng's life, he had also recovered his soul.

In the evening the two of them went to the public baths. As they came out Xiao Shi said that he was going to take some pork to Zhang Jian's family. A pig had died at the canteen, and all the meat had been handed out for free to the workers. He had grabbed a portion, to give to the kids to take the edge off their hunger.

'Can you give the children meat from a sick pig?'

'Oh, you just boil it a bit longer! Nobody's going to die of poison from that!'

'Look, the meat's gone blue, the blood's all blocked up inside. It looks horrible – and absolutely filthy!'

'Don't eat the blue bits then, it'll be fine! When the Jap devils were starving, they ate blue meat too. They ate raw sweetcorn and raw sorghum, they fished out worms from the rivers and ditches and put them straight into their mouths!'

'Did Duohe tell you that?' Xiao Peng asked. Duohe had told him that she had eaten worms on the road when she was a refugee.

Xiao Shi was struck dumb for a moment. The two of them stood there in the early-winter evening, moisture steaming from their freshly washed hair.

'She told you too?' Xiao Shi said.

'If you hadn't heard her tell of those miserable things, you'd think that all Japanese grew up drinking wolves' milk. And that Japanese women were all female wolves, who raised those monsters to murder, loot and destroy. I used to . . . to her . . . well, never mind. Once I'd heard her talking about those awful things, I really didn't want to hurt her any more.'

Xiao Shi listened in silence. After a while he opened his mouth to say in a casual voice, 'How come she didn't go back to Japan?'

'She doesn't have anyone in Japan.'

'Then how come we didn't lock her up here in China? There's loads of Japanese spies – haven't they all been rounded up?'

In an instant, Xiao Peng freed himself from his melancholy, romantic feelings, took a breath, and saw this short man for what he really was. He'd been had. The short-arse had tricked Duohe's story out of him.

You're swindling me, you sod! Xiao Peng thought.

Xiao Shi was laughing heartily. He struck up a defensive posture, and retreated out of reach of Xiao Peng's violent attack. 'You tell me how soft she is? Japanese tofu?'

'Bastard!'

'So what if I am? Bastards can tell the difference between their own people and the enemy.' He was prancing and throwing punches like a monkey, three paces away, 'It takes a bastard with patriotic feeling not to eat Japanese tofu.'

'You've got fuck-all patriotic feeling!'

'And you don't even have that much!'

Xiao Peng knew that the more Xiao Shi teased the more carried away he would become; all he could do was put his towel on his head and return to the dormitory on his own. By the time he was opening the door to his room, he could hear Xiao Shi's whistle echoing in the dark stairwell. There would be no peace for Xiao Peng that evening until Xiao Shi had learned everything there was to know about Duohe.

In the end the pair of them ate the blue meat. They borrowed a kerosene stove, scrubbed out a washbasin and stewed up a meaty soup. With six ounces of spirits, to wash down Duohe's cruel history. They kept drinking until Xiao Shi threw up all over Xiao Peng's bed, and no sooner had Xiao Peng cleaned up the mess than Xiao Shi had crawled onto his Sichuan room-mate's bed and vomited all over that too. Xiao Peng tended to Xiao Shi, cursing him for a 'bastard' with every breath, thinking to himself that this bastard had been shaken when he heard the story too, shaken until every organ in his body was turned upside down.

9

A heavy snowfall was a one in a thousand years' event in these parts. Xiaohuan leaned on the balcony railing and looked on, spellbound. The pine trees on the mountains had all turned white, and at first glance it might have been that mountain slope in the Zhu family village. She had gathered pine cones and picked hawthorn berries and wild grapes on that mountain since she was old enough to walk; she had lain on her stomach with her father in the snow, waiting for a fox to come out of its hole. The snow of China's North-east was wonderful stuff, it was warm, and when her father had built her a den, it had been so cosy inside. Since her parents had been classified as Rich Peasants in the Land Reform, she had only gone back to Zhujiatun twice in all these years, once for her father's death, once for her mother's. Her mother had said in the last few days of her illness that her eldest girl Zhu Xiaohuan was the one it hurt the most to leave behind, she had been spoiled by her in-laws and her husband until there was no doing anything with her, and what would become of her in old age? When all was said and done the children were not her flesh and blood; when they knew the true state of affairs, what kind of old age would Xiaohuan have at their hands? Her mother left reluctantly, her mind full of worries and concerns.

This was a fine, cheerful fall of snow, burying the filthy rubbish, and the racket from family quarrels and the loudspeakers that battered constantly against the ears. The children did not yet know that their block of flats was covered by heavy snow, as they were sound asleep. Xiaohuan hardly ever gave in to sentimentality like this, but now a powerful wave of nostalgia suddenly hit her. On her deathbed her mother had asked: Are the children close to you? Do they believe that you are their real mother? Is that Jap woman stirring up the children behind your back, driving a wedge between them and you? Xiaohuan told her mother to go in peace, Xiaohuan and Xiaohuan alone had the whip hand of the lot of them, children and adults alike. Her mother knew that her oldest daughter had become too accustomed to having the upper hand, and at one time this had worried her, but just before she closed her eyes, it was this flaw of Xiaohuan's that eased her mind the most.

In fact when she was having her last talk with her mother, Xiaohuan's confidence was just a front. The children had never suspected who their birth mother was, coming home from school they would still call 'Ma, Ma' as they came in through the door. 'Ma, I'm starving to death!' 'Ma, I'm bursting for a pee!' 'Ma, Erhai's been fighting again!' 'Ma, let me tell you something, I laughed myself silly . . .' Xiaohuan would reply: 'Starving to death? There's no point in feeding someone who's starved to death, he's already dead!' 'If you're desperate for a pee can't you go at school? Are you saving up fertiliser for home?' But they were getting bigger every day.

From a young age, Xiaohuan had been an avid collector of ghost stories. On Saturday evenings when Zhang Jian was on the night shift, they would all snuggle up to her, listening to her spooky tales, never the same one twice. The children were not only close to her, they admired her: because of Xiaohuan no one had ever picked on them, for fear that she would go storming and swearing to their door, cursing so vilely that they would have to escape out of the back window. Xiaohuan had a far-reaching network of contacts, she had friends in each of the dependants' residential blocks, so there was no way she could lose. The children were proud of her too; every time there was a parent–teacher meeting, Xiaohuan put on a frock – the only one she possessed – combed her permed hair into layers of waves, and wore a watch bought at a second-hand stall. Their classmates would say: 'Your mum's like someone from a Huangmei opera troupe' – the children's highest standard of beauty – or 'How much did your mum's watch cost?' The children were always very proud, and never let slip that their mother's gold watch did not actually work.

Of all the children, it was Girlie that Xiaohuan loved the best. Girlie was fifteen now, and could read people's expressions very well; Xiaohuan only had to be a little upset, and she would always ask quietly: 'Ma, who's made you cross? Ma, have you got a stomach ache again?'

Inside the flat, the radio started up. The first thing Zhang Jian did on waking was to turn on the radio. This new habit had replaced his former one of having a smoke on waking. During the three years of famine Zhang Jian had given up his bad habits of former years: namely smoking and drinking. He had had a pay rise the previous year, and immediately bought a radio.

When Xiaohuan came back after her father's funeral, Duohe and Zhang Jian noticed her making secret enquiries, in an attempt to ferret out any sign of the old flame reigniting. She would ask the children with feigned casualness, Did your auntie sleep with you every night? The look in her eye finally started to get on Zhang Jian's nerves, he told her that he just wanted the family to live their days out in peace together, beyond this, his heart was dead as a pool of stagnant water. Was she satisfied now? Did that put her mind at rest? Next time she went back to Zhujiatun there'd be no need to enlist the children as spies. Zhang Jian's unlucky words were soon fulfilled; two months after her father's death, Xiaohuan's mother took to her bed with her final illness. On her second return home, Xiaohuan saw that new arrangements had been made in the flat: Zhang Jian and his two sons were sleeping in the big room, while Duohe, Xiaohuan and Girlie had the small room. Xiaohuan asked Zhang Jian, What did you go and move everything about for? He said with a smile that from that day forth they would be divided into male and female dormitories, nobody need harbour dire suspicions of anybody else.

The song from the radio woke the whole family. The children ran to the balcony in their shirts, scooped up handfuls of snow, squeezed them into snowballs and threw them at each other in the room. Afterwards they ran out again to pick up more snow. Xiaohuan was shouting: If you're not wearing your padded coat you're not to go on the balcony!

Duohe said a few words to Dahai and Erhai in a low voice. The boys gave a cheer, and went to whisper to Girlie, who also started cheering. Girlie was starting to get curves in all the right places, but when she was in one of her crazy moods it was like she was six or seven years old again. There was a Japanese word in the sentence they were whispering, the word for glutinous rice balls with red-bean filling. Yesterday evening Duohe had spent several hours making two big steamers of rice balls. There was no granulated sugar in the shops, so Duohe had used blocks of low-quality brown Cuban sugar and saccharine pills for the red-bean paste filling. Whenever someone bit into a rice ball she tensed up, saying, 'Not good, better to be a bit sweeter.'

Whenever Duohe made a lot of dumplings, Xiaohuan would put a few on a tray to take to the neighbours' homes, so they could try her sister's handiwork. Duohe also cooked shrimps or fish in soy sauce, or cicada grubs the children had dug up: this little dish was a speciality of Shironami village. Xiaohuan would take these to the neighbours too, one dish for every family, a diplomatic strategy that always stood her in good stead, upstairs and down.

Erhai ate and ate and suddenly said: 'Save one for Uncle Peng.'

'Uncle Peng isn't coming,' Xiaohuan said. 'You have it.' Xiao Peng had not come for a long time. It was Xiao Shi who was still their guest at weekends.

Every time Xiao Shi came by now, he was always rather sneaky and furtive. What did he take Xiaohuan for? From the very beginning it had been clear to her what Xiao Shi and Xiao Peng had in mind. The pair of them could see Duohe, keeping herself pure, neither girl nor wife, and were overcome with outrage on her behalf, they both wanted Duohe to lose her purity at their hands. Xiao Shi had even stopped all his japes recently; every time he came he would bring a bag of crispy walnut biscuits, or some sesame oil, or four pig's trotters. Although Level Four Worker Xiao Shi had no family to keep, no parents or children, if he kept on coming to the Zhang family to play the rich uncle he would end up a pauper. One time, Duohe was scrubbing the floor, and Xiao Shi was staring in a trance at her bottom. Xiaohuan saw the blue veins in Zhang Jian's hands bulge out. Zhang Jian's precious darling was being stripped naked by a pair of dirty eyes. From that moment on Xiaohuan understood a great many things, that the time Zhang Jian and Duohe had shared could not be broken off, the feelings had just been set aside. Perhaps it had been wrong to cut it off while it was still alive, for that had helped it put down roots. As with all children's games, you should never stop while there is still life in it, it had started out as just a game, born of itself and destroying itself, but once you broke it off there would be pain, and it would become something that never changed until death. Xiaohuan could see through most human behaviour, but she had missed her step in the matter of Zhang Jian and Duohe. On seeing the back of Zhang Jian's hands as they held the newspaper, those veins standing out like tree branches, she got up, walked in front of Duohe, and found an excuse to send her out of the house. Xiaohuan took over the scrubbing brush, squatted down and scrubbed with a harsh scraping sound. In all these years, the Zhang family, young and old, had come to feel that the noise of that coarse brush on wet concrete was mellow and pleasing to the ear. Xiaohuan wondered if that floor was no longer scrubbed to a mirror-like smoothness, if the clothes were no longer ironed smooth, and those shrimps, whitebait and cicada grubs in soy sauce and red-bean paste dumplings were gone, whether the Zhang family could carry on living. Duohe had told Xiaohuan in fits and starts about her childhood and youth: Sakito and Shironami villages, flowering cherry trees, the Shinto temple; she had spoken many times of her mother, and of how the thing that the children saw most was her bent back: scrubbing floors, washing and ironing clothes, praying to the gods, bowing to her seniors, her husband and son . . . In the course of more than ten years, Duohe had brought the villages into their home, one piece at a time.

When breakfast was over, the children took the black dog out on the lead to play in the snow. Girlie had arranged with a few of the girls in her class to go together to watch the People's Liberation Army military skills competition – which was going ahead despite the heavy snowfall. Zhang Jian had changed onto the night shift, he could not sleep during the day, so he picked up some woodwork he had started earlier. He was making a desk for Dahai and Erhai.

A whistle sounded at the foot of the building. It was the little truck from the coal shop with a delivery of coal. Zhang Jian and Duohe collected baskets and buckets and ran downstairs, where they saw that Xiao Shi had just arrived, and had already taken off his padded jacket, borrowed an old iron bucket from a neighbour and started to fill it with coal.

The children in the block all gathered up buckets and basins to help the Zhang family carry coal. In this building, if any family had a delivery of coal, all the children would pitch in and help, and afterwards they would say to the grown-ups: 'This is what Uncle Lei Feng has taught us!' Then they would proceed to write letters about each other to the teacher, praising classmate so-and-so for learning from the selfless young soldier Lei Feng's example and helping the neighbours with their coal. The stairs were covered in dropped fragments, children were colliding with each other in the rush up and down the stairs, and slipping over them, until they were all human-shaped lumps of coal themselves.

Finally Duohe slipped and fell too. Xiao Shi hurriedly put down his coal bucket and helped her up. They were on the second floor, and the children were all drinking sugar water made by Xiaohuan. Xiao Shi's back was facing the stairs to the third floor. Suddenly, he kissed Duohe.

Duohe stared at him in surprise. She had hurt her knees in the fall, but now she promptly recovered, and she scurried straight down the staircase. Xiao Shi chased after her, put his arms round her waist from behind, and his mouth came up again. Duohe was just about to call out, when Xiao Shi said: 'Shout, if you dare! If you shout I'll shout too, I'll shout *catch the Jap devil*!'

Duohe was looking at his doll's face, but after ten years of looking at him, she could not tell whether he was really cunning and treacherous or just joking.

Xiao Shi took another mouthful of this Japanese delicacy. 'You're coming with me to the factory this afternoon.'

She did not move an inch, or react in any way.

'Or else I'll report on your relationship with Zhang Jian.'

Duohe's lips were moving slightly; Xiao Shi heard her repeating almost soundlessly '*report, re . . . port*'.

'Don't you understand *report*? Don't you Japanese report on people? We Chinese can't get enough of it. Especially when we're reporting Jap devils.'

Duohe nodded her head. She grasped what he meant, even though she did not fully understand any of the individual words.

'You Jap devils caused enough destruction and havoc in China, so now I'm taking revenge for them.'

Duohe was still looking at him. The corners of his mouth continued to twitch, as if he was teasing her, and also like he was threatening her again.

'How about it, Jap devil? Are you going with me or not?'

'Where d'you want her to go?' Xiaohuan's voice came floating down the stairwell as she came towards them. In fact she had been listening for some time.

'Aiyo, Sister Xiaohuan, what're you doing downstairs? Quick, don't you go getting your hands dirty!' Xiao Shi said.

'Where are you taking my sister off to?'

'I was just having a laugh!'

'Talk of Jap devils is no laughing matter.'

Xiao Shi sniffed, and shifted his feet, afraid that he would get frozen into a stalemate.

'Xiao Shi, that's enough carrying for now. Go and do something for your big sister.'

'What shall I do?' Xiao Shi had an opportunity to get on Xiaohuan's good side.

'Go and find Xiao Peng and bring him over. Such lovely snow, and in a while I'll make something nice to eat for you three brothers, and you can drink some wine.'

Duohe was looking at Xiaohuan. Xiaohuan whipped off the apron from her waist, and tried to dust off the two coal-black handprints on Duohe's clothing. Nothing she did could get it clean. Xiaohuan smiled and shook her head.

Xiaohuan said nothing to Zhang Jian when they went back upstairs. She got rid of the children, then fished out a couple of pickled cabbages from the earthenware pots on the balcony, and put on half a kilo of bean noodles to soak. The skins of the shallots had dried, leaving them soft as water and white as jade inside, so she chopped up a big plateful, and fried them up with eggs. She had dried aubergines and beans in their pods that autumn, and these went into a pot of red-cooked pork. By the time Xiao Peng arrived with Xiao Shi, three big dishes were already on the table.

Zhang Jian smelled a rat: Xiao Peng had apparently cut himself off from this family without trace (of course he was the only one who knew just how this had come about), and now he had suddenly come back. It would seem that there was a fragile side to Xiao Peng's character, he would hide himself away without a word, slowly licking his wounds, and not return until he had more or less finished licking. He made no great show of enthusiasm on greeting either of his guests, so that Xiao Peng would not feel that there had been a year-long gap in their relationship.

Xiao Peng told Duohe to sit down, but Duohe refused point-blank. A year earlier she had told Zhang Jian how Xiao Peng had taken her to the pictures, and Zhang Jian had wept. She remembered how he had squatted down, just the same way his father Stationmaster Zhang used to squat in the winter sunlight, his tears pattering on the ground. She did not know why, but as soon as she thought of him squatting there, forearms resting on his thighs, comfortably crouched there, solid and secure as his tears fell, she thought she had been wrong to blame him for anything. He had always had a deep-seated and long-lasting feeling for her, one that was without embraces, without kissing, without lovemaking. Sometimes Xiao Peng made her feel that it might be possible to forget Zhang Jian, that she might be able to find a different kind of happiness with him, but Zhang Jian squatting and shedding tears had shown her that it was impossible. When a man's teardrops fell on the ground, fast and hard, any woman would love him for his stubborn way of loving her. This was the reason why she was not willing to sit down with Xiao Peng.

Xiaohuan jabbed a finger at her head, saying in a light voice: 'Silly goose! It's not like we're stuffing you in a sack for the pair of them to pick up and bolt with – what're you afraid of?'

She could not persuade Duohe, so she left her there in the smaller room. Xiao Peng looked at that grey door, drank a mouthful of spirits and looked at the door again. He stared until it was ready to dissolve into cold, grey water with the strength of his longing. Xiaohuan thought that Xiao Peng and Xiao Shi went about their love affairs in such different ways; Xiao Peng would never corner Duohe on the stairs, or grab her with a pair of coal-blackened paws.

Xiaohuan poured out the wine, and filled everyone's bowls with food. Xiao Shi's mouth was never still, mimicking the Shanghai dependants' stinginess and formality, the way in which when offered oranges to eat they would politely decline each segment in turn: *Don't be polite, try some orange! Have some, do! I've peeled them all ready for you!. . . Help yourself, please help yourself!* All this fuss and palaver over a segment of orange! And when they've finished one segment, here comes the next one: *Don't be polite, have some orange!* He had both Xiaohuan and Zhang Jian chuckling along with him.

Xiao Peng drank two cups of wine, with a rather fierce look in his eyes. The food in front of him was piled high. Also imitating the Shanghai dependants, Xiaohuan took up a piece of meat in her chopsticks and thrust it towards Xiao Peng's mouth: 'Don't be polite! This pig was killed especially for you!'

Xiao Peng did not smile. He sullenly downed another mouthful of wine, put the cup straight down and said: 'Sister Xiaohuan, what have you brought us here to say?'

'Have something to eat first,' Xiaohuan said.

It was only then that Zhang Jian understood that it was Xiaohuan who had invited them over. He took a look at the two visitors, then at Xiaohuan, fearing that she would be unlikely to have anything good to say.

'Sister Xiaohuan, say it, we can eat again once you've spoken,' Xiao Peng said.

'Fair enough.' Xiaohuan was staring at her hands, as they shifted her chopsticks from left to right and back again. She was mentally beating gongs and drums to mark her entry onstage. She raised her head and quirked up the side of her mouth with the gold tooth, a charming and striking pose. 'You three buddies left for Ma'anshan together, on the same train. And at the station, Xiao Shi, your sister came to see you off. She told me your parents were dead, and she couldn't come south to take care of you, so I was to be your sister from then on. Do you still remember that, Xiao Shi?' Xiao Shi nodded his head. 'So, have I taken good care of you?' The two men nodded, more vehemently. 'Now both of you have come to know Duohe's life story, and you know Duohe's relationship with our Zhang family. You're our brothers, it was wrong of me to keep you in the dark, so take today's food and wine as an apology from me, Zhu Xiaohuan. Now there'll be no concealing of anything from anyone between the brothers. Isn't that right?'

The three men looked at her. Zhang Jian thought, That was rather prettily done.

'Since the three of you are brothers, and we've all opened our hearts to each other, from now on we mustn't go in for underhand tricks, or inform against each other, or anything of that sort. Still, there are blood brothers who fall out and become enemies. If you turn against us, Xiao Shi, and go and inform on us and destroy us, there's nothing we can do about it, isn't that right?'

'Hey, am I that kind of person?' Xiao Shi said indignantly.

'I know! I'm just using you as an example.'

Xiao Peng downed another two cups of spirits without a word.

'Xiao Peng, don't you go getting drunk!' Xiaohuan said. 'Aren't you working the night shift?'

'No,' Xiao Peng said, 'today I'm taking the night train.'

'Oh, where are you going?' Xiaohuan asked.

'I'm going to Shenyang on business. And I'm going home for a while since it's on my way.'

'And everyone's fine back home . . .?'

'Not fine at all. My dad's ordered me home, and he's going to beat me to death.'

'What for?'

'If he manages to beat me to death that'll be the end of it. If he doesn't then I'm going to get the divorce settled.' If he succeeded in getting a divorce he would continue to send maintenance money to his wife and child as before. He had taught himself Albanian, and he could teach evening classes at the technical school and earn a bit of extra income. As soon as he had finished speaking he stood up, and without giving any of them a chance to react, he was already over by the door. He said, as he put on his shoes: 'If I can't get a divorce, I won't see Duohe.'

Xiaohuan wrapped up two *mantou*, filled a lunch box with pork fried with dried aubergine and chased out after him. She had a sudden feeling of tenderness for this man: for more than a year he had been shut away who knows where beating himself up, so lovesick that his hair had started to go white.

'I wasn't getting at you just now,' said Xiaohuan.

He looked at her bitterly.

'Did you know that Xiao Shi was up to his tricks with Duohe?' She lowered her voice. 'If she didn't give him what he wanted, he was going to report her as a Japanese spy!'

Xiao Peng was struck dumb for a moment. Then he burped boozily, and raised his head to let the snowflakes fall on his face.

'That's him all over, not a serious bone in his body,' Xiao Peng said. 'He wouldn't turn her in.'

'And supposing he does?'

'I know him. You won't catch him doing anything if there's no advantage for him in it. If he turned her in, he wouldn't have anywhere to play Chase the Pig.'

'I heard him trying it on with my little sister with my own ears!'

'Don't worry.'

Xiao Peng pedalled away on his bicycle. The wheels sketched a huge S-shape, then on his way down the slope, he went head over heels, man and bike together, and Xiaohuan cried out and rushed down the hill after him, but he jumped back on and headed off into the distance, leaving a series of S-shaped trails behind him.

If people spend too much time together, it can be harmful in its own way, as unexpected variables can inexplicably arise. Xiao Peng's determination to pursue Duohe was one such variable. There seemed to be no malice in him, but Xiaohuan had no way of knowing whether there was evil concealed there. Nobody knew. Xiao Shi was different, his ill intentions had already revealed themselves. Xiaohuan couldn't say whether her heartfelt words, outwardly gentle but concealing a core of steel, had killed them off. Perhaps there was some great wilderness where no one was in charge, and where there might be a place for Duohe, Zhang Jian, Xiaohuan and the children to live out their lives, asking for nothing. Did this kind of wilderness exist? For the first time, Zhu Xiaohuan, who had loved noise and bustle all her life, found herself starting to detest them both. In these blocks of identical flats, dozens upon hundreds of them, all densely packed with windows and doors, everyone brought their noise and bustle into other people's lives. Your radio would sing into your neighbour's home, and when he flushed the toilet it would leak into your home. Carrying coal had become a source of noisy entertainment for dozens of kids too. Could they not have heard Girlie and her brothers' language, with its Japanese words mixed in? The children would often shout up and down the stairs: 'What's your family eating this evening?' 'We're having *baozi* dumplings!' What if Dahai and Erhai shouted back in reply: 'We're having *sikihan*'? From now on, slapdash Xiaohuan would be slapdash no longer, she would pay proper attention to the children's conversation. But wasn't it too late now? The snow had brought Xiaohuan a chilly clarity of mind.

She went back inside, to find Xiao Shi flat out on the bed, dead drunk. Zhang Jian exchanged a look with Xiaohuan; they had been thinking more or less the same thing just now. Both of them moved about stealthily, because neither could be certain whether Xiao Shi was truly drunk or putting on an act.

The door opened with a bang, and the two boys came running in, faces bright red. Xiaohuan bawled: 'Shoes off, shoes off!' She had become the sternest upholder of Duohe's rules. Xiaohuan put herself between the black dog and the inside, because he was covered in water and mud. As Xiaohuan was bending over to give wooden slippers to Dahai, the dog came in, and the first thing he did was to shake himself off, sending droplets of mud flying all over Xiaohuan.

Xiaohuan hauled the dog into the kitchen, dumped him in the sink, and turned on the tap to hose him down. Xiaohuan did not notice how vigorously she was defending the clean space that Duohe had created. The dog was big and the sink small, and one of his feet kicked out over the edge of the sink, and hit the balls of coal that had just been piled up so neatly. Xiaohuan, cursing, slapped the dog twice on his rump with the flat of her hand. Erhai came rushing in, wanting to snatch the dog away, but Xiaohuan pushed him outside. She put the dog back in the sink. The dog lost his temper in turn; the water was prickling his hair and skin like icy needles, he shouldn't have to put up with this any longer. He kicked and threw himself about like a mad thing, spraying a fountain of water black with coal dust onto the ceiling, spattering Xiaohuan's face, and falling into the leftover pickled cabbage and bean noodles in the pot, and into the stewed pork with dried aubergines in the basin.

Xiaohuan's brain was suddenly filled with darkness. She grabbed the dog's front paws and with flying speed carried him across the hallway and into the big room. Behind her, Erhai was shouting:

'What are you doing? What do you think you're doing?' Who could hold Xiaohuan back when the fit was on her? Xiao Shi had sobered up as well, and he went to restrain her, but she had already kicked open the door to the balcony, from where she flung the dog over the railing, and down to the ground.

Erhai hurled himself at her with a cry, grabbed hold of her hand and bit it.

The light came on in Xiaohuan's head, and at that moment she saw everything clearly: this was no son of hers. He did not take her for his real mother, perhaps he never had, because a child's instinct tells him that, no matter how wrong your true mother is, you can't sink your teeth into her like that. Zhang Jian and Duohe both came hurrying up, and saw that the ever-present pair of red circles on Xiaohuan's cheeks had disappeared, leaving her face the colour of wax. Erhai was lying on the floor, and his face was a waxy yellow too.

Xiaohuan knelt down and gently patted Erhai's arms and chest, but Erhai did not move or open his eyes; it was like he had fainted dead away. On Xiaohuan's wrist there was a purple blood bruise, surrounded by a circle of deep teeth marks, and she felt that the teeth marks in her heart were really very deep indeed, and the bruise there a blackish purple, deeper still. She was patting him, saying: 'My boy, Ma was wrong, wake up, quickly now! Ma has another arm, there, it's all yours! Have another bite! Wake up . . .'

Erhai really did appear to have fainted. Xiaohuan's tears were flowing across her face in all directions. Her mind was too unsettled today. That person who had thrown the dog down from the fourth floor was not her at all.

At that moment Dahai said: 'Blackie!'

They could hear Blackie's high-pitched whining outside the door.

This was the cry of a dog that had been wronged, accepted its fate and returned whimpering to its master.

They opened the door and, sure enough, it was Blackie. Just like Erhai, he had fallen from the same height, without harming a hair on his head. Uncertain of his welcome, he stood in the doorway with his head raised, weighing up every person in the family.

The sunshine returned to Erhai's face. Slowly, he sat up, turning towards the black dog. The dog, on the other hand, anxious at Erhai's appearance, cautiously walked closer to him, sniffed at his face, and rubbed himself against his head and licked his neck. It was only then that they noticed that the black dog's back leg was curled up. When he walked, his leg would touch the ground and shrink in, touch the ground and shrink away.

The black dog's broken bone would heal, but that hint of a limp remained. From that day onwards, Erhai never spoke to Xiaohuan. When communication became essential, he would speak through Girlie: 'Sis, you tell my mum that I don't want to wear that shirt, it makes me look like a hooligan,' or, 'Sis, get my mum to take Blackie for a walk, there's a school trip today and I won't be back until after dark.'

Xiaohuan thought that Erhai's temper must have been passed on into his blood from his uncle or his grandfather, or a great-grandfather on Duohe's side.

It'll all be better when Xiao Peng is here, Zhang Jian quietly comforted Xiaohuan: Erhai's bound to listen to Xiao Peng, because the black dog was a present from him.

But before Xiao Peng returned, Xiaohuan's misgivings were

confirmed. Zhang Jian was in trouble. He had been driving a crane carrying a piece of rolled steel, and it had lost its load, though the crane had been perfectly under control. Loads did occasionally come loose from their hook and fall, but it was a very rare occurrence. Zhang Jian was such a skilled crane operator, but there had been a terrible accident: the rolled steel had come crashing down and crushed a man to death. This man had been dragging an oxygen cylinder, in preparation to cut a piece of steel with a blowtorch: Fourth Grade Welder Shi Huicai.

When Xiao Peng returned to the factory, and heard that Xiao Shi had been killed by a piece of rolled steel from Zhang Jian's crane, his knees gave way.

Accidents happened, and Zhang Jian's explanation held water: Xiao Shi had suddenly emerged from behind a pile of rejected steel ingots, how could anyone have avoided him? But Zhang Jian was suspended from his work, and went home to await his punishment.

Xiao Peng felt that this whole business had become like a swamp of filthy mud; there was no longer any way to work out the rights and wrongs of it. He had endured a heavy beating from his father, and submitted the petition for divorce to the law court. When his wife heard that Xiao Peng would continue to send the maintenance just as before, not a penny less, she cried for a while and then agreed. But now he was free, Xiao Peng suddenly did not want to give up that freedom he had won. He suddenly became proud of his probity and self-control over this whole business with Duohe, Xiao Shi and Zhang Jian. It was a filthy swamp, and he was not about to go and roll in it.

Zhang Jian was back at work in the factory, having been demoted two grades to a common worker. If Xiao Peng saw him from a distance, he would go out of his way to avoid him.

One day he came out of the bathhouse, and saw Duohe's back in a crowd of female workers. These women carved Arabic numerals and Chinese characters such as 'Made in China' in a temporary shack made of matting. These would be stamped onto steel ingots, which were shipped to Vietnam, Albania and Africa.

He took several steps towards her, but in the end he came to a halt. The waters of that swamp were just too murky; once he set foot in it, would he be able to draw back again? He turned, and set off for the unmarried men's dormitory. Best to wait a while for the mud and sand to settle.

Just at that moment, Duohe felt a blast of heat from behind her. They were tapping out the steel again! Steel poured out at dusk was a scene that Duohe could never tire of watching. She stood there, looking up. The sky had become a golden-red colour, and she felt the air all around her twitch slightly, seeming to throb with a gigantic, invisible pulse. Slowly, she lowered her tired eyes, turned round and continued on her way. She had been so engrossed in watching the scene that she had failed to notice Xiao Peng walking away into the distance.

When Zhang Jian had been disciplined, his wages had been reduced by 30 per cent, and the family needed Duohe's temporary job in order to make ends meet. Cutting serial numbers was a technical job, and so beyond those rowdy, gossiping dependants; Duohe's colleagues now were young, single women, most of whom had been to middle school, not like those dependants, with their endless, persistent attempts to marry people off all day long. Duohe felt she was lucky to have been given this time of peace. She would bend over to cut a character or number, and when she had straightened up, an hour would have gone by. She could cut out seven or eight of these in a single day. Temporary workers got their wages once a week.

By the third week Duohe was earning half as much again as in her first week, because her daily rate of production had already risen to ten or more. Just as in the days when she had worked breaking ore, on returning home she would take the banknotes from the pocket of her work overalls and place them in Zhang Jian's hands.

The day of the accident, Duohe had been lighting the stove with Xiaohuan. Xiaohuan was very good at tending to stoves so that they would not go out once all winter. However, that day they had got up in the morning to find that the well-prepared stove had gone out. As they were cutting kindling and searching for waste paper, the two women saw Zhang Jian coming back. Xiaohuan thought the person following him looked familiar, and looked again: it was that official from the security office. The officer said briefly that someone had been crushed. Injured? Was it bad? Dead . . .?

Xiao Shi had died on the spot. Zhang Jian's white canvas overalls still bore the marks of Xiao Shi's bloodstains. He had taken him in his arms, calling out to him.

Duohe and Xiaohuan watched the security officer escort Zhang Jian into the big room. The neighbours were surrounding the Zhang flat in a half-circle, elbowing each other out of the way. The security officer told the two Zhang women that the factory was in a competition with brother factories, but they were bound to lose now: Zhang Jian's accident had lost them too many points.

'Did anybody see how that thing fell?' Xiaohuan asked.

'Only Xiao Shi and Zhang Jian. There aren't that many people about on the night shift in the first place,' the security officer said.

Zhang Jian had sat on the edge of the bed, one of his suede boots, trampled in machine oil and blood, pressing down on the other. Duohe knelt on the floor, and carefully undid the shoelaces made into dead knots by the blood.

Before the security officer had left he had spoken with Xiaohuan. Afterwards Xiaohuan passed on those words to Duohe: Keep an eye on Zhang Jian's emotions, try not to let him go out alone.

Zhang Jian had slept through the midday meal, and through supper as well. At midday on the second day, Xiaohuan carried a spring-onion pancake and a bowl of rice porridge into the big room, but he was still fast asleep. The children went in and out, heads down, the black dog had his tail between his legs and his tongue out, following the family throughout their funereal days. The children had heard classmates at school talking about how their father had crushed a man to death, news that was very soon supplemented by the neighbours' children: the man who had been crushed was their uncle, Xiao Shi, the one who often visited. Dahai did not want to go to school, because the other children in his class were avoiding him. In the past there had been a child in the class whose father was a rapist, and all their classmates had avoided him in the same way.

On the evening of the second day, Zhang Jian got up. He called Xiaohuan and Duohe together, saying, 'Don't be afraid, the children are big now.'

Duohe saw Xiaohuan's eyes suddenly redden with unshed tears. She had not yet fully realised what it was in these words of Zhang Jian's that had provoked Xiaohuan. Zhang Jian bent down, groping among all the shoes under the bed, and finally pulled out an ancient silk purse from a pair of cloth shoes, from which he produced a pair of gold earrings, a gold ornamental lock and a bank book.

'My parents meant these for the children,' Zhang Jian said.

The old couple had somehow skimmed off over two hundred yuan from their elder daughter-in-law's household, which they had kept back for the three children.

'There's been only a few seriously punishable incidents like this one in the factory since it was set up. You'd better be prepared.'

The two women were watching the lofty mountain on which they had depended crumbling into rubble.

'Xiaohuan, take this money and open a little tailor's stall, you're pretty good at making clothes . . .'

He kept his eyes half closed, doing his best to appear calm and ordinary as if nothing was wrong, forming the words languidly with his parched lips.

'Take these bits of jewellery and pawn them.' This mountain, on the verge of collapse, was taking charge of the women for the last time. 'Find a state-run pawn shop. They were my mother's dowry . . .'

The notes were old and dirty, bound with a piece of elastic into something that looked like a refugee's bundle. The two women's tower of strength was now this bundle of notes and these few pieces of gold. Zhang Jian was racking his brains to find the words, for a way to lay out the situation that might come to pass as tactfully as possible.

'That radio set is getting awkward to use – you'd better buy some spare parts and I'll mend it for you, otherwise later on you'll have to spend money when you take it outside to mend.'

'Mend what? We'll make do the way it is,' Xiaohuan said. 'If we don't have a radio we can listen to the neighbours'. What are you worrying about?'

'Then there's the bike. If it was done up you could sell it for a fair bit . . .'

Xiaohuan got to her feet, smoothing the creases out of her clothes.

'Give it a rest,' Xiaohuan said. 'Have something to eat.'

She dropped the silk purse carelessly on the bed on her way to pick up the apron from the bed rail, and tied its strings on her way out. Then the radio came on with a hissing noise, and a mob of children started to sing in rustling voices, evoking Ho Chi Minh: '*Look to the north, oh look to the north, Remember, oh remember Uncle Ho's words.*'

Xiaohuan set out the sausages and fried peanuts she had made yesterday. She also brought out a bottle of Daqu sorghum liquor, clamped down on the metal bottle top with her gold tooth and jerked upwards with her lower jaw, so that the cap was held on the point of the tooth, then she spat it out onto the tabletop, and took the first mouthful for herself, straight out of the bottle.

'That's good wine!' She filled up their three cups.

'Where are the kids?' After his first glass of Daqu, Zhang Jian had come back to life, and looked around him.

'Off visiting their classmates,' Xiaohuan said.

They ate their meal very peacefully; nobody spoke. The wine had been heated and was hot and fragrant, and they popped the peanuts fried in oil into their mouths one by one.

In the month that followed, Zhang Jian spent far more time asleep than awake. Each of these big sleeps ground down on his face, squeezing out more wrinkles. By the time his punishment was announced, he had become a little old man. Duohe spent a long time watching him sitting alone and hunched up on the balcony.

Duohe, who went to work on foot, felt that the road between the factory and the family quarters was getting shorter and shorter. She had enough thoughts and worries to think about all the way down the road, and enough nameless gratitude as well. Judging by the facts, the accident was pure coincidence, but Duohe felt it had brought Zhang Jian another layer closer to her. That it had been Xiao Shi, and no other, who was crushed to death had a certain inevitability about it. For a man to love a woman until he loses all control, and then to eliminate danger for him and for her, to kill a man for her, was entirely natural in the eyes of this woman from Shironami village. If it had been a man from Sakito or Shironami in his place, a brave man of her race, striking down with a samurai sword a man who had defiled her with his hands and was attempting to trick away her purity, was that not as natural as could be? What were words and objects of love without a little blood?

Dressed in big, baggy old work overalls, a peak cap on her head, Duohe walked this cracked asphalt road into the cherry-tree-lined lanes of Shironami village. Her knight loved her so desperately: a love that was without embraces, or kisses, or making love, yet could be aroused to murder. The bulky overalls became glorious raiment, a kimono; the peak cap a jewelled headdress; her knight's love for her was something that she alone knew. His punishment, his lost good looks, the strong build he no longer had, all made her love him more.

The red sunset of steel gradually expanded, until it had filled half the sky. Duohe tilted her head for another look, and watched until her cap fell off.

Her face flushed unnaturally red, Girlie started to shout from the communal walkway: 'Ma! Auntie!' She burst in, and came to an abrupt halt, realising that she could not enter the room until she had taken off her shoes, but unable to check the momentum built up in her headlong dash, she almost tumbled in. 'Ma! Auntie! I've been accepted!'

Xiaohuan had seen her running from the kitchen, and at once

turned off the tap and came into the corridor rubbing her hands. Girlie was on tiptoe, balancing on one leg stretching out her body and her arms, making a bridge of herself to straddle the distance between the door and the table to reach the teapot. She waved a hand – 'I'll tell you once I've had a mouthful of tea –' and clasped the teapot, put her lips to the spout and started to drink.

'Shoes off!' Xiaohuan said.

When she had drunk her fill, Girlie said that she had to go out again to her class teacher's house, to let her know that she had been accepted, so she had no time to remove her shoes. She put down the teapot and walked on the tips of her toes towards the small room, taking off her schoolbag, which was hanging askew, as she went.

'Oi, where do you think you're going? Shoes off! Look at those great mucky hooves!' Xiaohuan held her back.

Only then did it occur to Girlie that she had been keeping her mother in the dark the entire time. She drew out an envelope from her pocket, pulled out the letter inside, and handed it to her mother, but before Xiaohuan could unfold it, the girl threw both arms round her neck.

'I've been accepted by the Air Force Gliding School! Ma, you can't imagine, I've been suffering so much the last few days not knowing, every day I wanted to go up the mountain and hang myself!'

There had been so many hangings on the mountain during the past six months that any child who ventured into the deeper parts of the wood was liable to find themselves bumping into a pair of dangling legs. Work teams had come to the factories to clean out the landlords, rich peasants and historical counter-revolutionaries who had come to hide in their children's and wives' families after Liberation, and they would often take themselves off for a stroll to the mountain and hang themselves there in despair. It was not a big mountain, but the fame of its hangings had spread beyond the city, and a fair few counter-revolutionaries, landlords and rich peasants from the surrounding area would climb the mountain especially to go and hang themselves. So much so that when the neighbours were quarrelling, one of them might say: 'And if I'm telling you a lie I'll go up the mountain and hang myself!'

Now Xiaohuan opened the letter, to see a sheet of paper stamped with the seal of the Air Force Gliding School.

Girlie's face was wreathed in smiles. She was the only girl in the whole city to have been accepted. The examination candidates all had to have good grades, good health and a good moral character. None of the others could equal her for physical condition, and how can you fly in the sky if you don't have good health? She was going to fly? How was she going to fly? In a glider. What was a glider? A flying machine that was smaller than a plane.

Xiaohuan thought to herself, you'd never have known to look at her that Girlie could take the initiative and plan ahead, or how good she was at keeping her own counsel. A while back she had borrowed a wool coat from one of the neighbouring girls, and when asked why, she had said she was going to wear it to have her photo taken, when actually it had been to wear to the exam. You couldn't look down-at-heel for an exam. Xiaohuan felt a pang as she thought how sensible and considerate Girlie was, and that she had never had any decent clothes to wear, and she hurried off in search of the small bundle of banknotes Zhang Jian had saved. She had to buy real wool for Girlie, to make her a real woollen sweater. She turned over the shoes under the bed, looking in each one, as Girlie followed after her, telling her about the exams, and saying that with her dad in such trouble, she had thought that the air force was not going to take her. Her dad was awaiting disciplinary action while she was waiting for the notice of acceptance; these last few days she'd wanted to go up the mountain and hang herself every morning.

'Give it a rest.' Xiaohuan straightened up, looking at her daughter, whose eyebrows had run off her forehead with excitement. 'Did your dad get into trouble on purpose? If the air force hadn't accepted you because of that it would have been their loss!'

After Girlie came back from visiting her class teacher, Xiaohuan and Duohe had both made something to eat. Xiaohuan brought out the family's entire stock of food: half a bottle of oil, one bowl of peanuts and four eggs, and told Duohe to make something Japanese and tasty. There were no fish or shrimps, so she had to make do with deep-frying sweet potatoes, potatoes and lantern peppers together to make 'temperer'. Duohe had not been so lavish with oil for a very long time, she had lost her touch, and used it all up when she was just halfway through, so Xiaohuan went tripping off down the walkway to borrow oil from the neighbours. She had borrowed from three families in succession before Duohe had fried up a shallow basketful of 'temperer'.

In the evening the whole family sat down to a spread of seven or eight dishes, listening to Girlie talking them through the process of the testing over and over again. She said her eyes were the most tip-top pair of eyes in the whole city: the end of the eye doctor's nose had touched the tip of her own, almost choking her with his garlic breath, but even that hanging light of his hadn't turned up any problems with her eyes. Her face alight with excitement, she was chattering away like a magpie; sometimes she stood up to gesture with her hands, with their stubby, utterly childish fingers. Zhang Jian shot a glance at Duohe. It was unnerving – those hands could have been turned out from the same mould as hers.

Girlie brought laughter to the family for the first time in several months. Girlie also got Xiaohuan out and visiting of her own volition, which she hadn't done in ages. As soon as Xiaohuan put down her rice bowl, she went to take Girlie out to buy knitting wool, but she spent half an hour walking around the building. There were four families on every walkway, and she did not let one of them escape, knocking on every door and saying: 'Ai, now Girlie's in a special relationship with you, the Army to the People, eh?' . . . 'Our little air force pilot has come on a tour of inspection!' . . . 'Look, our Girlie's such a little thing, and she's going to be flying planes, d'you think they'll let her old mum come after her to wipe her nose?'

Her two younger brothers held their heads up again too. They stood flanking this future air force pilot, one on the right and one on the left, and from time to time they would give the tips of her plaits a tug. The Zhang family was going to bring forth an Auntie Lei Feng. The neighbours were a mass of noise and confusion, a great mass that grew and grew the further it rolled.

Finally the babble receded, retreating down the stairs. Duohe gave Zhang Jian a smile. He could see how satisfied she was. Although she did not understand every single sentence, she understood 'the best eyes', 'the best health', and this pleased her, because half of them had come from her.

She cleared away the empty dishes into the kitchen, and he carried in an empty cooking pot. The dim light of the kitchen bulb made his wrinkles appear deeper. She turned round, and their eyes were only fifteen centimetres apart. She said she had seen him smile: when eating supper he had laughed out loud. Laughed out loud? Yes, she hadn't seen him laugh like that for a very long time. Girlie had made something of herself, at least they'd brought one of them up successfully.

'What?' said Zhang Jian. He saw that her eyes were looking directly at him.

She said a few words.

Zhang Jian could roughly make out what she was saying: for her sake, he had come close to losing his smile. Just as he was about to ask what she meant, she said something else. He knew that she used more Japanese words when she let her feelings run away with her, and her lips and tongue would be more likely to trip over each other. He told her to take her time. She said it again. Then he understood. She said that now she believed he cared about her so much that he would fight tooth and nail for her. His eyes opened so wide that his heavy eyelids creased up, making it look like he had an extra pair of lids. She was still talking. She said that he had done away with Xiao Shi for her sake, which was the same thing as fighting for her.

Zhang Jian did not know when Duohe left the kitchen. The matter could be understood in that way too. Her words had slowly opened his eyes, and shown him that he had had the mind to kill Xiao Shi. Xiao Shi was not the only person he had wanted to kill either. That old fraud, the factory Party secretary, would often visit the workshop, bringing a bucket of sour plum juice against the heat of summer, and he got so fed up with him he was ready to murder him too. Because whenever the Party secretary brought sour plum juice, that meant he would have an hour's worth of beautiful but meaningless words to say, which in turn meant that they would have to do overtime to catch up on the work they had missed. Xiao Shi was not the only one who deserved to be killed. In the free market they had caught a young beggar stealing, and everyone crowded round to beat him. The beggar's skin was torn and his flesh hung in shreds as he rolled around, a man made of blood and mud, but fists and hands were still raining down on him from the crowd. It was like anyone who could not get in a blow had been unbearably wronged, like when emergency grain was distributed in the famine, everyone had to have a share or it would be unfair. He wanted to kill all of the people who had lashed out with their fists and their feet. When he was young there had been yet more people he wanted to kill: that old doctor who had delivered Xiaohuan's baby, and asked him whether to keep the mother or keep the child; how could he not deserve to die, asking something like that? Heaven should have struck him dead for pushing such a dilemma onto a husband and father! And then there were those four Jap devils who had chased Xiaohuan . . . From then on whenever he'd seen a Jap going about his business alone, he would meditate on how to kill him – should he hack him into tiny pieces or bury him alive, or thrash him with a cudgel? How many people had he killed in his heart? Too many to count.

Xiao Shi had been crushed by steel from his crane – had that been premeditated too? It was the day of the big snowfall, after Xiao Peng had left, and Xiaohuan had run after him. He and Xiao Shi had drunk until they were both red in the face. He had looked at Xiao Shi through half-open eyes. Xiao Shi had looked right back at him, then he had hurriedly shifted his gaze away, and smiled.

It was the smile of a stranger. Xiao Shi's smile was not like this: melancholy, dark and slightly shifty. Xiao Shi's smile had always been incorrigibly mischievous, the kind of smile that could never be provoked into anger. A stranger had taken over Xiao Shi's body. Whether this stranger would have brought Duohe good or bad luck in the future, it was hard to predict. But Zhang Jian thought that there would have been a great deal of bad luck and precious little good.

It was that stranger who had cornered Duohe in the stairwell, threatened her, and left black pawprints on her body.

It was that same stranger who in future would demand that Duohe submit to him, and pack her off to a labour camp if she did not give in.

That night Xiao Shi had picked up a piece of pork, with both the fat meat and the lean, calling to him, 'Brother Er, eat, eat!' He had not called Zhang Jian Brother Er for a very long time. He had used that name when they were at Anshan, but when they were transferred to the south, the Shanghainese and the North-easterners had all carved out their own independent fiefdoms, so Zhang Jian had forbidden him and Xiao Peng to call him this, in case it was seen as forming a clique of their own. 'Brother Er, it's been so many years, but it's Sister Xiaohuan who's suffered most.'

Calling him 'Brother Er' was a sign. And it was unlikely to be a sign of anything good. Zhang Jian had returned the meat Xiao Shi had picked out for him to the dish.

'And then there's that Xiao Peng, who studied for a few years at technical school, and now he's making himself out to be some sort of scholar. I dare say he's even written poems to my sister, all brave, fine, big words, better even than that great big book he gave Girlie. Look at him, all out of his mind with it –'

'And you're not?' Zhang Jian had said suddenly, with a faint smile.

Xiao Shi was startled, Zhang Jian very seldom adopted this tone.

'I . . . I heard Xiao Peng say she's Japanese. All those years we spent fighting the Japs – when did I ever get close to one of them?'

'So you want to try something fresh.' He had smiled again.

He had seen Xiao Shi's round eyes catch fire, as if he was waiting for the next sentence: *Then go ahead and try it*. He raised his wine cup, and drained the last mouthful, then looked at Xiao Shi, but the fire in those round eyes had gone out.

'Don't you worry, Brother Er, eh?'

Zhang Jian had seen that smiling expression that did not belong to Xiao Shi float up again. This time the smile awoke in him an urge that he had to force back down again. He did not consider the matter carefully until after Xiao Shi had left: how could he have had such an impulse to wring his neck? Because he had made those words 'Don't you worry, Brother Er' sound like a sinister warning? 'Don't you worry, here's the note I've made in my black books.' 'Don't you worry, any time you displease me, I can report this account upwards.' 'Don't you worry, Brother Er, there's plenty of bitterness in store for you yet!'

Now Zhang Jian was standing dumbly facing the dirty bowls and dishes in the sink. Duohe was scrubbing the floor outside, scrubbing away with her brush until even his heart got scratches. She had taken the accident to mean that he had struck the first blow and destroyed Xiao Shi, in order to protect her. To protect their secret love, to protect this unsatisfactory family, that could never hope to be at peace. He wanted to tell her that this was not the way it was, Xiao Shi's death had been preordained in the book of his life and death, and Zhang Jian was innocent of it. But he knew he would struggle to explain himself. In just the same way, if the security office, the Public Security Bureau and the law courts produced all kinds of reasons to maintain that he had had an ulterior motive with regard to Xiao Shi, he would find it hard to vindicate himself there too. He could not remember the last time he had engaged in a passionate argument over anything.

And of course it had happened on the night shift when there were few people about. Where had everyone got to? Were they on their meal break? And Xiao Shi just had to choose that moment to suddenly appear, just as he had suddenly appeared in the stairwell to block Duohe's way, his sooty hands crawling all over her body. Xiao Shi and the rolled steel Zhang Jian was carrying on the crane came into perfect alignment, matching positions like the cross hairs on the sights of a gun. Was he looking for death? Throwing himself on the barrel of a gun? And it had to be just that moment that Zhang Jian had let his mind wander, so that he was not paying attention to what was underneath the crane. The cross hairs and the target came together, flawlessly superimposed. And then the bullet was fired. The recoil had shaken him awake in an instant.

People gathered around a pool of blood, eyes averted from the body, speculating. He had cradled Xiao Shi in his arms. The bubbles of blood were so lively, emerging from that mouth that had used to bubble over with wisecracks like a pot on the boil. His round eyes, which had never once been serious, were closed, satisfied and content, and Zhang Jian felt a prickling feeling of grief in his nose. When all was said and done, he had spent over ten years looking into those eyes, and now they were closed, unable to accuse him with their white whites and black pupils.

But accuse him of what?

If that old fake of a Party secretary who brought sour plum juice to the workshop were to die in a sudden accident, should Zhang Jian find himself accused because he had killed him in his heart?

At this moment, Zhang Jian, who was standing by the sink scrubbing dishes, could sense that Duohe had entered the kitchen and walked over to the window, to rub the oil and smoke from the glass. The Zhangs were the only family in the whole building with a gleaming kitchen window; the other families' windows were begrimed with more than a decade's worth of accumulated grease and filth, which combined with dust to form a thick felt. Others had long since been covered with plywood or pages from colour magazines, which were replaced when the hygiene inspectors came round. But the Zhang family's kitchen window sparkled like crystal, one of the increasing number of eccentricities that people could discern in them.

'Give over polishing,' Zhang Jian said to Duohe.

Duohe's hands paused, and she looked at him. Then she raised the polishing cloth again.

'Stop polishing.'

He could not say for sure that he had not eliminated Xiao Shi for her sake. He pulled her away from the window and into his arms. How many years had it been since he last held her like this? The damp cloth in her hands was touching his back. He reached round, snatched the cloth away and threw it to the ground. What are you polishing? What are you polishing? That mouth of Xiao Shi's, gurgling as the bubbles of blood welled up, bubbles that were so supple, so warm, how could they have come floating up from the innards of a dead man? How could a lively man like Xiao Shi have got himself killed? Xiao Shi, who had had such a thick skin, such a brazen, cheeky grin, who had never been provoked to anger, nor blushed when he brought snubs down on himself – would such a man abandon his pursuit of Duohe of his own free will? Could such a man be killed by a malicious thought in Zhang Jian's mind? How many times had he brought beans or bean cakes for the children? Poor Xiao Shi's hopeless courtship of Duohe had been carried out with neatly tied bundles of pig's trotters. He had a naturally low and vulgar disposition, but he couldn't help that.

Duohe could feel he was shaking violently, and raised her head to look at him.

He had become a mass of truths and reasoning that he was not able to articulate. What he could do was clasp this beloved enemy in his arms, this woman who had come to him through wrongdoing and sin – how did she keep on looking like a young girl who never grew up into a woman? He had not kissed her so savagely for a very long time. Had they really become a pair of star-crossed lovers, close in spirit though far away in body, who had plotted to murder an eyewitness to their forbidden love? It seemed that was what they had become, for this was precisely the story he could see on Duohe's face, which was flowing with grateful tears. They fell into each other's arms: they had managed to avoid being struck down by lightning for their sins.

Their embrace was also because Girlie was going to fly. Thanks to her moral character, eyes and physical condition, all the best in the city. They hugged tightly, wanting each other to understand that Girlie had got half of all these 'bests' from each of them. He kissed her forcefully, almost suffocating Duohe. Finally he stopped. She looked at him through her tears. The first time she had seen him, it had been through pale brown fog.

She had been set down on the stage, and he walked towards her through the light brown fog. It was true that he was tall, but he did not have a tall man's clumsiness, and his head and face had none of that lack of proportion that one finds in big men. He was picking up the sack, her curled, numb legs and frozen body were dangling, swaying along with his footsteps, and from time to time she would bump into his calf. The total numbness had been broken, and as he strode along, pain started to revive with every step, and to move through her blood and flesh. The pain became countless fine burrs, creeping from the soles of her feet, the tips of her toes and fingers and the cracks of her fingernails into her arms and legs. He seemed to have noticed that the reviving pain was actually worse than numbness, so he made his steps steadier. He was carrying her, carving out a lane between a pitch-black crowd of dirty feet, and she suddenly was no longer afraid of those feet, nor of the braying laughter that issued from their owners. That was when she heard an older woman's voice begin to speak. An older man's voice replied. The smell of farm animals came in from the seams of the sack. After that she was put on the flatbed of a cart. Urged on by the whip, the animal pulling the cart broke into a run, faster and faster; a hand kept coming up, lightly patting her body to flick the snowflakes away. This was an old hand, it could not hold itself straight, and the palm was very soft. The hand of an old lady of fifty? Of sixty, even? . . . The cart entered a courtyard; again from within the pale brown fog, she saw it was a very good courtyard. The buildings seemed to be very good as well. She was carried through a door, straight from a snowy day to summer. It was a toasty, crackling warmth, she was thawing out, and the pain erupted all over her body . . . When she came round, a pair of hands were untying the knot of the sack, at the crown of her head. The sack was slipped off from around her, and she saw him. It was also just a fleeting glimpse. It was only afterwards that she slowly looked over that brief glimpse in her mind: He was not too bad-looking, no, he was good-looking. Not just that, his half-closed eyes were very good-looking, and half closed with pained embarrassment because of his own warmth and tenderness.

A week later, Girlie – Zhang Chunmei – left, carrying a yellowing grass-green bedding roll on her back, and dressed in a shiny new army uniform. She was like a cheerful green postbox in the cheerful crowd seeing her off from the building. They accompanied her as far as the bottom of the slope, where she turned off onto the main road. The people gradually thinned out, waving to this Girlie who in the future might become an Auntie Lei Feng. As they thought of what Girlie had left behind in their building – the sound of her laugh and her footsteps, her fine moral character – tears came into all their eyes.

Only the people closest to Girlie were left: the three senior Zhangs, the twins and a limping black dog, plus Girlie's class teacher and two girls from her school. They would see Girlie off all the way to the railway station. At that point the number of people accompanying her would shrink to two: her mother Xiaohuan and her aunt Duohe.

Xiaohuan and Duohe went as far as Nanjing. From here, Girlie would cross the Yangtze River and head north, to the gliding school eight hundred kilometres away. While they were waiting for the train, the three of them searched for a quiet place to say their farewells, making their way with difficulty through the waiting room, which was full of passengers lying on the floor. Many beggars were also picking across the ground covered with slumbering bodies, as if they were sweeping for land mines. What disaster were all of these people fleeing? Xiaohuan could only recall seeing such scenes in her childhood. That was when the Japanese had occupied the North-eastern provinces, and her parents had fled with her and her brother to unoccupied central China.

This was the first time Girlie had gone any distance from home. There was sweat on her brow and chaos inside her head; Xiaohuan could see it all at a glance. In the station waiting room a dozen or so children were crying, like huge cicadas, all competing to raise their voices louder and draw the sound out longer. Girlie said that she was meeting other new gliding school students in Nanjing, and they really should be here by now; there would be a group leader with them, they wouldn't be late. Xiaohuan plucked a plastic comb from her hair to untangle Girlie's fringe, which was sticky with sweat. She was also not satisfied with her long plaits, so she whipped off Girlie's new army cap, and combed her hair all over again.

Duohe and Xiaohuan took a plait each. Her head was first pulled to the left by her mother, then to the right by her aunt. At intervals she would complain that they were too heavy-handed, and making her plaits too tight. The two women ignored her, and just carried on plaiting. Tight is best, get them tight enough and Girlie would not need to comb her hair on the train, she wouldn't even have to do her hair the day after she arrived at the school. Best of all would be if she didn't have to do her plaits for a week, or a month, bringing her mother's and aunt's handiwork into her new life. (Afterwards Girlie mentioned her plaits in a letter: they had lasted right up until the fourth day, then all the students had their hair cut short in identical styles.)

They had only just got her hair nicely plaited when she let out a yell, and set off at a run, her nimble feet threading their way through the big waiting room packed solid with reclining bodies. When she had reached the ticket inspection gate, Duohe gave Xiaohuan's sleeve a tug: a file of boys and girls in identical uniforms to Girlie's were entering the station from a side door.

Xiaohuan and Duohe's eyes followed that ever-shrinking patch of army green until it disappeared from view. By the time they finally made their way to that side door, it was already shut. They watched through the glass as the two or three dozen new recruits headed towards the train. Xiaohuan beat on the glass door until her hands were numb. Her pounding brought a policeman over. He asked if she had a ticket. No. Then what are you banging away like that for? Be off with you!

With some difficulty, Duohe dragged Xiaohuan away, as it looked like she was going to start pounding on the policeman at any minute.

Xiaohuan sat down on the filthy floor, weeping and bawling that that so-and-so who'd torn her from her own flesh and blood wouldn't die a good death. She cried and shouted in just the same way as her mother and her mother-in-law. But nobody was alarmed. This station was a transfer point for trains from all over the country, from north to south, and shouting and crying of all kinds were entirely normal.

❖

Girlie was made Propaganda Monitor for her class.

Girlie came third in the mid-term test.

Girlie finally got some leave, and took a long-distance bus to the county town, dozens of kilometres away, to have her photograph taken. For some reason, her more sensible, adult expression left the whole family feeling dejected and subdued.

Xiaohuan took the photograph and said to the two boys: 'This sister of yours was different from you from the day she was born. If you put her down with her face to the wall, she'd sit there for three hours without any fuss or noise. You two should learn from her example, eh?'

Dahai listened, and looked at his sister's eyes, identical to their father's, half weariness, half laughter.

Erhai ignored Xiaohuan. His grudge against her had not yet run its course.

Only Zhang Jian was a little bit anxious and uneasy. So the family's luck would be good from now on? And Girlie was the lucky star who had turned fortune in their favour? Was Old Man Heaven really going to let him, Zhang Jian, get away with it as easily as this?

Zhang Jian knew from his colleagues that Xiao Peng had put in a good word for him with the people in the Public Security Bureau and the security office. Xiao Peng was now the Communist Youth League Secretary for the entire factory, and one good word from him was worth a hundred from anyone else. Xiao Peng had built him up as a benign, inoffensive person, perhaps a little slow on the uptake, who loved his family and friends and nothing else, not caring even about money. He also spoke of how many times Xiao Shi had spent Spring Festival and New Year at Zhang Jian's home, and the countless times he had shared pickled vegetable hotpot with them, nearly eating them out of house and home.

But Xiao Peng never uttered a word of greeting to Zhang Jian. One time Zhang Jian saw a bicycle key under one of the lockers in the bathhouse, knotted with a length of grubby red plastic. He recognised it at a glance. He took the key to Xiao Peng's dormitory, and gave it to his room-mate. Zhang Jian asked him to pass on a message to Xiao Peng, inviting him to come over to his house for a drink. Xiao Peng did not take up the invitation.

He invited him once a month, month after month, but Xiao Peng did not even send him a tactfully worded refusal. There seemed to be no romantic rumours about him either. Xiao Peng, who had become a bachelor for Duohe's sake, now did not want to see Duohe at all.

One day a meeting was held for the whole factory, where the Party secretary made a report. Halfway through somebody sitting in the front row slipped out, back bent, and walked towards an emergency exit at the side of the hall, only straightening up once he was behind the cloth curtain. From his seat in the eighteenth row, Zhang Jian could see that it was Xiao Peng. Xiao Peng too was fed up with this secretary and his interminable fine words. Zhang Jian thought, Xiao Peng was an ally, both in public and in secret, so why had he broken off the friendship so completely, just like that, never setting foot over the Zhang family's threshold?

10

Like floodwater in the mountains, a crowd of bicycles came pouring along the road every evening at five o'clock. On the east side of the railway, the workers from the steel-smelting plant and the workers from the rolled-steel plant came together, then went on to converge with the workers from the steel-plate factory, pouring along the sun-softened asphalt road, which seemed to buckle beneath them. The reed-filled ditch on both sides of the railway had dried out in the drought, and button-sized crabs climbed up onto the road, as if at the start of a great migration, only to be ground beneath the wheels of the advancing ranks of bicycles, exploding with a popping sound. Before too long, the flood of traffic had washed past, and all was peaceful again on the road, studded with drought-struck crabs that looked like designs heat-pasted onto pottery: shells covered with a delicate network of cracks, pairs of nippers that had never had the chance to be used in attack, pairs of eyes still staring up into the blue sky.

Duohe walked past, treading on these newly formed crab fossils. She had almost reached the dependants' area, where the big road split into criss-crossing smaller roads. The red bricks of the buildings were red no more, and the white-painted balconies were grimy and dull. These buildings, more than a hundred in all, identical when new, had mutated into all different kinds and varieties now they were old. Every family had added another balcony to the home by means of a big wooden plank, on which they placed bowls of onions or garlic, or flowers and shrubs, or bird or rabbit cages, or broken and decayed furniture. In some families the children collected waste paper, and piled it up in bundles on the balcony, covered with tattered fertiliser sacks, and this place made a good storehouse too. Duohe had put up an awning on their balcony's balcony, on which she stored a row of glass bottles containing pickled meat and vegetables. The Zhang family's balcony was so neat and tidy it dazzled the eyes, even from far away.

Duohe was carrying a canvas work bag on her shoulder, packed with more than ten steel stamps. Because wages were paid by the piece, she would take stamps home on Saturday to carve. She had withdrawn the head of the sewing machine, and squeezed on a table vice, which enabled her to work. She had been walking for twenty minutes, and her shoulders were becoming quite sore, and just as she had shifted her bag from one shoulder to the other, a bicycle passed her, sandwiched between several other bikes.

Zhang Jian was listening to some workmates discussing something. He rode on up the hill.

Duohe thought, she had been a very obvious sight as he rode by. Could he not have seen her? Or had he not wanted to see her? He was unwilling to acknowledge her in front of his workmates. When they were joking or quarrelling in the workshop, she became an invisible woman.

Duohe entered their home, and slowly took off her old cloth shoes, crusted with silvery steel dust. As she undid the toggles of the second shoe, her hands shook, and her actions lost all precision. It took her forever to get it undone. It was like this hand had crippled itself grasping the small steel file she used to make her serial numbers; every evening when she came home from work she had to rest for a while before the ability to fully extend and clench her hand returned to her.

She stripped off her bulky overalls, sickened at the smell that rose from the short-sleeved shirt inside, which had been soaked with sweat and warmed dry again. She went into the toilet, removed her clothes and hosed herself down with a rubber pipe attached to the tap. She could not bring herself to use the two bathhouse tickets issued every week by the workshop – that way Dahai and Erhai could have a proper bath with hot water once a week. Once she had had a wash, she went into the big room, and saw Xiaohuan and Zhang Jian on the balcony, talking. The two of them were lounging on the balcony railings, turned away from the room, and Xiaohuan was laughing as she spoke, Zhang Jian was listening and laughing along with her. If Duohe did not concentrate on what she heard, their words became a buzzing fog of sound. And their intimacy was another thing she could not work her way into, or join in. How could she not be distressed at their joy at this moment? There would never be any place for her in this happiness. They were talking and laughing, and from time to time they would call down to an acquaintance below: 'Come up and sit for a while!'

As far as a lot of people were concerned, there was no such person as Duohe in this world. It was necessary for Duohe to disappear in order to exist.

She tipped those steel stamps out of her work bag. The cement floor, polished excessively smooth, endured those rectangular lumps of steel with clunks and clatters that were painful to hear.

The two people on the balcony had not heard. They stood shoulder to shoulder, cracking jokes with acquaintances on the ground, chattering and laughing.

Duohe could not understand any of it. That laughter was also very hard to interpret, a quacking and cooing, everything a dense fog of speech and sound, from the sky to the ground. She thought, this is such a noisy race! She had lived among these people for so many years, how come this was the first time she had noticed that they were so noisy? How much time did they spend making this racket? If they weren't making all this noise perhaps the floor could be a bit cleaner, the furniture could be a bit tidier, the clothes could be a bit smoother. If they spent a bit less time making a noise, they would have no need to 'make do, eat', 'make do, wear', 'make do, live'.

She pulled out the sewing machine. In this household, every item had to fit neatly into its own space between other objects, which meant that you had to use precise movements when moving things around. If you were not precise, you would bring the sky tumbling down on your head all at once, like soldiers in a rout, or a landslide. The sewing machine's wheel twisted for a moment out of its customary invisible track, causing it to bash into the long wooden plank where shoes were kept, and the plank collapsed. One end bumped into one of the poles holding up the mosquito net over the bed, which promptly collapsed, enveloping Duohe. She wrestled her way out of the mosquito netting, but when she had finally got her head out, her foot in its wooden slipper kicked into the plank with the shoes, scattering them, and the wooden shoe on her foot along with them.

The two of them came running over. They did not understand the way she was behaving. They'd spent so many years living in the same dog kennel, if they were not willing to understand, they never would understand anything. Her intimacy with Zhang Jian was a hidden thing that never saw the light of day, that would only happen once in several years, while his and Xiaohuan's closeness was there every day, in front of an entire building full of people.

Duohe shouted some words. The other two struggled through a mass of 'don't understands' before they finally knew what she meant: Zhang Jian had seen her carrying a very heavy bag and had pretended not to see her.

Zhang Jian muttered a few words. Xiaohuan was afraid Duohe would not understand, so she started explaining before the sound of his voice had died away. What he meant was that his colleagues had been talking about how the bonuses were unfair, and they were going to speak to the leaders, and he could not jump off his bike at such a critical juncture. Besides, he'd had no idea that her bag was so heavy.

Duohe shouted another sentence, and this time Zhang Jian was struck speechless. Xiaohuan said to her: 'You say that again!'

She had quarrelled openly with Xiaohuan many times, and given her the silent treatment times beyond number, but she had never seen Xiaohuan look like this before: eyes narrowed to slits, one shoulder thrust out, lower teeth biting on the upper lip.

Zhang Jian was standing behind Xiaohuan. Xiaohuan gave him a push, looking at Duohe as she said to Zhang Jian: 'She says Chinese people are all born liars.'

Duohe said loudly, too right, and she understood just fine, there was no need for Xiaohuan to interpret. She had used this phrase to curse Dahai and Erhai, albeit in a jokey way.

'Who says Chinese people are all born liars?' Zhang Jian asked.

That was what they said in Duohe's village. They said it of their Chinese hired hands. Her mother had talked about Fudan in that way.

'Then your mother was a swine,' Zhang Jian said.

Duohe looked at his face. His eyes were still half closed, aloof from the rest of the world, nothing could faze him, no matter how strange, and the words came out from deep in his throat, and not from his lips. She struggled with what it was that he had just said.

'Don't understand?' Xiaohuan's shoulder thrust forward a little more, almost as far as her chin. 'What he means is: your mother says Chinese people tell lies, and that means that your mother was a swine!' Her slightly swollen eyelids, her cheeks, deep dimples and glittering tooth all came to her aid as she explained Zhang Jian's words.

Duohe swayed for a moment. From the dripping wet hair on her head to the centre of her body that had been sluiced in cold water, she felt the wild fires in her heart ignite with a roar.

She bawled out a volley of words.

Xiaohuan seized hold of her freshly washed hair, but could not get a good grip on it, so she made a grab for her clothes. The shirt had been worn ragged, and its collar had been cut off; this too was hard to catch hold of. Duohe backhanded her, and grabbed Xiaohuan's hair in turn. It was very easy to get a good hold on Xiaohuan's permed hair, and having done that she could drag Xiaohuan along. Zhang Jian came up and forced his hands between them, his arm trapping Duohe's neck from behind. Duohe's hands went limp, and she let go of Xiaohuan.

Duohe was panting so heavily that her chest was like a pair of bellows. She spoke in a loud voice, sentence after sentence. It didn't matter – if they did not understand she still had to say it. To them she was just a womb, a pair of breasts, and now both womb and breasts were useless, so come on then, throw them away, throw them down from the fourth floor!

Her jabbering away in Japanese brought the other two to their senses. In this building, if you farted on one side of the wall, it could be heard on the other side. Her Japanese speech was far more audible than any fart. Were they scared? Duohe was not. Her heart and body were full of flames of black fire. Since the bandits had come charging towards the girls on their horses, she no longer had anything to be frightened of.

She was a daughter of Shironami village, she should not have been a womb and a pair of breasts for people such as this. She threw herself towards the balcony. Two hands dragged her back from behind.

She kept jabbering away in her own tongue. The door to the balcony clanged in the neighbouring flat. She was calmer now. That pair behind her dragged themselves through their days, dragging up the children, and dragging her along with them too. Xiaohuan's 'make do' was a fearful thing. This big family had been thoughtlessly created by making do: if there was no wheat flour then make do with bran, if no red-cooked pork then make do with red-cooked aubergine, if there was no shampoo powder then make do with caustic soda. She, a Japanese, had somehow been making do along with them without ever quite knowing why, making do and making do again, and then sometimes it all hit her with a shock: from all these things beyond her control she could still gain a bit of satisfaction, and even steal a morsel of amusement.

After that evening, Duohe put down a straw mat in the corridor, and spread a cotton quilt over it. Although she was making do, she was also making a statement that she was not prepared to sleep in the same room as either one of that pair. The summer ended, the first rains fell, and the pines on the mountain slopes shed many cones. The autumn was getting chilly.

'You'll make yourself ill,' Xiaohuan said to Duohe. 'Move back in.'

Her expression was bland, as if all this was just the way it should be.

'Or else you sleep in the big room with the boys, and I'll come out and put a pallet on the floor?' Zhang Jian said. That smile of his could wear you out just looking at it, with masses of wrinkles on his brow, and two creases at the corners of his mouth that could have been cut with a knife.

Duohe bit her lip, and her heart softened somewhat, but she wanted to wait a bit longer, for him to drag Xiaohuan in, and to negotiate a proper, serious reconciliation.

'I'll give you stubborn! You'll catch your death of stubbornness on that cement floor!' Xiaohuan said, as she whisked her own quilt from the bed, and carried it to the corridor. Xiaohuan was so accustomed to quarrelling with people that she could not keep track of all her grudges. She was always sweetest towards the people she had just come to blows with. 'You're really this stubborn? I'll freeze you to death!' She laid out the quilt on the mat nicely for Duohe, patting it down here and there with her hands.

Duohe did not utter a sound, or move. Once Xiaohuan had gone, she knelt on the floor, rolled up the quilt which had just been laid out flat and tidy on the floor, and carried it back to Xiaohuan's bed. *She* was not about to muddle her way into a reconciliation.

'Look at her! A female mule, wouldn't you say?' Xiaohuan whispered in Zhang Jian's ear.

Duohe knew what they were whispering together.

Winter came, and Duohe moved herself into the big room, and laid out her quilt between Dahai and Erhai. The two boys, who were entering puberty, said in their hoarse, buzzing voices: 'Now Auntie's come, Dad's going to have to go, otherwise how are we all supposed to fit in?'

She immediately became accustomed to sleeping in the same room as the children. She often found herself with a boy's face tucked into each armpit, as they spoke among themselves the language that only they could understand. They had seldom spoken this language since they started at primary school, but it was their milk tongue, and it would come back to them after a few sentences. They had plenty of words, Chinese, Japanese and the speech of babies and young children, but now their vocabulary had increased, and they added new words into the mix. This was a secret language, one that excluded the other grown-ups in the family. They talked about all sorts of things: Dahai spoke of his dreams of being a centre forward in basketball, and Erhai talked about his Blackie. Sometimes the two of them chatted about some fine fellows called the Red Guards, who had turned everything upside down in the government. Here in the city and at the provincial capital, they had tied up the head of the provincial government and the mayor, and paraded them through the streets.

The three of them slept in one big bed: Duohe in the middle; Dahai, the larger of the two boys, slept on the outside; Erhai's place was next to the window; and Blackie had his den on the balcony outside the window. Sometimes after the two children were fast asleep Duohe could hear murmurings from next door. Xiaohuan would chuckle in her smoky voice, and Zhang Jian would add a few words from time to time. Let them laugh, let them talk, it no longer grieved her.

A couple of times she woke up to find that Dahai had wormed his way into her quilt, and was sleeping in her arms. She put him back, half pushing, half lifting. Dahai's body was a fine sight, he was already putting on flesh, and Duohe could not imagine how such a big boy had come out of her own body.

One day, the schools closed. Dahai and Erhai came back at noon, saying that they were going to go out and 'link up' with other like-minded revolutionary youths. Link what? It's the Great Revolutionary Link-Up, don't you even understand this? It doesn't sound like good news to me, you're not going. Mum's so backward! Oh, you've only just noticed? I've been backward for decades!

The Zhang family were the same as all the other families in the building. They all grounded, beat and cursed their children, whose hearts and feet were itching to go out and 'link up', even though they had not reached the required age. There had never been such a wave of the younger generation attacking their elders. Walk past the door of any household, and you would hear the mother roaring: 'You dare! I'll rip you to shreds, you little rat, just see if I don't . . . Kneel! Who said you could get back up? If you go off "linking up" again I'll make you carry two baskets of coal on your head as a punishment.' But the children left anyway. They stole money for tickets and slipped away, mixed in with the older students.

Dahai and Erhai ran away together. But they lost each other in the crush on a crowded train, where they couldn't eat, drink or use a toilet for three nights, and one of them ended up going to Guangzhou, the other to Beijing. Erhai went to Guangzhou, and came back a month later with five Mao badges pinned to his clothes, bringing a few pineapples with him. He started speaking again to Xiaohuan after years of silence, as if he had never stopped speaking at all. As soon as he came in the door, he said with a cheerful expression: 'Ma, I'm back!'

Dahai, however, was still in Beijing. From there he sent a volume of the *Quotations of Chairman Mao* with a letter inside, as posting a copy of this book carried no charge. The letter informed them that he had had two audiences with Chairman Mao himself, and had gone on to the great North-west to have an audience with someone else, and to sow the fiery seeds of the revolution there.

When Dahai came back he was a 'little red devil'. A suit of army clothes speckled with grime, a mouth full of new words, he always had a definitive statement for every occasion. His voice had become quite beautiful, and he had grown a full five centimetres taller. Xiaohuan was so happy that she kept shedding tears, saying over and over again: that damned little pig demon, how could he have turned himself into such a talented young man for free, living without money or grain coupons?

That night Duohe wanted to speak to her two sons in their own language again. Erhai responded with a sentence or two, but Dahai just turned his back, and very soon he was asleep. From then on Dahai never spoke their secret language again.

For several weeks there had been no letters from Girlie. Generally, she would write once a week with a few bits of good news. If there was no good news, she would send a few caring words: Mummy, don't smoke too much, I've heard that smoking is bad for you; Auntie, don't tire yourself out with the housework, the more you do around the house the more there is to do; Daddy, don't spend all your time brooding, go fishing with this or that uncle when you have the time; Dahai, don't be too shy, go and try out for the youth basketball team.

Now writing to their elder sister was the thing the two brothers were most happy to do. One after the other, they asked her why had she not written home for such a long time. The letter came at last, slipped between the pages of the *Quotations of Chairman Mao*. Usually when Girlie sent home two or three yuan in notes, she would slip them into the plastic cover of the *Quotations of Chairman Mao*, with the Great Leader watching over them so they would be quite safe. She asked if her mother could buy a few feet of homespun cloth, the kind the peasants made themselves, and make her a shirt. This request of Girlie's was highly eccentric, but Xiaohuan did as she was asked. More time passed, and she asked them to make her a pair of shoes, saying specifically that she did not want her mother or aunt to make the kind that the city people wore – she wanted them to be made out of true, authentic homespun cloth. Girlie was becoming increasingly peculiar, no one in the family could guess what she meant by it, apart from Dahai: he knew wearing shoes made by peasants showed that she hadn't forgotten the army's great strategy for the countryside and how its people would rise up against the cities. Although Dahai came across as painfully shy outside the home, with the family everything he said was well reasoned and argued, and he could sometimes reduce even Erhai to silence.

Girlie seemed to be getting stranger all the time: she asked her father, who had some experience of farm work, how wheat was planted, how to hoe, how to harvest, and when in the old Chinese solar calendar millet and sorghum were sown. After replying to each of these questions, he discussed it with Xiaohuan. 'Tell me, isn't there something a bit off about this business with Girlie?'

'Like what?'

'Isn't she going to be flying planes? Has she become one of those soldiers who does farm work?'

'Just so long as it doesn't get in the way of her being a Five-Good Soldier.' When Xiaohuan had received the metal 'Five-Good Soldier' merit badge which Girlie had sent, she showed it to all sixteen families in the building. Once everyone had looked it over, she brought it to Duohe. Duohe listened in silence to Xiaohuan talking of how she was such an outstanding meritorious worker, looking on wordlessly, huge-eyed, as Xiaohuan took the badge away. The next day, Xiaohuan found the badge pinned to Duohe's pillow.

'This proves that my sister's ideology is red, that she has a sound work ethic, and she hasn't forgotten that the peasants are the poorest class in our nation!' This was how Dahai explained it.

Erhai seemed to have a rather more suspicious mind. He read his sister's letters repeatedly, trying to find the answer to the riddle.

This was an era when the answers to many riddles were rooted up. One day a crowd of Red Guards came charging up for one of the neighbours, and they exposed his secret: he was a covert agent for Taiwan, who listened to a Taiwanese radio station every day. A woman in the building opposite had also been exposed: before she became the wife of a working-class man, she had been married to a company commander in the Kuomintang. In Dahai and Erhai's school there was a teacher who had seemed perfectly decent, but a short investigation by the Red Guards revealed him to be a rightist who had avoided classification in the Anti-Rightist Campaign.

There were more than a hundred blocks of dependants' quarters, all appallingly broken-down and shabby, but the daily reposting of large posters gave them a certain unity. Any block of flats that had produced several undesirable persons would get a simple makeover: banners would be hung from the front and back balconies, floating and dangling down, their slogans blocking the breeze and keeping out the sun.

The twins felt that life in this Great Era was more fast-paced and dramatic than life at home, and they were often so busy that they were never to be seen from dawn to dusk. This was especially true of Dahai, who was the leader of a Red Guard brigade, and now dressed in a worn army uniform he had swapped with dependants of the army depot for a set of his father's old work overalls. To the three members of the older generation back home he was full of impatience: 'What do you know about it?'

In July a vicious drought came, the kind you meet with just once in a hundred years. People moved their bed frames, or carried up straw mats, and slept on the roof of the building. In the middle of the night Zhang Jian was awoken by the muffled sounds of a struggle. Fights broke out between boys every night. He was just about to go back to sleep, when he realised that this time the combatants were his sons. Although Dahai was tall, Erhai's stubborn temper generally made up for his inferior strength, and allowed him to turn defeat into victory. Most importantly, he was not afraid of pain: bite down hard on his skin and it was no different from biting his shirt. When Dahai could not win a fight he often used his teeth, which were currently deep in his brother's shoulder, yet this did not hamper Erhai from delivering blows with his fists and feet. The most remarkable thing was that the two of them were fighting in almost total silence, in deadly earnest.

Zhang Jian pulled the brothers apart. Dahai's nose and mouth were a bloody mess, and he took off his vest to block his nostrils, but Erhai didn't even bother to rub the bite on his shoulder. Their father waved his hand, signalling his sons to go downstairs with him. Dahai didn't move; Erhai took two paces, then saw that his brother remained where he was, and he stood still too. He was not prepared to leave on his own with his father, for then he would be the one telling tales, or giving his own, biased version of events. Zhang Jian understood his younger son, and did not force him, for fear of waking the neighbours. He gave a ferocious gesture: go back to sleep for now, I'll deal with you later, in my own good time.

The following morning, Zhang Jian was eating breakfast, preparing to set off for work, when the boys came downstairs, sleeping mats under their arms. Dahai was walking in front, Erhai behind, six or seven paces separating them. You could see at a glance that they had not worked off their bad feeling.

'Stay where you are,' he said.

With immense reluctance, the boys stood still. Two bare chests, four fierce and intransigent eyes, a pair of living statues of rebel heroes. The Great Age had drawn this family in.

'Stand up straight.'

They did not move.

'Don't you know how to stand?' Zhang Jian roared.

Xiaohuan came out from the kitchen, to see what trouble the father and his two sons had brought on themselves. Duohe was still asleep on the rooftop. She was bringing home too many pieces of steel for carving each night and, having worked herself to exhaustion, she could not get up in the morning. Before coming down from the rooftop, Xiaohuan had tucked in Duohe's mosquito net for her again, to keep out the flies when they started to move about in the morning air.

The two boys puffed out their ribcages.

'Why were you fighting?' Zhang Jian began his interrogation, munching a crisp pickled cucumber.

Their father's words might just as well have been spoken to the wall, there was not the slightest response.

Xiaohuan shoved her oar in. Wiping the bloodstains from Dahai's face, she said: 'Have you had differences with your brother over your revolutionary standpoint?' These days Xiaohuan's banter was full of words taken from those big black-and-white posters. 'Why don't you debate the matter first, for God's sake? We could listen, then we'd be progressive too.' She was laughing and joking as usual, but Dahai thrust out his hand and knocked the facecloth away.

Zhang Jian's hand lashed out in turn to box Dahai's ears.

'Outside you may be the rebel chief of staff, but try any of that back home and see what you get!'

In his fury Dahai puffed out his ribcage even further, causing a deep and terrible valley to form underneath his ribs.

'Erhai, you tell me, why were you fighting?'

Erhai also resolutely played dumb.

Zhang Jian sneered at the two boys in front of him, trying to ape revolutionary martyrs. 'I already know.'

The twins were not wise in the ways of the world, and both glanced at him. This time Zhang Jian could pretty much confirm his guess. There had been a difference in the expressions in the boys' eyes: Erhai's was pure curiosity, whereas Dahai's was guilty and terrified. When neither of them would speak, nine times out of ten Dahai was the one who was in trouble. When Dahai got in trouble, Erhai seldom told on him. It was different the other way round; Dahai would tell his parents all about Erhai's various misdeeds at school. And Erhai's misdeeds really were so numerous that they needed Dahai to keep track of them all.

So what kind of trouble had Dahai got himself into in the dead of night? Zhang Jian was very fond of Duohe's pickled cucumbers, and he crunched on while he turned over the facts of the case in his mind.

'Erhai, if you don't say, you won't be going anywhere today.'

Erhai considered this for a moment, his eyes full of confusion: the Great Age was waiting for him outside, and he was going to be imprisoned for Dahai's sake.

'You ask my brother.'

'He doesn't have the face to say,' said Zhang Jian.

The two of them stared at their father, the great detective. Dahai's face went pale, then red, and then from red back to white again. The old scar on his forehead was bone white.

'Tell, Erhai! Your dad'll back you up!' Xiaohuan took away the boys' breakfasts.

Dahai's spirit was already broken; he had pulled in his ribcage and his eyes were fixed on the elastic ties on his wooden slippers.

'Dad, make my brother say it himself.'

'Then you won't be getting anything to eat. My food isn't for people who harbour Bad Elements,' Xiaohuan said, smiling away.

'Fine, I won't eat then,' Erhai glanced briefly at the steaming hot bread.

Zhang Jian could not continue to waste his breath on the pair of them, and he got up to put on his work clothes and shoes. He waved his hand at his sons. 'Get lost, both of you!'

But Erhai did not move. 'Dad . . .'

Zhang Jian raised his eyes from his shoelaces.

'Don't let Auntie sleep on the roof.'

Zhang Jian could hear that the noise of Dahai brushing his teeth in the toilet had stopped.

'Why?' he asked his son. The answer to the riddle was about to be revealed.

'There are . . . hooligans on the roof,' Erhai said.

'Hooligans? Was Dahai being one too?' Xiaohuan put the rice bowl down on the table.

Zhang Jian's heart suddenly started to pound, as if some ugly secret of his own was being exposed, a little at a time.

Erhai wrinkled his nose, furious that Xiaohuan was forcing him to talk about such awful things, his two cheeks so red they were nearly purple.

'He'd lifted up Auntie's mosquito net! And he was lifting up Auntie's clothes.'

A fit of nausea hit Zhang Jian. He had eaten too many pickled cucumbers, and now he was going to pay for it, the sour cucumbers and that repulsive scene came rolling up together, and caught in his throat. He dashed into the kitchen, grasped the concrete edges of the sink with both hands, and threw up. This revolting image, with its accompanying pungent and unpleasant smell, poured over him in waves – a boy, transformed by the light of the moon into a skinny black shadow, a black shadow that prowled to the side of a plank bed, and pulled aside the mosquito net to see a white, soft female body, whose shirt had become rolled up in her sleep . . . and the black shadow, feeling that it had not rolled up far enough, quietly stretched out a hand, and gradually lifted up that shirt that was almost rotted away with age, to reveal two soft, white, rounded objects . . . and it did not stop there, that young boy was reaching out towards those white, soft things . . .

No amount of vomiting could cleanse him of this vile vision, which was eroding his stomach from within. He had somehow ended up with both elbows propped on the sides of the sink, his head drooping low between his raised shoulders, and he was breathing in deep, heaving gulps. The repulsive image had already taken up residence deep within his guts, and he could feel it gradually eating them away to form a revolting scar. This was followed by a spasm of heart-piercing pain.

He wanted to grab hold of that unworthy creature, and tell him that those two objects were the first mouthful of food he ever took.

He exchanged heartsick looks with Xiaohuan, shivering, but not with cold.

'Erhai, do you like your auntie?' Zhang Jian asked. He cursed himself inwardly: what kind of damn stupid talk was this, what had it to do with the matter in hand?

Erhai did not speak.

'Auntie is closest to you two. She didn't even want to get married for your sakes.' In his heart he was bawling: where the hell do you think you're going with all this talk? What do you want the children to know? To know that there's a monstrous secret right next to them?

At work, the sound of gongs and drums could be heard from time to time, on top of the ear-shaking, deafening sounds of metal striking metal. When a furnace was tapped, the metal somehow became 'Anti-Revisionist Steel' or 'Anti-Imperialist Steel' or 'Loyalty Steel', and then people would beat gongs and drums, play musical instruments and sing, announcing the good news to Chairman Mao. There was enough good news to announce for one or two hours, and those were hours when you did not have to do any work. In all this noise and bustle, Zhang Jian still tried to hear the discussion that was going on in his own heart: was he going to beat Dahai to within an inch of his life for his vile behaviour? Then how grieved would Duohe be? If she had been able to make public her status as a mother, this ugly thing might never have happened.

People had got hold of some red silk from somewhere, and big silk pompoms were hanging all over the place, with another four red embroidered balls dangling from the crane. Zhang Jian was deeply grieved for Duohe: all her life she had lived as a mother and yet not a mother, a wife and not a wife. The coloured silk fluttered up and fell down, the loudspeaker was singing 'Steering the Seas Depends on the Helmsman'. A crowd of people who did not look like workers entered the workshop. Zhang Jian saw from the crane that the person at the head seemed to be Xiao Peng. And sure enough, it was.

Xiao Peng was chief of staff of one of the rebel factions in the factory. Today he was going to send a telegram of congratulation to the Party Central and Chairman Mao, to inform them that they had exceeded their quota of 'Loyalty Steel' by such-and-such a figure. Every worker had to listen to the text of Xiao Peng's telegram.

Zhang Jian was watching him; he had a real man's air about him now. For the first time he longed to speak to him about Duohe. If he still loved Duohe, then he should take her away with him. For better or worse, this ill-fated woman could be a wife for a while, and perhaps she could still be a mother. He had known Xiao Peng for many years, and thought he had a decent moral character.

Xiao Peng shook hands with the workers. He really had become a chief of staff. He was dressed in a set of newish summer canvas work clothes, the blue kind, rather tight at the waist, with a passing resemblance to an army uniform. In the height of summer the factory floor was like a blast furnace, but Xiao Peng was still wearing a helmet, not a hair out of place. He commended them all for their hard work, saying that the workers were the most dependable class of the Revolution. He said that he had nothing decent to give them as a token of his appreciation, but he would show willing anyway. Then he walked to the side, and dragged over a mobile ice-lolly box. He went up to every worker, and handed out two milk ice lollies apiece.

The heartfelt words that Zhang Jian had wanted to share with him were all gone, not a sentence left. He had thought that, like him, Xiao Peng hated that Party secretary who brought sour plum juice. Zhang Jian was standing right at the back, so it would have been relatively easy to sneak away, but just as he had taken two steps, Xiao Peng said: 'Zhang Jian, you have worked hard! In a while let's have a chat!'

He had gone from longing to talk to dreading it, with only a box of ice lollies in between. Nor did he know whether this counted as buying people's hearts, or whether buying off people's hearts justified his feeling of revulsion, but at that moment all he wanted to do was stay out of the way until it was all over. Out of sight out of mind, it was cleaner that way. Xiao Peng's eyes had homed in on him, but he persisted in avoiding him. He went into the toilet, where he squatted drily for half an hour. When he came out, the others told him that they had eaten his share of the ice lollies, and expressed gratitude to the commander-in-chief on his behalf.

The factory ceased production for several months, because too many new people were coming into power at the iron and steel company, and all the factories had been thrown into confusion. Zhang Jian and a friend in the building opposite took up pigeon fancying. That day he and Erhai went out to release some pigeons, taking the dog with them, when they saw a young fellow in an air force uniform looking around in all directions.

Without knowing why, Zhang Jian came to a halt, waiting for him to turn from the main road onto the smaller road in front of their building. He did not know what basis he had for knowing that he would turn this way. The air force soldier moved towards them, looking for the numbers on the buildings. Between smoke from fires and the giant posters only a few traces remained, and he asked Zhang Jian if he knew where number 20 was.

Erhai's eyes immediately lit up, and he stared at the young air force officer.

'Who are you looking for?' Zhang Jian asked.

'My name is Wang. There's this girl called Zhang Chunmei – is this her home?'

Erhai could no longer contain his pride as the younger brother of Zhang Chunmei, and said: 'Zhang Chunmei's my sister! This is my dad!'

The man from the air force shook hands with Zhang Jian. He realised at once that Wang had brought news he was finding hard to break to the family. He stared intently at the young officer, he had to make him understand that his spirit was strong, he could bear anything.

'Zhang Chunmei is in very good health, you needn't be afraid,' the soldier said.

Could it be that this man had seen his inner self-command as fear? So long as Girlie was still alive and in good shape, he did not care about anything else.

'However, the matter is not quite that simple.' The soldier was looking at him, with that fire shining in his eyes that one seldom sees outside the military.

Zhang Jian told Erhai to go back and tell his mother that someone had come from his sister's school, and that she should get the tea ready.

'Best if I tell you briefly first. Mothers tend to let their feelings run away with them. If you feel that her mother can bear it, there'll still be time to go and discuss it with her, how does that sound?'

Zhang Jian was anxious, upset and confused: how come this soldier had such a womanish way of speaking? If you've got something to say then say it, if you've got a fart coming let it out! He flapped his hand savagely at Erhai, told him to take himself off, and squatted down himself. The air force officer squatted down alongside him, four-square and stable just like him; clearly he too had grown up squatting under the eaves of a house somewhere in the North-east, drinking porridge made from maize stalks.

Once Erhai had gone, the soldier offered Zhang Jian a cigarette. He waved it away. Was there ever such a sluggish soldier in the whole world?

'Uncle, the reason I've come is to do some investigation into Zhang Chunmei's early life.'

Where was her father supposed to start?

'She was always a good child, from when she was small – pick any ten people, and all ten of them would praise her as a good child.'

'Has she ever suffered from any kind of mental abnormality?'

Zhang Jian did not understand. Surely he couldn't mean mentally ill?

The young officer smoked his cigarette as he began his tale. When she arrived at the gliding school everyone had thought Zhang Chunmei was a good girl too. The problem was with her personal file. There were several dozen young students in her group of new recruits, and three squads had taken the train from Nanjing. The person in charge of the group was responsible for managing the files for all the students. When they arrived at the school, Zhang Chunmei was the only one whose file had been lost. That did not matter, as a high-school student of fifteen or sixteen was unlikely to have any complex or difficult social experience or family connections, right? So they made her fill in a new form: she would have to recreate her own file piece by piece. When she had filled out the form, the personnel department put it into a new folder, and her life in the school started from this form, this one sheet of paper.

Nobody had a bad word to say about Zhang Chunmei. She was not afraid of hard work, and the first time she sat in a training glider she threw up, but she still did extra practice, just the same as usual.

She was too young to join the Party, but she was very quickly singled out as a young woman of potential by the Party branch. And most of all she was popular, she related to people in a relaxed and natural way. That was what everyone recalled about her before the trouble started.

What trouble was this?

It was her file. Her file was completely faked. Because she knew that losing her file on her way to join the army was the perfect opportunity to make use of a loophole.

What did she fake in her file?

In the form she filled in, she said her father was a worker in a rural commune, so was her mother, and all her brothers and sisters worked the land. The family was extremely poor, and both her grandparents were bedridden. No one would have noticed the forgery, but she shared a dormitory with seven other girls, and sometimes one of them would wake the others talking in her sleep. One night a girl was woken suddenly by Zhang Chunmei. What language was that? There seemed to be some Chinese words in it, and also some foreign words. The following morning, in front of all the girls in the dormitory, this girl said: Hey, Zhang Chunmei, you were jabbering away last night, all this stuff in a foreign language! Zhang Chunmei said she was talking nonsense. The girl said, You wait, one of these days I'll get someone to listen in with me, to prove it wasn't nonsense.

Zhang Jian felt like an aeroplane was running in his own head, the noise was so frightful that he could barely hear what the young officer was saying.

. . . After a while, one of the other female soldiers noticed that Zhang Chunmei did not go to sleep at night; she would sit on the bed. Someone else noticed that she would take her quilt and go to sleep in one of the classrooms. When asked why she was breaking the school rules, she said that the other girls in her dormitory made too much noise, and it was impossible to get to sleep. They could not allow people to sleep in the classrooms, no matter what the circumstances. If there was an inspection the school would be blamed by their superiors for this scandalous thing. But it would be possible to put up a canvas cot in a room with two female teachers, and even if the teachers had something to say in their dreams, it would not be a babble of voices talking noisily at once. And so they moved Zhang Chunmei into the dormitory with these two female teachers.

When Zhang Jian had heard this far, he could tell already what was coming next.

One of the teachers heard Zhang Chunmei speaking Japanese in the dead of night. Although the teacher had not studied Japanese, she had worked out what it must be. She quietly got up, and shook the other teacher awake. The two women sat on their beds, and heard Zhang Chunmei come out with a string of muddled, unclear talk and laughter, interspersed with a series of Japanese words. They reported the matter to the school. Where could a peasant child from an impoverished family, living in the poorest part of the remote countryside, far from any other settlement, have learned Japanese? That was how the suspicions of her file and her birth began.

Zhang Jian thought to himself, how could Girlie, with her fine brain, have done something so stupid? She had faked herself a family of peasants: peasants weren't as good as the working class!

The two female teachers did nothing to alarm Zhang Chunmei. They asked her casually, what crops do your family grow? How many rice crops do you plant every year? Do you keep pigs? Zhang Chunmei did pretty well, all told, and her accounts of farm work were all quite near the mark. At this time her classmates gossiped about her a lot: Zhang Chunmei isn't a bit like a country girl, when she had a wash on first coming to school, there were still marks from a bathing suit on her body! Country girls' hair was different, always dryish and yellowish at the tips, burned by the sun. Her classmates even thought she might be the daughter of some high-ranking army official; sometimes senior army officers were concerned that their subordinates would try to curry favour with them, and therefore would not subject the officers' children to enough hardship, meaning their child would emerge from the experience still a privileged child of the powerful. The teachers borrowed a tape recorder, and when Zhang Chunmei started to talk in her sleep again they secretly recorded her. They found a translator for these Japanese terms, which baffled them still more – sweet potato, potato, skirt, dog, auntie, pine cone, red-bean rice ball . . .

All these kinds of words, trivial things. Zhang Jian did not seem to be particularly disturbed.

Sometimes it was like a little child talking, with a child's intonation and pronunciation. The school doctor had a word with Zhang Chunmei. He asked about her environment from when she was small, how many people there were in the village, and whether anyone in those few families had gone to university to study foreign languages. Zhang Chunmei gave a detailed reply: the village was very small, just twenty households, and on one side was a mountain, which they had terraced for fields. When she went to high school she had to walk for more than two hours before she could catch a bus. The doctor said, Your family's so poor, and they still sent you to school? She said all the families sent their children to school, there was a very positive atmosphere in that village. You see, all those details, the way her story pretty much hung together? She had taken her tests in the Nanjing region, and one of the examiners from the school remembered very clearly the clothes Zhang Chunmei had worn the day she was tested: a very smart red wool coat, with a black fur collar and gold-rimmed buttons, clothes that could not conceivably belong to a country girl. The school security office, alarmed, spoke to Zhang Chunmei, and the true state of affairs came out. Why would she want to fake her family background? She did not speak. Not speaking would be severely punished! She still did not speak. Could it be that this was a case of parental cruelty? She shook her head, vigorously and sadly, as if to say *Trust you to think up something like that.*

'So where's my girl now?' said Zhang Jian.

'You know that in the army fabricating a file is a criminal act; she will receive her punishment through the military court.'

'Where will she be punished?' So long as Girlie came back alive, any punishment would be all right.

'They have temporarily suspended her from classes, and sent her to hospital for a spell to see how she gets on. Delusional psychosis can be cured. First they'll try her with a course of medicine.'

Zhang Jian's grief-stricken face turned towards the ground. What medicine were they using? Let them not be turning a perfectly healthy girl into an idiot! A file of ants were cheerfully crawling along the ground, some of them carrying a moth's wing between them. Weren't ants supposed to be 'bringers of good news'? His little girl was being treated as a madwoman and shut up in the mad hospital, his heart was pierced through with agony, and the ants were still bringing their good news, just the same. He could not hear what the young officer was jabbering on about. He would go to the hospital and bring Girlie back: Forget about the army, if there was any dying to do, they'd die together, as a family!

'. . . the school told me to go and talk to her parents, to take a look at the environment in which Zhang Chunmei lived. The experts in the psychology department thought that Zhang Chunmei's case was unlike other people: her delusions were not at all that kind of . . . For example, suppose she were to say she had been born into a general's family, that kind of delusion would be understandable. Do you see what I mean?'

Zhang Jian nodded.

'I also visited your factory. The local Neighbourhood Committee spoke quite highly of her mother too. However you look at it, everything about the environment in which she grew up was very good. Before she came to the gliding school, she had always been an excellent student – I have seen all her teachers. Could I have a word with her mother now?'

By this time, the balcony of the communal walkway had become a viewing platform, with a row of people leaning on the railings. Everybody was watching the stage to see what kind of drama a soldier from the air force of the People's Liberation Army and Zhang Jian were going to act out. The air force comrade must certainly have told Zhang Jian something very upsetting: he was squatting with his back hunched and his neck drawn in, and you could see at a glance that it was as upsetting as upsetting could be. Something must be the matter with his Girlie. What had happened? Couldn't be anything good! Let her not have become a revolutionary martyr, another Auntie Lei Feng!

By this time a couple of female neighbours had dragged Xiaohuan to a place on the communal walkway where there was a gap between the banners hanging from the roof of the building, pointing out to her the two people squatting at the bottom of the building.

'Has something happened to our Girlie?' Xiaohuan called out.

Zhang Jian turned his head and found that everyone in the entire building had arrived on the scene. Even if there was nothing the matter with Girlie, she was already on public trial. He saw that Xiaohuan's words had brought Duohe over too, her startlingly white face was looking first at him, then at the officer.

He hurriedly came to a decision. For the moment he would keep the child's mother in the dark. He, the head of the family, would take responsibility for when to tell her, and how to tell her.

The officer was a little surprised by this sudden display of dogmatism. He stood up, and Zhang Jian raised his face and waved. As he walked onto the main road, he could still see him squatting there. He thought this was such a simple, honest working man, he had even forgotten the courtesy of inviting him in for a cup of tea, and he had been so hard hit by the shock.

The neighbours saw Zhang Jian get to his feet and stand for a while, dizzy and half blinded, then walk to the entrance to the staircase, his back and legs like those of an old man. The dozens of bicycles in the stairwell were as old and broken as the building itself, and he knocked several of them over, with a noise like a pile of scrap iron collapsing. Zhang Jian made no attempt to pick up the bicycles, but went slowly up the stairs. He said to the mother and aunt of his children when they came to meet him on the second floor: 'What've you both come running down here for? Nothing to see here! Girlie's sick and in hospital, isn't she, that's all!'

The audience on the balconies all heard clearly and whispered in each other's ears: 'What d'you think's the matter with her?'

'Look at Zhang Jian, he's old with worry!'

Zhang Jian continued to berate Xiaohuan and Duohe loudly, looking over at the neighbours too: 'Go home, the lot of you! You just had to come out and join the fun, didn't you?! You won't be content unless something bad's happened, none of you!'

The people whispered quietly among themselves: 'Listen to that, something has happened after all!'

They did not hear Xiaohuan ask urgently in a low voice: Just what disease has Girlie caught?

They walked to the fourth floor, and Zhang Jian experienced a surge of dread. They would have to pass all the way along the communal walkway, surrounded on all sides by concern and questions, before they could reach the door of their home. The curious eyes lining the corridor would suddenly notice the oddness of this family with its one man and two women. This Great Age had no place for oddity.

Zhang Jian stiffened his resolve, put a peaceful, unperturbed expression on his face, smiled at the concerned neighbours lining the way, and said to Xiaohuan: 'The comrade from the air force was here on business, and brought us news since we were on his way. Girlie isn't in good health, she's being treated in hospital.'

The corridor of neighbours was still not entirely satisfied. But as soon as they saw that Zhang Jian was only talking to his wife, and was not inclined to pay them any attention, they had no choice but to go their separate ways.

All the neighbours managed to find out was that Zhang Jian had not bought a train ticket until five days later. There was a power struggle going on over one section of the line, two factions had come to blows, and no trains ran for quite a few days. Zhang Jian was going to see his daughter. She was not seriously ill, she just could not sleep, as Xiaohuan reassured the neighbours, household by household. Nothing the matter at all. Xiaohuan went out visiting, to console the neighbours a bit, and herself as well. Twenty neighbouring families had the wool pulled over their eyes.

Only Auntie Duohe, invisible and unseen, sensed that matters were not so simple.

More than a month later Zhang Jian came back, dried up and thin. Like a camel that has walked for dozens of miles on short rations and no water, his eyes had become two little patches of desert. The neighbours wondered, what could have put him in this state?

Zhang Jian had no account to give of whether Girlie had managed to go to sleep, whether she had returned to her lessons, or whether she was flying in the sky in the training glider once more, or playing basketball for the girls' team at school. The neighbours would have to wait for Xiaohuan to give them a proper account, one at a time. Leaving the neighbours without a proper account was unheard of, not one family, upstairs or down, had had any business that was left hanging without a proper explanation.

But not a sound came from the Zhang home, and no one came out to ease their minds over Girlie. Xiaohuan came and went, but surprisingly did not mention her daughter. In the beginning when Girlie had gone to the gliding school, hadn't they all been so sad to see her leave? The neighbours started to become dissatisfied with the Zhang family. You're going to need more than a few red-bean rice balls to hoodwink us, Xiaohuan.

Xiaohuan continued with her jokey nature, just as usual, going upstairs with a bunch of leeks in her hand, saying with a laugh to anyone she met, These old leeks smell horrible now, but when I've made them into dumplings they'll smell just great. Come up and have some, won't you?

The Zhang family's Auntie Duohe was quieter, standing, all white and clean, at the corner of the stairs, to make way for people coming up. Sometimes when people were carrying things in their hands or carrying a bicycle upstairs on their shoulders, there she would be, standing soundless in the dim light, like a white shadow. It could give you quite a shock. Duohe's excessive politeness, her silence and the way in which she had consistently not given any bother for more than ten years, now were starting to become troublesome. In the eyes and minds of the neighbours, she was a source of doubt and suspicion, one for which the Zhang family had never given a proper account. They suddenly felt like the Zhangs had been keeping them in the dark for years over the matter of this mysterious maiden aunt. How could this be? There was no keeping back anything from the families in the building, in their going up and coming down, going out and coming in, not of their motive, aim or destination – 'Going out?' 'Yep, off to buy some salt.' 'Are you cooking? What're you making?' 'Steamed cornmeal bread!' 'Carrying your bike upstairs? Are you going to repair it?' 'That's right, the brakes are loose!' 'Where are you off to so late?' 'I've been nagged to bloody death, it's driving me crazy!' This aunt came and went with never a word, rushing off who knows where, to do things that she never disclosed to them. At the very most she would ask with a half-bow: 'Come off work?' but you could tell just by looking that she did not plan to give you a chance to detain her any further.

The neighbours noticed that she had put on her work clothes and peak cap again, shouldered her bag and gone down the stairs. The factory had returned to work. They were going to bring out the first steel for several months, which made it a matter of great moment, and gongs and drums and coloured silk were everywhere, spread over the heaven and covering the earth.

11

In her canvas work bag, Duohe carried the steel serial numbers that she had cut while the factory was out of action off to the workshop. There were more than fifty of them. There was a woman in charge of the workshop now, and she asked how she could carry so many. She smiled briefly and nodded. The workshop director said that some more workers had come, so Duohe's workbench would be moved to under the tree outside the door. Once the workshop's reed-matting shelter had been enlarged, she would get a good place. She nodded again. A few poles had been put up beneath the tree, with azure plastic sheeting stretched over them to keep out the rain. Duohe was delighted with her new surroundings.

Now it was the characters 'Made in China' that she carved the most every day. Because these four characters were hardest. Her work was never rejected: one character on each piece of steel, which were to be stamped onto wheel hoops for trains or sheet steel destined for Vietnam, Africa or Albania. Duohe's unusually focused eyes and handiwork had been sent to three continents. The workshop director would call out to her occasionally when she needed something, and Duohe would raise her head from the workbench, but the director suspected that Duohe did not recognise her at all. Sometimes the director thought of telling her that the name Zhu Duohe should be on the list of commendations on the workshop blackboard, but because she never spoke out at meetings they had to pick someone else to commend instead. On the whole, the director reflected that this might be a step too far; if she did not make Duohe aware of it, she would have no idea of the existence of this 'roll of honour', so she just said 'You've worked hard, well done!' and dispensed with the rest of the guidance. The director reckoned that Duohe did not know the vast majority of her colleagues in the workshop; when she looked at their faces, all she saw was 'Made in China'.

One afternoon in April, the factory's new leader came. He had locked up the factory head and Party secretary, and after demoting them to the status of paroled criminals, had himself become leader. Director Peng of the Factory Revolutionary Committee, who had only just turned thirty, had no easy task ahead of him. He had to maintain the output of steel in the steelworks, while at the same time launching counter-attacks against a youth who wanted to be leader. That young man was the chief of staff of another big rebel army, which was organising general offensives every day, and attempting to snatch power out of Director Peng's hands in a *coup d'état*.

Director Peng was just passing through, when he happened to glance sideways out of the window of the Volga car that had belonged to the old factory head, and immediately told the driver to pull over. He saw the sky-blue awning suspended between two trees, and the half-stooped figure beneath it.

When he had got out of the car and was walking towards that figure he regretted it a little: if the old things which he had already dealt with tidily and set aside were to become chaotic again that would be bad. But Director Peng was no longer the green Xiao Peng of those years, he was confident that he could seize the reins of two thousand workers who were in chaos and master them all, and if he allowed a little bit of chaos into his own emotions too there would be no great harm done. If he wished to master his emotions again he could do so at once.

He was surprised to find that Duohe was thinner and smaller than she had been in his memory. She raised her face, as if dazzled, and it took her roughly ten seconds to focus. Director Peng held out his hand to her, and she bowed to him, turning over two hands covered in steel filings to show Director Peng, as her face blossomed into a smile. There were threadlike wrinkles on her face when she smiled, but there was more life to it than to her former absurdly pale and clear skin.

Director Peng suddenly became the green boy Xiao Peng again; he pulled her hand over to the other side of the workbench and shook it vigorously. The old intimacy and warmth was still there, separated by just two layers of thin calluses and one layer of steel cuttings.

He became very chatty. And not one sentence of it was of an appropriate level for a man of his status: he said that he'd seen her from a very long way off, and thought she looked familiar, but did not dare to be certain it was her, it seemed that she had got thinner, nothing else had changed. His talk was no more elevated than that of the dependants.

As she was listening to him, she picked up a small steel file, and worked on the serial number clamped in her table vice, trimming a bit here, tidying a bit there. After a couple of strokes of the file, she stood up, and gave him a smile.

He thought, where else could I find such a good woman? At her work all day long, eyes fixed straight ahead, not nagging or fussing at all. Part of the reason he had been so fond of her in the past was her lack of words. His childhood and growing up had been too full of women who were good talkers, but there was no one who had such a talent for silence.

The workshop director came with a crude, mass-produced stool and invited Director Peng to sit. The stool was for workers to sit on, so it was not much lower than the workbench, and as soon as Director Peng sat down, he immediately got up again; when he sat his eyes and Duohe's were no longer on the same level.

When he was about to leave he invited Duohe to drop by his place for a visit. The pounding of Duohe's heart was audible even to him. How many changes had the nation and its people been through in the past few years? Could it be that his invitation was still exactly the same as a few years previously?

Duohe walked with Xiao Peng back to the Volga. The fact that Xiao Peng rode in a Volga must have left a very deep impression on her, and out of all the great matters this was one that was bound to register with her. Duohe was no longer as free with him as she had been at her workstation. A man who rode in a Volga casually asking her to drop by and sit for a while was no longer as straightforward as she had imagined, and the more casual he was, the less straightforward the situation became.

Although Xiao Peng had the status of a man who could ride in a Volga, he still lived in the same dormitory room as before. The difference was that the entire corridor had become a dormitory for Xiao Peng's bodyguards. These days Xiao Peng's safety was a matter of concern to a great many people.

Xiao Peng made the bodyguards give his room a good clean. They carried an old sofa over from the factory headquarters, but the cover was filthy, so he had them spread a blue-and-white-striped towel from the bathhouse over it. He thought that there could be nothing more offensive to Duohe than to make her 'sit for a while' on this squalid sofa, reeking of cigarettes and feet. The Party secretary whose power had been wrested away was so white and clean to look at, yet he often used to sit on that sofa picking at his feet. Duohe's cleanliness and tidiness was the characteristic that Xiao Peng found most appealing – when he saw her in front of her workbench, her work overalls might have been so big they were like a blue sack of grain, but she had washed and ironed them in such an orderly, precise way. Although the whole gang of women had been wearing the same blue grain sacks, Duohe's was still a beautiful grain sack.

Perhaps because she was Japanese?

The secret that Duohe was a Japanese woman had remained with Xiao Peng. Xiao Shi had been silenced by death. So long as Xiao Peng overlooked this fact, Duohe could probably occupy her fraudulent place among the countless women of China in safety, to the end of her days. Every time this secret floated up from within his mind, it horrified him, but at the same time it gave rise to an indescribable tenderness. She was a foreigner! She was a woman born of the enemy, one who had come close to breeding up more of the enemy herself. The taste of a daughter of the enemy must be a unique experience, it was sure to be a delicacy.

Sometimes his tenderness had its source in pity for all she had suffered in the course of her life, sometimes in anger on her behalf at the unfairness of her life in the Zhang family, neither a wife nor a concubine.

Sometimes he was sentimentally attached to her, if only because he secretly sensed that they would never actually become a couple. Even if everyone in the world approved, he himself would not necessarily do so.

Sometimes he was confused and bewildered for a moment. He

had endured heavy wrongs: for her sake he endured a blow to the face from his father, and no doubt betrayal by his own son, for as soon as he was an adult, the first thing he was going to do was expose his father Xiao Peng. For her sake, he had stood fast against his wife's forgiveness as her tears flowed – his wife's weeping forgiveness had hurt his heart so much that a part of it had died. He had endured all of this, just in order *not* to marry this daughter of the enemy Duohe? Xiao Peng thought that it was his own freedom that he had ransomed from his marriage; it was in order to love Duohe freely without getting married. Women who could marry were everywhere, women who could be courted without marriage were exceedingly rare. The fact that she was the daughter of the enemy alone was enough for Xiao Peng to indulge in heart-stirring romance, but without any danger of getting completely drawn in.

He had the guards scrub the glass until it was as clear as air. The windows in the Zhang family home were so transparent that you could mistake them for empty frames. He also made them scrub the floor, bottoms wiggling. The floors in this building were made of wood, and when he dragged out all the shoes and cardboard boxes from under the bed he discovered that it had once been painted dark red. But the rest of the floor inside the room was full of bumps and hollows, and its surface was rough and ridged, well on its way to returning to its original state as a log – one felled by the water's edge, to be slowly eroded away for years by the sun and rain. The guards did all they could to make the floor a bit cleaner, to scrub the grime, and to chip out the dry grains of rice, melon-seed husks and finger- and toenail clippings from the cracks.

It turned out that this room could be made bright and very sweet-smelling. In April and May, the slopes of the mountain were covered with red, downy wild lilies, so Xiao Peng had his guards pick a large bunch. Fiddling around with flowers and plants did not fit in with his status as Director of the Revolutionary Committee, but red flowers could be understood in another way.

This afternoon Duohe was going to come to 'sit for a while' after work. Around five o'clock the factory's alarm suddenly let out a long wail, and a guard reported to Xiao Peng that the opposition faction had launched a new offensive. They had gone to the outskirts of the city to mobilise a great mob of peasants, and now peasants with farm tools in their hands were converging from all sides: from the mountain, from trucks, from tractors, gradually pressing closer to the steelworks.

The members of the opposition faction were from Shanghai and the south, and made up the minority in the factory; as things stood they had no hope of occupying the factory Revolutionary Committee by force of arms. They had gone to the peasants to stir up divisions, saying that the steelworks had drawn off the water from their reservoir, having originally agreed to lay on running water for them, but after many years they had failed to make good on their promise. The steel factory dumped piles of rubbish on their land, and paid no rent for the land they used in order to do so. As soon as the opposition had snatched the power from the Revolutionary Committee, the peasants could depend on them for water pipes and land rent.

Xiao Peng strapped on his brass-buckled leather belt, slung his .54 calibre pistol over his shoulder, donned his steel helmet and left. At this moment Duohe did not exist, until she bumped into him on her way up the stairs.

'You can't go back home, the factory's surrounded! It's dangerous for you to go home now!' said Xiao Peng, pulling her along. Duohe followed him as he sped down the steps, crossed the courtyard and got into his Volga. All the guards jumped onto their bicycles behind him. In an instant they had become contestants in a bike race, following hard on the heels of the Volga.

Duohe followed Xiao Peng into the factory headquarters. A great red flag had been raised on the roof, and Xiao Peng stood beneath it, a loudhailer in his hand, shouting in all directions: 'Comrades, workers of the Revolution! The reactionary faction wants to force us to cease production! Our answer to their counter-revolutionary attack, their sabotage of anti-imperialism and anti-revisionism is this: Hold your ground and remain at your post! If any of them should dare to set foot on the base of the furnace, a rolling flood of molten steel will transform them into a puff of black smoke!'

All the main gates of the factory had been closed, and workers from Xiao Peng's faction stood inside the boundary wall, holding all kinds of spears and big knives, ready to cut down anyone who came over.

Several cranes drove to the foot of the factory headquarters, and lifted sack after sack of cement used for repairing the workshops to the roof of the building. Soon, work on the fortifications was under way.

Duohe had been ordered to take refuge in the meeting room, with two elderly secretaries as her companions. After dark, voices could be heard very clearly shouting outside, telling Xiao Peng to stop resisting, and to surrender as quickly as possible, otherwise they would not guarantee his unworthy life.

Xiao Peng had stopped fighting a war of words with the people on the other side of the wall. The big floodlights in the factory had all been extinguished, with only a few searchlights sweeping back and forth in the darkness. Every time the searchlights swept into the meeting room, Duohe would look at the clock on the wall: eight o'clock, ten o'clock, eleven o'clock . . .

Duohe's two companions were close to tears. They were just a couple of years away from retirement: a time to enjoy their old age in peace with their grandchildren in their arms, and now this, there was no chance of a good end for them now. Even if the opposition faction did not storm their way in, they would be surrounded anyway, and would starve to death inside the building.

It occurred to them that when meetings were held in the factory headquarters, they would sometimes bring out a few peanuts and melon seeds for their visitors. Sure enough, they groped in a cupboard and found a packet of peanuts. They invited Duohe to eat, and shared a fistful with her. Douhe packed peanuts into the pocket of her overalls, and hurried up to the roof.

As soon as Xiao Peng saw her arrive, he immediately shouted at her to go down. She paid no attention, and poured the peanuts into the pockets of Xiao Peng's coat. A map was still spread out on the ground in front of him, a hand-drawn relief map of the factory area that he had drawn from memory, as he deployed the people around him in attack and defence.

He raised his head, and saw that Duohe had not left; she was watching him gesticulating and waving his hands. He could not see her face clearly, but he could tell that his appearance as a great commander in this age of great deeds had left a deep impression on her.

If he did not eat those peanuts she would not leave, so Xiao Peng chewed hard and issued commands with peanutty breath. Group after group left after receiving their orders, only for new groups to gather, waiting for him to issue further commands. After he had given out all the orders he had one remaining for Duohe: 'Quick, downstairs! What's it going to look like if you're here?'

At this moment the disaster occurred. The opposition outside the factory had no plans to attack the main gate, or the side gates, nor did they climb the walls. They had somehow got hold of a train, which they used to enter the factory directly along the rail tracks. The people inside the factory had no time to react, and they did not realise it was too late until the train had been driven inside, overturning an empty truck parked on the track.

From the train a black mass of the Great Peasants' Army came pouring out. The southerners of the opposition faction were not prone to sudden flare-ups of temper like the North-easterners, who would fling themselves into fights without a thought for their own lives. Their aim was to seize power, whoever helped them was fine by them, and the peasants had time on their hands, so why not turn them into an army of volunteers? Under the direction of a small number of workers, the peasants immediately occupied the strategic parts of the factory area. The North-easterners all retreated into a workshop and the factory headquarters building. Before long the peasants had occupied another workshop, and the club opposite the factory headquarters. The club building was not as tall as the headquarters, but it offered a better line of fire.

The iron staircase leading to the roof was sawn away. So long as they held fast, no one could think of climbing up there, and Director Peng's safety was ensured.

The gunshots started in the small hours of the morning.

The firepower of the opposing side was very fierce. One after another of the cement bags were pierced through, and the fortifications gradually started to shrink.

Xiao Peng said, through gritted teeth: 'Did that gang of dog fuckers rob the munitions depot or what? How can they have enough ammunition?'

They fought until dawn, when both sides ceased fire. After a brief inspection, Xiao Peng ascertained that there had been no casualties, and even Duohe was as calm and peaceful as usual. Now she could not leave. Their date had become a drama of life and death, and the emotions that came with them. How much longer would they be together? Staying on this bald rooftop with nothing to eat and nothing to drink, two locusts tied by the same piece of string, or two plants linked at the root, kicked into the mud by a cow's hoof, where they would have to struggle on slowly together. Xiao Peng felt that so long as they were not shot dead by a bullet from the other side, this assignation was the kind of thing you could only find on a stage.

'Are you thirsty?' Xiao Peng asked Duohe.

Duohe hurriedly looked all around her; the big bucket of water that had been brought up had already been completely drained.

'I was asking you!' Xiao Peng thought to himself that she really was a good woman, thinking at once about his thirst.

Xiao Peng very quickly became immersed in preparations for a new battle. Duohe kept looking at him, hoping he would notice that her worst discomfort was not hunger or thirst, but the need to relieve herself. When he had made all the arrangements as best he could, Xiao Peng beckoned to her. She ran after him, their backs bent, to the edge of the building, where there was a shallow, concave trough for rainwater to drain away. Xiao Peng ordered his subordinates: 'Close your eyes, all of you, and turn your faces away!' His own eyes were squeezed tight shut, but he did not avert his face. He squatted in front of her, and held open a set of overalls.

Her face was scarlet to the neck.

Right up until the opposition faction withdrew its troops, Xiao Peng continued to make temporary toilets for Duohe. After a time they did not run to the edge of the building, Xiao Peng just used a set of overalls to shield Duohe's lower half, and the thing was done. It was just as well that there was nothing to eat or drink, so this embarrassing event only took place once every seven or eight hours.

One after the other, the peasants recalled that the rice in their paddy fields would be ripe soon, and they had to go to let the water out. Some of the peasants' wives and children came looking for them, saying that if they got themselves killed in battle the family would lose a source of work points, and who would foot the bill? The peasants' great attack on the city came to an end early in the morning of the third day.

The iron ladder was welded back into position, and Xiao Peng and his allies retreated one by one back down from the roof. As they were withdrawing it started to rain heavily, soaking the cement, which was well on the way to becoming a permanent fortification. Xiao Peng told all the others to leave first, and he and Duohe remained until the very last.

The rain hissed down, flowing onto both of their faces. Xiao Peng looked at Duohe looking at him as if this was more romantic than any action.

'Thank you.'

She did not understand what he was thanking her for.

'Thank you for the peanuts.' For two days and two nights he had directed the campaign with verve and energy, struggling to save a dangerous situation. Had all this depended on a handful of peanuts? He did not know himself.

She also said: 'Thank you?'

'What are you thanking me for?'

Through a curtain of rainwater he saw her face blush scarlet again.

Xiao Peng had matters of vital importance to attend to, and when they came down from the building he and Duohe parted company.

❖

When Zhang Jian and Xiaohuan saw Duohe staggering home, they both came downstairs to meet her. What had become of her in the fighting? She looked terrible – what had happened?

Duohe just said that she had been trapped on the roof of the factory headquarters with no food. She had never properly reconciled with them after their quarrel, and the conversation for the most part was Xiaohuan answering her own questions: 'What've you been doing to yourself? Nothing to eat for two days? For sure you've not eaten! And not washed your face either? How could you have, stuck in that place?!'

Afterwards Xiaohuan said to Duohe that she too had more or less eaten nothing for two days. She thought that Duohe had been laid low by a bullet in some hole or other, and who knew what she was going through! One moment she was pushing and shoving Duohe, the next dragging her, and at the kitchen window of every family they passed, no matter whether the window was open or shut, she would announce her good news to those inside: 'She's back! Right as rain!'

When she came across an open window, a reply would come from inside: 'His sister-in-law's back? Well, that's good!'

Some neighbours passed the three Zhangs in the stairwell, and they all had questions about Auntie Duohe's escape from danger. By the time they were disappearing from view, each neighbour was thinking: Well, you're not keeping *this* business from us all. So how come you're not giving us a clear answer on Girlie? For all we know she's caught some shameful disease!

Xiaohuan knew they owed the neighbours an explanation with regard to Girlie. But she faced down the eyes that seemed to be pursuing her, cracking jokes and cursing the same as usual. Whatever they owed, they would have to keep on owing. Zhang Jian had been back for a good few months, looking dark and thin, before he had told her and Duohe the truth. Girlie had already been withdrawn from the gliding school. She was not willing to face the questioning neighbours who lined the way home, so Zhang Jian had taken her back to his old home in the North-east. Thanks to Stationmaster Zhang's connections, he had found her a job in the county town without too much difficulty. When Xiaohuan heard this she almost came to blows with Zhang Jian, and told him to go at once to bring Girlie back. She had never heard of any shame in the world that could crush people to death. Zhang Jian told her that Girlie had said that if he forced her to return she would beat her head against the wall until she bashed her brains out.

The day after Xiaohuan had learned where Girlie had gone, a cadre from the Neighbourhood Committee asked her: 'I hear Girlie was talking Japanese in the air force school, and she got expelled?'

Xiaohuan, who had been chattering away idly with several old ladies in the Neighbourhood Committee, continued in the same bantering tone: 'Yes, and your mum's been expelled too! It was our little girl who expelled the air force. That's the air force's loss!'

When she left the Neighbourhood Committee she did not go home, but went up the mountain. She had never climbed up there: why would a lover of noise and bustle like Xiaohuan take herself off up the mountain? She found a place to sit out of the wind, and suddenly she felt like she could see for miles. What did Girlie and Zhang Jian know? So afraid of people whispering in each other's ears, nudging each other with their elbows. Let them whisper, let them nudge, no shame could last for long. Other people will get into some new trouble soon enough, then they'll have a new shame, and once there's a new shame, the old shame will die down, like nothing had ever happened.

When she came back down she brought this vision with her, along with a brain full of cool, clean mountain wind. At supper she announced to Dahai, Erhai, Duohe and Zhang Jian that she was going to take action, and bring Girlie home herself.

'Even thieves and loose women have the face to carry on living, and eat three square meals a day!' Xiaohuan said. 'Look at the counter-revolutionary in this building, doesn't he spend all day at the market in his white counter-revolutionary's armband, buying vegetables for his wife?'

Dahai's dark, heavy eyebrows wrinkled up into a bunch.

'Dahai, what're you doing?' Xiaohuan rapped with her chopsticks on Dahai's bowl.

'What am I going to tell my classmates? That my big sister was talking Japanese in her sleep, and she faked her identity to boot . . .? My classmates even clubbed together to buy her a diary as a gift!'

'Tell them just that!' Xiaohuan said.

'Tell them what?' said Dahai. 'Say my sister was punished by a military court?'

'Oh, so when your sister was glorious you shared her glory, but when your sister's punished she's not your sister?'

'I never said she wasn't.' Dahai ate a mouthful of porridge, and through the slurping added: 'If it was me, I'd fake my identity too.'

'Why?' Zhang Jian asked.

Dahai kept quiet.

'He said he'd make up a family background too. Our family's not good enough for him!' Xiaohuan said. 'He'd prefer to make up a family background, say his dad drags a stick around begging for his dinner. Even that's better than our family!'

Dahai sunk his teeth deep into Duohe's pickled cucumbers, and said: 'Too right!'

Xiaohuan was just about to put him in his place, when it suddenly hit her that he and Girlie were the same; willing to choose a family that was even poorer, and parents who had still less to boast about. All too likely, she and Dahai had sensed from a very young age that there was something dark, tangled and messy concealed in their family, a tangle whose threads could never be set in order again, and they had been born right into the middle of it. That was when everything had only just begun to be a mess; Uncle Xiao Shi's death had also been a turning point, and Uncle Xiao Peng's disappearance was another. The adults had always been evasive about the true relationship between them and they had guessed that there was something not entirely clean about these two women and this one man.

There was a persistent feeling of awkwardness. Poor Girlie, you would think she was so cheerful, with her rosy cheeks that showed nothing but happiness, and a mouth that was always smiling or laughing, whether open or closed. Yet inside she was so timid, and full of self-contempt. In all likelihood, from when she first began to make sense of the world, she had been waiting with extreme caution for some disaster or tragedy to befall this family. Because of this she felt so inferior that all she wanted was to be a peasant girl from some remote, backward village. None of the adults had noticed her continual state of fear and worry, or all the mental suffering she had endured. Perhaps she had even guessed her own bloodline: who was to say that she hadn't unconsciously noticed Duohe's hands, with their stumpy fingers and rounded joints, each chubbier than the last . . . the same in every detail as her own? Who could say that she hadn't seen her Aunt Duohe's expression shining out of her own camel's eyes, so like her father's, as she looked in the mirror? And noticed the baby-fine hair that grew on the back of her neck below her hairline, so that whenever she wore a high collar, furry wisps were squeezed outside? Had Girlie realised that this baby hair was identical to that of her aunt? And when she realised, had she broken out in a cold sweat? Girlie had never cried or made a fuss. Ever since she was very small, she had been an undemanding child, but all along she had soundlessly, wordlessly taken in everything with her eyes and ears. All the adults' trouble and scheming had been for nothing. Don't think you could hide anything from her.

That day Xiaohuan sat in front of the table, her heart full of that baby Girlie, wrapped in a cherry-red cloak. As the young Xiaohuan carried her about in her arms, wherever she went, she would always hear people say 'Girlie's got a lucky face!' and the young Xiaohuan would forget that she had not given birth to Girlie herself. At such times, she would never have believed that Girlie would grow up to have such bitterness in her heart. That the moment she started to understand the world would be the moment she started to live in fear, to bear a burden of shame.

Dahai finished his meal, wiped his mouth and got up, saying: 'Humph. All over the nation, the people are waging revolution. If there's anything wrong, best to come clean while there's still time.'

The three adults did not move a muscle. They listened to him leaving them behind, squeezing himself into the crowded ranks of the populace of the entire nation.

In the two days when Duohe had vanished without trace, a great many terrifying thoughts had passed through Xiaohuan's mind: perhaps someone had informed on Duohe, and she'd been taken directly from the workshop, taken away to some place that never saw daylight. She had also thought that since the quarrel, Duohe had become estranged from her and Zhang Jian, never speaking to them, and if she had something to say she would say it through Erhai and Dahai. Perhaps she had finally had enough of this kind of life, and put an end to it herself. This was a great age for suicide. And Duohe came from a race that glorified taking their own life.

Now Duohe only had Erhai to talk to. Sometimes Xiaohuan heard him next door, replying to her in a few short sentences. She did not know what Erhai said that caused Duohe to give a gurgle of laughter. Erhai was not popular, he was prone to use his fists before he opened his mouth, so there was no one for him to talk to outside either. Often people came to the door to complain, saying that Erhai had been wrestling, and had brought his opponents down so heavily that they could not get up again. Now and again Erhai would leave Blackie at home, so Duohe would talk to the dog, in the same language she had used with the children in their infancy, half Japanese, half Chinese, heavily interspersed with words that only the most barbaric spirits could understand.

12

The factory ceased production again.

In the increasingly sultry days, gunshots would ring out from time to time, silencing the pigeons and cicadas. At such times a hush would fall over everything; you would hear the gunshots and echoes pile up, then fall away. Soon the pigeons only dared to circle round their own rooftops.

The neighbours had heard that Director Peng of the Revolutionary Committee had been captured by the opposition, which was now back in power. Several months passed, then Director Peng's faction rescued him, returning power once more into his hands.

The army dispatched a division to garrison the city. They put all the factories under martial law, and then the factories went back to work.

The new hut for the serial-number cutting was erected at last. With great reluctance, Duohe took her leave of the sky-blue tent. After work resumed she was always hoping to encounter Xiao Peng's grey Volga again, but the chance had not yet come.

Just as Xiao Peng had predicted, those two days on the roof six months earlier had become a unique experience in both their lives, and this experience naturally gave Duohe much to think about. Whenever she sat alone, facing the workbench, she saw Xiao Peng's silhouette in the night: he had led her to the edge of the building, ordering his subordinates to turn their faces away and shut their eyes. Xiao Peng was half squatting, neck and shoulders curled in, spreading out those work overalls for her, in fact he cut almost as sorry a figure as she did. At first, Duohe did not dare to think about this embarrassing predicament, but later she started to enjoy her recollections of the scene. She seemed to remember that Xiao Peng had hurriedly turned back in the misty light to give her a fleeting smile. Just like a man and a woman who had had no secrets between them, only he (or she) could serve this unromantic physical need. She felt that all sound had vanished, even the words that he had been shouting without a pause were silent. There was only the sound of her relieving herself, like rain beating urgently on the concrete. Xiao Peng had been closest to that sound. Xiao Peng could even hear her involuntary long sigh of release. He had just held up the work overalls to hide her shame – whose overalls? Were they his own? She had no way to find out. He had shut his eyes tightly. *Were* they shut tightly? What if they weren't? Then what could he see? He would not have been able to see anything on such a dark night. Duohe would not have cared even if he could. Her relationship with Xiao Peng had changed in a single night.

Every time Xiao Peng held open the overalls, half squatting on the edge of the roof, his life was in fact under threat. He was not behind the barricade, which left him exposed to any sniper's bullet. For this reason the people inside the fortifications with their faces turned away and eyes shut were hurrying him along in hoarse voices: 'Director Peng! It's not safe! Hurry up, come back!'

She now thought that Xiao Peng, curling up his body to make a temporary screen for her out of the overalls, had not cut a sorry figure at all, he was deeply romantic.

Xiao Peng's Volga appeared. Duohe's workbench had been carried into the new mat shed, directly facing a window. Outside there was a stretch of wild grass, and on the far side was the road that led to the main gate. Xiao Peng's grey Volga drove past, reducing its speed, as it prepared to park on the stretch of level ground outside Duohe's window. Duohe waved to the car. The roadbed was a lot higher than this row of reed huts, and the wheels were just level with the top of the window frame, making her invisible to anyone sitting in the car.

The grey Volga stopped briefly, and then drove away again. Not long after, the workshop director said to Duohe: 'Director Peng of the Factory Revolutionary Committee phoned just now, he wants you to go and see him.'

Duohe carefully washed the steel filings from her hands, took off her cap, considered for a moment and put it back on again. She had been wearing the cap all day, and her hair was certain not to be up to much, better to keep the cap safely on.

As soon as Director Peng saw Duohe, he said to her: 'Go to the hot-water stove outside the back gate and wait for me. I'll be there soon.'

An assignation in a boiler room?

Duohe had already seen Xiao Peng use his extensive powers to call the wind and summon the rain, a little assignation would certainly be even more thoroughly planned and executed. Duohe overcame a moment's hesitation, and walked towards the back gate of the factory. She had only just reached the shop that sold hot water, when the Volga braked to a stop beside her. It was Xiao Peng himself who was driving.

He asked her where she wanted to go for a stroll.

Overwhelmed by the unexpected favour, she shook her head with a smile.

Xiao Peng drove in the direction of open country. The tarmac road gradually narrowed. Half an hour went past, and it became a country road, laid with stones. He told her that the parks were all closed, forcing him to treat the open country as a park. He then asked her whether she often visited parks. She shook her head again, gave another smile. How many times had she been? Twice. Who had she gone with? With Zhang Jian.

He did not say any more. At that moment the car entered a wood. It seemed to be a tree nursery, whose saplings had not been transplanted in time. There were more dead ones than living, but some had grown into big, tall, almost mature trees.

'Nobody's bought any saplings to plant for the last two years. Look, they're all spoiled.' He stopped the car and they got out.

He took a military canteen from the boot, and slung it on his back, walking straight ahead down the road between the saplings. Duohe followed him, wanting to walk alongside, but the road was very narrow and she found herself squeezed off the road and into the nursery below.

'Tell me, look at these saplings, some of them just died, but some carried on living, and even grew into trees, why is that? It must be the survival of the fittest, the ones that survived were all strong, able to snatch the little bit of nourishment in the soil for themselves,' Xiao Peng said.

Duohe's mouth was silently reciting words that she had not quite made out. Xiao Peng continued; from the theory of evolution he moved on to materialism, and in what way he himself was a materialist. Duohe was finding it increasingly hard going. He suddenly noticed her lips, secretly working away. She had always had this habit. He had been twenty the first time he noticed it, and he did not know whether he liked this habit, but he had always been captivated by it. Deep inside the nursery it suddenly hit him: he had never liked her, but he was captivated by her. Being captivated was more terrible still.

That day the factory had been holding a competition on the baseball court. The factory team versus the Red Guards. He had happened to be passing, and wanted to watch for a while. Just as he had entered the seating area the second half began, the players from both sides came onto the court, and Dahai, who was playing centre on the Red Guards' team, caught sight of him, somehow missed a step and slipped, scraping off a strip of skin from the outside of his thigh and calf. In an instant half the leg was covered in red. Xiao Peng did not even stay to watch the game, but walked into the players' changing room, where he found a member of the team bandaging Dahai, in a very careless and sloppy fashion. Xiao Peng walked up, took his place, stripped off the bandage and retied it.

'Uncle Xiao Peng, I know why you've stopped coming to my house. It's because of my auntie, right?'

'Your auntie?' He was deliberately being obtuse.

'Because you know about the skeleton in her cupboard.'

'What skeleton would that be?'

'Why are you asking? It's not like you don't know.'

'How would I know?' He smiled guiltily at this youth.

Dahai lapsed into silence. Xiao Peng felt that this silence was deeply murky and obscure. He had no choice but to pick up the thread of the conversation, saying: 'Just what secret background does she have?'

Dahai did not reply directly, but his words were like a prophecy. 'That's the thing about this Great Cultural Revolution, it's going to expose everyone's dirty secrets. Nobody should think of hiding in a corner.'

How many cruel, morally complex things did the Director of the Revolutionary Committee of a steel factory have to deal with? But at this moment he could not come up with any ideas.

'Uncle Xiao Peng, I'm willing to work with you.'

'You're a schoolboy.'

'The Revolution makes no distinction between old and young.'

'What do you plan on doing for me?'

'Do you need someone to cut stencils for your duplicator? I can do that.'

'If you want to come to the newspaper agency, you'd be welcome there.'

'Can I have a bed there?'

'You're not planning on going home?'

'That home's just foul, a complete mess. The Neighbourhood Committee has even written to our original home town back in the North-east to investigate – before long no one need think of concealing anything.'

Xiao Peng's hands slowed in their bandaging. Several days later, Dahai's words still made him feel ashamed. Even a teenage boy could understand that the greatness of the Revolution was its intolerance of personal considerations of any kind. And yet he had become captivated by a daughter of the enemy, infatuated by that warped delicacy. Of course he had always been on the lookout for a chance to sample it. His opportunity had arrived, and she had finally presented herself at his table, body and soul. Well then, tuck in, you've waited for years, only unwilling to take a step past Zhang Jian, who was standing in your way. Now she clearly had made that step herself, or else Zhang Jian was no longer blocking his path. Even with the tastiest delicacy, there will be moments when your stomach rebels against it. In Zhang Jian's hands this tasty morsel had probably changed into an autumn aubergine, its stomach pregnant with seeds, rind as chewy as rubber.

Xiao Peng and Duohe sat down on a mound of earth in the nursery. Xiao Peng poured out cherry wine from his flask into the cap, passed it to Duohe, raised his canteen and clinked it briefly against the cap. The thrushes were singing, and the setting sun cast thread-like shadows from the skinny saplings, living and dead, sketching a beautiful pattern on the grass speckled with wild flowers. If it hadn't been for that speech of Dahai's, Director Peng would have been able to enjoy the tasty dish that was Duohe.

In one pocket of Director Peng's overalls was a greased-paper packet, containing sweet and sour garlic cloves; in the other pocket was a packet of peanuts. Dye had been added to the cherry wine, turning it a deep red, like watercolour paint, and very soon Duohe's two silently reciting lips were a deep cherry red. Xiao Peng drank a mouthful of wine, and hurriedly wiped his lips with the back of his hand; if his lips were stained too, it would cause Duohe's attention to wander. Once again he started to enquire about the situation in Shironami and the other Japanese villages.

'When you were little, did your father do farm work at home?'

She said that her father had enlisted in the army not long after she was born. He had come home several times on his way to new postings, and that was why she had a younger brother and sister.

'What rank was your father?'

She replied that she thought he was a sergeant.

Xiao Peng's heart sank. If Duohe's father had been a colonel or a major, his opportunities to kill people with his own hands might have been somewhat fewer. But sergeants killed all the time; all the most bloodthirsty scenes in films had sergeants in them, didn't they?

'Were all the men in the village forced to be soldiers?'

She said that they had not been forced. If there was a man in any family who was unwilling to be a soldier, the women of that family would not be able to look their female neighbours in the face. All the men of the village were brave, and they had never produced degenerates who were greedy for life and feared death.

There were many gaps in Duohe's speech, and she spoke slowly, but she was doing much better than the first time he saw her, and he could understand 80 per cent of what she said on her first attempt.

The wine was wafting around in Xiao Peng's stomach, floating like a soft silk ribbon, twisting in coils and then rising, slowly curling into a soft, supple whirlpool in his head. That was such a fine feeling. He looked at Duohe, and he could see the cherry-red whirlpool in her eyes too.

A daughter of the enemy.

Look at the way the Japanese sergeants had massacred the Chinese common people in films. Xiao Peng's parents and grandparents could have been among those hundreds and thousands of ordinary folk, they had just been more fortunate than those who were slain.

Duohe's cherry-red lips should taste kisses. They were so soft, so sweet, they were like kissing itself, and all that kissing implied.

He lowered his head, and planted a kiss on those two lips. Lips that had fermented into wine. That silk ribbon in Xiao Peng's brain coiled into an ever more powerful whirlpool.

A hand reached into Xiao Peng's clothes, and a cool palm was laid on the place between his shoulder and his neck. Xiao Peng thought better if it were a knife: kill him, then he would have no choice. If she could not kill him, he could retaliate and seize the knife, and he would still be left with no choice.

Like a soft knife, Duohe's hand felt its way up and down Xiao Peng's neck. Was this a hint? That she wanted him to undo his clothes? Xiao Peng's heart was full of fervent hopes, and he thought, to hell with it! He rolled her over, beneath his body.

Dahai, or Zhang Tie as he was now known – named for the iron made in the town of his birth – fled to the factory headquarters for shelter, and from that day he cut himself off from his family. Not long after, the cadres in the Neighbourhood Committee received the reply from the North-east confirming Duohe's identity as a Jap devil. This female devil had been concealed in the Zhang household for more than twenty years: what had she been doing? Zhang Jian and Xiaohuan were not stupid enough to say that Duohe had spent the last twenty years giving birth to children and raising them. For the sake of the children's future this was not the kind of thing they could reveal. They would say that when the Zhang family bought her all those years ago, it was out of pity, and as a source of labour, to make coal bricks, carry water, sweep the station. Just that? So why take her south with them, and conceal her status as a Jap devil from everyone? Why had they smuggled her over a distance of several thousand kilometres in order to hide her forever, to conceal a Japanese in this city whose iron and steel industry was used for national defence, and all just in order to have her wash and iron clothes, scrub the floor, and go to the factory to earn a bit of extra money? The majority of the steel produced in this factory was put to important uses, such mighty uses that no one dared to ask what they were. So this female Jap devil had been infiltrating the factory for several years: how much intelligence had she got her hands on? And how much damage had she caused the nation?

❖

At the moment when Xiao Peng's passion was at its height, Duohe rolled out the way. She had grass clippings in her hair, and her eyes were wide open and staring. It seemed that this had not been the feeling when he kissed her. The feeling had turned into something else as he acted on it, and in doing so had become lost before he realised it.

'What's the matter?' Xiao Peng asked.

Duohe stared at him, like this was just what she wanted to ask him: 'What's the matter with *you*?'

He shifted closer to her. Soon the darkness would be complete. The mosquitoes were buzzing. All these flowers and plants and grasses would soon be covered in shadow. The whirlpool in his head lost its focus, leaving him listless. Once the whirling stopped, he would no longer have the courage to take his pleasure from this daughter of the enemy.

Duohe got up and took a step back. By an odd coincidence, the light was the same as it had been that day on the roof of the building, so that all she could see was his face. It was still the same face from the roof, but she sensed that the face was all that was left. She retreated another step.

Xiao Peng thought regretfully that if he had not gone to watch Dahai's basketball match that evening, if he had not gone to the changing room to bandage him and heard him say those words, it would have been so much better. Dahai would have said those words to him eventually, but how much better if he could have said them at some later date. Xiao Peng could not see her as an enemy and enjoy her at the same time: that was animal behaviour.

On the road they did not speak. He took her as far as the junction next to the Zhang family's building, and watched her walk away in the light of the street lamps, all alone. Her footsteps were always so childish, clumsy and absurd, almost like she had had polio as a child. She could not even walk gracefully, so how could she be capable of any wickedness? Xiao Peng's heart bled.

But by the time he had returned to the factory headquarters, Xiao Peng's heart had completely healed. He went looking for Dahai who was still cutting stencils in the offices of their small newspaper, and made him talk about the atmosphere in the home when he was growing up, and the relations between his father and mother and aunt. Dahai said that his parents had mentioned one thing when they were fighting: that Auntie had once been dumped by his father, abandoned by the side of the river, and had wandered all over the place and suffered great hardship for over a month before she came back home. At that time he and his brother were not yet weaned.

This black night became a ball of contradictions that he had no easy way to resolve. Xiao Peng did not know whether he wanted to eliminate the daughter of the enemy, or whether he wanted to eliminate Zhang Jian in order to uphold justice. Not just for Duohe's sake, but for Xiao Shi's too.

He sat in the deep autumn night of 1968, his head, light under the influence of the cherry wine, clutched in his hands. Oh, Xiao Shi. That monkey who had entered the factory with him, and who had brought him so much laughter; Xiao Shi, who was prepared to set at naught his own sense of shame in order to amuse him. Xiao Shi's elder sister had seen him off as far as the station, and had left him in the care of Zhang Jian and Xiaohuan, her eyes swimming with tears as though she were handing over an orphan. The result was that Zhang Jian had cut off the last single sprout of the Shi family line, root and branch. Zhang Jian had driven a crane for so many years without ever letting anything slip from its hook, and yet the load just happened to fall in the moment when Xiao Shi was walking past?

Xiao Peng just wished that he could have been there, so he could have pushed Xiao Shi out of the way.

Just as Xiao Shi had dragged him from the railway track.

Xiao Peng saw in his mind over and over how Xiao Shi had jumped onto the iron rails and pulled him back, as he went charging off blindly in the wrong direction. With that helping hand, Xiao Shi had rescued a new leader of the steelworks – Director Peng.

Xiao Peng considered Xiao Shi's attitude: Xiao Shi had known perfectly well that Xiao Peng was competing with him over Duohe, but he still gave him a hand up. And he himself? For Duohe's sake, how many times had he cursed him, in public and in secret?

The result was that he fell victim to Zhang Jian's plan. Was this not obviously a sinister plot? And it just had to happen at the time when he was returning to his home town.

This was a case of murder. This murderer Zhang Jian had evaded the net of the law, going to work and taking his wages, coming off work and messing about with his pigeons; outside the home he was a member of the working class, but behind closed doors he was two women's man.

Xiao Peng fell asleep at three o'clock. In the morning someone came in with hot water, and saw Xiao Peng on the sofa, dozing sweetly, and did not dare to call him. He was awakened by the arrival of the first batch of documents at nine. He stared at a big pile of documents from the centre, the province, the city and the factory, and said to himself: 'Xiao Shi, my brother, I've wronged you.'

He asked the army representative to come to his office, closed the door tightly, and told him about the death of a worker called Shi Huicai, and the history of a crane driver named Zhang Jian.

❖

From his crane, Zhang Jian saw the army representative go up to the director of the workshop, several policemen walking behind him. It was the way the workshop director involuntarily turned round that put Zhang Jian on his guard. They had said just a few words to the director, and the director had swivelled as if on a spring to look behind him. He had looked across at the crane.

The workshop director walked over, and beckoned to Zhang Jian. Then something suddenly occurred to him, and he retreated, flustered, to one side.

That was enough. Enough for him to judge what was coming. He stopped the crane, and let out a breath. The roof of the workshop was just above his head, and all the people and objects down below were tiny. He had never looked at the way the rails curved together, and turned out in their own separate ways, but in this instant he saw it all clearly. Perhaps this was the last time he would see these rails from this position: the roof of the workshop, the people down below. The workshop director was afraid that he would be up to his old tricks again, and squash him into a second Xiao Shi.

Zhang Jian came down and walked up to the security officers, looked at the army representative who had always treated him well, and said to himself: I'm innocent, I can explain everything, and once I have, it will all be over and done with. But it was precisely because he held such hopes of explaining clearly that he was consumed with fear.

They took him to the changing rooms and told him to clear out his locker, then hand over the key. Two workers had sneaked into the changing rooms for a nap, but as soon as they saw what was happening, they slipped out, pulling the peaks of their caps down low. Zhang Jian took out a pair of wooden slippers, a soap box, a comb and a change of clean clothes. If they took him directly into custody without letting him go home first, these things would be very useful. He thought: They can't shut me up for too long, I'll explain it all, from start to finish. I'll start from the day Duohe was sold into the family. We're an ordinary family from the common people, and my father was an old worker, he only wanted to save a starving girl's life. Don't try to tell me that you shouldn't save Japanese, that he should have let her leave and starve to death. The Zhang family was not the only good-hearted family in the surrounding villages, many people had saved those starving little Japanese girls and taken them back home! You can go to Anping village and investigate! As Zhang Jian was handing over his key to the workshop manager, he realised that his hand was shaking. The greater his hope the more full of dread he became. By the time he had finished cleaning out his locker, his hands seemed useless to him. Then a pair of iron handcuffs appeared and cuffed them together.

The detention centre was the dormitory of a cadres' training centre, because the real detention centre was overflowing. The cadres' training centre was on the other side of the city, and Zhang Jian remembered that he had visited this part of town when his romance with Duohe had been at its height. The dormitory had been simply and crudely constructed, and there were tiny mushrooms growing in the cracks in the brickwork. The floor was also laid with bricks, which moved against the sole of your foot when you trod on it. The windows were the most basic kind, barred with strips of scrap iron rejected from the sheet-steel plant, and to stretch even an arm outside was out of the question.

The first day Zhang Jian sat on his bed mat and familiarised himself with his surroundings. He had a clear and eloquent response in his mind to every question that might be asked. He had spent the best part of his life in silence, but that was because he could not be bothered to engage in debate.

Early on the second day, the questioning began. He was led under escort across the courtyard, and walked towards a row of single-storey buildings. Through the windows he could see that every room had six or seven prisoners in it. It could not have been easy, searching out so many convicts. Suddenly he found himself reconsidering his ideas: other people had six or seven cellmates, while he was in solitary confinement, which showed that his crime was either too serious or too trivial. It must have been too serious. They were confining him as a prisoner condemned to death. They wanted him to pay for Xiao Shi's life with his own. All hopes were dashed in that instant. And now hope was gone, he had become a brave hero.

A group of orioles dropped onto the tree, calling out to each other. On their assignations Duohe would lie in his arms, as they listened to the songs of all kinds of different birds. There would never again be a time to listen to birdsong with her in this life.

The interrogation room was temporary too. There was a ping-pong table turned on one end resting against the far wall. They were discovering enemies everywhere, day and night; the population outside was shrinking, while the population inside was increasing.

The interrogator was thirty or so. When Zhang Jian came in he was reading his file, and said, 'Sit there,' pointing to a long bench on the opposite side of his table, without even bothering to look up.

'When asked questions, you must reply honestly,' said the man. 'Because we already know your circumstances like the palm of our hands.'

Zhang Jian did not utter a word. Half his life was behind him, but he had only done a few things, did it really warrant such diligent reading?

The questioner finally raised his face. It was actually rather like Xiao Shi, but larger. You felt that he was sitting behind this table for his own amusement. There was no air of stern impartiality about him, no sense that the law was mightier than a mountain and should be vigorously enforced. Perversely, this caused Zhang Jian to lose the sense of self that he had just grasped hold of. This couldn't be an amateur interrogation, could it? These days there were many amateur roles: amateur factory heads, amateur workshop directors, amateur soldiers, amateur performance troupes, all people from outside the profession doing things they had always dreamed of doing. Zhang Jian felt that this amateurism was rather an alarming thing: in its attempt to make up for its own deficiencies everything was taken to still greater extremes, and for this reason was even more amateurish.

'Where were you born?'

'Heilongjiang province, Hutou township.'

'. . . and that's it?'

Zhang Jian waited in silence for him to enlighten him. What did he mean by 'and that's it'?

'Just "Hutou township" counts as a full confession?'

He continued to wait in silence for the man to explain himself. Was that not clear? Is it the number on our door plate you want? The name of our district?

'Hutou township was a township where there were more Jap devils than Chinese. Why did you not confess this voluntarily?'

He felt even less inclined to speak. Firstly, he had not counted the Japanese population against the Chinese population of Hutou township. Secondly, he had been barely two when his father was transferred to Anping. If the interrogator had read the file attentively, he should have known this.

'Your father was an employee of the puppet regime in Manchuria?'

'My father –'

'Just answer yes or no!'

Zhang Jian made up his mind to ignore him.

'So your much-vaunted working-class status is fraudulent!'

'There were several thousand railway workers in old Manchuria, are you saying they were all fake working class?' Zhang Jian discovered that he had an extremely glib tongue when he needed one.

'You could say that.' The investigator had not been thrown by Zhang Jian's comment – in fact, he was very happy to have an opponent who would quibble with him.

'Then what about Li Yuhe?'

'Who?'

'Li Yuhe, the hero in *The Red Lantern*.'

'He was an underground Party worker. It's different for underground Party members; they were even among the high officials in the Kuomintang.'

Zhang Jian was silent. It looked like his interrogator was starting to attack Zhang Jian from Stationmaster Zhang's generation. Indeed, he might posthumously confirm Stationmaster Zhang as a traitor, a Japanese running dog.

'After you moved to Anping, did you have close dealings with Japanese people?'

'No.'

'I can demonstrate at once that you're lying.'

Zhang Jian thought, sure enough, he's an amateur.

'Is not Zhunei Duohe, concealed by your father after the War of Liberation from Japan, a Japanese woman? She was hidden in your home for more than twenty years. Does your relationship count as close or doesn't it?'

'She was only sixteen years old at the time –'

'Just reply "yes" or "no"! I'll ask you again, is this woman you concealed in your home Japanese or isn't she? Well?'

'Yes.'

'In the twenty years and more she has been here, exactly what things did she do to harm Chinese people?'

'She hasn't done anything to hurt anyone.'

'Then why did you conceal her identity? We've made inquiries in the North-east, and there are genuinely a few peasants – peasants with a low level of awareness – who rescued Japanese women, or married Japanese women and had children by them. But they did not conceal the truth of the matter. In those years when the North-east was liberated, there were purges, and organisations responsible for the punishment of traitors and Japanese spies. Only a handful of individuals never went on file. Not going on record only demonstrates that you harboured evil intentions. Why did you bring Zhunei Duohe to Anshan, and then here, always concealing her identity?'

Zhang Jian had thought that, in truth, this single act of concealment would make people suspicious. In the beginning his mother and father had just wanted to appease Xiaohuan, to conceal the fact that the Zhang household consisted of a man and two women, thereby setting in train a series of huge and glaring lies. Once Duohe had borne three children to the Zhang family, their relationship had relied even more heavily on lies to keep itself hidden. How had Zhang Jian, a new worker in the New Society, avoided being found out as a bigamist? Not to mention that the three adults and children had been living together for so long that each had become a part of the other. You can break the bones but the tendons are still connected. If they had concealed nothing, Duohe would certainly have suffered the most, no matter how she was plucked from the Zhang family, because she would have been forced to leave her own children. And if she was separated from the three children, she would have been cut off from everything in her world.

'When Zhunei Duohe went to the steel factory to cut serial numbers, were you the one who introduced her?' the interrogator asked.

'Yes.'

'Impersonating a Chinese woman, and sneaking into a key site of Chinese national defence, is surely the reason why this Japanese endured all those hardships, concealed her true name and hid for over twenty years?'

Maybe they should not have tried to get away with the deception. Not have hidden anything, right from the start. By making her have children, while at the same time wanting to make these children his own with no tinge of Japanese blood in them, Zhang Jian had deceived all the people in Anping village. Could it be that when they had dragged Duohe along with them to Anshan, and then to Ma'anshan, they had not wanted her to continue to bear and raise children, because they wanted a concealment that was so effective that they would never need do it again? They had dragged Duohe along with them on their journey south because of an uneasy conscience, because they did not want this Japanese woman whose fate was already so bitter to have an even more bitter fate thanks to them. He should be grateful to that interrogator, he had made Zhang Jian interrogate himself, and brought him clarity. Where Duohe was concerned, he was guilty.

'In fact a few people had their suspicions of Zhunei Duohe. Shi Huicai was one of them. Did he ever confront Zhunei Duohe directly?'

'No.'

'I have cast-iron proof that he did.'

Zhang Jian knew who the proof came from. It could only be from one of two people: Xiao Peng or Dahai. Xiao Shi must have mentioned something to Xiao Peng in the past. Dahai might have figured out a rough version of the truth from quarrels between his parents.

'In any case, resistance is useless. I have proof. Shi Huicai did privately confront Zhunei Duohe. By asking you now, I'm giving you an opportunity, don't bring down destruction on yourself.'

'When the two of them had their confrontation, was I present?'

The interrogator gave a start. After a while he came out of his trance, and said: 'According to reports, you were not present.'

'If I wasn't there, how would I know the two of them had had a confrontation?'

The interrogator paused again. Then he said: 'You are much more cunning than we had supposed. Zhunei Duohe told you after the fact. She is your mistress, what could she not tell you while you were sharing a pillow?'

Zhang Jian thought that it was people like this who had forced him into his persistent silence. This kind of person kept on talking and talking in a completely outrageous fashion, with no sense of decency at all.

'And thus you determined to commit murder, to silence the witness.'

Zhang Jian did not make a sound. Whether he debated or not, it would make no difference at all.

'You made up your mind to murder Shi Huicai when you were working the night shift together – is that not the case?' Zhang Jian did not react. If the interrogator couldn't get him into an argument then there would be no fun in it, and he would give up in annoyance. It would be just like diarrhoea after a laxative, with none of the writhing and struggles of the intestines which could culminate in spasms of pleasant sensation. 'You picked the perfect time, waiting until most people were eating – isn't that right?'

This was an age when wrongful accusations could come back to life. Debating would bring on such a wrongful accusation, while refusing to engage would lead to the same result with a lot less effort. In this instant Zhang Jian understood how the people who had jumped off the chimneys or gone up the mountain to hang themselves had reconciled themselves. They had endured a succession of fleshly and spiritual troubles and distress. And yet Zhang Jian had reconciled himself to this logic so quickly. Save them the trouble, and save himself too. The most important thing was saving himself the trouble. Take a look at that ping-pong table: if you have one person hit the ball over, a vicious blow with the whole strength of his arm, if there is nobody to hit it back the table must be put aside and propped up vertically, for the game is at an end.

'You must answer my question!' The interrogator pounded viciously on the table. A vicious swipe at a ball with no one to return it.

Zhang Jian was gazing into the far distances of his heart.

'So by your silence, you're admitting to your criminal act?'

'What criminal act?'

'The criminal act of killing Shi Huicai in order to silence his testimony.'

'I have not killed anyone.'

'But was not Shi Huicai killed by you?'

'Of course he wasn't.'

'You faked an accident, correct?'

He retreated once more into silence.

'You calculated the time well, so that you happened to be on the same night shift as Shi Huicai, correct?'

His eyelids closed a little more. Let this world slip away into unreality, let all the facts vanish into darkness. The reason he had got into the habit of drooping his eyelids since he was small was that he wanted to make the world unreal. That way was best: to let all these restless, mischief-making people dissolve into a patch of grey. Many years ago, one day in August, Duohe had gone with him to the side of a pond near the cemetery to celebrate the Japanese festival of '*Obon*', lighting paper lanterns to call her father, mother, brothers and sister back home for the festival. But she could not bring them home to the Zhang family, so she set up a home beside the pond: a grass awning stuck with water lilies and with wine and rice balls set out. The awning was made from reed mats bought from the peasants. Perhaps next year, Zhang Jian would be among the relatives she called back home. He had already successfully missed the next string of questions. By now it must be time to end this game of amateur interrogations.

13

They had last had any news of Zhang Jian at the end of November. A notification had arrived, ordering Xiaohuan to prepare cotton padded clothing and bring it to the factory. They also wanted a pair of knee protectors. Xiaohuan and Duohe discussed this. 'What does he want knee protectors for? He doesn't have rheumatism.'

In fact Xiaohuan had not been particularly despairing. Once she had cried a little, she had done her best to console Duohe, who was shuddering all over, unable to weep: What family doesn't have someone locked up these days? There are two people in this building alone who got put away and then let out again. She had noticed that the people who got taken away were generally a bit kinder than those who locked other people up; she had also found that the people who had been locked up and then let go had all improved somewhat, in personal character, and in attitude.

Xiaohuan fluffed up a bed's worth of cotton wadding, and made a lovely, warm overcoat for Zhang Jian. The outside was dark blue, with Zhang Jian's name embroidered on the collar, and 'Chunmei', 'Erhai', 'Xiaohuan' and 'Duohe' embroidered inside in small characters. She bundled up the big coat with a dozen or so salted duck eggs inside, and pushed it to the factory security office on Zhang Jian's bicycle.

She dropped off the coat, and found Dahai, at work on his stencils.

'What are you doing here?' he asked.

Without another word, Xiaohuan grabbed his arm and dragged him off the chair. He cried out 'Ow, ow, ow!', as Xiaohuan's fists and feet shot out. Every time she came with things for Zhang Jian, she would tell Dahai to take her to Xiao Peng, and Dahai always refused. This time it was going to be different; if she got into a fight there was a good chance it would bring out that man Peng. To the people who came to pull her away, it felt as if this woman had more than one pair of hands and feet; they were holding her back from the left and from the right, but blows continued to rain down on her son's shoulders and bottom.

Sure enough, Xiao Peng appeared, brought out by the sound of a beating.

'What do you think you're doing, beating people up in the offices of the Revolutionary Committee?' Xiao Peng asked drily.

'I'm beating my son! Wait till I get my breath back, I've got a grandson to beat as well – are you ready?!'

'If you've got something to say, let's talk,' Xiao Peng said blandly.

Xiaohuan fluffed up her hair and pulled out an iron cigarette box, which she opened to reveal shreds of tobacco, charred at one end. You could tell at a glance that they had come from cigarette ends. She had gone back to smoking a pipe again. As she stuffed tobacco into the bowl, she announced: 'Listen, all you low-down riff-raff who wrongly accused that good man Zhang Jian. The night of the accident, Xiao Shi had been down for the afternoon shift, he swapped to the night shift at the last minute. How could my husband have plotted in advance? That night, the factory was producing its own electricity, there wasn't enough power and they turned off two of the big lamps, how could he see clearly whether it was a dog or a cat walking about down there? Don't assume that we of the common people are idiots, we know how to make inquiries of our own, and we can find witnesses too!'

Xiao Peng watched Xiaohuan. She was smiling flirtatiously one minute, smiling grimly the next, then sneering coldly, the tip of her gold tooth flashing bright then darkening; every sentence addressed her full audience, but the full stops always landed on the tip of Xiao Peng's nose, his forehead, lips and his great Adam's apple. Everyone immediately understood that a glare from Xiaohuan's little eyes would hit home, right on the pressure point.

'If I can't cry out for justice here, I'll do it before the city government, or take it to the province! I'll go and let Chairman Mao hear me shouting out my wrongs!' As Xiaohuan was speaking, she knocked the pipe onto the already filthy corridor floor. She knew that now they were carrying out the mighty Revolution, the cleaners had a Command Centre of their own too, so people had to sweep their own floors, just like they had to carry their own dishes in small restaurants.

'Exposing people's pasts is all the rage. We can set up an Exposing Command Centre too!' Xiaohuan said to the crowd of faces, while still allowing the full stops to land heavily on Xiao Peng's face. 'There are people, aren't there, who fancied a traitor-to-the-Han-race love affair, chasing after a Jap woman like their lives depended on it? Well, he didn't catch her, and got himself in such a state that his eyes turned red, so off he went to make revolution, and then he came here to become a chief of staff!'

Xiao Peng's glance shifted away. Xiaohuan noticed it at once. The crowd of faces were already exchanging glances; they could tell that

Xiaohuan's innuendoes were aimed at Xiao Peng, but they still felt inhibited from looking directly at him.

'Don't think you can weasel out of it. We know all about you – every wart and mole in places too shameful to be seen! And there's no weaselling out of *that*!' Xiaohuan saw Xiao Peng's expression darken. She'd got him!

People started to titter. Xiaohuan sensed that all her skills as a performer were being cheered on by an appreciative audience, and she felt her spirits revive as she fell still more into character.

'Yes, we concealed my sister's identity, so what? If we hadn't, you'd have given her the devil of a time years ago. She's a Japanese woman: should she just have let you ruin her? Even the People's Liberation Army treated their Japanese prisoners of war well, and gave them wheat cakes to eat! I kept things from you, so now you're going to see how you can punish my crime, eh? I'll be waiting for you back home!' She walked away, and turned her head. 'Director Peng, we've been making red-bean sticky rice balls, why don't you come by for a taste, see if they're any sweeter than the ones you used to eat in the old days?!'

As Xiaohuan walked towards the stairwell, she could feel a chill on her back. It was Dahai's gaze, full of loathing and despair. It did not bother her, playing the role of a female clown in her son's eyes. She wanted to let people know that the Zhang family was not a lump of meat for them to carve up any way they pleased. When Xiao Peng brought down his knife, he should feel very nervous inside.

She walked to the courtyard of the factory headquarters, where she saw a row of towels hanging on a wire, with the red characters for 'guest house' printed on one end. Cut off the red characters and they'd still be perfectly good towels. With the family breadwinner in prison, they had had precious little food to go with their rice over the last few months, and there was no oil, salt, soy sauce or vinegar or other such basic condiments. You could forget about getting hold of any meat. Anything you could snatch up in passing you should grab immediately, and the day was not far away when they would be short of towels.

By the time she had squeezed her way under the wire, she was clutching six towels to her bosom. She left at a quick pace, hastily groping at her long sleeves, pressing the towels into her arm, and against her chest. The trick was never, ever to turn your head, looking made you a focus of suspicion, and wouldn't solve anything. She had to make something out of nothing: to find food, drink and clothes to wear without spending a fen was no easy thing, but take a bit of trouble and it could still be done. So in summer, when she went out of the main gate of the factory she would not take the main road, rather she would walk out along the railway line which ran through the fields on both sides, first plucking a handful of trailing water-chestnut stems, then hiding aramanth and other leafy vegetables she had secretly stripped from their stems inside. There were often ponds by the side of the fields, which always had water chestnuts in them, and no one could see that she was actually picking vegetables, and not gathering a few water chestnuts to idle away some time. Once she had picked enough vegetables, she would bundle them up in her headscarf, with water-chestnut vines poking out at the corners.

Duohe had lost her job at the same time that Zhang Jian lost his. The only one left in the family who was qualified to work was Xiaohuan. She had applied to lots of places: the ice-lolly factory, the processed-food plant, the slaughterhouse, the soy-sauce factory, and they all told her to wait to hear from them, but nothing ever came of it. The reason she went to those factories was because they were all places where you could pick up fringe benefits with minimal effort.

The benefit in the lollipop factory was Cuban sugar, the slaughter-house would always have pigs' offal, and the processed-foods factory spoke for itself. Xiaohuan's waist was narrow, and she could steal a few links of sausage or a pig's lung and stuff them into her waistband, and still have a waist pretty much the same as normal people.

Pushing the bicycle, Xiaohuan headed away from the steelworks towards home. A woman with a basket of eggs slung over one shoulder walked up. Xiaohuan greeted the peasant woman warmly and heartily as 'big sister', saying she had a lucky face. The peasant woman cackled and said that she was all of forty-nine years old. Xiaohuan gave a start, thinking to herself that she looked at least sixty-three. Having chosen six eggs, Xiaohuan patted her pockets, saying that she'd left for work in a hurry that morning, and forgotten her purse, such a shame after all that work choosing the eggs! The peasant woman said: No hard feelings, we've made friends even if we can't do business, who's to say we won't get another chance to meet in future? Just as she was leaving, Xiaohuan took out the six towels from her clothes, printed with red peonies, Little Red Books, bedbug blood and 'guest house'.

'These are all good cotton yarn, have a feel, thick, isn't it?'

The peasant woman did not understand what Xiaohuan was up to, taking her hand and running it over the towels. She hurriedly replied: 'Yes, nice and thick.'

'Since we sisters met by this lucky chance, I'll make you a present of two of them!'

The peasant woman's face wavered on the point of a smile.

'Much better than the ones they sell in your Supply and Marketing Cooperative in the countryside. You can lay them over a pillow, and it'll be like entering a bridal chamber!' Xiaohuan pressed the towels into her hands.

The peasant woman said: How can I accept a favour like this when I've done nothing to deserve it! Xiaohuan said that the place where she worked was always getting rid of towels, sometimes after just a couple of mild washes, and they weren't worth anything, she had just thought it was a rare thing to have found herself an elder sister like this. When Xiaohuan had finished speaking she got up and took her leave, but after two steps the peasant woman called her to stop. Since they were friends now, the warmth couldn't be all on one side, she should give her something too. The eggs were from her family's own hens, they weren't worth anything either, so Xiaohuan should take the six eggs that she had just selected as a passing gift.

'Aiyo, that would be trading goods with you!'

The peasant woman asked if an exchange of gifts wasn't just the same as a trade? She put the six large, shining eggs on the edge of the basket, and urged Xiaohuan to take them away. Xiaohuan looked askance, her lips pursed as if in complaint, while slowly squatting down. The peasant woman asked her what the three characters on the towels meant. Xiaohuan said they meant 'Make Revolution'. Aiya, that's good, good, fashionable characters!

Xiaohuan thought to herself that she really did have a good eye: as soon as she came near this woman she had seen that she was a total illiterate. On the way back, she thought that when the woman got home and laid out the towels on the bed, and other people told her that those three red characters meant 'guest house', she was bound to think: looks like that poor girl didn't have the first idea how to read.

She made a bag for the eggs with her headscarf, tied it onto the handlebars of the bike, and strode away with elegant steps. The road was covered in potholes, the tarmac having long since been carried away on the rolling wheels of passing vehicles, and trampled by the soles of people's shoes. The Ministry of Roads was busy making revolution too. The bicycle kept bouncing up and down, and she felt that her heart was more fragile than an eggshell, and thinner; she had to carry it as she walked. She could not remember how long it had been since the family had last eaten eggs. After Zhang Jian's salary was stopped, she had resolved to learn how to run her life properly. But very soon the money in the bank book, which had not been that much to begin with, had all gone. She chastised herself; as soon as she got hold of money she was a fool, but on the other hand she could live very cleverly without it. Zhang Jian had been saving new fur-lined boots, overalls and cotton gloves for many years, and these she took to swap with peasants for rice and flour. He had saved two whole cartons of the soap issued by the factory, all dry and cracked. There had been a desperate shortage of soap these last few years, and you could get enough maize flour for two months in exchange for a single carton.

Zhang Jian was bound to be cleared before all the things had been exchanged or sold off. And if he was still not cleared by that point, she would have to find work. It wasn't as if she had reached the end of the road. Even when the people from Duohe's village had fled disaster only to find disaster wherever they turned, hadn't Duohe at least come out alive?

Bicycle after bicycle brushed past her. People were coming home from work. The crowd was far removed from its former grandeur, when it had resembled a vast army storming a city's gates. Now only two-thirds the number of people were working, the rest were either under observation or doing the observing. The bicycles had got old as well, clanging their way along the aged road, bumping three times for each pothole.

She had to keep shouting, to keep people out of her way. Six eggs would make a nice, thick sauce for six pots of noodles. There were wild edible yellow lilies in the fields, it was exactly the season to eat them, to have a pre-New Year feast with dropped eggs. Erhai could eat three big bowls in surly silence. Right now he was the only child, and the two women were half starved as he ate everything.

Before Zhang Jian was taken away, Dahai had come home to collect his quilt and clothes, for all the world like a stranger who had come to the wrong door. He had charged into the room, his feet covered in sloppy mud leaving a trail of yellow footprints. There were also two little youths who had come along with him. Xiaohuan was not yet aware that he had hardened his heart to sever relations with his family, and as soon as she saw him she yelled: 'Young master, how come you're not taking off your shoes?' When he had finished trampling through the big room he stomped to the little room, as if he had never known this long-standing family rule. Duohe lowered her head to look at the string of muddy yellow footprints, but said nothing at all, and just went off in search of socks. She turned out a pair of incomparably folded, flat, snow-white socks, and walked to the corridor. Dahai had already rummaged out his own clothes, leaving things strewn all over the bed and the floor.

'You, out of there, get your shoes off!' Xiaohuan grabbed him, and dragged him to the doorway. Dahai's two companions could see that the situation had taken a turn for the worse, and retreated outside.

He sat down on the long bench where all the Zhang family changed their shoes.

'Shoes off!' Xiaohuan said.

'No!' The two kids behind him were standing in the open doorway, peering inside.

'You dare!'

'They're still on, aren't they? I *have* dared.' Dahai stuck a muddy shoe up in the air, crossing his legs and waving it from side to side to show Xiaohuan.

'Then you just sit right where you are. You take one step into the room, you just try it!' Xiaohuan picked up the broom, which was lying nearby.

'Pass my quilt and mattress out to me! I can't be bothered to go in anyway!'

'Where are you going?'

'Out!'

'If you don't explain yourself, don't think you can take so much as a needle from this house!'

'I'll get them myself!'

Dahai had no sooner stood up from the stool, than Xiaohuan's broom handle was raised again.

'Shoes off.' The broom handle rapped at his feet.

'I won't, so there!'

At this moment Duohe came to his rescue. She walked up level with his face, then knelt, neatly and squarely, intending to untie those mud-encrusted shoelaces. Xiaohuan was on the point of telling her not to wait on him, to let him take them off himself, but at that moment Dahai lashed out with his foot, exactly level with Duohe's solar plexus.

Duohe was wearing a white apron over her clothes, and a white headscarf on her head. The sole of Dahai's size 43 Huili sports shoe immediately left a print on the apron. His Red Guard basketball team issued him with a pair of shoes every six months, and usually he couldn't bear to wear them for fear of ruining them, let alone in the mud on a rainy day. Duohe's white apron was new, with the marks of the sewing machine's needle still on it, and she had just been putting it on, ready to go into the kitchen, when Dahai came back. It seemed like everything was prepared for this kick and the evidence that the kick left behind.

Xiaohuan still remembered how Duohe had looked down at herself. Actually, the imprint of that size 43 shoe was pretty faint, but Duohe brushed at it several times with her hand.

What Xiaohuan could not remember was her own reaction. Whether she had succeeded in hitting Dahai with her broom, and whether he had shielded his face. She had no clear memory at all of how he had got out of the door. It had taken half an hour before she realised that he had not taken anything with him at all. The following morning, she had noticed that Duohe kept nursing her chest. She had tried to persuade Duohe not to give that little swine the satisfaction, as she rubbed her faintly bruised chest with *baijiu* liquor.

That same afternoon, Zhang Jian had been taken away from the factory.

Since the departure of Zhang Jian and Dahai, Duohe had been even more silent. Xiaohuan discovered that whenever she was on her own she put her hands protectively to her chest. It was as if another foot was going to lash out at any moment, and she was already on the verge of ducking out the way. It also seemed that the injury wasn't healing, and she had to carefully work around the pain in her chest and in her heart. Whenever Duohe thought no one was watching her, when she could relax and let herself go, she fell into just that kind of posture. It aged her by several years.

Xiaohuan kept wanting to set her straight: Zhang Jian's case is an injustice, pure and simple, he won't be locked up there for very long, there are people who've been unjustly accused in every family, and if not in the immediate family, then distant relations or close friends have been affected. But Duohe said nothing. She only spoke to Erhai, and to him no more than: have some more to eat; you should change your clothes; Blackie's had a bath; your socks have been mended; you play the erhu really well.

They did not know when Erhai had started to learn how to play the two-stringed fiddle. Erhai was like the old Erhai, Zhang Jian; he preferred to wait for other people to find out things. When asked about his erhu he'd said impatiently: 'I studied it at the Children's Palace, didn't I?!'

It turned out that this was true, and he had kept on playing, just never in front of the family. He had also joined some group called the Propaganda Troupe, which Xiaohuan had deduced from the characters printed on his erhu case. Xiaohuan suspected that the only reason Erhai came back home was out of respect for Blackie's feelings, otherwise who was to say that he too would not be like Girlie and Dahai, harbouring a secret resentment towards this family in his heart?

By the time Xiaohuan got home with the eggs it was already six o'clock. All the way up the stairs was a hubbub of vegetables falling into hot, oily woks. This evening they would have a similar hubbub in their kitchen too. When Xiaohuan came in, Duohe was scrubbing the floor again.

'Give over scrubbing,' Xiaohuan said.

She stopped for a moment, then returned to her scrubbing with a swishing, scratching sound.

'If you don't care about wasting energy, I'm afraid of wasting water. It's not like it's free!'

Duohe paused once more, and when she took up her scrubbing again the sound was different, hot and fierce. Its meaning was clear to Xiaohuan: the water has been kept back in a bucket anyway, you're not trying to tell me that pouring it out is called wasting money? These days, there was no goodwill between Xiaohuan and Duohe, they would grudgingly but politely pass a mouthful of something tasty to the other one, grudgingly urge the other to wear more clothes, and not catch her death. When Xiaohuan had finished making the noodles in their thick sauce and set the table, she started to eat her own noodles, and shouted out at Duohe, who was still scrubbing the floor: 'Now I've made them do you expect me to feed you by hand? And I'll have to waste gas reheating them!'

Duohe carried the water she had been using to scrub the floor to the toilet, gave her hands a wash, went over to the dinner table, picked up the noodles with their scraps of egg and edible lilies on top and walked into the kitchen. Xiaohuan stood up in her turn. Duohe had her hands up to her chest again. As soon as Xiaohuan saw that painful sight, she felt even more full of unspoken rage and frustration.

'Just eat, relax and eat properly!'

Even Blackie, lying in a corner of the kitchen, could hear that Xiaohuan was being unfriendly, and rolled his eyes at her.

The door banged open, and Erhai, who was now known by his proper name, Zhang Gang, came in. He was named for steel, as his brother was for iron. He might be a silent person, but his actions made plenty of noise. When he took off his shoes he would not sit on the bench, but one leg would kick in mid-air, his bottom leaning against the door, causing the door to clatter and bang. His wooden slippers were the same thickness and weight as everyone else's, and yet when he walked the sound was much louder, filling the room with clacking like the bamboo clappers in a beggar's ballad. Normally when he came back home he only said two things: 'Ma, Auntie,' and after that it was up to the others to ask him questions. Moreover you had to ask provocative questions, so he was forced to contradict you, as this was the only way to get answers flowing without too much effort.

'So I hear you've been wrestling with people at school again today?' Xiaohuan said.

'I never went to school!'

'Then you went out somewhere and ended up wrestling someone?' She put a bowl of noodles in front of him, piled up high in a little mountain.

'I was rehearsing! I was in the auditorium the whole time!'

If Xiaohuan's next question had been 'What were you rehearsing then?' he would certainly not have deigned to reply. So Xiaohuan said: 'What's there to rehearse? It's just the same old tunes!'

'New songs! An army representative wrote them.'

If she were to ask him 'So when are you performing?' again he would be certain to give no response. So Xiaohuan adopted the same dismissive tone of voice, saying 'What are you always rehearsing then? It's not like there'll be anyone watching!'

'Who says? We're performing next week in the City Government Auditorium.'

Xiaohuan nudged Duohe's knee with her leg. Life returned to Duohe's eyes, which alighted briefly on Xiaohuan's face, then on Erhai's. Xiaohuan's meaning had been transmitted to Duohe: You see? I've wormed out the boy's secret. Let's go together to the City Government Auditorium to see the show!

When he had finished eating, Erhai pulled out five yuan from his pocket and left them on the table.

'What's this – dinner money?' Xiaohuan looked at the neatly folded notes, smiling broadly.

He did not say anything, just went to put on his shoes.

'Next time you're stealing money, steal a bit more. It'll be worth it, even if you do get caught!' Xiaohuan said.

'Rice is free in the Propaganda Troupe, and they give out a subsidy of 1.2 jiao per day for the rest of the food!' Erhai was bristling with rage. He gestured to Blackie, and two shadows, one horizontal, one vertical, left by the dimly lit corridor.

Duohe did not fully understand what he meant, and looked at Xiaohuan. Xiaohuan's mouth opened slightly, then she decided to let it go. Best not to interpret for her, why make both women sick at heart? It was enough that this fine young man, who was eating just plain rice at every meal, saving the money for meat and vegetables to give to his family, made Xiaohuan alone feel painfully ashamed, she didn't need to drag Duohe into it. But Duohe had caught up. Her eyes were lifeless again and her expression abashed, she seemed to be examining her conscience, questioning whether she should have eaten a whole bowl of noodles just now.

The following day, bright and early, Xiaohuan slung a vegetable basket over her shoulder and set off for the farmers' market. Most people got here before seven o'clock, and the more people there were the greater the advantage to Xiaohuan. The dependants all went before work to buy vegetables. Xiaohuan's bamboo basket was not big, but it was deep, shaped like a wooden barrel. Duohe had bought the bamboo herself one summer, chopped it into thin strips, and woven this oddly shaped basket. Her handiwork was both dense and delicate; you could fill it with rice, shake it and not a grain would leak out. It was also impossible to see from outside what you had put in the bottom once she had wedged an enamel bowl inside. Practically everybody buying food did this, just in case they came across tofu, mince or anything of that sort that you could buy without ration coupons, as there would be no time to go off looking for a container. Occasionally the food-processing plant would be selling off egg yolks by the ladle (she had no idea what they did with the whites, so very much inferior in taste to the yolks), and if you did not have a bowl a great opportunity would pass you by. Xiaohuan wandered up to a three-wheeled goods tricycle selling eggs. This was the distribution point for the Egg and Poultry Company. Quality was not guaranteed with any of the eggs, and often there were customers standing by the side of the three-wheeler, cursing loudly for all to hear, saying that when they cracked the eggs they had bought at home, out came a moribund chick or duckling. If they met with a salesperson in a good mood, he would educate you: slit open the chick's stomach, and you could get half a spoonful of egg yolk that had turned into chicken giblets. But most egg sellers would say in exasperation, Well, what were you doing earlier? Didn't you hold the egg up to the light? So the Egg and Poultry Company's sales outlet was surrounded on all sides by people picking up eggs, and holding them up to rays of light that streamed in horizontally and vertically through the gaps in the reed matting. There were a lot of eggs and not much light, and Xiaohuan's pair of knife-blade shoulders came into their own as she nudged aside the crowds and made her way directly to the holes in the matting walls. At this moment someone would shout: 'Oi, lady, how come you're standing in my light?' She would say, 'Sorry, sorry, I didn't know your family had bought up all the rights to this light,' at which point an argument would become inevitable. While engaging in her verbal battle, Xiaohuan would return rejected eggs one by one to the stall's big basket, but actually she would have already sneaked four or five eggs underneath the enamel bowl. The sales assistant would dart a brief look towards her basket, taking in everything inside it at a glance, but apart from a white enamel bowl printed with 'Glorious Model Worker' there would be no eggs there at all. Once people had seen their fill of the performance, they would slip past the peculiar basket on Xiaohuan's arm, and carry on checking eggs.

Other times she would go hunting at the cooked-food stall. The state-run stand was just a stall, but it took as many liberties with the customer as a big shop would. Behind the signboard were several greasy chopping boards, a row of rectangular aluminium dishes filled with red-cooked pigs' heads, hearts, liver, lungs and different types of tofu, and a big fat lady who ignored everyone. Every dish of meat products was covered by a piece of gauze that had started out white but was now a dark reddish brown. When a buyer appeared, the lady would say on the third time of asking, 'Got meat coupons?' If the answer was 'yes', she would slowly heave herself to her feet, saying: 'Yesterday's.' She meant this as a warning: the meat products had come out of the pot a day earlier, eat them if you've a mind to, but if you make yourself ill you've got no one to blame but yourself. She had a disturbing habit of looking all around her while she was working, even when chopping meat. This made people think that she might have been a model worker in the past, so effortlessly practised that she could do it with her eyes shut. Going on the hunt there could not be described so much as requiring skill as needing magic. Because of the big fat lady's habit of looking all around her, the best Xiaohuan could do was to whip a hand under the gauze covering a lump of meat, grab it and whisk it into the basket when her face was turned, and then stuff the meat under the enamel bowl as she sneaked away. The enamel bowl was gradually exchanged for other bowls in ever larger sizes, because the things they had to keep covered kept on increasing in number. One time Xiaohuan found someone selling pullets, and she wanted to buy a few to take home and raise. When they had grown up they would lay eggs, and so she changed the enamel bowl for an aluminium cooking pot. There were so many uses for an aluminium pot; sometimes she could open it up to reveal all kinds of things: several heads of garlic, a lump of ginger, four eggs, a pig's ear . . .

The day of Erhai's performance, Xiaohuan chopped up a dish of pig's ear, and wrapped it up, ready to take backstage, to give him some extra nutrition.

When she and Duohe arrived at the gate of the City Government Auditorium, they saw a rabble surrounding the main entrance. It was a joint gala performance by the army and civilians, and no ticket was required, all you had to do was enter with your work unit. Before long Xiaohuan and Duohe had muddled their way through. Inside, the chaos was terrifying: male hooligans and female loafers, separated by neat columns of the People's Liberation Army, flirted, catcalled and threw sweets, summer radishes and rice cakes. The PLA were singing song after song in hoarse, tuneless voices, conducted by a soldier right at the front, who was digging and scooping away like he was frying food in a giant wok, first with one hand, then the other.

Xiaohuan saw a little stand in the foyer selling melon seeds. She bought two packets, and stuffed one into Duohe's pocket. Duohe stared at her, and she said with a laugh and a grin: 'Our son gave us this filial gift of five yuan, we're hardly going to eat ourselves out of house and home with a few melon seeds!' But she felt a pang of shame: she was being a wastrel again. Her son had not even been able to eat a proper lunch to save this money, and she couldn't wait to bring it out and waste it.

After the performance was over, the loafers and hooligans all retreated from the scene, and the army left too, still singing their tuneless songs. A short fat officer in the second row beckoned to the students on the stage, and everyone gathered together at the front. Xiaohuan and Duohe's eyes looked over each one in turn, but they could not find Erhai.

The senior officer said: 'Who was the one playing lead erhu just now?' He spoke Mandarin with a heavy southern accent. 'How many of you were playing the erhu? Put your hands up!'

Four hands went up at once. A young man who looked like a teacher dragged up another hand from beside the curtains, and held it high. Xiaohuan gave Duohe a poke with her elbow.

'That's the one!' the senior officer said.

Xiaohuan turned to Duohe, and raised her eyebrows.

'Hey, I've got something to ask you! When you play the erhu, why d'you have your bottom facing the stage?' The senior officer walked up in front of Erhai.

To their surprise, Erhai did not bother to reply to the officer.

'There were people dancing on the stage, and you turn your back on them like this, with your bum pointing at them, is that a proper way to behave?' the officer asked again.

Just like his father, Erhai did not respond.

'I was listening to you offstage, and your playing is great! So I went into the auditorium, and the first thing I saw was this lad fiddling away, watching the performers dance through the back of his head! I'm asking you, why didn't you look at the stage?'

The senior officer's face was full of interest, and he turned from Erhai's left to his right, like he was looking for a cricket in a crack in the stone.

'Are you dumb?'

Unable to stop herself, Xiaohuan said: 'He's not dumb! He's just not much of a talker!'

The student performers on the stage laughed, and they all started talking on Erhai's behalf. This one said that Erhai was extremely feudal, so when his female classmates were dancing onstage he turned his back on them. That one said: If a girl cracks a joke, he goes on strike. A pair of teachers, one male and one female, came out to say that Erhai's erhu was effectively leading the ensemble, everyone followed his rhythm, and if he stopped playing performing became impossible, so let him have his back to the stage if he wanted to.

The senior officer was even more intrigued. He clasped his hands behind his back and studied Erhai in detail.

Xiaohuan started to be afraid: what did this senior officer have in mind for Erhai?

'What else can you do?' he asked.

Erhai looked at the senior officer, and nodded to indicate that there were a great many things he could do. The officer asked the students around him: 'What else can he do?'

'Accordion, Beijing-style erhu . . .' the male teacher said.

'Swimming, ping-pong,' a male student added.

'Wrestling,' Erhai suddenly said. Everyone, including the senior officer, gave a start and then laughed.

From her seat below the stage, Xiaohuan said urgently to Duohe: 'Now the cat's out of the bag!'

'What kind of wrestling?' asked the officer.

Erhai's face was purple with suppressed emotion. 'The army has a Reconnaissance Unit, don't they? That kind of wrestling.'

The officer said: 'Wrestling? That's good. We have a Special Operations Unit. How about I find an arrest and capture specialist to give you a competition some day?'

Erhai was silent once more.

The senior officer walked off the stage and then looked back, smiling to himself, his face tilted towards Erhai. Xiaohuan watched the man and a crowd of soldiers walk down the aisle and out of the door, and said to Duohe: 'The little wretch! If that officer's memory is any good, and he really finds someone to compete with him, he'll get himself wrestled to mincemeat!'

That evening Erhai returned home with his mother and aunt, in a rage all the way, blaming them for turning up without an invitation, and sneaking in to watch him perform. This time it was Xiaohuan who did not speak. She had got what she wanted, so there was no need to say anything. She was puzzled: when people meet with disaster they think they can't carry on, but after a while they discover that's just the way things are, and you have to plough ahead. When Zhang Jian had been locked up, she had thought that she would never again be happy, the way she was today, not for the rest of her life.

That army officer was the head of the Military Control Commission. He was known as Division Commander Hao, and he had an unusually good memory. Over a month later he really did find two experts in capture and arrest in the Special Operations Unit, and sent to the Red Guard Propaganda Troupe for Erhai. The wrestling competition was held at dusk before New Year. The division commander made his people spread a layer of special sand on the empty ground beneath the building where he lived, and he leaned on the railings of the second floor spectating.

The first capture specialist announced that he was withdrawing from the competition after a couple of rounds. He said that Erhai did not even understand basic footwork, and was just lashing out at random.

The senior officer gave a wave of his hand, and summoned the second capture specialist. This man had a long face and a bulky frame, and when he came into the ring he pulled the peak of his cap, which was already worn crooked, to the back of his head. Erhai watched him without moving a muscle, legs crossed, the upper half of his body bent very low. The capture specialist did not attack, but shifted his way gradually to Erhai's left, who moved along with him, a fifteen-year-old boy, with a great bundle of wrinkles piled up on his forehead. The man started to move to the right, and Erhai followed him, but with smaller and more stable movements.

The senior officer's wife walked out from their flat onto the balcony, glanced at the scene below and said in a loud voice: 'Ooh, what's going on down there?'

The brawny capture expert immediately glanced upwards. Erhai remained motionless, as though he had not heard.

The big man was losing patience, and threw himself on Erhai. He had unusually powerful legs; Erhai attacked him three times without bringing him down, so he very quickly fell into lashing out at random. The result was that the big man won two bouts, and Erhai won one.

'The way I see it, the little devil won today,' the senior officer said. 'By fighting at random he drove one away, and still won a bout with the strength he had left. Besides, you say that he doesn't know the basic footwork, but he beat you into this state without that knowledge. If he'd known, would you still be alive?' The senior officer started to clap for Erhai.

Erhai remained still and expressionless. He thought that the big man had won by a narrow margin. If he had not wasted so much energy on him, he might actually have won.

'Do you know why the little devil beat you?' the officer asked the competitors and spectators down below. 'He concentrates. Didn't you see the way he was concentrating? His eyes could have bored holes in a stone!'

The senior officer's wife responded with a chuckle, 'I think this little devil's a handsome chap – if I didn't have any sons I'd adopt him as my godson!'

The onlookers heckled: 'So you can't take him as a godson if you have a son?'

'I'd have to ask his parents. Little devil, stay for supper, hey?'

Erhai shook his head.

The senior officer had not finished his commentary on the wrestling match. He pointed to Erhai and said: 'Moreover, the little devil fought with style. Just now, when my wife called out, his opponent lost focus. That was the perfect moment for him to attack, and he let it go, because he was not willing to take advantage through trickery, and win when his opponent was off his guard.'

Having failed to get Erhai to stay, the commanding officer's wife seemed even more kindly disposed towards him, and left him a phone number and an address, telling him to contact her if he found himself in any kind of difficulty. She had come to this city to visit her husband whose regiment was here in support of the Leftists; normally she and her mother-in-law lived in the division headquarters, several hundred kilometres from this city. All her children had joined the army. She walked with him all the way to the main road before taking her leave.

Afterwards Erhai heard that the commanding officer's wife had visited the Red Guard Propaganda Troupe, but by then he had already been expelled. When it became known that Erhai's father had been given a suspended death sentence, they whispered about him all day, and he kept knocking down the people who whispered about him, laying them out flat.

The big public sentencing was held in the city sports ground. Xiaohuan went alone, without telling Duohe. There were three long rows of people to be sentenced to death or to be given the chance to reform through a suspended death sentence, and Xiaohuan was sitting towards the back. All she could see of Zhang Jian was his silhouette. They always had to drum up a big batch of people to kill in the run-up to Spring Festival. The people in the front row were dragged off, crammed into trucks, and after being displayed to the whole city would be taken to the execution ground unless the sentence was suspended. Zhang Jian was one of those in the first row. Xiaohuan's hands were pinching at her thighs, wanting to pinch herself awake from this nightmare. When she was little she had had similar nightmares, where the Japanese had tied up her father or brother and were going to kill them, and she had been watching in just this way, unable to make a sound.

When they read out Zhang Jian's sentence, Xiaohuan could hear nothing, apart from something falling down her throat with a great gulp. Afterwards she realised that heavy thing was her own saliva, mixed with blood. She did not know if it was her tongue she had bitten, or her lips. It had been close to six months since Zhang Jian had been put away, and she had not seen him once. His head had changed from a black chestnut to a white one – more than two centimetres of hair had grown back since they had shaved him bald in a convict's haircut, as they probably lacked the manpower to shave their heads clean again before sentencing. A couple of decades ago,

Zhang Jian, with his chestnut head of black hair, had been the kind of young man who could make a woman love him! After the matchmaker had left all those years ago, Zhu Xiaohuan had shamelessly written a note and had it taken in secret to Zhang Jian, telling him to meet her at a restaurant, as she wanted to measure his feet to make him a pair of shoes. Zhang Jian, who at that time was still Zhang Erhai, had turned up with two young men from the village. Similarly, Xiaohuan had brought a sister to the meeting: with more people there they could let themselves go, and say anything, proper or improper. Zhang Jian had barely had a word to say for himself, but by the time everyone had finished eating and asked for the bill, they found that he had already settled up. And later, in the instant when he had pulled aside Xiaohuan's red wedding veil, the thought had come to Xiaohuan that she would be certain to grow old with this man who was so reluctant to open his mouth you would think he was carrying gold in it.

Xiaohuan thought that she would be kept very busy in the two years of Zhang Jian's suspended sentence: she would wear out iron shoes looking for a place where she could have wrongful cases re-investigated. Zhang Jian had lifted Xiaohuan's red veil, and she had silently pledged to him that they would stay together. She had to stand by her pledge.

In the stadium, Xiaohuan squeezed her way below the stage, where convicts were being loaded, knees buckled and faces like death. Zhang Jian's expression was darker than other people's, but his knees and legs were like a dead man's too. On such an occasion, any brave man who claimed not to be afraid had to be faking. Xiaohuan did not cry or scream. She was afraid that Zhang Jian would get distracted comforting her. She called out: 'Erhai!' She had not called him by his childhood name for many years. Zhang Jian raised his head, and promptly burst into tears. Now she was that big sister who liked to rumple his hair again, saying: 'What are you crying for? Bear up, now! They even let Lao Qiu out!'

Lao Qiu was their neighbour from the flats opposite. He had been sent to prison for the crime of communication with secret agents of the Kuomintang, his hands sticky with the lifeblood of underground Party members. He had originally been given a suspended death sentence, but somehow he had got out of prison.

Xiaohuan followed the prisoners and their escorts, talking to Zhang Jian over the heads of three ranks of armed police. She said that everyone back home was well: Duohe was well, the boys were well, and Blackie too! They all told her to ask after him. Zhang Jian was much calmer now, and nodded repeatedly. The convicts' handcuffs and leg shackles were very heavy, and got in the way of their hands and feet, so when mounting the trucks they had really become piles of freight to be shifted by the policemen. This gave Xiaohuan a longer opportunity to shout.

'Daddy, they've notified me – once you've entered the labour reform camp, I'll be able to come and visit!'

'Daddy, we've had a letter from Girlie, she says she's found a boyfriend, he's a conductor on a train, she sent money last month, so don't you worry, eh?'

'Daddy, we're all fine at home. I'll send you another new pair of cotton padded trousers at Spring Festival!'

She did not let up until the words she was shouting could have no longer possibly reached Zhang Jian's ears through the great cloud of yellow dust and smoke from the truck. She had told her string of lies in a loud, strong voice, but now she started to cry. If only their life was like the lies. No one had notified her when she could visit the prison. Girlie had said in a letter that someone had introduced her to a man whose wife had died, a conductor on a train, but she had never sent any money. The only promise Xiaohuan might make good on was a pair of new padded trousers; she would get hold of a metre of new cloth even if she had to steal it. Now she understood how useful the knee protectors were; he spent all day kneeling and wore out the knees of his trousers. She was going to add a bit of extra padding to the knee area.

From the city stadium to home there were more than twenty stops on the bus route, and tickets cost one jiao. On her way there, Xiaohuan had not bought a ticket, but stood directly in front of the ticket collector's counter, like a worker who had spent half her life with a monthly ticket tucked away in her pocket. On the return journey, she forgot all about the bus. By the time she noticed, she had already walked halfway home. She just wished that the way was a bit longer. If she had a bit more time she would have another set of lies ready to tell Duohe and Erhai.

Erhai had gone from spending all day outside to not setting foot out of the door once. School had started up again some time ago. He would go for a few days, then get sent home for beating up half his classmates. If his classmates shouted anything at him about his father he would knock them down, leaving them unconcious. It took a lot of classmates uniting together to finally bring him down and frog-march him back home. Two months earlier, he had gone out with the household registration book, and come back with a big red certificate of merit for 'Voluntarily Going Up the Mountains and Down to the Countryside'. As soon as Spring Festival was over, Erhai would no longer be eating rations from the household registration book, he was off north of the Huai River to be a peasant. By the look of him, he could only make a little peasant boy of twelve or so.

When Xiaohuan came back from the stadium, Erhai had not yet

got out of bed. She said to herself: Don't ask me what kind of sleep this is, last night's sleep or a midday nap. He did not move a muscle, pillow clamped down over his head. The radio was on, though, scratchily playing the city radio station: how such-and-such an article in Chairman Mao's latest directive had created an overwhelming tide of enthusiasm in such-and-such a factory. Something suddenly occurred to Xiaohuan, and she walked over and lifted up the pillow. Underneath was a face that had been crying all morning. He had plainly heard the sentencing meeting, and his father's sentence.

Xiaohuan hurriedly looked towards the balcony, then went to check the big room and the kitchen. Duohe was nowhere to be seen. Had Duohe heard the news on the radio too?

'Where's your auntie got to?' she asked through the pillow cloth.

Beneath the pillow, Erhai did not breathe a word.

'Did she hear the radio too? Are you dead?'

And indeed, it did look like a child revolutionary martyr was lying there under the pillow.

Xiaohuan pushed open the door of the toilet, with its iron bucket full of half-dirty water for scrubbing the floor – water that had first washed the faces of everyone in the family, then washed their feet, and then washed the cotton socks of the day. There were no obvious traces to be seen of any abnormal behaviour on Duohe's part. So what was making Xiaohuan so anxious and fearful?

At this moment Blackie started calling to be let in with piercing howls. Xiaohuan went to the door. Since Erhai had stopped going out, taking Blackie for walks had fallen to Duohe. She would walk him once in the morning, then at noon and at dusk, and the length of the walks kept increasing. Once Xiaohuan had had many friends, wherever she went there were people to be friendly with, but now, although she affected a cocky, spirited air when she appeared in the corridors of the building and on the stairs, she did not even have a decent neighbour. Occasionally she would bump into someone and they would exchange a few words, but Xiaohuan knew that in no time that person would be telling other people: Oh, oh, I've caught that Zhu Xiaohuan in the act – the family's eating noodles with an eggy sauce, looks like convicted criminals get by better than when they were drawing a wage! With friends gone, Xiaohuan started to pay attention to Blackie's whereabouts, whether he was warm enough and getting enough to eat, and his joys and sorrows. Occasionally, when Duohe did not go out, they let Blackie take himself for a walk. By the looks of things Blackie had given himself a very good walk, for steam was coming off all over him.

Xiaohuan saw that the patterned cloth bag that Duohe often carried was still hanging on the wall. She opened it, looked inside and found a wad of small change, the biggest note two jiao. Recently, she had observed that a pair of canvas gloves that Zhang Jian had used at the factory had been drying on the balcony from time to time, with the fingers slit open. She had asked Duohe whether she had been scavenging glass for the rubbish recycling depot, and if so she should disguise herself well, so the neighbours wouldn't see the Zhang family lose face. Duohe had made a surly retort. It had taken Xiaohuan a long time to work out what she meant: in this building Duohe didn't count as a human being anyway, what face did she have to lose? Now she looked at these notes, which confirmed why Duohe was spending more and more time airing the dog.

By four in the afternoon, Duohe had still not returned. Xiaohuan took out two two-jiao notes from the pile, in order to go to the market to rummage for bits of vegetable in the bottom of baskets. Once she had got as far as the ground floor, she realised that Blackie had followed her, panting and whining away in his doggy language, but she did not know what he was saying. She said: 'What did you come down for? Haven't you been running about like crazy all day?'

The dog whined and turned his head in the direction of a path to the left of the slope.

'Get lost, I'm not taking you for a walk!'

Blackie was still walking towards the path, whining. She went straight ahead down the main road, and Blackie followed her again. Xiaohuan thought: In this family, apart from the ones that don't talk, we have the ones that don't talk human language, and then we have the people who say things we don't really understand.

She entered the food market and saw that a big fish head had been set out at the fishmonger's, the size of a small pig's head. She went up and said, pointing: 'Weigh it!'

The fish head weighed in at six jiao, and she only had two. After she had used up her entire stock of flattery, the attendant agreed that she could bring the rest of the money the following day. As she walked out of the door carrying the fish head, her nose stung with tears: if Zhang Jian had been dragged straight out of that public sentencing meeting and shot, she would not be buying any fish heads. By stewing this fish head, she was giving the whole family a chance to celebrate that Zhang Jian had not been shot dead. This was such a wretched celebration. And she had splashed out all this money for fish-head soup to coax the family to be happy, to coax them all into believing that in the two years of the suspended death sentence there were seven hundred and thirty days, and each day had twenty-four hours, and in every hour things changed and chances were made for him to have his sentence commuted. She had to coax Erhai and Duohe not to take it too hard; however things turned out they had to carry on living a day at a time, and as they lived on they should eat fish-head soup when they got the chance. Even if Zhang Jian had been taken from the public sentencing meeting to the execution ground, if he knew that without him his family could still have fish-head soup to eat, would that not be the greatest comfort of all? In the evening when they were all eating the soup together, she would tell her lies to Duohe and Erhai: she'd found a way to get Zhang Jian's case commuted. After Spring Festival she would get moving, and get his suspended death sentence changed to life imprisonment as soon as possible. And once it had become life imprisonment, it might not be an actual life sentence anyway.

When she returned home Blackie was still whining away in his doggy language. Xiaohuan looked at the sky, confused in her mind and troubled in her heart. If Duohe was gathering glass this late, could she even see? If she got her finger cut off that'd mean still more money to go on medical fees!

By half past six, the stewed fish head was already done. Xiaohuan suddenly felt that she understood Blackie's dog language a little. She called to Erhai, and went down the stairs, Blackie walking in front and mother and son behind, shining a torch. Once they had left the stairwell, Blackie trotted towards that big slope in the road, where he waited for the others to catch up, and then hurriedly turned left.

Following Blackie, they came to an iron door, half buried in the ground. Erhai told his mother that this was the air-raid tunnel that his school had dug together with another school. The door at the other end of the tunnel was inside the school.

Blackie sat down outside the iron door, waiting respectfully. Xiaohuan thought, Duohe must have made Blackie wait for her outside the doorway, she had gone in and not come out again. Every hair on Xiaohuan's body stood on end, and she picked up a fist-sized rock from the mouth of the tunnel. Erhai broke his silence, saying, 'Ma, you've got me and Blackie!'

More than two kilometres later, the three of them walked out from the tunnel. There was nothing inside at all but turds and condoms.

'Your auntie must have gone to the toilet inside, and lost her bearings in the dark. She must have come out that door.' As soon as the words were out of her mouth, she thought that this could not be right. Duohe did often lose her bearings, but to get herself lost in the way she had conjectured, she would have to be an idiot.

'My auntie didn't want Blackie to follow her.'

Then what was she up to? An assignation? On an important day like today, when there was fish-head soup to be eaten? But still, if it was an assignation?

They continued onwards, following Blackie. The dog seemed to know what he was doing. After half an hour, they arrived at the research institute of the iron and steel factory. The boundary wall had collapsed in many places, and they crossed it walking on shattered bricks. Blackie came to a halt, and looked at the two human members of the group, almost like he was explaining the situation to them. Here was a jumble of fire-scorched ruins: several months earlier a fire had started in a third-floor laboratory, and an entire building had burned down. Now and then a streak or a dot of brightness would appear on the ground, shattered test tubes and experimental bottles, buried under the bricks and soil.

Xiaohuan and Erhai understood why Blackie had brought them to this place, and what it was that he wanted to explain but could not. He was showing them that this was the place where Duohe dug up her broken glass. Through Blackie, they finally understood why Duohe's fingers had been inexplicably bound up in gauze or sticking plaster and why the gloves were slashed.

They continued to let Blackie be their guide. This time Blackie took them to a place halfway up the mountain. Several years ago work had begun digging an air-raid shelter on the mountain that could hold hundreds of thousands of people; the stones that had been blasted out were piled up into another mountain, and rainwater had accumulated in the hollowed-out part to form a pond. Neither had expected to find a pool of such crystal-clear water in such a place. Erhai threw a stone into the pool, and they could both hear that it was very deep.

Blackie had become the master now. He took them striding from rock to rock, to arrive at last on a very flat stone that protruded from the pile, and hung suspended above the water of the pool.

Blackie sat down on the stone and turned his head to look back at Xiaohuan and Erhai. The two humans walked over. From where Blackie was they could see right into the centre of the lake. Now a star was reflected in there.

Blackie often came here with Duohe. Their conversations were either strangely ill-assorted, or else entirely without words. In that case had Duohe used the air-raid shelter to prevent Blackie from following her, and come here by herself? The water was extremely still, it seemed so limpid that there was not a speck of life to it. In the light of the torch they could see the pale stones in the water, criss-crossed and interlocking like dogs' teeth. Throw yourself in head first and your head would be split open like a melon. Xiaohuan walked with Erhai around the pond of stones. From time to time the beam of the torch illuminated the water. Had the news of Zhang Jian's suspended death sentence caused Duohe to give up hope and become a new ghost for Shironami village? She asked Erhai how Auntie had reacted when she heard the announcement. He had no idea, the radio broadcast of the public sentencing had been bawling and bellowing in the street like lions and tigers, first the propaganda vehicles had passed by, then the convict trucks from the sentencing, for miles around the loudspeakers that normally played 'The East is Red' and 'Sailing the Seas Depends on the Helmsman' were broadcasting slogans from the sentencing. He had buried his head in the pillow and even then the quilt was full of the sound of slogans. He did not know how his aunt had been. He did not even know how he himself had been.

If she really had jumped in the pool they would not be able to fish her out before morning. Xiaohuan had no choice but to take her son and Blackie back home. They could see from the ground floor that the Zhang flat was in darkness. Duohe had not returned. And yet when mother and son and Blackie reached the second floor, Blackie darted up the pitch-black stairs. Erhai understood, and hurried up the steps after him, three at a time.

By the time Xiaohuan arrived and pulled on the light cord, in the greyish light of the lamp they found Duohe sitting on the bench for changing shoes, wearing one wooden shoe and one cloth one. They did not know whether she was about to go out of the door or come inside.

'I've spent so long outside trying to find you that I've walked my feet swollen,' Xiaohuan said, half smiling, half complaining.

She promptly tied on her apron and busied herself about the kitchen. The fish-head soup was puttering merrily away. She chopped up a handful of coriander from a flowerpot, scattered it on top, and carried the pot to the table. 'Don't just sit there! Bring me that grass mat! Or else the heat'll spoil the table!'

Duohe was still sitting there, stupefied.

Erhai ran into the kitchen to fetch the coiled grass mat to put underneath the iron pot.

Xiaohuan doled out a big bowl of fish meat and soup for everyone, and began to drink. Duohe took off her cloth shoe, stepped into the other wooden one, and sat down very slowly at the table. The light in the corridor was just ten watts, and it was enveloped in the steam from the pot, so none of the three could see anyone else's face clearly. Xiaohuan had no need to see Duohe; she knew that she had left that terrifying thought outside the door, at least for the moment.

Through the steam, she started to tell the two shadowy faces that she planned to launch an appeal against Zhang Jian's wrongful conviction. Her lies completely convinced her audience, and from the sounds of their eating she could hear their sense of taste gradually returning, and their appetite gradually reviving. When Erhai was helping himself to his fourth bowl of soup, Xiaohuan intervened, telling him not to eat until he was sick. The leftover soup could be used to boil up a pot of mixed-grain 'cats' ears'.

Sure enough, the next day a big pot of 'cats' ears' appeared. Not even Xiaohuan had realised that when she was not being lazy she was actually a fine household manager. She had no intention of repaying the four jiao she owed to the fish stall.

She went to the local police station, talked her way into a business licence and set up a sewing machine at the foot of the Neighbourhood Committee building, mending clothes and tailoring simple new pieces. She brought Duohe along with her, to do the buttonholes and sew on buttons. In fact she did not feel easy leaving Duohe on her own, in case she took to thinking mad thoughts again and started wanting to take herself off to join the rest of her Japanese village in some strange underworld.

After Spring Festival Erhai set off to join a production team in the countryside north of the Huai River.

But after the festival Dahai came home. The factory's Revolutionary Committee had been regularised, and underage volunteers like him had been sent home covered in glory. The Red

Guard basketball team had also been regularised; some of its members had been incorporated into the army garrison basketball team, others had been organised into a city youth team. Dahai was already too old for the youth team, and the army team physical had identified a pair of exceptionally flat feet, which meant that he was not a good long-term prospect. All they could do was encourage him to go back to the school to play amateur basketball. The day Dahai returned home, Erhai was just preparing to leave. Dahai called out affectionately to him: 'Erhai!'

Erhai watched him walk up casually, wearing his outstandingly tatty running shoes which looked like they must stink to high heaven, and immediately said: 'How come you've not taken off your shoes?'

Dahai appeared not to have heard.

'Take your shoes off!' Erhai was seized by a fit of stubbornness and blocked his brother's way.

'Shoes off? Bollocks to that!' Dahai suddenly turned hostile.

Erhai turned hostile in his turn. From then on he did not mention so much as his brother's name in his letters. At home and at school, Dahai affected the high and lofty attitude of a genius whose talents were unrecognised. Although he retained his good looks he kept losing weight until at last he fell ill, and a medical examination revealed that he was already in the second stage of tuberculosis. He would often say to Xiaohuan that there were too many regrets in his life, and the greatest of these was that he had inherited this pair of exceptionally flat feet, from who knew where. Perhaps his uncle or his grandfather had planted rice sprouts, brought in the harvest and gone to market in Shironami village on identical flat feet, Xiaohuan thought.

14

The sewing stall Xiaohuan had set up at the bottom of the Neighbourhood Committee building was proving a big headache for the female cadres. In the past they had been on good terms with Xiaohuan; now she was the wife of a condemned criminal, staying on good terms with her was out of the question, but they still had to pass by her sewing machine every day. Fortunately Xiaohuan was a late sleeper, and it took her until ten every morning to get her stall set up, so they could slip in and up the stairs while it was still early.

One day Duohe had swept up the ends of thread and scraps of fabric that could not be pieced together into a pile; she could not find the dustpan anywhere, so she went upstairs and took a dustpan from there, meaning to borrow it for a while and return it later. She had just picked it up, when a female cadre from the Neighbourhood Committee started shouting: 'What are you doing – stealing our things?' Duohe was so anxious that she kept shaking her head. The female cadre said: 'No wonder things are always going missing around here!'

Xiaohuan, who had heard every word, yelled loudly: 'Who's nicked a piece of my twill? Me and my sister had just nipped out to the loo, how come it just disappeared?' She had remembered that the female cadre was wearing a pair of brand-new twill trousers.

'Zhu Xiaohuan, you can't go spreading vile slander like that!' The female cadre came rushing down from upstairs, her fingers fiddling with the legs of her trousers. 'Is this stolen from you?'

'That's between you and your conscience,' Xiaohuan said. 'I bought a strip of blue twill, I was going to make a pair of trousers to sell.'

'Don't you make false accusations!' the female cadre said.

'You know very well whether the accusation is false.' Xiaohuan chatted away, leisurely and casual, watching the woman fly into a foot-stamping rage. It was plain to see how furious she was.

Since Xiaohuan had lost her friends among the dependants and female cadres, she very soon made herself a crowd of friends with no status at all: pot-menders, people who exchanged eggs for flour coupons on the black market, makers of popped rice, women who had been paraded through the street for a loose woman with broken shoes around their necks, people who ran rat-poison stalls, all of whom worshipped her as a goddess. All the hoodlums on the street with their dark glasses, zip-up shirts and big sideburns, all the educated youths who stubbornly resisted being sent down to the countryside, would run Xiaohuan's errands for her, always respectfully addressing her as Sister Xiaohuan. The cadres in the Neighbourhood Committee maintained that Zhu Xiaohuan had become degraded to an elderly social butterfly, flitting among the dregs of society.

In the beginning the cadres had enquired of the provincial and municipal Public Security Bureaus how they should deal with a Japanese like Zhunei Duohe. Neither the province nor the city had handled such a peculiar case, so they sent people to Heilongjiang to see how the public security organs there had dealt with the Japanese women who had been sold into Chinese families. The investigation found that all of this group of Japanese women were still the daughters-in-law, wives and mothers of Chinese families, still doing the heavy work of Chinese peasants and the heavy chores of the household. Apparently they had not found any punishment that was heavier than the work in a Chinese family. There was just one Japanese woman who had quarrelled with her neighbours and been declared a Japanese spy, and her punishment was to make her carry on with her usual farm work and housework, but they also gave her a white armband, on which was written her name and her crime. The female cadres had been dithering for some time over whether to make a white armband for Duohe, and when Xiaohuan suddenly turned hostile, they immediately set to work, then delivered the white armband to Xiaohuan's sewing stall. On the white armband was written: 'Japanese spy Zhunei Duohe'.

Xiaohuan shot a glance at the armband, and said to Duohe, who had not yet had time to react: 'They're making you wear it, so you go ahead and wear it. Look at that needlework, I could do better with my toes. Put it on, make do.'

Duohe still did not move.

'Or else I could give it a frilly border?' Xiaohuan said, poker-faced. She took up the white armband in her hands, looking it over, and then picked up a strip of blue-striped fabric from the ground, comparing them from all angles. 'How about this colour for the frill? Could you make do with that?'

In the blink of an eye, the frill was attached. Duohe slowly fitted the armband onto her arm, and Xiaohuan pinned it in place. When the female cadres saw it, they reproached Xiaohuan loudly, and asked what she thought she was doing.

'Don't you know she's Japanese? Over there in Japan all the white armbands they wear are frilly.'

'Rip it off!'

'No!'

'Zhu Xiaohuan, you're sabotaging and making trouble!'

'Where's the central Party document or latest instructions from Chairman Mao that says that a white armband can't have a frill? If you can find it for me, then I'm sabotaging and troublemaking!'

'What do you think you're doing? Is this a proper way to go on?'

'Don't like the look of it? Keep on looking, make do, eh?'

The next day, the female cadres announced that from then on Zhu Duohe had to sweep clean the stairs, offices and toilets of this building three times a day. And if they found a fly or a maggot in the toilet, Duohe's crimes would be increased by one level of magnitude.

'If they're making you sweep, then sweep,' Xiaohuan said. 'Just think of yourself as a zookeeper, mucking out the pigsties.' As she spoke she raised her eyes from the sewing machine.

Wherever Duohe went, Blackie went too, so Xiaohuan was not afraid that she would get picked on, or that she would take some new notion of killing herself, for Blackie would report to Xiaohuan at any time. There was just one thing that worried and irritated her: Duohe did all her work very earnestly, without a hint of dawdling or slacking, and washed the toilet as clean as the one in her own home. She made a special trip to the toilet in order to teach Duohe how to cut corners in her work: not to start sweeping until she saw the female cadres coming through the holes in the pierced concrete wall. She also said to her: the Neighbourhood Committee get their water for free anyway, so splash it out by the bucketful, and you won't even need to sweep. She told her not to forget to bring a bucket of water home with her when work was over, to save on their own water bill.

Not long after Xiaohuan set up several folding chairs and a folding table outside the Neighbourhood Committee, on which she laid out a pot of tea made from fried seeds, drawing in those dregs of society that the cadre ladies would rather die than approve, who clustered around, chatting and laughing. Her business promptly began to boom.

'How's the tea?' Xiaohuan kept asking.

'Really tasty!' Her dubious friends praised it extravagantly.

'Japanese tea!'

'Really? Well, no wonder.'

Then Xiaohuan would call Duohe over, and say that she could make Japanese food, only they did not have any red beans or glutinous rice. The following day, the hoodlums would come bearing rice and red beans. Xiaohuan got Duohe to make rice balls at home and then bring them to the sewing stall. Having enjoyed this Japanese hospitality, the hoodlums brought out even more of their shadily acquired things to eat for Xiaohuan. They were all around seventeen years old, precisely the age to appreciate an auntie like Xiaohuan, with her charm, her skill and her belly full of barely suppressed 'wickedness'. They included Duohe in their generous treatment: 'Auntie, how can you do stuff like rinsing down toilets? You're an International Friend! Leave it to us!' All the long-haired loafers, boys and girls, helped Duohe to sluice out the toilets three times a day, singing revolutionary songs in the sleaziest way imaginable. The female cadres forbade them from helping the enemy redeem her crimes, but they would say, cigarettes dangling from their mouths: 'And you think you can keep me in order, do you?' One day a cadre threatened to send Duohe to the Public Security Bureau. The loafers said: 'Go ahead, send her, and after that there'll be plenty of people to put holes in your bike tyres! You'll need new glass for your windows at least once every two days! And your children too, we know where they go to school.' Then the female cadre threatened to send the loafers to the Public Security Bureau. A tall hoodlum said: 'I'd just finished raping this woman, and she dragged herself back up and said: thank you, see you next time!'

Everyone around him told him he was vile, some roared with laughter, others cursed and laughed at the same time.

Duohe had not understood all of it, but she started to smile along with them. She found to her surprise that she was smiling from inside to out. A few months ago, sitting beside the stone pool, how could she have thought that she would still be able to lift her head and laugh out loud; that, having written herself off as hopeless, she could continue to muddle her way through each day?

The public sentencing had indeed come dangerously close to reuniting Duohe with the people of Shironami village. That day, as she went down the road with Blackie on his lead, the streets were full of the excitement that comes with killing people. It flooded the space like electricity, it hit her as she walked until her whole body was numb. The loudspeaker tirelessly read out the names of the condemned, and the names did not dissipate in the air, but congealed in the chilly, damp winter of the Yangtze delta. Zhang Jian's name condensed on top of Duohe's head, covering her.

She walked to the mouth of the air-raid tunnel, and ordered Blackie to wait for her at the entrance. Blackie understood that whenever her hand gently pressed down on his bottom, she was telling him to sit. Normally telling him to sit meant telling him to wait. When she went into a shop to buy a packet of tobacco or salt, or to the grain store for rice or noodles, she would always give his bottom a push, and he would sit down at once. Once she had shaken off Blackie in the air-raid tunnel she had walked to the side of the pond halfway up the mountain slope. The sky was an afternoon sky, greyish-white layers laid out evenly as far as the eye could see, and through the layers of cloud the dazzlingly white sun shone through.

How many times had she come here with Blackie to be at peace, and to chat to the dog in the language she spoke with the children? They were all grown up now, and were getting out of practice at this babyish language that was neither one thing nor another. She could only speak it with Blackie now. She talked and talked, and after a while it was like she was talking to the three children.

This black dog was a link between three people: Xiao Peng, Erhai and herself. Xiao Peng had bought Blackie in order to make Erhai happy. How important Erhai's happiness had been to Xiao Peng in those days! Because he knew that Duohe would give him a few smiles just for making Erhai happy. Xiao Peng had no way of knowing that Duohe spoke more to Blackie than anyone else. She could see that the dog was worried to death about her; he saw that the notion of suicide was forming in her mind. When a person is in a state of utter despair, there is a smell to them. There must be, otherwise how had Blackie sniffed it out?

She sat down on the stone, looking at the water, so clear that you could see the bottom. Any one of the jagged stones would be fine, it would be a help to her when she threw herself in head first, shortening the time of her struggle.

She had not chosen a different method, such as hanging or throwing herself under a train, because this pool resembled a pond in the neighbourhood of Shironami village which had also been created by blasting a mountain to make a railway. Going into this pool, she would enter that one too.

It was a pity that they had not yet started to construct the air-raid shelters and that this pond did not exist at the time of her secret meetings with Zhang Jian. This place was so clean and tranquil. She could never forget those days even now, and whenever she saw a place with pleasant scenery she could not prevent herself from thinking of Zhang Jian, and of when she might be able to bring him there. Even that time when Xiao Peng had taken her to the tree nursery, she had dreamed afterwards of visiting the place with Zhang Jian.

She sat next to the pool until she was chilled to the bone. She made up her mind that she would put an end to herself immediately. It would not be hard; at this moment both her race and her family gave her courage, resolution and strength.

She got to her feet. She had forgotten what month and what day it was. She thought: how could she not even know the date of her own death? How could she be certain that Zhang Jian would be able to find her in the netherworld? The underworld was bound to be bigger than the world of the living; if you did not have a date for your death it might be like being unable to find your household registration.

She stood on the stone, and finally recalled the voice from the public sentencing on the radio: today was a Sunday. Very well, Duohe would meet her death on a Sunday early in 1970. It had been two years since she and Zhang Jian had spoken. Over two years. Because she had been carrying a heavy tool bag on the slope and he had ignored her, and because he had been standing on the balcony with Xiaohuan, shoulder to shoulder. And she was actually going to leave without making up with him. Would they still be able to make up when she reached the underworld? Possibly not.

With hurried steps, Duohe went down the embankment of stones. It was too dangerous, she had almost gone without breaking her sulky silence. She had to find a way to see him once, for a reconciliation. The only person who would be able to arrange this was Xiao Peng. He was bound to have a lot of very important connections, which would mean she could see him as soon as possible and then finish what she had started today. She was certain that she would be able to kill herself; just now there had not been any turmoil in her mind, only impatience to see her father, her mother and all her kin.

Duohe went from the pond to the steelworks. She found Xiao Peng's dormitory, but the door was locked. She waited for hours, but when someone finally came back it was not Xiao Peng, but a young married couple. They told Duohe that Director Peng had moved to the house of the former factory head, but they did not know the address.

She went back again to the main factory administration building, and found the Revolutionary Committee Chairman's Office. All the doors were locked because it was Sunday, and also because everyone had gone to watch the condemned criminals being paraded through the streets. She went to the guest house at the foot of the building to borrow a pen and a piece of paper, on which she wrote '*Meet with you tomorrow. Duohe*'.

She went back home, and Xiaohuan returned shortly afterwards with Erhai and Blackie. She did not know why, but by the time she had finished eating Xiaohuan's fish-head soup, she rejoiced inwardly that she had not jumped into the pond today. Erhai was going north of the Huai River, whatever else happened she still had to celebrate New Year with the child, and see him on his way before doing away with herself. That last time she and Xiaohuan had quarrelled it had been very heated, and if she left like that Xiaohuan would be certain to think she was partly responsible. She did not want Xiaohuan to feel guilty for the rest of her life.

The second day she went again to the factory headquarters. The Revolutionary Committee Chairman's Office was still locked, and when she asked why, they said that Director Peng had gone to a meeting in the provincial capital. A month passed, and she went again, this time she was told that Director Peng had gone to Beijing for a meeting. Duohe thought that there was something odd about this, and found an out-of-the-way place to wait. Not long after she saw Xiao Peng leave the building, and stride into the grey Volga. She hurried over. There was an intense expression on her face: Hide if you can! Born liar!

'Do you have business with me?'

'I want to talk!'

She had already plucked open the car door, and that was how she made her demand, one foot planted in his car, allowing no room for doubt.

'I'm too busy, I don't have time for this,' Xiao Peng said coldly. 'Drive on!'

With one hand Duohe held onto the back of the driver's seat, her foot hooked firmly under it. Before the car had lurched five metres, it was dragging Duohe along on the ground.

The car was forced to stop. Duohe still did not get up. She knew that as soon as her foot relaxed its hold, the car would drive off and leave her in the dust.

Xiao Peng was afraid that people would see him with Duohe, so he told her to get into the car to talk. This was Duohe's strategy: to let people see that Director Peng's car had come close to killing someone.

Xiao Peng had no choice but to agree to take her to his home to talk.

Xiao Peng was still living a bachelor existence. His home was like an office, hung with big photographs of Marx, Engels, Lenin, Stalin and Mao, and with various editions of Mao Zedong's works on display, furnished with government-issue furniture. When the two of them were alone together, Director Peng became Xiao Peng once more. First he brewed a cup of tea for Duohe, telling her that it was Maofeng tea from Huangshan.

The two of them sat on the government-issue three-piece suite, Xiao Peng on the central sofa, and Duohe on the easy chair to the left. He asked just what it was she wanted. She said that it was Xiao Peng who had put Zhang Jian inside, so he had to find a way to let her see Zhang Jian once more.

'It's not fair to say that.' Xiao Peng's face darkened.

She spoke another sentence.

After a bit of mental effort, he understood what she was saying: that he knew in his heart whether or not he had done right by Zhang Jian.

'Oh, so if I cover up the crimes of a criminal, then I'm doing right by him? Then how can I do right by Xiao Shi, the victim?'

Duohe did not speak again. The truth of the matter had been twisted too far out of shape, and she had not come here to invite Xiao Peng to get his thoughts in order. There was nothing she could ask of him, she just wanted to see Zhang Jian, and have a decent, final parting. Her tears beat on the patched legs of her trousers, pattering as they fell.

Xiao Peng remained silent, he seemed to be listening to the sound of her tears. Suddenly he stood up, walked to the window and wheeled round.

'Are you still thinking of him?'

She stared at Xiao Peng. What kind of strange question was this?

He walked back to the sofa, sat down, and then patted the place beside him. 'Come on, sit here.'

Could it be that he wanted to finish what they had started in the tree nursery? If he would arrange matters afterwards and let her see Zhang Jian, this was a price she was prepared to pay. In any case she had already made up her mind to kill this fleshly body.

She sat down next to him.

He tilted his face towards her, with a slightly mysterious smile, examining her features.

'Your father must have killed a good few Chinese, right?'

She said that her father's unit had been in South-East Asia.

'There's no difference – in any case he was the enemy.'

There was nothing Duohe could say. He was very close to her.

'Suppose you were to think that I framed Zhang Jian on a trumped-up charge because I envied him. Then that would make me as base as you two women and Zhang Jian,' he said.

Duohe thought, the reason she had been infatuated with him for a time, and they had nearly become lovers, was precisely because she had seen him come so very close to a semblance of nobility.

'There's a scent to your body.' There he was again with that mysterious smile. 'Could Zhang Jian smell it?'

She found him slightly alarming, as if a cold wind had blown over the pores of her skin.

'He never noticed it.' He leaned his head back against the sofa, and closed his eyes, seeming to be inhaling that scent with all his heart and soul. 'The year I was twenty, the first time I came to your house, you were putting tea beside me, and out it came from a gap at the back of your collar, a fragrance came floating out . . .'

Was he hysterical?

'At that time I didn't know you were Japanese. So I thought, this woman is certain to be mine one day. That scent of hers makes me . . . oh, bloody hell. After that I had my suspicions about your relationship with Zhang Jian.'

His finger rubbed lightly over her hair.

'Xiao Shi couldn't smell this scent either. How could he? He clearly was so . . . let's just say, this scent was clearly emitted for me alone. That Zhang Jian couldn't smell it just proves that he is a pig, a mountain pig, he can't appreciate a delicacy! And he's the one who's always on your mind.' He turned towards her, staring neurotically. 'Is he always on your mind? But someone like me, who appreciates you so much, how can I not be on your mind? Eh?'

Duohe thought, if there were no empty words at all, just a quick battle to be fought to get a quick result, get it over and done with, she would not mind so much, but if he planned to make her say that he was always on her mind, she would rather die than say it.

But those were the words he was waiting for. Like a desperately thirsty man waiting for water from a pipe that had rusted solid.

She slowly shifted towards the far end of the sofa, and when she was most of the way there, she stood up all at once and rushed for the door.

'What the hell are you running for?' He picked up an ashtray and hurled it over.

The ashtray shattered, but she was unharmed.

'Fuck it, would I go to bed with you? *I'm* not a pig, and I'm not that stupid!'

She continued to scrabble hastily at the door.

'You listen to me, he's a convict under suspended sentence of death, I don't even know where they're keeping him. I'll have to go and make enquiries first. Wait and you'll hear from me!' he said from behind her.

She was already in the corridor. Once she was out of the door she was safe. She had been prepared for anything, but not to hear a madman talking about love. It had been over two years, what had driven him out of his mind? Did he not have power and position? Where had that young boy gone, king of his army of children, who had once led the fighting from the rooftop, and had encircled her with his overalls? How could such an overpoweringly sinister monster have occupied the shell of Xiao Peng's body?

By then Xiaohuan's sewing stall was doing a roaring trade. Shortly after, Duohe was fitted with a white armband, and was kept extremely busy every day, cleaning and rinsing everywhere. In a flash a year had gone by.

One day at the stall, she was suddenly taken aback at the thought of the decision she had made by the stony pool, it was like a dream. One of Xiaohuan's idler friends, a girl, said, What's so difficult about visiting prison? She could get in touch with the quartermaster of the labour camp any time. The quartermaster was actually more powerful than the governor of the labour camp, he could speak directly to the criminal's brigade leader and the thing was done. There's this to be said about big revolutions, they create a lot of very useful loopholes. Xiaohuan asked this girl whether she had a special relationship with the quartermaster. Naturally the girl knew what Xiaohuan was implying. She said that the quartermaster would be happy enough to have one; when she had been inside he would grab a handful here today, tweak a handful there tomorrow. For the sake of her Auntie Xiaohuan, she would establish a 'special relationship' with him right away.

Before many days had passed, the prison visit was all settled.

Xiaohuan repaid the girl with a pair of trousers made exactly the way she wanted. A few years previously the loafers' trousers had encased the legs tightly, but in recent years they had taken to copying the People's Liberation Army, favouring the loose-crotched trousers of a soldier.

In those hot summer days, it felt like the entire city was being forged into steel. Spend more than a few minutes outside and you would feel sick and see stars. Xiaohuan took Duohe all over the town making purchases, preparing the things to take to Zhang Jian when they visited him in prison. There was a severe shortage of food products, every family was short of coupons for cake, and the cakes in the glass cases of the department store had gone mouldy for want of a buyer. Xiaohuan spent all the coupons she had collected from her dubious friends on a kilo of cake covered in a faint layer of green moss. The things she was most satisfied with were two big pots of fried bean sauce, containing pork skin, pork fat, dried tofu and soya beans and generously salted, so that it would not go off even if the weather became hotter still. In this way, whether you were eating rice or sweet-potato cakes, noodles, slabs of boiled wheat dough or thin rice gruel, this sauce would always make for a good dish.

The old man who popped rice and corn filled a sack of popcorn for Xiaohuan. The shoe mender gave her a pair of newly made cloth shoes. The ice-lolly seller gave her a set of toothpicks whittled from lollipop sticks.

In the evening, as Xiaohuan and Duohe packed each of the articles into a bag, the outside door opened, and Dahai came in. His head was covered in blood, and his clothes were soaked through with it.

Duohe hurried over and took his arm to support him, asking what the matter was. He shoved her out of the way.

Xiaohuan looked at Dahai, and saw at once that he had shaved his eyebrows. She knew what was going on. Several days earlier Dahai had asked her where the tweezers were which the family used for pulling out pigs' bristles. She had said that they'd had no pigs' trotters to eat for years, who could still remember a thing like tweezers? Now she understood how he had solved the problem of his heavy, dark eyebrows: by shaving off the greater half with a razor, leaving two thin, asymmetrical lines and a strip of bloody wounds. The hair on his lip and on his temples had also been shaved. He had made himself over into a little old granny. Looking further down, he had run the knife over the sparse hairs on his chest too, and the hair on his legs was shaved clean away until they were almost like those of a girl. Xiaohuan felt both sorry for him and sickened by him. She could imagine how hard it must be for him to spend his days as a hairy Jap brat, and how dangerous. She could imagine him facing the mirror, grinding his teeth at that handsome lad with his heavy eyebrows and elegant eyes, delicate skin and white flesh. Those naturally red, glossy lips would be bitten white, bitten purple and finally bitten ragged. The only small mirror in the house was hanging on the water pipe in the toilet, and he would tug at his head of unreasonably thick, heavy, black hair, hating that he could not pluck it out by the handful, like weeds. But you would never be done weeding out something like this, because there were also those Japanese hairs on his legs and chest. He had stopped going to the public bathhouse because of this. Finally, he made up his mind to take a knife to himself. One ferocious swipe of a blade after another, willing to drive the knife in deeper still if he only could cut the Japanese half of himself out of his body. Did anyone else in the world detest themselves like this? Was there anyone who hated themselves so much that they would lay violent hands on their bodies like this young boy? See how viciously he had treated himself. His eyebrows were so ridiculous now, like strokes from a poorly wielded calligraphy brush. They were exactly like bodged pen strokes that had been rubbed out and rewritten, but rubbing out had only made things worse; a whole series of seemingly smart moves that just left him looking foolish. And he had had the nerve to take his young granny's face out of doors. If it had been Xiaohuan who saw such a face, she would have catcalled and beaten him too.

Duohe brought mercurochrome. With a great effort Xiaohuan kept herself under control and did not betray his shaving of his eyebrows and body hair. She said as she washed his wounds: 'Let them call you a Jap brat, your flesh won't drop off just because they call you a few names in the street! What'd we do if you got yourself beaten to death?'

'Better to be dead!' He drew his voice out in a long sigh.

'And then they'd be satisfied.'

Xiaohuan threw the facecloth into the blood-red washbasin and did a brief mental calculation: there was a total of three injuries on his head.

'You've got lung disease – is it easy for you to produce all that blood? How much meat-bone stew and fish-head soup are we going to have to feed you to get it back again? Look at the state of you – call this a head? I could chuck a bit of oil in the pot and fry it up as meatballs!'

'You should see their heads after I'd finished with them!'

'If you have to fight, wait until we've come back and take Blackie: when you've got Blackie you're not going to get beaten into such a state, and they'll be the ugly ones!'

Once Dahai's wounds were salved and bandaged, Duohe came out with two pieces of mouldy cake. She put them on a little saucer, and carried them over to Dahai's bedside.

'I'm not eating that!' Dahai said.

Duohe said something briefly in explanation. What she meant was that the cakes had been steamed, so the specks of mould did not matter.

'If you can't speak Chinese, don't talk to me!' Dahai said.

Without turning a hair, Xiaohuan whipped out the broom and rapped Dahai twice on the thigh. Afterwards she carried the cakes back to his hands again.

'Anything a Japanese has touched, I won't eat!'

Xiaohuan took Duohe by the hand, walked out of the room, and slammed the door shut. Then she shouted at Dahai inside: 'Well, Auntie, as of tomorrow, you're in charge of the cooking, eh? I won't even set foot in the kitchen. So the little swine isn't eating anything Japanese have touched now? If he had what it takes he wouldn't have suckled on a Japanese nipple before he was even weaned! If he'd been such a brave hero back then, an Anti-Japanese Resistance Baby, that'd have saved me the bother of putting rat poison in his food, wouldn't it?'

At one point she had even considered getting Dahai to come with them to visit his father, but judging from this, Xiaohuan could see that he would not acknowledge him. In these years disowning one's parents was all the rage. If you got lucky you could even use turning your back on your own flesh and blood to find a job, or join the Party and rise to become an official. Now Erhai had gone down to the countryside, Dahai had the right to stay behind. To use his gross lack of family feeling to get a job in the city; to join the Party and rise to become an official by his determined anti-Japanese resistance to his aunt at home. Xiaohuan looked at that tightly closed door, and a bleakness such as she had never experienced before welled up in her heart.

The following day she and Duohe got out of bed before daybreak, and walked to the long-distance bus station. The sky did not start to get light until they were on the bus. Duohe was turned towards the window, and in the sunlight the paddy fields had become fragments of a broken mirror. Xiaohuan knew that Duohe was still upset about Dahai.

'These trousers are a good material.' She fished out a trouser leg from inside the bundle. 'They'll last him three years, or maybe five, even if he does hard labour every day. Have a feel, this is Dacron khaki, there's more wear in it than sailcloth.'

Look at her, riffling through the bundle, full of satisfaction. Since she started to prepare things for Zhang Jian, each day she would rub her hands over all the clothes, trousers and shoes, and admire them, and get Duohe to join her in fondling and admiring them. She would be in excellent spirits: it was often only after she had said 'they'll last him three or five years' that it would occur to her that these might be years he did not have. But she thought again that she had to buy things to last, regardless of whether he actually had that long. Things changed quickly in times like these – a few months were a dynasty. Weren't there people once again sticking up posters attacking the head of the Revolutionary Committee, Director Peng? The posters called him a 'white brick', someone only good in his area of expertise, saying that they should choose a 'red brick', a revolutionary expert, to sit on the director's throne.

The next stop was the labour reform camp. Xiaohuan suddenly shouted out: 'Stop the bus! Stop! I want to get off!'

The driver instinctively hit the brakes, and a busload of pedlars carrying chicken eggs, duck eggs and musk melons all cried out together: 'My eggs . . .'

The conductor said with a forbidding scowl: 'What d'you think you're doing, howling like a ghost?'

'I've gone past my stop!' said Xiaohuan.

'Where do you want to go?'

Xiaohuan named the second stop after the long-distance bus station. The ticket she had bought was only good for two stops, and now they were at the twelfth stop. The conductor checked the tickets at the door at every stop, to save her the bother of clambering over the hens' eggs, duck eggs and melons.

'What's wrong with your ears? I called out the stop – are you deaf?' The conductor was barely twenty, but took the tone of a grandmother chastising her grandchild.

'Eeee, we don't understand that accent o' thine! You've been weaned for a while, how come you've not learned to talk like a decent human being?' Xiaohuan stood up. You could tell at a glance that she was the kind of middle-aged North-eastern woman who cared nothing for face when quarrelling, and nothing for her life when she got in a physical fight. Seventy per cent of people in the city were North-easterners, and the southerners took care never to cross swords with them directly. 'I told you to stop the bus!'

'You'll have to wait for the next stop,' the driver said.

Xiaohuan thought, of course we'll have to wait for the next stop, otherwise we'll have to walk a long way in the sun.

'Does this bus of yours do a return journey?' Xiaohuan asked.

'Of course it does,' replied the conductor.

'Then you have to give me and my sister here a lift back.'

'Sure – on February the thirtieth. Wait, if you think you can hang on that long,' the conductor said.

'Then you'd better give me back the money for both our tickets!'

'You come with me to the company offices to get the money back!'

As the two of them were arguing pointlessly back and forth, the bus pulled in at the stop. Xiaohuan got off, dragging Duohe along with her, pinching her hand hard. Once the bus had disappeared in a rolling cloud of dust, she said with a laugh: 'That saved us two yuan. We spent two jiao to come all this way!'

The labour reform camp did not have an official visitors' room. Xiaohuan and Duohe were taken to the prisoners' canteen, which was full of low wooden-plank benches, set out as if in readiness for an official report. Xiaohuan pulled Duohe to sit down on a bench in the first row. Soon, a snaggle-toothed pair of glasses came walking in, and said that his name was Zhao. Xiaohuan remembered that the girl had told her the quartermaster was called Zhao, and immediately drew a multipack of cigarettes from her bundle. Quartermaster Zhao asked how Xiao Tang was getting along outside, and Xiaohuan praised Xiao Tang as a lovely girl, pretty as flowers and jade, and invited Quartermaster Zhao to go and meet Xiao Tang when he had time, to eat Japanese food and drink Japanese tea, Xiaohuan's treat.

When Quartermaster Zhao first came in he was all defensiveness, but Xiaohuan's easy familiarity quickly put him at his ease, and he said to Xiaohuan that this was not a convenient place for talking, he could have the guards take her husband to his office. Xiaohuan immediately said: 'It's perfectly convenient, it's fine! An old married couple like us, we used up all our inconvenient words years ago!'

Quartermaster Zhao had never had such a jewel of a relative on a prison visit before. He forgot his position and smiled broadly, exposing his unruly riot of teeth.

Xiaohuan had been making her own internal calculations. Quartermaster Zhao was capable of helping out in a big way, so she had no intention of accepting the small favours he handed out. If she was going to owe him, then let the final bill be an astronomical sum.

After Quartermaster Zhao left, two guards carrying rifles escorted Zhang Jian in. He had just passed through open country in powerful sunlight, and when he came in he stood dumbstruck in the doorway. He clearly needed a moment to see who was there to receive him.

'Erhai, we've come to see you!' There was a prickling, constricting feeling in Xiaohuan's throat, and it cost her a lot of effort to force out this approximation of a cheery voice. Duohe, meanwhile, stood in front of the low benches, not daring to be sure that this white-haired thin black shadow was Zhang Jian.

'Duohe!' Xiaohuan called out, turning her head. 'See how sturdy he is!'

Duohe took a step forward, and suddenly bowed to him. From her expression, she still seemed to be stuck in the process of recognising him.

The guards made the two women sit on the front row of benches, and Zhang Jian sit on the back row. That's no good! We can't hear each other speak! Yes you can, when the high-ups read out documents, all the convicts sitting down below can hear! But this isn't reading out documents! Documents or no documents, that's where you have to sit! The clock starts from now, whether you can hear or not! Visiting time is set at one hour, after that they have to serve lunch in here, and after lunch they'll be reading documents!

Xiaohuan and Duohe were looking at Zhang Jian across rows and rows of benches. The windows were small and high up, and in the dim light that came through them Zhang Jian appeared dark and faintly smudged.

The guards present were separated from them by another dozen benches, so they talked about things they might just as well have left unsaid: 'Everyone's well back home', 'Erhai writes often', 'Girlie writes often too', 'Everything's fine!'

Zhang Jian only listened, sometimes he said 'Oh', and sometimes he would give a snort of laughter. Although his silence had not changed, Xiaohuan thought that the nature of his silence was different from before. It was an old man's silence, nattering and scolding away in his heart.

'People in the factory are putting up posters about Xiao Peng. They want to kick him out of office, they're calling him a white brick.'

'Oh.'

'That'd be good, if he got thrown out.'

Zhang Jian was silent. But in his old man's silence, Xiaohuan could hear him nagging away: What's so bloody good about that? Does any decent person become an official these days? You old women, kicking up a fuss over stuff you know nothing about, what's so good about that?

Xiaohuan thought, to think that he was three years younger than her: he had already begun to nag and scold in his heart. Only a person who did not believe in anything, and who had lost his taste for everything, could have a heart full of nagging like this.

'Did you hear what I said? As soon as that Xiao Peng is out of office it'll all turn out right, for certain,' Xiaohuan said.

Let those two guards exchange suspicious glances, she was not afraid, she had to make him recover his lost appetite for life.

He sniggered. He had understood, it was just that he did not think things would get better.

Xiaohuan thought that in Duohe's memory Zhang Jian had remained not even the way he was before he was arrested, but from earlier still, the way he was when they used to creep into the little wood, and climb the wall into the primary school. The way he had been backstage at the club. As for the present Zhang Jian, she feared that she, Xiaohuan, was the only one who did not reject him.

Xiaohuan stood up slowly, the joints in her body creaking.

'Erhai, don't hoard your clothes and food, who's to say that we won't get another chance to visit you, and bring you some more, eh?'

She asked one of the guards where the toilet was, and then walked into the heartless July sunshine. She would give Duohe and Zhang Jian some time alone. She resented her bitter fate; bitter because she was tied up together with two people whose fate was more bitter still. No one wanted either of them, no one cared for them, and so all of this fell on Xiaohuan's shoulders, didn't it? What were the odds of meeting such a pair of ill-fated lovers in a whole lifetime?

On the road back, the two women both stared at their own scenery. After the bus had gone five or six stops, Xiaohuan asked Duohe whether Zhang Jian had said anything. Nothing at all.

In Duohe's serenity, Xiaohuan could see her own wisdom. She had been right to leave the two of them alone together. A part of his life belonged to Duohe, which could only come out when Xiaohuan was not there.

By the time they got home it was the middle of the night. They had had nothing to eat all day but a few dry *mantou*. Duohe hurried into the kitchen and put two bowls of hanging noodles on to boil. Duohe was deeply tranquil, much more serene than before they went. She and Zhang Jian must have talked about something. What important words had these two people who no one wanted and no one cared about said to each other, to make Duohe so serene?

❖

Xiaohuan had left Duohe and Zhang Jian behind her in the room, and had gone out alone into the cruel midday July sun. All the cicadas were bawling out at the tops of their voices. Several rows of benches and a guard lay between Zhang Jian and Duohe. She said a sentence which an outsider would struggle to follow. She had to talk over the shouting of the cicadas, so her words were shouted too. She told him to think of her every evening at nine o'clock, and she would be thinking of him at the same time. She and he would be thinking of each other, concentrating all their heart and will, and in this way they could see each other every day.

His half-closed camel's eyes widened for a moment, and settled for a while on her face. She knew that he had understood. He also understood that she regretted falling out over two years before: if she had known then that the next half of their lives would be spent with one of them inside the prison wall and the other outside it, she would have treated him well, spent every day with him, every hour. Now she repudiated all her accusations against him.

'Erhe . . .' She was gazing at the floor.

He was looking down too. They did this: looking at the floor, or the sky, or some place in their minds, and yet it was each other that they saw. It had been like this right at the very beginning too. A fleeting glance, then turn the eye away immediately; then magnify the thing they had seen in their minds' eye, and examine it closely, over and over again.

Her first glimpse of him was from a white cloth sack. The white cloth had become a layer of fine, closely woven white fog. They had put her on the stage, and he came walking towards her through the white fog. She was curled up in the sack, and only looked at him once. After that she closed her eyes, storing that image of him, so she could look over and over again. He was tall, true enough, but when he moved his movements were not as loose and sloppy as most big-bodied men, and his head and face were perfectly proportioned. He picked up the sack in his arms, so that her chest was pressed against his chest. He carried her, forcing a way through the black crowds of filthy feet, and she was suddenly no longer afraid of these feet, or of the quacking laughter emitted by their owners. Then she was carried into a courtyard. Through the clouds of white fog, she saw it was a fine courtyard. The house was good too. A very good family. They passed through a door, and it was like they had gone from a snowy day straight into summer. The air was crackling with warmth, and very soon she fell asleep. When she woke a pair of hands was untying the knot of the sack, which was at the crown of her head. The sack fell down all around her, and she saw him. This, too, was just another fleeting glimpse. It was only after that that she took time to look slowly at what she had seen so fleetingly: he wasn't bad-looking. No, he was very good-looking. A very masculine type. And not just that, his eyes were half closed, because his goodness and tenderness were making him embarrassed and uncomfortable. Then . . . he picked her up in his arms again, and laid her down on the kang . . .

She often recalled this beginning. Sometimes she suspected that her memory was not accurate. But then again, when they had got to know each other in such a way, how was it possible for her not to remember accurately? It was only twenty years, no more. Even if it was fifty years, or sixty, she would still not be able to forget this beginning.

At this moment one of them was a prison visitor, the other a prisoner being visited. He nodded to her invitation to meet. Let the guards hear her invitation: *Every evening, nine o'clock, think of Duohe. Duohe will also think of you. So you and Duohe, meet.*

From then on, every evening at nine o'clock, Duohe always thought of Zhang Jian with all her mind and heart. She could feel him keep the appointment, right on time, right in front of her, his eyes exhausted like a camel's, indifferent to human slaves. Even if she was in another world, he would still arrive at the meeting on time.

One day, Duohe felt amazed: the notion of suicide that she had never been able to dismiss from her mind was suddenly not there any more. There was Xiaohuan, every day shouting 'Make do', smiling 'Make do', complaining 'Make do', and the days muddled on by. And she was muddling along with her. According to Duohe's standards, if things could not be done perfectly and elegantly, then she would prefer not to do them at all, yet Xiaohuan mended a stitch here, did a little repair there, one eye open and one eye closed, and anything could be dragged along, sloppily and grubbily. This was not living well, but she could still make do and not live too badly. In the blink of an eye she had muddled her way through a month, and in another blink a summer had passed. Then she had muddled her way into autumn. It turned out that 'making do' was not unpleasant at all. Once you were used to it, it was actually extremely comfortable. Duohe in the early autumn of 1976 found to her great surprise that in all this making do the last faint spark of suicide had been extinguished without her even realising it.

She learned to find excuses to carry on living, just as risible as Xiaohuan's. Duohe's excuse was that she could not miss her assignation; she had an appointment every day with Zhang Jian at nine o'clock, and she could not stand him up.

In October, propaganda trucks were driving all over town, gongs and drums were beating to shake the heavens, and the loudspeakers were bawling all over the place, celebrating that a new director of the Revolutionary Committee had assumed office. It turned out that Director Peng had been kicked out, and had become a new enemy. Xiaohuan laughed and chatted away at her sewing stall. 'They've got themselves another new enemy, and they beat gongs and drums to celebrate?'

The new enemy's old accounts were going to be settled again. The new enemy's old enemies were going to be reviewed one by one. Before long the police, public prosecutor and law courts re-examined Zhang Jian's case, and changed his suspended death sentence to twenty years' imprisonment.

Xiaohuan said to Duohe: 'We'd better make the most of it and get Zhang Jian out before this new director has changed into a new enemy. Who knows if some person mightn't drag down this new director, and bring the score back to where it was.'

She and Quartermaster Zhao were already calling each other 'Sister-in-Law' and 'Little Brother'. Quartermaster Zhao was still taking Xiaohuan's gifts, but slowly he started to give gifts to her. Like all of Xiaohuan's dubious friends, he felt that Xiaohuan had some sort of magical power that could not be put into words, and was delighted for her to make use of him. It was his good fortune that she could get something worthwhile out of him. Every time Xiaohuan's family came to visit, sesame oil, sausages, dried mushrooms and bean noodles would appear on the tables of the officers' dining room. He had long since forgotten that his original intention in getting close to Xiaohuan had been to get close to the girl Xiao Tang. When he saw the people surrounding Xiaohuan's sewing table, fawning on her, competing eagerly, scheming and jockeying for position, resentment arose in his heart. 'Who do they think they are? Are they fit to contribute their efforts to Sister Xiaohuan? They bring along a packet of turnips in sauce and think they can spend the whole afternoon with her!'

There were more pickings to be found under Quartermaster Zhao's fingernails than if those people emptied out their entire purses. He got Dahai a job teaching PE in a small, locally run school. Dahai moved into the school, and that was the end of his anti-Japanese resistance in the home.

Throughout all this Xiaohuan never mentioned the possibility of Quartermaster Zhao using his connections to have Zhang Jian's case reviewed. She still had to wait for the right moment. Her grasp of the way to lay her psychological groundwork was always superb. She did not plan to open her mouth until after Spring Festival, by which time the Mao suit she was making for him out of pure wool gaberdine would be finished.

A few days before Chinese New Year, Erhai came home. To Duohe's and Xiaohuan's surprise, he had grown big and burly. He came in through the door, drank a cup of tea and ran outside again. Xiaohuan asked him where he was going, and he did not speak a word, he was already on the stairs. Leaning on the rail of the communal walkway, Duohe and Xiaohuan saw a bedroll containing all his personal effects lying at the foot of the building. When Erhai came up with the bedroll, Xiaohuan asked him why he had moved all his possessions back, wasn't he just here for the new year? He pursed his lips without replying, smiling at Blackie who was following behind him.

He carried the quilt and cotton padded mattress to the balcony. Blackie put his paws on his chest, the dog's mouth splitting open from ear to ear with happiness. Erhai shook the quilt and beat it crisply. Blackie's paws landed on his back.

'Why're you making such a fuss of me, silly? I'm home and I'm not going away again!'

It was only now, thanks to Blackie, that Xiaohuan and Duohe found out about his long-term plans. If he was not going back, his only choice was to be an idler, like the ones who clustered round Xiaohuan's sewing machine all day long. These young people who resisted pressure from their schools, Neighbourhood Committees and families started out being regarded by others as loafers, and in due course became loafers because no other choices were available to them. Xiaohuan looked at Erhai's hands, covered in chilblains, his fingers swollen red and translucent like carnelian, and thought to herself: If he has to be a loafer then so be it.

On the night of Spring Festival Dahai came back too. At the dinner table, he tipped the rice that Duohe had dished out for him back into the pot, took a new bowl, filled it with rice and sat down again. Everybody pretended not to see. Erhai spoke to Duohe, saying that he had met an old man who had a genius for playing the erhu, and that he had spent his year north of the Huai River under his instruction.

Xiaohuan knew that Erhai was drawing up battle lines between himself and Dahai: If you're going to ignore Auntie, then I'm going to be friendly to her, so there! She thought: We're finished, that's the end of peace in our family. Before the Spring Festival dinner the two brothers had actually exchanged a few words, now they were back in bitter conflict. A problem emerged when it was time to sleep. Dahai made the corridor his bedroom, and announced that no one was permitted to cross his room on the way to the toilet.

Everybody ignored him.

Xiaohuan said with a smile: 'It's even more fuss than the puppet government in the North-east, old Manchuria as was. They had the Japanese Army, the puppet government's army and the Anti-Japanese United Army!'

The following morning, Xiaohuan got up last, to find that the two boys had gone out. They came home at midday, separately, Dahai sporting a black eye. He had been no match for Erhai when they had fought in the past, and now Erhai had grown tall and filled out. If ever they were to fight in earnest, Dahai would be lucky to walk away with his life.

Dahai hung a cloth curtain across one side of the double bed in the little room: one side was his territory, the other was Erhai's. He announced that he was not going back to teach PE at that school: since Erhai had come back home to eat for free, he could do so too. His PE teacher's salary of eighteen yuan was not worth having to listen to the students call him a 'Jap brat' every day.

Xiaohuan was forced to work day and night making clothes in order to keep this large household going. Fortunately, people were starting to get tired of wearing khaki army uniforms, and were beginning to wear blue-, grey- and cream-coloured clothes again. Young women also started to bring purple and sky-blue cloth to Xiaohuan's stall for spring outfits. It was a pity that the department store only had these few types of cloth. If one girl, a bit braver than the rest, took the lead and put on a purplish-red collarless shirt with white spots, over a dozen other girls would immediately buy the same kind of cloth, and get Xiaohuan to make them identical collarless shirts. Hundreds, even thousands, of girls passed along the road in front of Xiaohuan's stall every day, she kept count, and altogether there were only a dozen or so patterns for them to wear.

The loafers were loafers no more. Their parents had retired, relinquishing their jobs for them to take over. They shaved off their big sideburns, little moustaches and quiffs, changed out of their zip-up shirts, skinny trousers and baggy trousers, put on white canvas jackets, and off they all went, carrying their parents' aluminium lunch boxes. It turned out that they were not natural-born ne'er-do-wells at all. They still remembered their Auntie Xiaohuan, though, and they would often stop for a cup of Japanese tea as they passed her stall after work, and bring her the latest fashions. The trend among Shanghai and Nanjing people was to embroider a certain kind of pattern wherever there was a hem or seam. Sometimes they would bring national or international news, and discuss it for a while.

'The Japanese prime minister, Tanaka Kakuei, memorises a page of a dictionary every day!'

'What does resuming diplomatic relations between China and Japan mean? Doesn't that mean we're talking again?'

'Auntie, China and Japan have actually resumed diplomatic relations, so when are you going back to Japan for a visit?'

Duohe gave all of them a big smile.

One day in September, Dahai ran to the sewing stall to demand money from Xiaohuan. A nineteen-year-old has many calls on his purse: eating, drinking, smoking and amusements. That day he was after money to change the tyres on his bicycle. Zhang Jian's bicycle had been given to Erhai, so Dahai had bought a racing bike, and often went for long rides on it. Xiaohuan fished out several two- and five-jiao notes from her purse. Duohe produced a one-yuan note which she had originally intended to spend on thread. Dahai took it from her.

'Put that down,' Xiaohuan said. 'Whatever happened to not wanting anything a Japanese has touched?'

Dahai hurled the note straight to the ground.

'You pick that up for me,' Xiaohuan said.

He stood firm.

'Pick that up for your auntie!'

'In your dreams,' said Dahai.

'I'll have your hide for this when we get home,' said Xiaohuan, coming out from behind the sewing machine holding the pile of small notes that she had gathered together. 'Go on, take them.'

Dahai walked up to Xiaohuan, and realised too late that he had been had. Xiaohuan grabbed the front of his clothes with one hand, while at the same time dropping the notes and reaching out behind her with the other for the wooden ruler on the sewing machine.

'Are you going to pick it up or not?'

Dahai's eyes were blinking.

Several dozen people had already gathered round, and four or five female cadres from the Neighbourhood Committee were leaning on the railings upstairs to watch.

At this moment a voice said in an unfamiliar accent: 'Let me through! Let me through!'

The people reluctantly gave ground to admit a man of about thirty, with an official look about him. He looked up and said to the female cadres: 'I'm from the Provincial Office of Civil Affairs, where is the Neighbourhood Committee?'

The female cadres promptly shouted down: 'Zhu Xiaohuan, go home to beat your son! It makes an awful impression if you let the provincial leaders see!'

Xiaohuan hauled Dahai in the direction of that one-yuan note.

'Pick it up!'

The cadre from the Provincial Office of Civil Affairs hastily crossed the stage where the performance was in full swing, and went up the stairs.

Dahai needed the money Xiaohuan had dropped on the stall and that one yuan on the ground, so he bent down under Xiaohuan's quivering ruler. His face was scarlet with the pain of lost dignity. When his hand touched the money, someone laughed quietly. He withdrew his hand, but the wooden ruler pressed down on the back of his head, he could neither go up nor down, and the people laughed loudly.

Dahai carefully counted up the money. 'I'm still two yuan short!'

'Sorry I'm sure – your mum and your auntie have been slaving away for a whole morning, and this little bit is all we've earned.' Xiaohuan's sewing machine was running briskly.

'Then how am I supposed to get my tyres changed?' he asked.

Upstairs, one of the female cadres stuck her head out, and called: 'Zhunei Duohe! You come up here a minute!'

Xiaohuan looked up. 'What's the matter? Haven't we swept the office clean for you?'

'A comrade from the Provincial Office of Civil Affairs wishes to speak with her,' the female cadre said.

Xiaohuan found her polite tone deeply suspicious.

'She can't go. If the leading cadre from the Provincial Office of Civil Affairs has something to say, he can come down and say it; Zhunei Duohe is also Zhu Duohe. She's got a big sister called Zhu Xiaohuan, and if anyone's going to sell Zhu Duohe, her sister wants a cut as well!'

After a while all five women were leaning on the balcony trying to persuade Duohe to come up: it was good news.

Xiaohuan did not bother to reply, but focused all her concentration on working her sewing machine. She made a sign to Duohe to sew on her buttons in peace, she would deal with everything.

The cadre from the Provincial Office of Civil Affairs came downstairs, accompanied by the five female cadres. Xiaohuan and Duohe looked at them.

The women urged all the people away in loud voices, like they were shooing away chickens. Dahai was about to leave too, but one of them told him to stay behind.

The cadre from the Provincial Office of Civil Affairs brought out a letter. It was in Japanese. He put the letter into Duohe's hands, saying to Xiaohuan: 'We have already looked into Zhunei Duohe's circumstances in some detail. The letter was passed on to our province all the way from Heilongjiang.'

Xiaohuan saw Duohe's coal-black eyes chewing on the characters of the letter, devouring them.

The cadre from the Provincial Office of Civil Affairs said to Xiaohuan: 'One of the members of Prime Minister Tanaka's retinue was a nurse called something Kumi. As soon as this Kumi arrived in China she made enquiries about Zhunei Duohe. Of course her enquiries came to nothing. Before she went back to Japan, she wrote two letters. One was to the Chinese government, telling how Zhunei Duohe had saved her life all those years ago. The other letter is this one.'

Xiaohuan was thoroughly familiar with the three-year-old girl called Kumi, who had been one of the main characters in that tragic, cruel story that Duohe told. Now she had come back to see Duohe, and the story that had been broken off for many years was taken up again. Duohe's tears fell rapidly onto the characters written in Kumi's hand.

The cadre from the Provincial Office of Civil Affairs said: 'You really weren't easy to track down. Still, it's good that we found you.'

The female cadres from the Neighbourhood Committee stood on one side then; they all felt that by bringing this letter the Provincial Office of Civil Affairs had put them in an awkward position. Zhunei

Duohe had been an enemy, but now her political status had become ambiguous. Who would sluice out the toilets every day?

Dahai thought that he was now faced with a big problem as well: over these years he had become accustomed to things being either black or white. Now here was this cadre from the Provincial Office of Civil Affairs, whose attitude was neither black nor white; what kind of attitude would he have to adopt with Auntie Duohe from now on?

Xiaohuan packed up early, so she could accompany Duohe home. This was a great day for Duohe, she had to be with her in her astonishment and sighs. Yet Duohe had forgotten that Xiaohuan was there, walking by her side, as her two hands pinched and twisted at that letter written in her own language. She would walk a few steps, then stop again for another look at the letter. The pedestrians on the road saw this woman in her forties weeping as she walked without a morsel of shame as just one more interesting street scene for them to watch.

Even once she was inside, Duohe failed to notice that Xiaohuan had come in with her, and she sat down by herself on the balcony, reading the letter over and over again.

Xiaohuan made a dish of fried dried tofu, red-cooked aubergine, beansprouts braised with shrimp skin and wood-ear mushrooms stir-fried with dried lily flowers. This was a great day for Duohe.

The boys sat at the table in prickly silence, not knowing how to take this aunt who seemed to have acquired a new status. Xiaohuan took food in her chopsticks and passed it to Duohe's plate, and saw that her eyes were swimming as she chewed her food, and her mind was obviously elsewhere. Xiaohuan glared at the two boys who were looking right at her, speculation in their eyes.

Duohe ate practically nothing, and went back to the balcony in a daze. Blackie was concerned about her, and sat down by her side. Nobody understood the words she spoke to Blackie, but Blackie did. Blackie's understanding went beyond language, beyond Chinese and Japanese.

As Xiaohuan was washing dishes in the kitchen, Erhai came in. For some reason, he briefly put an arm round Xiaohuan's shoulders. Dahai came in after him. It seemed that this momentous thing that had happened to Duohe had brought about something of a thaw in the brothers' relations. The two of them had become a bit steadier.

'You do know, don't you,' Xiaohuan said suddenly, 'that Auntie is your birth mother?' She fished the bowls out of the hot water one at a time, and scrubbed them carefully according to Duohe's method. Duohe was very particular about cleaning bowls.

Neither of the boys had a word to say to this. Of course they knew. They had known for years. They had had to put up with all kinds of ill-treatment because of it.

'It looks like Auntie is going back to Japan.'

Actually this had only just occurred to her. Of course Duohe was going back. Was it possible that Prime Minister Tanaka's nurse would not come to fetch her?

15

September nights are cool and dark; the air is perfect for clearing the head. Duohe was sitting on the balcony, holding Kumi's letter. Kumi had no family either, she wanted Duohe to be her family. Duohe had given her another life, so she had always been like one of her relatives. That was what Kumi had written in her letter. Kumi, Kumi, was her face round or oval? She had been so ill when they met that she had lost her normal appearance. Oh, it was so careless of her, Kumi should have sent a photograph, so that Duohe would have something besides a blur in her brain when she thought of her.

Kumi told her that when the scattered remnants of the great flight reached Dalian, their numbers had been reduced from over three thousand to a few hundred. The adults waited in a concentration camp, where their numbers were soon further reduced by a bout of typhoid. Kumi and more than four hundred children from other settler villages took the boat to South Korea, from where they were transferred to Japan. Many children on that ship had died of illness, but she was one of the survivors. In the orphanage, aged six years old, she resolved to study medicine. At fifteen she entered the nurses' school, and at eighteen she became a nurse. When she heard that Tanaka was going to visit China, she wrote down her experiences and sent them to the prime minister, and as a result was selected to be one of the nurses in his retinue.

The first day she came to China, Kumi asked Prime Minister Tanaka to hand the letters she had written over to the Chinese government. Kumi's letter to Duohe, which was five pages long, said that she hoped that Duohe was still alive. Duohe was such a lucky name. There were tens of thousands of paper cranes wishing that she would come back soon to her homeland.

When Kumi's second letter arrived, the cadre from the Provincial Office of Civil Affairs visited again. There were all kinds of forms for Duohe to fill out. The hardest answers were where she had been on such-and-such a year, month and day, what she had been doing, and who could testify to it. Duohe and the boys clustered together under the ten-watt bulb, filling in a column at a time. The boys were only twenty, yet their fingers shook slightly: if they miswrote one character, the form would be spoiled.

From filling in the forms to filling in further forms to receiving the passport took just three months. The Provincial Office of Civil Affairs had never dealt with a case of this kind: Prime Minister Tanaka Kakuei's nurse had come up with the funds herself, and wrote continually, urging them on.

The five female cadres from the Neighbourhood Committee came together to the Zhang home. They said that the Provincial Office of Civil Affairs had telephoned the office of the Neighbourhood Committee, asking them to accompany Duohe as far as Beijing. Duohe would be met in Beijing, and then put on the plane for Tokyo. Xiaohuan said that there was no need for them to do that, though they appreciated the thought. The female cadres had never taken any responsibility for Duohe, let her spend her last few days without anyone taking responsibility for her, right up until the very end.

The two boys and their mother did not know what attitude to take with Duohe. They discovered that all attitudes were very awkward. Xiaohuan would sit down beside her for a while, then stand, but she found that she was somewhat surplus to requirements; Duohe was already using Japanese to turn her ideas over in her mind. So she walked away sheepishly, to let Duohe be by herself. But before long Xiaohuan would feel that this was not fitting either; here she was, a family member who was going to travel so far away, and they had no idea how long she would be gone, so how could she not keep her company in these last days? Even if she kept her company without saying anything, that was just as good. Xiaohuan sat next to Duohe again. If her mind was far away, following those Japanese characters, then let it go, she wanted to be with her anyway. Very quickly Xiaohuan realised she needed Duohe to keep *her* company.

In any case, after all these decades, whether being together as good companions, or quarrelling and fighting together, she was used to her company, with goodwill or without it.

Xiaohuan rushed up two outfits. One was a suit of dark blue, suitable for spring and autumn wear, the other was a grey Mao suit. The polyester they had nowadays did not require starching or ironing, the pen-straight creases in the trousers would be with you for a lifetime.

All this time, they had been waiting for news from Quartermaster Zhao. He had gone to arrange a prison visit, and the original plan was that he would definitely write in the next day or two, but it was not until the very day that Duohe was due to leave that Quartermaster

Zhao finally telephoned the Neighbourhood Committee. Two convicts had escaped recently, and arranging this prison visit was beyond even him, with all his power and guile.

Duohe told Xiaohuan and the boys that she was going to Japan to see what it was like; perhaps she would be back very soon.

Duohe did not return to this now unspeakably shabby dependants' building until five and a half years later. She had heard that Zhang Jian had been seriously ill in the labour camp, and after his release he had lost the ability to live independently.

The train from Nanjing drew to a halt. Xiaohuan recognised Duohe at once amid a crowd of grey, dark passengers. Duohe had squeezed to the door of the train ahead of time, and she was the first to jump down, seconds after it had come to a stop.

She was wearing a cream-coloured Western-style suit with a skirt over a white gauze blouse that tied in a bow at the neck; her face was narrower than when she left, but her skin was gleaming like pearls and smooth as jade, and her eyes and lips had been touched with colour. The highish heels on her shoes were making her walk rather awkwardly; Xiaohuan did not recall that Duohe had such big feet. Her hair, cut neatly just below her ears, had not changed, but she certainly no longer washed it in caustic soda, for it appeared soft, supple and startlingly bright. This was the face Takeuchi Tatsuru should have had all along. Decades of oversized, baggy canvas work overalls, patched shirts and trousers, drab checks, stripes and dots, their dingy colours bleached away by water and sun – all of this had been a long and unfair diversion, full of twists and turns, unnecessary but unavoidable. The present Duohe was superimposed on the

Duohe of several decades earlier, showing Xiaohuan how senseless and how easily erased those decades had been.

Duohe came up and embraced Xiaohuan. When all was said and done, those years together fighting and quarrelling was still time shared. How Xiaohuan had missed this time together. Duohe had a great quantity of luggage, and the seven-minute halt before the train left the station was barely enough to get all her cases down. As they walked out of the station dragging big cases and small bags, Duohe chattered away without stopping. Her voice was pitched a key higher than before, and she spoke Chinese both quickly and sloppily.

As soon as Zhang Jian heard the neighbours calling out loudly 'Back, are you, Auntie?' he got up from the bed. He had already changed into a new shirt, made for him by Xiaohuan, white poplin printed with a design of thin, pale grey lines. If you looked closely you could see that they were little aeroplanes. When Xiaohuan dressed him in it he had resisted, saying that this cloth must be for little boys. But Xiaohuan said: Who'd go sticking their nose right up close. Put a waistcoat on top, so there's only a collar and two sleeves, who cares about a few little aeroplanes? He let Xiaohuan arrange him the way she wanted, because he had no strength to arrange himself, and no confidence to do it. He had spent so many years shut up in the labour camp, everyone outside was more fashionable than him. When Duohe came to the door, he suddenly wanted to find a mirror. Still, the only mirror in the family was Xiaohuan's little mirror, which she carried with her in her bag. As the sounds of neighbours' greetings came closer, he grasped the walking stick leaning next to the bed, and with an effort made the next few steps a little bit more hearty.

A woman entered in a waft of perfume. Her teeth were so white. Did Duohe's used to be this white? Let them not be false – the person, or the teeth. An overseas visitor. A Japanese woman. Zhang Jian thought that his face must look exceedingly peculiar, caught between all kinds of different expressions, like his feelings. Ranging across happiness, anger, grief and amusement, all his flesh was stuck in an in-between state, neither stretching forward nor shrinking back.

Duohe could not disguise her shock. Was this thin, sun-blackened old man the person she had single-mindedly remembered every night at nine o'clock (ten o'clock in Japan), the man she had believed she could see by thinking about him?

Xiaohuan told Duohe to sit down, don't just stand there! Sit down and change your shoes! She added that Dahai would be back soon, he had asked for leave today, he had not gone to work in the factory.

Zhang Jian thought that he must say a few words to Duohe, pleasantries about the hard journey she'd had, something of that kind. She bowed so very deeply. This bow alone had already made a stranger of her. She must have enquired about his health and the state of his illness, because he heard Xiaohuan reply that they had checked everything that should be checked, and the tests had found nothing, it was just that he couldn't get his food down, see how thin he was!

Duohe suddenly stretched out her hand to grasp Zhang Jian's, which seemed unnaturally large because he was so thin. She rested her face against that hand, and with a wail burst into tears. Zhang Jian had thought that he would need another thirty years and more to lose this strangeness, but now he found that the layer of strangeness that separated him from her had already become familiar and intimate.

Xiaohuan had gone out into the kitchen, and she returned, carrying a teacup in each hand. She saw them, and tears flowed from her eyes. After a while, the lids of the two teacups began to clatter against the cups with her trembling. She retreated from the room, carrying the rattling, shivering teacups, hooked her foot round the door and closed it on them.

When Dahai came back, the family had washed away their tears and started to look over the gifts that Duohe was setting out. Duohe had changed into a short kimono, and the slippers on her feet had come from Japan. Everyone had a share in the gifts she had brought for all aspects of daily life, including Girlie, far off in the North-east, and Girlie's husband and children. The thing that caused the greatest sensation was a transistor television, even smaller than a magazine.

She also produced a tape recorder, saying that Erhai enjoyed playing the erhu, and he could listen to tunes of the erhu on this tape recorder. It was only then that everyone told Duohe that after two years spent hanging around at home, it suddenly occurred to Erhai to write to the wife of that army commander who had been in charge of the military occupation of the city – who had once promised to help him. She had not forgotten him, and sure enough, she had arranged for Erhai to enlist in the army, and got him into the song-and-dance troupe at the headquarters as an erhu player.

Duohe looked at the photograph of Erhai in military uniform, and said that of all the three children, Erhai was the one who looked the most like her, especially when he laughed loudly. It was a pity that Erhai laughed too seldom.

And so the clothes Duohe had bought for Erhai became the property of Dahai, and Dahai had two identical sets of clothes for spring, summer, autumn and winter. Duohe had remembered their measurements in her heart, and they were not out by an inch. Dahai tried on each item in turn, and kept walking in front of Duohe for her to give a tweak here, a tug there.

Xiaohuan suddenly let out a snort of laughter. They did not

know what she was laughing at, and raised their heads together to look at her.

'You little sod! What happened to not wanting anything a Japanese has touched?'

Dahai promptly gave a shameless laugh. Right now the whole thing was just a joke. Between family members, fighting was just one step on the path to agreement, beating was tenderness, cursing was love, once the thing was past everything became a joke, and making up saved so much effort. Were not those children who had stuck up posters everywhere exposing their fathers for hiding gold bricks in the home or concealing transmitters, all their fathers' sons again now? That half of Duohe's blood flowing in Dahai's body had determined that he would make up with Duohe one way or another.

At suppertime Duohe spoke of Kumi's goodness. She depended on Kumi for everything. On her return to Japan, Duohe had suffered from crippling culture shock, and could not understand the Japanese the city people spoke. There were many things she did not understand: machines for washing clothes into which you put coins, machines for cleaning and sweeping the floor, machines selling train tickets, machines selling food and soft drinks . . . Kumi had to teach her about them one at a time, sometimes she had to instruct her many times over. Often she would teach her to use them in one place, then she would go somewhere else where the machines were different, and all she had learned was useless. Without Kumi she would have gone nowhere, not even daring to enter the shops. And there was another reason for not entering shops, which was that there was nothing she needed to buy: her clothes, shoes and everything she used were hand-me-downs from Kumi. Picking up clothes for free was just lovely. Luckily Kumi was only half a head taller than her, and she could make do and wear all her clothes – if she had been a full head taller, how much trouble would it have been to cut the clothes down to size? Even more fortunately, Kumi's feet were two sizes bigger than hers, so if she stuffed cotton wool in the toes of her shoes she could wear them and make do very well. If Kumi's feet had been smaller than hers, she would have been properly in for it.

Everyone noticed that Duohe's mouth was full of Xiaohuan's language, a 'make do' here, a 'just lovely' and a 'properly in for it' there.

Duohe still scrubbed pots and washed dishes, just as she had in the past. While she was scrubbing she said to Xiaohuan that the concrete sink was not very hygienic; once the dirt had become ingrained it was easy to make it look clean without being really clean at all, and she should cover it in white tiles, that was the thing. And since they were putting up tiles they might as well do the whole kitchen. Chinese people used too much oil when they fried food, and when porcelain tiles got oil on them they were easy to wipe. Once she had cleaned up every corner and crack of the kitchen, she returned to the big room and looked it up and down. Throughout all this, Xiaohuan felt guilty and ill at ease: an inspector had come from a Japanese 'Patriotic Hygiene Committee', what comments would she come out with next? But Duohe did not say anything, just wrinkled her forehead and gave up. Duohe took out a roll of ten-yuan notes from her leather handbag and handed it to Xiaohuan, telling her to go tomorrow and buy tiles to cover the sink.

Xiaohuan dodged out of the way, saying: 'Ai, how can I take your money?'

At this Duohe pressed the money on Dahai, and told him to go and buy them.

'You dare take your auntie's money!' Xiaohuan turned on him fiercely. She thought about how Duohe was wearing shoes with big wads of cotton wool stuffed in the toes, it must be unbearable on her feet. Xiaohuan could make do in all things but not in this one. Nothing made a mark on its home more than a person's feet, and once they had lain for a while in a pair of shoes, the shoes became their nests, shaping themselves to them, with all their bumps and hollows, highs and lows, duck feet or pigeon toes, like sand poured into a mould. If another pair of feet came in, well, sorry, the shape of that original pair of feet might be ugly or beautiful, but it made no difference, they would bulge up against you and rub everywhere, they had to break your feet into them. Part of Duohe's money had come from savings made by inflicting suffering on her own feet. Xiaohuan was just not prepared to put her feet through that in order to make the walls of the kitchen feel good.

Dahai smiled shamelessly again, and took the money from Duohe's hands. In order to save face, Xiaohuan left it at that.

Zhang Jian was lying on the bed, weak and feeble, yet he felt that in spite of everything there was a strangeness there, which could inflate, increasing the tension in this thirty-odd-square-metre flat. The tension would grow until he wanted to duck out the way, but there was no place to hide.

Duohe was not wrong in anything, she contributed the money and strength for everything she did, and they were all constructive things, but the household still became ever more tense. Even Duohe herself realised it, and she kept explaining that she was not rejecting them, she only wanted to bring in a few small improvements, so that they could live a little bit more comfortably and hygienically.

Xiaohuan and Duohe accompanied Zhang Jian for a thorough physical examination: all the major and minor organs were essentially healthy. At this point Duohe spoke up, saying that before she came back, she had made plans to take Zhang Jian to Japan for testing and treatment. Now she had seen how he was, she believed that this plan was the only way forward. How could he possibly not have anything major the matter? Weak and feeble as he was, and skinny as a bag of bones: could he be healthy?

How many people went to Japan for treatment? He was very lucky to be able to go! If he was cured, he could make up in latter years for the time that had been wrongfully lost. Otherwise he'd be wronging her, not to mention wronging himself. This was how Xiaohuan persuaded Zhang Jian.

They had to get going straight away if they wanted to get everything done. Zhang Jian and Duohe needed to get married, and they had to apply to both countries at the same time: to leave the one country, and to enter the other.

Dahai took time off work, and carried his father on the back of his bicycle, with Duohe walking by their side. As soon as they left the gate of one government office they turned straight into the door of another one.

The neighbours had seen Dahai coming and going in a great hurry in his new clothes, and they all admired his Japanese jacket, asking him to lend it to them so they could have a copy made to the same pattern.

'Did your auntie bring it back for you?' A neighbour tweaked the fabric. 'It's different, right enough!'

'It was brought back by my mother.'

'Ooh, you're not calling her "auntie" now?' The neighbour smiled knowingly.

Dahai, however, was completely in earnest. 'She was my mama in the first place!'

The neighbours heard him dragging out the space between the two characters of *ma . . . ma* in a minor key, like an actor in a play.

'Then will you be going back to Japan with your *ma . . . ma*?'

'I most certainly will!'

'When you come back in the future, you'll be a Japanese!'

'I was Japanese in the first place.' Dahai walked off. He was desperately busy, and these neighbours had no tact at all, asking questions whenever they saw him.

By the time Zhang Jian and Duohe had dealt with all the formalities, and were on the point of leaving, Dahai's Japanese life story had already circulated widely among his contemporaries. The story went like this: when his father was in the North-east, he had worked as a hired hand for a very wealthy Japanese family, and in that family there was a beautiful little Japanese princess called Zhunei Duohe. His father had secretly loved this young Japanese girl, watching her grow up day by day, and finally become promised to the son of a Japanese high official. His father had been so hurt by this that he had come close to taking his own life. He resigned his job, returned home, and married a peasant's daughter called Zhu Xiaohuan. One day when he went to market, he bumped into the Japanese girl, who was now fifteen years old. She asked his father heartbrokenly why he had quit his job and left her family, giving her no choice but to consent to the marriage agreement with the high official's family. Only then did his father discover that Zhunei Duohe had loved this Chinese hired hand from a very young age. After that the two of them began a passionate affair. That was when his elder sister Zhang Chunmei was conceived.

And then?

And then Dahai's father never stopped his assignations with Zhunei Duohe.

And after that?

After that the Great War came to an end. The Japanese were defeated. That Japanese family were killed in revenge by Chinese, and all the people of their village fled. Zhunei Duohe came with her daughter Chunmei to the Zhang family, and they took her in. Because Zhu Xiaohuan, the official wife, could not have children, everyone in the Zhang family knew that Zhunei Duohe was the true wife of the Zhang family.

Dahai's love story with its hundred holes moved the young people until they could not stop themselves from sighing. If now had not been a great age of revolution, they believed that Dahai could have written this story down, and become famous overnight.

When the day finally came, Zhang Jian slowly came down the stairs and into their hired car, leaning on Duohe's arm, and the neighbours all congratulated them, gazing on these 'lovers who became family at last'. 'What's Zhu Xiaohuan playing at? She's actually going with them as far as the station?' 'Can't she even let them be together as a family?' 'All the same, it's been really hard for Zhu Xiaohuan!'

As they said this, the people started to feel sorry for Xiaohuan. There they were, flying off wingtip to wingtip over the seas to Japan; what must she be thinking?

But Xiaohuan was just the same as ever. Dahai became the only target for her laughter, curses and nagging. Every day when he went to work, she would pursue him onto the walkway: 'Don't spill the sauce from your lunch box, it's all oily! Don't try to barge ahead when you're crossing the railway line! If there's a train coming just wait a bit if you have to . . .' Sometimes she chased after him so hastily that she had one foot in a cloth shoe, while the other was wearing a wooden slipper.

One day, a month and more after Zhang Jian and Duohe had left, people saw that Xiaohuan's eyes were heavily swollen. Without a doubt, she must have cried long and hard last night. People wanted to ask her what had happened, but they were also embarrassed to do so. There had been disagreements between them and her family, and even now Xiaohuan had not forgiven them. With great difficulty they caught hold of the listless Dahai.

'What's up with your ma?'

'What's up with who?'

'Have you had a fight with her?'

'Oh, you mean *that* mother? Nothing's the matter with her, she's just had a good long cry.'

Dahai considered that he had already given a reply to the riddle that was keeping them in suspense, and that it was unreasonable of them to keep on staring at him. So he scrunched up his eyebrows and walked away.

A few days later Erhai returned, wearing an army uniform. If they'd called him back too, something bad must have happened in the Zhang family.

After all these years, they had figured out the trick of talking to Erhai, for all that he was like a teapot with no spout, keeping everything inside.

An old lady said: 'Oho, have you come back to visit your sick mother?'

'My mum's not ill.'

'Then it must be because you've found yourself a nice girl!'

'My dad was sick.'

'Did they find out what it was in Japan? Nothing too serious, I hope?'

'Myeloma.'

When Erhai had nothing else to do he would sit on the balcony and play his erhu, and from his playing the neighbours understood something. They asked Erhai again: 'You're going to Japan to see your dad?'

'Too late for that.'

16

Before Girlie left for Japan, she went to visit Xiaohuan. She already had the look of a middle-aged woman. Her family was going to emigrate to Japan. Girlie, who had felt ashamed to go home, now felt that she had recovered at least some of her dignity. Before he passed away, Zhang Jian had told Duohe that Girlie and her family should be the first of them to be brought over, as she was the one with the most unsatisfactory life in their home town. Duohe worked as a cleaner in an office block, and had no money to act as guarantor for all of Girlie's family, but Kumi had helped out.

Girlie did not bring her husband and two children with her to see Xiaohuan. Xiaohuan understood that she was not willing to spend money on travel expenses for three more people, and perhaps the money was just not there to spend. Girlie was as painstaking and sensible as ever, and she never opened her mouth without a smile. As she went past neighbours' doors arm in arm with Xiaohuan, they all said they were like a real mother and daughter. It was only Dahai's temper that worsened when Girlie came back. If a child was crying in someone's home when he passed by the door he would say, 'Having these people for neighbours is enough bad luck for eight generations.'

Blackie would come down the stairs to meet him, only to be kicked until he whimpered.

No one knew that since Girlie had come back there were quarrels in the Zhang family every day. In fact it was mainly Dahai doing the quarrelling, but sometimes Xiaohuan heard more than she could take and joined in, and they hurled abuse at each other.

'What's she ever done for them to send her a form to go to Japan? What's she ever done for my mum? What's she done for our family? All she's done is lose face –' Dahai said.

'And what have you done, you little shit?'

'At least I've never lost face for our family by getting expelled from school! When my mum was cleaning toilets wearing a white armband, where was she?'

'You wanted to lose face but you couldn't. Back then, if you'd really been able to lose that Japanese face of yours, you certainly would have. You couldn't. And that's why you took a razor to those two Japanese eyebrows of yours, and your Japanese temples and Japanese chest hair – you shaved them off, into the toilet and down the drain! Every day when you stood in front of the mirror, all you could think of was how you could get rid of the face your own mother gave you.' There was a jeering smile on Xiaohuan's face as she laid bare his most secret sore point, and suddenly it occurred to her that recently the little mirror had been hanging from the water pipe in the toilet once more. Gazing at his thick, dark hair, thick, dark eyebrows and fair skin, the boy had started to love himself. The more he looked the more he loved himself, the more he looked the stronger his blood connection with Duohe. Or was he still looking into the mirror, grinding his teeth, hating himself for a Japanese who didn't have a full beard or complete eyebrows, hating his father's expression that would suddenly appear in his own gestures, that kindly, tender-hearted look to the eyes? Or did he hate even more the words bottled up in his stomach, of which the vast majority were the language of his Chinese mother Xiaohuan? If he could still lay violent hands on himself, would he slash open his stomach to let all those decidedly unrefined Chinese peasant words come tumbling out?

'Now you acknowledge your mother?' Xiaohuan said. 'So where were you earlier? The only thing you didn't do was join in shouting *Down with the Japanese spy*! You little toad! I was the one who delivered you when you were born, on that very mountain out there – why didn't I throttle you back then when I had the chance?'

Girlie came up to pacify Xiaohuan, saying that she did not see eye to eye with her brother, but there was no point in arguing with him, and telling her mother not to lose her temper.

'Who are you to argue with anyone?' Dahai switched opponents, aiming his spearhead at his sister. 'You married out of the family, you shouldn't be counted as a member of the Zhang family at all! And *you're* the one who's going to Japan – what've you ever done to deserve it?'

'It was your father's wish,' Xiaohuan said.

'I don't believe that for a moment.'

'If you don't believe it you can piss off and die, then once you're dead you can ask your dad.'

'Oh, so she's not living a happy life! So I am? Working eight hours a day in the factory in the dark, never seeing the light of day! What's she ever done to deserve special treatment?!'

Xiaohuan started to snigger.

Dahai stopped shouting, to see what she was laughing at.

'I'll tell you what? That you've rotted away your guts with regrets. Once you'd finished breaking your auntie's heart, did you think she wouldn't remember?'

'Any real mother would forget!'

'What do you mean by that?' Xiaohuan asked. She was starting to become afraid, nervous of this question.

'Only someone who isn't my real mother would remember a grudge.'

Xiaohuan thought she had brought this answer on herself. She should have stopped when she got close to that question, or avoided it. Now it was too late, she had taken her own heart and driven it onto the point of a knife.

Girlie kept on with her words of comfort: Dahai didn't really think in that way; once the words had been forced out there was no reining them back in. Once he had said all he had to, and got it out of his system, he would regret it deep down for sure. Xiaohuan just smiled weakly.

Dahai wrote a letter to Duohe, and read it out loud to Girlie and Xiaohuan. In the letter he spoke of how as a boy he had been cursed so many times as a Jap brat, of how many times he had wept under his quilt, unable to bear the humiliation. How many times he had hit out in defence of his mother's dignity, and his own, and how many times he had been injured as a result. However, all these grievances that he had suffered had not won him the slightest reward! His sister had suffered no such deep spiritual injuries, still less her family, and yet they were the ones that got the reward! *He* was the most unhappy member of the Zhang family . . .

When Xiaohuan had heard Dahai read his letter to the end, she said in a level voice: 'You go and find out how much it'll cost to get you to Japan. Your mother in Japan can't raise all that money, so I will. I'll make sure you go even if I have to sell every pot in the kitchen for scrap.'

Xiaohuan's feet worked day and night, and after a year she had earned around three hundred yuan. When Erhai came back on his promotion to platoon leader, he broke his silence as soon as he saw Xiaohuan. 'Ma, how come your face is so sallow? And thin! Your eyes are all red! What's the matter?'

Xiaohuan told him about how Dahai was to go to Japan. Erhai did not speak.

'Erhai, do you want to go too, is that it? I've heard that they don't let you go abroad if you're in the army, you'll have to lose that uniform before you can go,' Xiaohuan said.

'I'm not going,' he said.

'The neighbours are all half dead with envy. When your big sister went, it was like they were seeing her off to school all over again.'

Still he did not speak.

'The Gang of Four fell ages ago, and it's not just peasants, workers and soldiers who can do well for themselves, I've heard about a student in this city who's gone off to study abroad in Britain. Everyone in the city knows about it.'

Still Erhai said nothing. Before he went back to his unit, he told his mother that he would earn the money for the plane ticket to Japan, so there was no need for her to slave away all night. The brothers barely saw each other, because Dahai was taking intensive language classes at night school, and when not at school he would lurk on the mountain memorising vocabulary. He said that the neighbours were just so ill-bred, the entire building was as noisy as a poultry farm. His companions were different from before, they were all genteel, scholarly classmates from the night school. Sometimes they would pass in a gaggle at the bottom of the building, every one of them like a Japanese with a ghastly speech impediment.

One day, four young people knocked on the door of the Zhang household, two of them girls. On seeing Xiaohuan, they apologised, saying they had come to the wrong door. Xiaohuan said they were not wrong, she had seen Dahai going up the mountain with them from the balcony.

'Come and wait inside, he'll be off work in a while,' Xiaohuan said.

'Oh no, we'll just wait downstairs,' said one of the girls.

The door shut, and Xiaohuan heard one of the boys ask: 'Who was that?'

'I don't know,' the girl said.

'Dahai's family's maid, perhaps?' said the other boy.

Erhai came out of the big room. When Xiaohuan saw his looming stance, she moved smartly to restrain him. Erhai said loudly towards the door: 'Dahai is a bastard, is he fit to hire a maid?'

Everything went quiet outside.

The day before Erhai was due to return to his unit after his month of family leave, he called his brother over to the big room. Xiaohuan heard the bolt shoot home with a rush. Then came a low-voiced argument that she could not hear, try as she might. It seemed that Dahai was explaining himself, and Erhai was hurling accusations at him without pause.

Xiaohuan tapped on the door. They both ignored her. She circled round to the window, and opened it. The door that led to the balcony from the big room had not been closed, and Xiaohuan could hear the brothers' quarrel from beside the open window in the other room. Dahai was saying that if the neighbours had made up stories, what could he do about it? Erhai made no attempt to reason with him, all his replies were: Brother, you're talking bollocks, you're talking bollocks, you're talking such a load of old bollocks. Erhai had already made enquiries among the neighbours, who all said that Dahai had told them that his father had worked as a hired hand for a Japanese family, and seduced the daughter of his Japanese employer . . .

'That is such a load of old bollocks! And you have the nerve to deny it . . .' he said.

After that Xiaohuan heard muffled groans from Dahai. At first she worried that Erhai might be too heavy-handed and actually cripple him, but she also thought, let him hit him a bit first, then we'll see. About five minutes passed, and only then did she shout through the window: 'Erhai! How can a member of the People's Liberation Army beat people!'

Dahai opened the door and rushed out, straight into the toilet. Xiaohuan saw on the cement floor, which had been polished until it shone blue, a trail of blood.

'How could you hit him in the face?' Xiaohuan asked Erhai. 'How's he supposed to go to Japan if you spoil his face?'

Mother and son exchanged a look. In the toilet, water was rushing through the pipes.

Epilogue

Duohe often wrote to Xiaohuan. She always talked about her dreams. She dreamed about herself in this family. She dreamed of that road at the foot of the building, that big slope. She said that she often went to Chinatown in Tokyo to buy vegetables; the food was cheaper there, and the people took her for a Chinese. She said that when Dahai came to Japan she would give up her own little room for him to live in, and she would squeeze in with Girlie's family. Once she had saved up enough money they would work something out. She said that when she came back to Japan it was already too late for her, there was no place for her there. She only wished that the children would learn Japanese, and find their place. Duohe's letters were full of 'wishes'. A considerable number of orphans and women left behind after the war had petitioned the government to demand equal rights with Japanese citizens to employment and welfare. They also called on the government not to be prejudiced against the orphans and left-behind women who had been abandoned in a foreign land, nor to treat them as incapable, because their slow understanding had been created by the war. Duohe wished these petitions would succeed, so Girlie and her husband could find decent jobs. Duohe said she herself would just make do earning a cleaner's salary, but she wished she could save up a bit of money.

Reading Duohe's letters was hard work, but it gradually became an important part of Xiaohuan's life, especially after Dahai left for Japan. Girlie seldom wrote, and Dahai not even once, so Xiaohuan's only way to read about their lives was from Duohe's letters.

Duohe's letters grew longer and longer. For the most part she talked of how she had been reunited with so-and-so who was originally from Shironami village, or of how the petition was progressing. There was no progress. So the people who had returned from China became the poorest people, and those most subject to prejudice. She spoke of a fellow villager from Shironami who had come back from China: his children were beaten up at school every day, and their classmates called them Chinks. Just as he had been called a Jap devil by his Chinese classmates in his youth. Xiaohuan realised that Duohe was starting to get on in years, and often forgot things that she had already written. Duohe wanted Xiaohuan to make notes of her daily life, and tell her all about it, including how she quarrelled with people. She said that you could probably walk from one end of Japan to the other without finding anyone who could quarrel the way Xiaohuan did, or who had such a talent for quarrelling. She thought that Japanese people had rage and anxiety, yet they did not let them out properly, so they were not happy. Someone like Xiaohuan, who could quarrel until her opponent burst out laughing, would certainly not be wanting to kill other people all the time, or to kill herself.

Although Duohe took forever to get to the point, Xiaohuan chuckled: Duohe seemed to understand her very well.

Actually she did not quarrel that much now. She had come to realise that most of her arguments and fuss throughout her life had been on behalf of her family, and now she was the only one left, she could not find anything worth arguing about. She even spoke more easily now, though Blackie would always listen incomparably seriously, the same as always, gazing at her with eyes that were now clouded by cataracts. The three children were all doing very well; at least their prospects were better than those of the children of the other inhabitants of the building. This was one of the main reasons why Xiaohuan no longer quarrelled with people: what would I quarrel about with you? Do you have three children as good as mine? People who are satisfied with what they have do not quarrel.

Three years after Zhang Jian's death, Xiaohuan finally brought herself to tear open the envelope that held his last letter. It had been placed in a big parchment envelope, and sent back together with his old Shanghai brand watch, a little silver lock and a house key. The little silver lock was a relic from his babyhood, and he had always kept it tied to his keys. The key he had forgotten to give to Xiaohuan before going to Japan, and he had taken it away hidden in his pocket. The old watch was very accurate, it had stopped at exactly the moment when Zhang Jian's heart had stopped beating. Duohe had told Xiaohuan this specially in a letter.

Zhang Jian never finished his letter. He said that just recently his stomach had improved a little, and Duohe always made him noodles, cats' ears and other wheat dishes just like Xiaohuan used to make. He said that once he had recovered his health, he would go and find work that did not require him to speak Japanese, like the job Girlie's husband had, polishing the glass in a department store. Once he had earned some money he would bring Xiaohuan over to Japan, he had already discussed it with Duohe. The three of them could not do without each other, they had fought and quarrelled for a lifetime, but they had all fought themselves into a single lump of flesh and bone. He was staying in hospital now, and once he had had his operation tomorrow he could leave.

It was only then that Xiaohuan realised that he had been completely unaware that his life was drawing to a close. It would appear that Duohe and the children had kept him in the dark all along, right up until he was wheeled to the operating table.

This letter of Zhang Jian's had been left unfinished. He wrote propped up on a pile of pillows, and went to sleep thinking of the way Xiaohuan had looked when she married him, that was how Xiaohuan imagined it. He had not even had the physical or mental energy to write a complete letter. He must have slipped it underneath his quilt, for fear that Duohe would see. He still had to continue with his cautious games between the two women, just like many years earlier. The children and Duohe had pulled the wool over his eyes very successfully, and he had believed them: that he still had plenty of time left, and there would still be no shortage of troubles to deal with, such as his two women, and the need to be cautious with them both. He must certainly have believed that once he had gone under the surgeon's knife he would be the old, strong, vital Zhang Jian once more. Otherwise he would not have set out such a long and far-off future for Xiaohuan. His apologies to Xiaohuan could be seen at a glance.

She said to Blackie with a smile: 'Well, we appreciate the thought, eh?'

Every day the neighbours would still see Zhu Xiaohuan walk from the bottom of the building down the big slope to the Neighbourhood Committee, carrying the chest that held her sewing machine. She had rented a triangular room under the stairs, where she kept the frame. But she was afraid the sewing machine itself would be stolen, and every day carried it stubbornly there and back. Blackie was old and blind, but he followed her, swaying his rump.

Blackie would often hurtle down the big slope, he had no need for eyesight to turn the right corners in his headlong dash. Xiaohuan knew that meant the postman had come. If there was a letter from Erhai, the postman would let Blackie run up the hill holding it in his mouth to present it to Xiaohuan. He never lost heart, he would always throw himself ebulliently down the slope, staring at the postman with his grey-white, sightless eyes, mouth split open from ear to ear in his beaming doggy grin.

Erhai had been transferred to the South-west, where he had married and had a child. He wrote to his mother Xiaohuan whenever he had time, but there was no letter from him today. Yet Blackie's smiling face never turned away from the postman, he would remain standing in the same spot, wagging his tail, right up until the postman got on his bike and rode up the slope.

All Xiaohuan could do was console him: 'Blackie, there'll be a letter tomorrow, hey?'

Geling Yan is an award-winning Chinese novelist and screenwriter. Born in Shanghai, she published her first novel in 1985. Since then she has written numerous short stories, essays, scripts and novels including, in English, *The Flowers of War, The Uninvited* and *The Lost Daughter of Happiness*. Several of Geling Yan's works have been adapted for the screen, among them *The Flowers of War* which was filmed by acclaimed Chinese director Zhang Yimou and stars Christian Bale. Geling Yan currently divides her time between Berlin and China.